"You have n... pecial it has b...

"Dare I hope," she gasped, clutching her heart, making him laugh. Shaking her head, she smiled. "There's no way this truce is going to last."

"I'll try if you will," he said, his eyes twinkling with mischief, and she had to laugh in return.

"I'll try, I promise."

"I keep waiting for a pitch from you to get me to agree to something. You all but admitted that was the purpose of your bidding for me tonight at the auction."

"Maybe I've shelved that original agenda," she said in a sultry voice. "I'm having fun, Tony. Fun that I don't want to spoil. The night is magical. For a few hours, let's enjoy it."

He raised her hand and brushed a light kiss on her knuckles. His breath was warm.

"I'm glad you feel that way," he said. "I'm not ready to tell you good-night and watch you walk away."

* * *

That Night with the Rich Rancher
is part of the Lone Star Legends series
from *USA TODAY* bestselling author
Sara Orwig!

THAT NIGHT WITH
THE RANCHER

BY
SARA ORWIG

MILLS &
BOON

First Published in Great Britain 2016
By Mills & Boon, an imprint of HarperCollins*Publishers*
1 London Bridge Street, London, SE1 9GF

© 2016 Sara Orwig

ISBN: 978-0-263-91845-8

51-0116

Our policy is to use papers that are natural, renewable and recyclable products and made from wood grown in sustainable forests.The logging and manufacturing processes conform to the legal environmental regulations of the country of origin.

Printed and bound in Spain
by CPI, Barcelona

Sara Orwig lives in Oklahoma. She has a patient husband who will take her on research trips anywhere, from big cities to old forts. She is an avid collector of Western history books. With a master's degree in English, Sara has written historical romance, mainstream fiction and contemporary romance. Books are beloved treasures that take Sara to magical worlds, and she loves both reading and writing them.

With many thanks to Stacy Boyd, Senior Editor

One

Tony Milan felt ridiculous. Standing in the wings of the wide stage of the elegant Dallas country club ballroom, he promised himself that next time, he would be more careful making bets with his oldest brother. Losing at saddle bronc riding in a rodeo last April had put him backstage tonight at this gala charity event, which included a dinner dance as well as an auction. One that would auction *him* off. At least it was all for a good cause, he reminded himself. The funds raised would go to Parkinson's disease research.

As he'd made his way to the stage earlier, he had seen some of the attendees: beautiful women dressed in designer gowns accompanied by men in tailored tuxedos. The highest bidders would win a night with "Texas's most desirable bachelors," according to the brochure that had been mailed to a select group wealthy enough to afford the event. He couldn't imagine any woman bidding much for an evening out with a guy she won in an auction, but after the opening bid, he realized he was wrong. The Texas ranchers who'd gone before him had stirred up high prices.

Looking out at the latest bachelor who now pranced offstage, Tony could not recall ever feeling more out of place. And then he heard his name called.

Taking a deep breath and forcing himself to smile broadly, he stepped forward, striding out of the darkened shadows into the blinding spotlights in front of a glittering audience. Applause was loud as he waved at the audience, most of which he could no longer clearly see because of the spotlights shining in his eyes.

After a spiel about his bachelor status, the master of ceremonies opened up the bidding. Tony was startled by the number of women who jumped into the bidding, but as the amount climbed, first one and then another dropped out until only three women were left.

Shocked yet pleased by the amount he was going to draw, he grinned and walked around the stage as the bidding climbed.

When a woman in a front table bid, he glanced down and saw it was an ex-girlfriend. He hoped she didn't win. As far as he was concerned, he'd said a final goodbye to her when she'd started getting serious. No long-term relationships for Tony Milan. He liked to flirt, play the field, just have a good time with no strings attached. Thankfully, after a flurry of bidding, his ex-girlfriend dropped out and only two women were left.

Tony couldn't see either one of the women, hidden by the blinding lights, but he heard their competitive bids. They were calling outrageous sums of money—all for an evening with him. When one graciously dropped out, the MC brought down the gavel.

"We have a winner," he said, not able to hide his out-right glee at the final amount for the charity. "Would our lucky woman please come up onto the stage?"

Tony couldn't contain his curiosity. He scanned the audience for a glimpse at her, and then a spotlight found her at a table off to the right. His pulse jumped when a stunning blonde stood up. Her hair was piled atop her head with a few spiral curls falling about her face, and she wore a fiery red dress as she threaded her way to the stage. Even from a distance he could see the dress clung to a breathtaking figure. Jeweled straps glittered on her slender shoulders and her full breasts pillowed above the low-cut neckline.

One of the auction's ushers took her hand as she climbed the steps to the stage and Tony's gaze finally swept over her from head to toe, taking in her long, shapely legs revealed by a high slit in the skirt. Instantly Tony began to feel immensely better about the entire auction and the upcoming evening.

As the blonde crossed the stage, his gaze swept over her features. She wasn't a local resident, he thought, be-cause he didn't recognize her. But then as she neared center stage to give the MC her name, he had a niggling feeling that he did indeed know her. He looked at her again. Something about her features seemed familiar. Perhaps... There was a faint resemblance to a local—his neighbor and lifetime enemy, Lindsay Calhoun.

He shrugged away that notion. The woman talking to the MC could not be Lindsay Calhoun. For one brief moment, a memory flashed through his mind of Lindsay dressed in skintight jeans and driving her muddy pickup, her long sandy braid bouncing beneath her floppy old hat. That was followed by another memory—Lindsay wag-ging her finger at him and accusing him of taking her ranch's water—something unethical he would never do to any neighbor, even Lindsay. She was mule stubborn, never took his advice and wouldn't agree with him if he said the sun set in the west.

Most of all, she was serious in every way, all business all the time. With their many confrontations, he had wondered if she'd ever had any fun in her life. So there was no way on earth that the vision who had won an evening with him was Lindsay.

Curiosity ran rampant as the MC took the mystery woman's hand and she turned to the audience, shooting a quick glance at Tony and then smiling at the audience while the MC held her hand high like a boxer at a heavyweight fight.

"Our winner—a beautiful Texan, Miss Lindsay Calhoun!"

Tony was stunned. His gaze raked over her again. Why had she done this? Their families had maintained a perpetual feud since the first generation of Milans and Calhouns had settled in Texas, and he and Lindsay kept that feud alive. Besides, she didn't even date. Nor would she spend a dime for an evening with him. She never even spoke to him unless she was accusing him of something.

He squeezed his eyes shut as if to clear them, and then looked at her again. Actually, he stared, transfixed. Not one inch of her looked like his neighbor.

She turned as another man in a black tux came forward to escort her toward Tony while the MC began to talk about the next bachelor.

"Lindsay?" Tony's voice came out a croak. The woman he faced was breathtaking. He wouldn't have guessed all the makeup in Texas could have made such a transformation.

Her huge blue eyes twinkled and she leaned close, giving him a whiff of an exotic perfume—another shock.

"Close your mouth, Tony," she whispered so only he could hear. "And stop staring."

The tuxedo-clad man stepped forward. "Lindsay, it seems you've already met your bachelor, Tony Milan. Tony, this is Lindsay Calhoun."

"We know each other." Tony hoped he said it out loud. His brain felt all jumbled and he couldn't force his gaze from Lindsay. He still couldn't believe what he was seeing. He had known her all his life. Not once had she even caused him to take a second glance. Nor had he ever seen her as anything except a colossal pest. Saying she wasn't his type was an understatement.

But was there another side to her? Why was Lindsay here? Why had she bid a small fortune to get the evening with him? No doubt she wanted something from him— and wanted it badly.

Would she go to this length to get water? He ruled that out instantly, remembering her fury and harsh words when she had accused him of buying bigger pumps for his wells to take more groundwater from the aquifer they shared. He had told her what she should do—dig her wells deeper. She had charged right back, saying she wouldn't have to go to the added expense if he wasn't depleting her water with bigger pumps. And there it went. Once again her usual stubborn self refused to take his advice or believe him.

Then she had started calling him devious, a snake and much worse. She pushed him to the edge and he knew he had to just walk away, which he did while she hurled more names at him.

That was the Lindsay Calhoun he knew. This Lindsay tonight had to be up to something, too. Surprisingly, though, he couldn't bring himself to care much. Thoughts of ranching and feuding fled from his mind. He was too busy enjoying looking at one of the most beautiful women he had ever seen.

How could she possibly look so good? They were being given the details of their evening, beginning with a limousine waiting at the country club entrance to take them to the airport where a private jet would fly them to Houston for dinner. He barely registered a word said to him; he couldn't focus on anything but the sight of her.

"Excuse me a moment. I'll be right back," their host said, leaving them alone momentarily.

"You've got to give me a moment to come out of my shock," Tony said with a shake of his head.

"You take all the time you want. I've been waiting for this," she drawled. "If necessary, I would have paid a lot more to get this night with you."

"If you'd come over to the ranch dressed the way you are now and just knocked on the door, you could have had my full attention for an evening without paying a nickel, but this is for a good cause."

"It's for two good causes," she said in a sultry voice, and his heartbeat quickened. He still couldn't quite believe what was happening. Before tonight, he would have bet the ranch he could never be dazzled or even take a second look, let alone willingly go out with his stubborn neighbor.

"Lindsay, I've never fainted in my life, but I might in the next thirty seconds, except I don't want to stop looking at you for anything."

"When you saw I had won, I was afraid you'd turn down this evening."

"I wouldn't turn down tonight if I had to pay twice

what you did," he said without thinking, and her smile widened, a dazzling smile he had never seen in his life.

"If you two will follow me, I can show you to the front entrance," their host said, returning to join them. "First, Miss Calhoun, you need to step to the desk to make arrangements about payment."

"Certainly," she answered. "See you in a few minutes, Tony," she added in a soft, breathless voice.

Where had that sexy tone come from? He recalled times when he had heard her shout instructions to hands on her ranch. She had a voice that could be heard a long stretch away and an authoritative note that got what she wanted done. As he watched her, she turned to look at him. She smiled at him, another dazzling, knee-weakening smile, and he couldn't breathe again.

Holy saints, where had Lindsay gotten that enticing smile? It muddled his thoughts, sent his temperature soaring and made him want to please her enough to get another big smile.

He had seen her stomping around horses, yelling instructions and swearing like one of the men, the sandy braid flopping with her steps. He had faced her when she had yelled furious accusations at him about dumping fertilizer. How could that be the breathtaking woman walking away from him? His gaze ran down her bare back to her tiny waist, down over her flared hips that shifted slightly in a provocative walk.

With the tight dress clinging to her every curve, he caught a flash of long legs when she turned and the slit in her skirt parted. That's when he noticed the stiletto heels. He would have sworn she had never worn heels in her life, yet she moved as gracefully as a dancer. He wiped his heated brow. This was rapidly turning into the most impossible night of his life.

Befuddled, totally dazzled by her, he tried to remind himself she was Lindsay, and he should pull his wits together. That might not be so easy. He would never again view her in the same manner.

Why hadn't he ever really looked at her before? He knew full well the answer to his question. He had been blinded by their fights over every little thing, from her tree falling on his truck to his fence on her property line. Not to mention her usual raggedy appearance when she worked.

If she had gone to such lengths tonight to wring something she wanted out of him, he had better get a grip, because it was going to be all but impossible to say no to the fantastic woman in red standing only yards away and writing a check for thousands of dollars for an evening with him. Not even a night— just a dinner date and maybe some dancing.

But Lindsay Calhoun wasn't interested in dinner dates and ballroom dancing, boot scooting or even barn dances. He eyed her skeptically. To what lengths was she prepared to go tonight to get what she wanted?

He gave up trying to figure her out.

Still, he couldn't take his eyes off her. The skintight red dress left little to the imagination. Why had she hidden her gorgeous figure all these years? Why had she always pulled her hair back in a braid or ponytail? He looked at the beautiful silky blond hair arranged on her head, some strands falling loosely in back. He had never seen her hair falling freely around her face—would he before this night was over?

She looked seductive, like pure temptation, and he knew he should be on his guard, but there was no way he could be defensive with the woman standing only yards away. He wanted her in his arms. He wanted to kiss her.

And, if he was truthful with himself, he wanted to make love to her.

When she finished writing and handing over her check, their host led them to a garden, where they had pictures taken together. As he slipped his arm around her tiny waist while they posed for the camera, the physical contact sizzled. He was so heated he thought he would go up in flames.

He made a mental note to get a picture. His brother-in-law and sister were in the audience, so they had seen her tonight. So was his oldest brother, Wyatt. He was certain Jake Calhoun had seen his sister look this way before, but Wyatt was probably as shocked as he had been.

Talking constantly, their host escorted Lindsay and Tony through the wide front doors of the country club, where a long white limousine waited.

As soon as the door closed on the limo, they were alone, except for the driver on the other side of a partition.

"Maybe you've been using the wrong approach," Tony remarked.

She smiled another full smile that revealed even, white teeth that made him inclined to agree with whatever she said.

"That's what I decided. So we'll see how it helps letting my hair down, getting out of my jeans and into a dress, smiling and being friendly. So far, it seems to be working rather well, don't you think?"

"Absolutely. I don't know why you waited this long. I keep reminding myself not to give you the deed to my ranch tonight."

She laughed with a dazzling, irresistible smile on her lips. "The other way is a more direct approach. You know where you stand."

"And this is a sugarcoated enticement to get what you want?"

"Oh, my, yes. I'm just getting started. When I walked up on stage, I'm sure you wanted to refuse keeping your part of the bargain."

"You're wrong. Not the way you look tonight," he said in a husky voice. "With you in that red dress, there's nothing that would cause me to turn down an evening with you."

When had he reacted like this to a woman? He escorted beautiful women, was friends with them, had them continually around in his life and yet never had he been dazzled senseless as he was tonight. He wouldn't ever have guessed Lindsay could generate such attraction and make him overlook all their battles.

It had to be the shock of who she was that was setting him ablaze. He'd better get a grip on reality and see her as the person he knew her to be. But that wasn't going to happen tonight. His thought processes worked clearly enough to know that.

She smiled sweetly. "Penny for your thoughts."

"I'm wondering why I haven't ever heard from anyone about how gorgeous you can be."

"I suppose because I rarely go out on dates and never with anyone in these parts."

"Why not?"

She shrugged. "I've just never met anyone around here I wanted to go out with very much. And there's nowhere close by here to go dressed up."

"There's Dallas."

With a twinkle in her blue eyes, she answered, "In Dallas, our paths probably wouldn't cross."

"I've known you all my life and I know your family

well. Tonight I feel as if I'm spending the evening with a complete stranger I've just met."

She looked amused. "In some ways, Tony, we are strangers. There's a lot you don't know about me," she said in the breathless, sultry voice that made the temperature in the limo climb again.

"I should have asked you out long ago," he said.

"You know how likely that was to have happened, and what my response would have been."

He nodded. "Our past is better left alone and forgotten tonight."

"We fully agree on that one," she answered as the limo slowed. "Tonight is filled with illusions."

"The way you look is no illusion. You're gorgeous," he said, and was rewarded with another coaxing smile.

The limo turned into the airport and in minutes they slowed to a stop. While the chauffeur held the door, Tony took her arm to escort her to the waiting private jet. The moment he touched her, awareness burned in a fiery current. Her arm was warm, her skin silky smooth. He caught another whiff of her exotic perfume, and he couldn't wait to get her to their destination so he could ask her to dance and have an excuse to hold her in his arms.

In the plane he was aware of how close she sat. It was difficult to keep from staring because her red dress had fallen open, revealing those beautiful, long shapely legs. He took a deep breath.

"I need to keep pinching myself to make sure this is actually happening," he said. "And I keep reminding myself you're the same neighbor I see across the fence with your horses."

"I love my horses. You should come visit and really look at them sometime. I have some fine horses."

"I've seen them across the fence. Everyone in the county knows you have some of the finest horses."

"They're working horses or horses for my riding. I like to ride."

"We have that in common, Lindsay."

"I've never seen you riding just for pleasure."

"If it's for pleasure, I don't ride in the direction of your ranch." He smiled sheepishly. "I figure we're both better off that way."

"We're in agreement there, too," she remarked in a tone that was light and held no rancor.

"Have you attended one of these charity bachelor auctions before?"

"Sure, because it's a good cause." She held up a hand but stopped before it touched his arm. "I don't need to ask, I know you haven't. What prompted you to agree to participate in the auction tonight? You seem to be more the type to just donate the money."

"I lost a bet with Wyatt over bronc riding in an Abilene rodeo."

She laughed. "So because of your brother you're trapped into a night with me now."

"I was filled with thoughts of revenge until you stood up to walk to the stage. Since then, this night has taken the best possible turn."

She smiled. "I must admit I'm pleasantly surprised by your reaction. I never, ever thought I'd hear you say that. But you know, underneath this red dress, I'm still me."

He inhaled deeply, his temperature spiking at her mention of what was beneath the red dress, even though she had intended a different meaning.

He cleared his throat. "I have a feeling I better not say anything about what's underneath your red dress."

She looked as if she held back a laugh. "I knew there

had to be another side to you besides the one I always see. I've wondered how the evening would go and so far, so good. I think, Tony, we've set a record already for the length of time we've been civil to each other."

"I intend to be more than 'civil to each other.' We're just getting started," he said. "Frankly, Lindsay, it's damn difficult to remember that you're the same woman whose ranch adjoins mine. I feel as if I'm with a beautiful woman I've just met," he said softly, taking her hand in his and rubbing her knuckles lightly with his thumb. His brows arched and he turned her hand over to open her palm, looking up at her.

"You have soft hands. I know how you work with the cowboys. You should have hands like mine—with scars, calluses and crooked bones from breaks. How did you get these?" he asked, running his thumb lightly over her palm.

"I wear gloves most of the time," she said. "And I haven't been out working quite as much for the past two weeks because I was shopping for a dress and getting ready for tonight."

Her voice had changed, becoming throaty, losing the humor, and he wondered if she had a reaction to his touch. That idea made the temperature in the limo climb again. He gazed into her big blue eyes. "I hope tonight will be far better than you dreamed possible and worth all the effort you put into it," he said softly, and raised her hand to brush her palm with his lips.

His thumb brushed across her wrist and he felt her racing pulse, making his own pulse jump again in response. As he looked into Lindsay's eyes, he wanted to pull her close and kiss her. He couldn't help the thought that came to mind. How much was this night going to complicate his life?

He couldn't answer his question, but he was glad for the auction and thankful she hoped to win him over with sweet talk. It was a dazzling prospect.

He tried to pour on the charm and avoid any topics about the ranch, their relationship or their families. The feud between their families had been far stronger when they had been children and their grandparents had influenced the families. As a small child, Tony was taught to avoid speaking to any Calhoun, and she'd been taught the same about the Milans. In fact, they hadn't spoken to each other until they became neighboring ranchers and had their first dispute over her tree falling on his fence and hitting his truck.

The plane ride seemed to take mere minutes. Before he knew it, they touched down in Houston and were ushered to another waiting limo. A short while later, they pulled into a circular drive lined by manicured shrubs strung with tiny white lights and stopped in front of a sprawling stone building he recognized as an exclusive club.

When they stepped out of the limo, Tony took her arm to walk through the canopied entrance. Inside, when he told the maître d' they were from the Dallas auction, they were welcomed and led to a linen-covered table by a window overlooking the wide patio that held hundreds more twinkling lights and a splashing water fountain.

A piano player sang as he played a familiar old ballad and several couples danced on a small dance floor.

In minutes they were presented a bottle of Dom Pérignon champagne. As soon as they were alone with drinks poured, Tony raised his glass in a toast. "Here's to the most beautiful woman in Texas."

She smiled. "A very nice exaggeration, Tony," she said, touching his glass lightly with hers and taking a sip. "Actually, you look rather handsome yourself."

He smiled and wondered if she felt any real attraction. "Lindsay, I can't imagine why you've been hiding that beauty all these years."

She laughed. "Not so many years, Tony. And thank you. I'm far from the most beautiful woman in Texas, but it's nice to hear."

"You could have had most of the single guys in the county asking you out if you'd wanted," he said.

"Actually, that's not my aim in life," she remarked. "And I do get asked out."

"To talk about someone's horses. If they could see you tonight, though, horses wouldn't come up in the conversation." He waited a second and then asked the question that flitted into his mind. "Speaking of which, Lindsay, will you go to dinner with me next Friday night?"

She grinned at him. "Aren't you jumping the gun? You don't know if we can make it through tonight and get along the entire time."

He leaned across the table to take her hand again. "I promise you, we're going to get along tonight," he said, his tone lowering as it did when he was aroused. "A lot of people saw you at the auction tonight. I think you'll be inundated with invitations from guys when you get home. I want you to myself," he added softly, and something flickered in the depths of her eyes as her smile vanished and she gazed at him solemnly. Electricity flashed between them, and he wanted to be alone with her and kiss her more than ever.

As their waiter appeared, Tony released her hand and leaned back in his chair, listening to a menu recited by the waiter. When they were alone again, Tony raised his flute of champagne. "Here's to a fabulous evening that we'll both remember and want to repeat."

With a seductive smile, she touched his glass with hers

lightly, causing a faint clink, and sipped again, watching him the whole time with a look that made him want to forget dinner and find somewhere to be alone with her.

"I'm beginning to see that you have a sensual side you've kept well hidden."

"Well, yes, Tony. I've kept it hidden from *you*," she said with good humor, and he laughed.

"I suppose I brought that on," he said, wondering whom she had allowed to see this aspect of herself. He sat back to study her. "As well as I know your family, I really don't know much about you. You went to Texas Tech, didn't you? And you were an agriculture major?"

"Yes, with a minor in business. I knew I'd come home to run a ranch."

"Good background. Do you ever feel overwhelmed with the ranch?"

"Sometimes the problems seem a little overwhelming, but I love the ranch too much to feel at odds with it. It's my life."

"I agree, but it's different for you. Don't you want a family someday?"

"Owning the ranch doesn't mean I can't have a family," she retorted.

"I suppose." He nodded as he considered her remark. "Everyone in the county knows you work as hard as the guys who work for you. It's difficult to look at you now and remember how tough and resilient you are."

"Did you know my big brother came out to the ranch, sat me down and lectured me to try to get me to be nicer to you?"

"The hell you say. Is that why you're here tonight?" he asked. Still, he couldn't believe that the gorgeous creature flirting with him now was only here to make nice.

She leaned over the table, reaching out to take his

hand in hers, and his heart jumped again. Every touch, her flirting, the looks she was giving him, all stirred responses that shocked him. No other woman had ever had the same instant effect on him from the slightest contact.

"No," she replied, her voice lowering. "Before the night is over, you'll know this was all my idea and not one of my brothers had anything to do with my plans for tonight."

Her plans? His mind began to race with the possibilities and they were all X-rated. His blood pulsed hot through his veins. "I'm beginning to wish we were alone right now."

With a satisfied expression, she sat back. "Mike and Josh weren't at the auction and I haven't talked to them lately. They have no idea what I'm doing tonight. Jake was in the audience, with Madison, but across the room from me. Otherwise, I'm sure he would have tried to stop my bidding because he would have suspected my motives. But he more than any of my brothers should know you can take care of yourself."

Tony nodded. "I'll bet it was Jake who tried to talk you into being nicer. Mike has had his own problems with losing his first wife, caring for four-year-old Scotty and getting married to Savannah. And Josh is too busy making money with his hotels."

"You're right about all three." She glanced down to their joined hands. "Although I don't think this was exactly what Jake had in mind when he told me to be civil to you."

Tony couldn't help but smile. "I'm sure it wasn't." He turned his hand so that his was holding hers and rubbed his thumb across her smooth skin. "You know, I've heard little Scotty adores his aunt Lindsay. I'm beginning to see how that's possible."

"I don't think Scotty sees me the way you do."

He laughed. "No, I'm sure he doesn't. But you have a whole different side to you that I'm seeing tonight." And he was still having quite a time wrapping his mind around this Lindsay. If this auction night had happened when she first moved to her ranch, would they have avoided their big clashes? Or would that same stubborn Lindsay still have been lurking beneath this beauty?

"I've gotten the same lecture from my brother Wyatt about cooling our fights," he told her. "As county sheriff, he just wants peace and quiet in his life and he doesn't want to have to continually deal with our battles—which will be less in the future, I promise you."

"I hope we can end the clashes altogether."

"If you're like this, you'll have my complete cooperation. You know, I have to tell you. Over the years, some things you've wanted or accused me of destroying, I had nothing to do with. Hopefully, after this, you'll listen to my side a little more. But enough about our past. It doesn't exist tonight, Lindsay."

"That suits me fine," she said softly as she licked her lower lip.

"That does it." He pushed back his chair and went around to her. "If you do one more sexy thing, I may go up in spontaneous combustion." He held out his hand to her. "Let's dance. I don't want the table between us anymore." He also needed to move around and cool down.

Her blue eyes sparkled. "Ah, so I have your attention."

"You've had my full attention since that spotlight revealed you."

He led her to the dance floor, where he turned to take her into his arms. He was intensely aware of her enticing perfume, of her soft hand in his, of her other hand skimming the back of his neck. She was soft, lithe and a good dancer, one more surprise for the evening.

"You have really hidden yourself away from a lot of fun and a lot of attention."

"I have a life. Around the ranch and in Verity, I don't think I've missed a thing. You don't know what I do when I go to Dallas, Houston or New York."

"No, I don't, but I'm curious now."

"I have a lovely time. I have friends in other places besides Verity and the ranch, you know."

"I'll bet you do," he said, smiling at her.

He had seen Lindsay in one of the bars in Verity, playing poker and downing whiskey like one of the men. Now he had a hard time reconciling that image with the woman in his arms. He stared at her, amazed it was her and wondering how long this facade would last.

Even when she returned to her normal self—and she eventually would—he knew he'd never look at her in the same way again. Discovering there was an enticing side to her changed his entire view of the woman who took life too seriously.

For once, she wasn't so serious and earnest. He knew that was her nature, though, and he warned himself not to have high expectations of partying or lovemaking. She was not the type of woman he wanted to get entangled with, but for tonight he was going to break one of his basic rules of life.

Tonight he was going to stop thinking about the past and their problems. Tonight he was simply going to enjoy being with a stunning woman whose intention was to please him. And he wanted to return the favor.

When the dance ended, he took her hand. "I think our salads have been served. Shall we go back?"

As they ate, he listened attentively while she talked about growing up a Calhoun. She avoided mentioning the family feud or any touchy subject. Instead, she related childhood memories, college incidents and ranch success stories. The whole time she spoke, he couldn't stop picturing her blond hair long and soft over her shoulders. He wondered if she would let him take it down later. He wanted to run his fingers through the long strands, hold her close and kiss her. He wanted seduction.

Again, he wondered about her plans for the night. She had surprised him constantly since the bidding began back at the auction. In a way she was being her most devious self, but he hoped she never stopped. So far, he had loved every minute of this night since the spotlight first picked her out of the crowd.

Over their dinners, which were a thick, juicy steak cooked to perfection for him and a lobster for her, she asked about his life, and he shared some stories.

Finally, their desserts were brought out, fancy, beautifully crafted dishes that they both ignored because they were more interested in each other.

"Would you like to dance again?" he asked when she sat back.

"Of course."

The piano player had been joined by four more musicians, and the group played a ballad that allowed him to hold Lindsay close in his arms.

"Remember," he whispered in her ear, "for tonight, we'll forget our battles."

"I already have," she said, squeezing his hand lightly and making his breath catch.

The band changed to a fast number and he released Lindsay reluctantly. Instead of returning to her seat, she began to dance in front of him, and he followed suit. As he watched her, he could feel his body heat rising. She was like a flame, her hips gyrating sensuously, her blue eyes languid and heated as if thoughts of making love were inspiring her every movement. She was sexy—another shocking discovery. She had to know the effect she was having on him. While her eyes glittered, a faint, satisfied smile hovered on her face. He wanted to yank her into his arms, lean over her until she held him tightly and plunder her soft mouth.

He danced near the wide glass doors overlooking the veranda. He opened the doors and whirled her through them onto the patio, where warm night air enveloped them.

"We can dance out here?"

"The night has cooled enough and we have this to ourselves," he said, moving to the music that was only slightly muted. He danced out of the light spilling through the glass doors, into the shadows and stopped, looking down at her as she tilted her face up.

She was taller than most women he had gone out with, but still shorter than he was. His eyes adjusted to the August night and he could see her looking up at him as he tightened his arm around her, feeling her softness press against him.

"Ever since you walked across the stage at the country club, I've been wanting to do this." Slowly, inch by inch, he leaned in closer, taking his time to steal the kiss he craved.

He wondered if it would be worth the wait.

Two

As Lindsay gazed into Tony's eyes, her heart thudded—and not just from desire. Wanting his kiss disturbed her because it was not part of her plans for enticing him. Still, there was no denying it. Some crazy chemistry burned between them. Actually being attracted to Tony Milan had not even occurred to her as a remote possibility when she'd initially come up with her plan to get him to be friendly and to influence him to stop overpumping his groundwater, which was taking water from her wells. Somewhere in the back of her mind, a question formed in the sultry haze. Could he have been truthful when he said he wasn't using bigger water pumps?

From the first encounter they were at odds. The initial confrontation was over the boundary between their neighboring ranches. Each had come armed with over a century's worth of documents to prove their property lines. Tony had been the condescending Mr. Know-It-

All, telling her she was wrong and how to run her ranch. He'd changed little since that first meeting. He was still a classic alpha male who had to control everything and when it came to ranching, that attitude was annoying. Tonight, though, was a whole different matter.

She was in control.

Or so she planned.

Right now she had to admit she was nearly speechless, because she had never planned or considered an attraction to Tony. She thought she could have a fun, pleasant evening and get on better footing with him. He had lots of friends, so she figured he had to have a nice side and that's what she hoped to get to know tonight with her bachelor-auction ploy.

She had hoped to entice him, make him see her as a desirable woman, have fun and maybe even share some kisses with him so their battles would not be so bitter and he would stop doing annoying things. Instead, she was breathless around him. An attraction between them that she had not expected had flared to life.

How could he be so attractive to her? She knew already that it was because of his charm, his seductive ways, his same alpha male that annoyed her with his know-it-all, take-charge attitude, but now it thrilled her. It was aimed at her, like a missile locked on its target, and, incredibly, she found it appealing…and sexy. She was definitely seeing him in a whole new way tonight.

Still, she couldn't help feeling her carefully laid-out plan was going off the rails a bit. Now wasn't the time to analyze her feelings, though. Not while she was in his arms. She knew this could never continue past tonight. Feelings for Tony Milan could complicate her life big-time. But for one night only, she would go where her heart and body led her. She could only tilt her head back and go with them. And right now they were taking her closer and closer to Tony. She wanted his kiss.

Her heartbeat raced as her gaze lowered to Tony's mouth, and she closed her eyes when his lips finally touched hers.

All thoughts fled and her heart slammed against her ribs as Tony's warm mouth moved on hers. His lips brushed hers lightly, a tantalizing touch that heightened her need for his kiss. Every inch of her tingled as desire electrified her nerves, hot and intense.

Another warm brush of his lips and she tightened her arm around his waist, sliding her hand behind his neck to wind her fingers in his thick, short hair. Every contact was unique, special, something she'd never expected and would never forget.

His mouth settled on hers, parting her lips as his tongue thrust deep and stroked hers, slowly. It was a kiss to make her moan and cling to him, to make her want him more than was sensible and beyond what she had set as limits for tonight's "date." His kiss set her ablaze with desire, making her quiver for his touch and dare to touch him in kind. How could Tony's kisses do this to her? How could he cause responses that no other man ever had?

Her knees felt weak while desire was too strong. Her heart pounded and she moaned softly against his lips. She felt as if she could kiss him for hours and still want so much more from him. As her hand slipped down over his arm, she felt the hard bulge of solid muscle even through the sleeves of his tux and shirt. The feel of that strength, that powerful maleness, rocked her. She felt as if she was hanging on to her senses by a thread.

What she was doing? Somewhere in her mind the question formed, but her thoughts were too scrambled and hungry with need to articulate an answer.

Nearby voices dimly reached her ears, barely registering in her thought processes. Tony released her slightly and for a few seconds they stared at each other. He looked as dazed as she felt, his half-lidded eyes smoky and dark, his lips wet and smeared with her lip gloss.

His voice was thick and deep when he finally spoke. "Damn, Lindsay, there's another side to you I never knew. You're a stranger that I've never met before tonight."

"I think I can say the same thing about you," she whispered. "All I hoped was to get you to talk to me."

He dragged his eyes away from hers and cast a glance to the side of the veranda. He frowned slightly as voices grew louder.

"We're not alone out here anymore," he whispered, still studying her solemnly as if she were the first woman he had ever kissed. But she knew better than that.

"Logic says we should go inside," she replied without moving. For seconds they continued to stare at each other until Tony took her arm and led her silently back inside. The small band was playing another fast number and they moved to the dance floor, stepping out in time to the throbbing beat. Still stunned by his kiss, she watched him dance, his black tux jacket swinging open as he moved with a masculine grace that was sensual, sexy, his hips gyrating and making her think of being in bed with him.

She felt her cheeks flame and looked up to meet his gaze. It was as if he read her mind. Desire was blatant in his eyes.

The band slipped into a slow ballad and Tony took her hand, drawing her into his arms to dance close. Their bodies were pressed together, his hardness against her curves, and she didn't know how long she'd be able to stay in his arms like this before she would combust. He pulled back ever so slightly to look down at her, and she was caught in his solemn gaze. For the first time, she realized his eyes were blue, with green flecks in their depths. He had thick dark brown eyelashes, straight brown hair that was neatly cut and short.

Tony Milan was *handsome*.

Down deep she had always thought that, in spite of how annoyed she had usually been with him. But up close like this now, she could no longer view him in any such detached manner. Not after that kiss. Tony Milan wasn't dime a dozen "handsome." No. He was drop-dead gorgeous.

And she wanted him to kiss her again.

The realization surprised her on top of the other jolting shocks of this night. Was she going to regret her decision to see if she could win him over with enticement and sweetness? It wasn't sweetness Tony was bringing out in her tonight. It was desire. She wanted to be alone with him and she wanted him to kiss her again. She wanted to kiss and hold him, to run her hands over him. There was no way she was going to bed with him—she'd established that boundary from the start—but she wanted more than she'd originally planned.

The night had lost its sense of reality and become a moment out of time. Everything had changed. Desire was hot, constant. Tony was sexy, virile, charming, appealing, and tonight he was the most desirable man she had ever known.

She had never expected or planned on a night like this one. Since she had decided to own a ranch, she had never wanted to date other ranchers or cowboys. She knew them too well and she didn't want them telling her how to conduct her business on the Rocking L Ranch. She loved her ranch—it was her whole life. No one had the right to come along and tell her how to run it. How many times had Tony done exactly that?

Tonight was different, though. Tony was different. How much would tonight change their relationship as neighboring ranchers? Or would they go back home with the same attitudes they had always had?

She knew she wouldn't and she didn't think he would, either.

And then she couldn't think anymore. Tony moved her hand against his chest and covered it with his own, pulling her even closer, as if wrapping their joined hands in the heat from their bodies. She inhaled the scent of his woodsy aftershave, a musky scent that was all male. She gave herself over to him and let him lead her with his sure steps. They were totally in sync as they moved, their long legs pressed against each other's. The contact was electrifying. She wanted to keep dancing with him for hours, almost as much as she wanted to be alone with him, in his arms and kissing him. Was that where the evening would lead, or would he follow the auction itinerary and go back to the Dallas country club, kiss her goodnight and each of them drive away? To her surprise, that wasn't the way she wanted to end the evening.

For the next hour they danced and she realized Tony was fun to be with when he wanted to be. He had her laughing over things he had done with her brothers over the years. She knew he was friends with them even though they were older. She was the only Calhoun who actively fought with him, but she had always blamed Tony for being such a know-it-all and so uncooperative as a neighbor. For tonight, though, she saw none of that. Far from it. He looked as if he was having a wonderful time and he helped her to have a wonderful time.

There was one rational part of her that cried out a

warning: she needed to remember why she bid on him. She couldn't let her plan backfire on her. When this night was over, she'd still need what she came here for—and that wasn't a relationship with Tony Milan. A relationship was the one thing she needed to avoid at all costs, because it would vastly complicate her life. She was here only to win his friendship so he would discuss their problems with her. If possible, even talk about their water situation.

From her earliest memories she had been taught by her grandparents not to trust Milans. Now her brother had married one and he was blissfully happy. She had to admit that she liked and trusted her sister-in-law Madison. And a distant Calhoun cousin—Destiny—had married a Milan—Wyatt, who was sheriff of Verity. Wyatt had been a shock because he proved untrue everything Lindsay had been taught by her grandparents and mother about Milans. In all her dealings with Wyatt, she had found him to be honest, friendly, fair and definitely trustworthy.

She gazed at Tony's handsome features and wondered if he could be trusted, as well. As they danced, he constantly touched her, looked intently at her. He paid her compliments, got her whatever refreshment she wanted. All his attention, his casual touches, increased her awareness of him, as well as her desire for him. She fought the temptation to tell him that she wanted to go someplace where they could be alone. She had a hotel room in Dallas for the night provided by the auction board. She could invite him back for a drink.

As much as she told herself she wanted to kiss him again, she knew where the kissing might lead. And she couldn't make love with Tony. Difficult as it was to curb her desire, she had no other choice.

Finally, as the band took a break, Tony turned to her.

"It's time for us to meet our chauffeur so we can take the plane back to Dallas. It's all arranged to get us back by midnight, so we should go now."

"Let me pick up my purse," she said.

On their flight home, Tony embodied the perfect gentleman, continuing to surprise her. She'd known he had to have a good side to him, but she'd never expected to be charmed by him or even find him such enjoyable company. Certainly not once had she thought she would be attracted to him or see him as a sexy, exciting man whose kiss set her heart pounding.

As they flew back to Dallas, Tony reached for her hand, holding it in his. "The evening will still be young when we get home. We can go dancing or just go have a drink and talk. Better yet, I have a condo in Dallas. Come back with me. I'll take you to your hotel whenever you want. We can have the place to ourselves."

Eagerness to draw out the evening made it easy to answer. "Let's go to your place," she said. "I don't want tonight to end yet. It's been fun, Tony. I know things will go back somewhat to the way they were because that's reality, but this has been a special night."

"You have no idea how special it has been. Things may go back to sort of like they were, but they won't ever again be the same as before. You'll no longer have an antagonistic neighbor. I promise."

"Dare I hope," she gasped, clutching her heart, making him laugh. Shaking her head, she smiled. "There's no way this truce is going to last."

"I'll try if you will," he said, his eyes twinkling with mischief, and she had to laugh in return.

"I promise I'll try, too," she said, looking into his eyes and again feeling an electrifying current spark between them.

"I keep waiting for a pitch from you to get me to agree to something. You all but admitted that's the purpose of your bidding for me tonight."

"Maybe I've delayed that original agenda," she said in a sultry voice. "I'm having fun, Tony. Fun that I don't want to spoil. The night is magical, a trip into a world that doesn't really exist. But for a few hours, we can pretend it does and enjoy it."

He raised her hand and brushed a light kiss on her knuckles, his breath warm on her hand.

"I'm glad," he said. "I'm not ready to tell you goodnight and watch you walk away." He placed his hands on the arms of her seat, facing her and leaning close, his voice dropping to a whisper as he said, "I want to hold you and kiss you again."

Her heart thudded and for the first time she realized she might be in trouble. Was Tony the one who would get what he wanted out of tonight instead of her? She'd planned to wring concessions from him, but now it seemed he was once again in control and she was under his spell. Not once had it crossed her mind that she could be so beguiled by him.

And she was powerless to stop it.

His gaze lowered to her mouth and suddenly she couldn't get her breath. She tingled, feeling as if she strained to lean closer to him while she actually didn't move at all. He moved closer, until his mouth settled on hers. He kissed her, another kiss that set her heart racing and made her want to move into his lap, wrap her arms around him and kiss for the rest of the flight.

Instead, in seconds—or was it minutes?—she shifted away. "This plane isn't the place," she whispered reluctantly. She had to keep her wits about her. Had to mind her goal of working out her water problem, at least par-

tially. Still, her breath came quick and shallow, matching his own.

Looking at her mouth, he didn't move for a moment
and her heart continued to drum a frantic rhythm. He
leaned closer to whisper in her ear, "I want to kiss you
for hours." His words caused a tremor to rock her. Another shock added to the continual shocks of the night.
She had no choice but to admit the truth—she wanted
him to kiss her for hours.

As his gaze met hers, he scooted back into his seat
and buckled his seat belt again.

When her breathing returned to normal, she tried for
conversation.

"Why do you have a condo in Dallas? I thought you
were as much into ranching as my brother Mike, that
both of you had devoted your lives solely to ranching."

"I'm on two boards that meet in Dallas—for my brothers. Wyatt has recently acquired a bank and I'm on that
board. Nick recently became owner of a trucking company with two close friends and I'm on that board, too.
In Dallas, I have a small condo and I like having a place
of my own I can go relax when I'm in the city. It's convenient even though I don't spend a lot of time there. I
don't have a regular staff in Dallas unless I plan to stay
a long time, which rarely happens. Then I hire from a
local agency to cook and clean."

"That makes sense."

"I spend most of my time on my ranch. When we're
back in our regular routines, I'd like for you to come over
to the MH Ranch sometime. I have a new horse and I'm
boarding a new quarter horse that Josh bought. You're
welcome to come see them, ride them and tell me what
you think."

"Sure," she said. "I suspect you better let all the guys

who work for you know that you invited me or they'll tell me I'm trespassing and toss me off your ranch."

He laughed. "I'll tell them. Now if you'll come wearing a dress with your hair down, they'll be so dazzled, there's no way they'll mention trespassing. Far from it. We'll all welcome you with open arms."

Smiling, she shook her head. "Nice try, but I don't wear a dress to ride a horse." She shrugged. "In fact, I don't wear a dress anywhere around home. But you can tell them I'm coming."

"Sure. Better yet, let me know beforehand and I'll pick you up. I probably should do that anyway, so they all know we have a truce of sorts." He turned more so that he faced her in his seat. "And it is a truce, Lindsay. Definite and permanent. I'll never again be able to fight with you."

"Don't say things you don't mean, Tony. Your intentions might be good, but there is no way this side of hell that you'll be able to stick by that statement."

Once again he leaned in closer and her heartbeat quickened as it had before. "Yes, there is definitely a way that I can be influenced to stick by that statement. You can wind me around your little finger if you really want to."

"I don't believe that one."

"You should," he said, settling back in his seat again. "Before tonight, did you ever think we would get along as well as we have?"

"Of course not." She tilted her head to study him. "In some ways, we're strangers. There's a lot I don't know about you."

"That's true and a lot I don't know about you. But strangers? No way, Lindsay. There is much I want to explore and discover about you and I intend to do that tonight," he said in a husky voice that made her heartbeat jump again.

Cutting into their conversation, their pilot announced descent into Dallas, and in a short time Lindsay looked out at the twinkling city lights spread far into the distance.

"Do you have your car at the club?" Tony asked.

"No. I left it at the hotel and took a cab."

"Good thinking," he said.

Once they arrived back at the country club, a valet brought Tony's car around and in minutes they drove through the iron gates to his condo complex.

As soon as Lindsay entered his unit, she walked through his entry hall to cross the spacious living room and look out over the sparkling lights of downtown Dallas.

"You have a gorgeous view."

"Do I ever," he said, and she smiled when she turned to see him looking at her.

"I meant the city lights," she explained, knowing he understood exactly what she had referred to.

"Want a drink?" he asked.

"Yes. White wine, please."

He removed his jacket and tie, dropping them on a chair, and walked to a bar in a corner of the room.

"This is a large living area. It's very nice," she said, looking at comfortable brown leather chairs and a long leather sofa.

"It's convenient when I'm here, which is not too often. A few days here and I'm ready for the ranch."

"That I understand," she said, crossing to the bar to perch on a stool and watch him pour her wine.

"I have a full bar if you prefer something else."

"The wine is good."

He handed her the glass and picked up a cold beer. "I figured you for a cold brew," he said, smiling at her.

He set his bottle on the counter, his gaze skimming over her legs when her skirt fell open just above her knees. "Lindsay, it's a crime to hide legs like yours all the time."

"You have no idea what I do all the time. We see each other about once every four or five months at best."

"That I intend to change."

She shook her head. "You know as well as I do that we'll go right back to our usual way of life when the sun rises in the morning."

"I hope to hell not," he said, holding up his bottle of beer in a toast. "Here's to the most beautiful neighbor I'll ever have and to a night I'll never forget."

Laughing softly, she touched his bottle with her wine-glass and sipped her wine.

"Here's to the day we can both be civil to each other," she said.

"I'll drink to that." He touched her glass, took a sip of beer and set his bottle on the bar. "But we're going to be much more than civil to each other," he said, the amusement no longer visible in his expression. With his deep blue eyes gazing intently at her, he took her drink from her hand and placed it on the bar. Her heartbeat quickened in anticipation while desire burned in the depths of his eyes.

"I've waited all evening for this moment—to be alone with you," he said, stepping closer. His arm circled her waist and he lifted her off the bar stool easily, standing her on her feet and drawing her into his embrace as his gaze lowered to her mouth.

Desire made her draw a deep breath as he leaned closer, and then she closed her eyes, winding her arms around his neck, surrendering to his kiss.

The moment his mouth settled on hers, her heart slammed against her ribs as passion ignited and desire overwhelmed her. Tony was hard, his chest sculpted with muscles, his biceps like rocks from constant ranch work. She breathed in his scent and knew she would remember it forever. She wound her fingers through his short hair and returned his kiss, wanting to stir him as much as he did her. She tightened her arms around him without having to stand on tiptoe to kiss him because her heels added inches to her height.

As Tony drew her more tightly against him, his warm hand played over her bare back and then up to her shoulders. Dimly she felt him push away her straps as they slipped down on her arms. In seconds she was aware of slight tugs to her scalp when he removed the pins and her hair fell over her shoulders and down on her back.

Slowly, while he kissed her senseless, he drew away each pin until finally her hair framed her face.

He raised his head to look at her, running his fingers slowly through the long locks. "You're so beautiful. You take my breath away, Lindsay," he whispered, sounding as if he meant every word. How could she find this pleasure with Tony? Or want him so desperately?

She had meant this night to be lighthearted, friendly, seductive, so afterward he would be civil to her and try to cooperate with her. She hadn't considered there could be this unbelievable, fiery attraction that he seemed to feel as much as she did.

No matter what he said, they'd go back to their old ways after tonight, though maybe not as contentious. This blazing attraction was for one night only. Tonight she wanted this time with him because she had never before desired or reacted to a man the way she did Tony.

His gaze shifted to her mouth and he leaned down to kiss her again. How long they stood kissing, she didn't know, but at some point, Tony picked her up to carry her to the sofa, switching off the overhead lighting, leaving only the bar light glowing softly.

She planned on some kisses and caresses and then she'd stop. Truthfully, she had never even planned on this much. Dancing, some laughs, a good time, maybe some flirting as she tried to soften him up so he would be more receptive to what she wanted.

She had never dreamed it was possible for Tony's kisses to turn her world upside down, to make her heartbeat race and cause her to desire him more than any other man. She was on fire. As if of their own accord, her hips shifted slightly against him, pressing tightly and feeling his hardness. He was ready for her.

Astounded by the need she felt for him and the response his kisses evoked in her, she kissed him wildly, her fingers unfastening the studs on his shirt, finally pushing away the fabric. Wanting to touch him, she ran her hands over his warm, rock-hard chest, growing bolder when she heard him take a deep, trembling breath. He set her on her feet while he continued to kiss her.

She felt his fingers at her waist at the back of her dress and then felt him tug down the zipper. He ran his hand lightly over her bottom and she moaned softly as her desire intensified.

While he kissed her, his hands slipped lightly up her back and across her shoulders and then came down to push her red dress over her hips so it fell softly around her ankles.

Tony stepped back to look at her. She wore only lacy bikini panties.

His eyes had darkened to a stormy blue-green and he let out a ragged breath. "I'll never forget this moment," he whispered, and stepped to her to crush her against him, kissing her deeply, a kiss that made her feel wanted and loved. She knew she wasn't loved by him, but he made her feel that way, as if he needed her more than he had ever needed any other woman.

He showered kisses on her throat while his hands cupped her full breasts and his thumbs circled their tips. His kisses moved lower until his lips met one breast while his hands caressed the other.

Running her fingers in his hair, she gasped with pleasure when his tongue circled her nipple. She was awash in desire, wanting him more than she had ever dreamed possible. She wanted his loving; she wanted all of him.

She had made a decision much earlier to end this night before it led to lovemaking, and she'd stuck with it even as they flew back to Dallas. But now desire forced her to rethink her decision, instinctively feeling that this moment would not come again.

Common sense told her that, come morning, they would go back, at least partially, to the arguments they had had all their adult lives. Tonight was special, a once-in-a-lifetime magical night that would never come again, and what they did tonight, all their loving, would carry no ties after dawn.

Tony was incredible. No man had ever excited her the way he had, and no man would ever make love to her the way she knew he would. Beyond that, she was unable to think when his hands and mouth were on her. But she was able to make a decision. She pulled back and looked into his eyes.

"Tony, I'm not protected."

He raised his head, kissing her lightly. "I'll take care of it," he whispered, and leaned down to kiss and fondle her other breast.

She wanted him with all her being, wanted to make love with him for the rest of the night. With deliberation her fingers unfastened his trousers. He grasped her wrist and she paused as he released her to yank off his boots and then his socks. He dropped them carelessly to the floor and returned to kissing her while she pushed down his trousers and then peeled away his briefs.

Her heartbeat raced as her gaze swept over his muscled body. His manhood was thick and hard, ready to love. Stepping closer, she caressed him while he stroked and showered her with kisses.

He picked her up again, kissing her when he carried her through his condo. She clung to him with her eyes closed as they kissed. He touched a light and she glanced quickly to see they were in a bedroom. She returned to kissing him until he stood her on her feet. He reached down to yank away the comforter covering his high, king-size bed.

Watching him, she felt her heart drum in anticipation of the pleasure he would give her. As her gaze swept over his muscled body, she trembled. He stepped back, looking at her in a slow, thorough study that made her tingle as much as if his fingers had moved over her in feathery caresses.

"So beautiful, so perfect," he whispered, drawing her into his embrace as he leaned over her to kiss her hungrily. His hard erection pressed against her, his hard body hot and solid against her.

Why did she want him so desperately and respond to him so intensely? His slightest touch set her quivering and his kisses rocked her, building in her a need unlike she had ever felt before. How could she have found this with Tony?

She couldn't answer her question. Nor did she care. She just wanted Tony and his loving for the rest of the night.

He lifted her into his arms again and placed her on the white sheets, kneeling beside her, his knees lightly pressing against her thighs. Then, as if in a dream—or a fantasy—he rained kisses from her ankles to her mouth.

She writhed, her hips moving slightly as blinding need built inside her until she wanted him more than she ever thought possible.

"Tony, make love to me," she whispered.

"Not so fast, darlin'. We're going to take our time and love for hours," he whispered, still showering her with kisses.

His endearment, spoken in a tender voice that she had never heard before from him, was as effective as his caresses.

"Tony," she gasped, sitting up to grasp his shoulders. "Make love to me. Let me love you."

"Shh, darlin'," he said softly while he kissed her breasts between his words. "Lie down and turn over, let me kiss you," he said, pushing gently.

She rolled onto her stomach and he picked up her foot to kiss her ankle lightly and then brush kisses higher up the back of her leg. He traced circles with his tongue on the back of her knee.

Digging her fingers into the bed, she raised her head slightly to look over her shoulder. "Tony, I can't touch or kiss you this way."

"You will soon," he whispered, and returned to his tender ministrations, trailing his tongue slowly up the back and then along the inside of her thigh.

Aflame with longing, she twisted and rolled over, sitting up to wrap her arms around his neck and kiss him, pouring all her hunger for him into her kiss, wanting to drive him as wild as he had her.

They fell back on the bed with Tony over her, his weight welcome against her. While she moved her hips against him, he kissed her as he rolled beside her. "Do you like me to touch you here?" he whispered, fondling her breast. "Do you want me to kiss you here?" he whispered, moving to brush kisses on her inner thigh, watching her as he did. "You're beautiful."

His words heightened the moment, making her more aware of him and what he was doing while she was lost in sensation and desire.

While he kissed her, his hand trailed up her leg to the inside of her thighs. When he stroked her she gasped with pleasure.

His hand moved against her, driving her to new heights. She didn't think she could take more and she reveled in the feelings he evoked in her. Needing him, she reached out and took him in one hand as her other played over his chest.

She wanted him to feel the same heady sensations he was strumming in her, so she caressed him, eliciting a growl deep in his throat. He stopped her, but he continued to love her, driving her to the brink, lifting her to the precipice of release. And then, when she was about to fall over, he pulled his touch away, shifting his hands to caress her breasts as he also showered them with kisses.

Her fingers wound in his hair. "Tony, I want you. I'm ready," she gasped, moaning with pleasure as he continued to kiss each breast, his tongue drawing lazy circles over each nipple. His fingers dallied on her stomach, but when they slipped lower, she arched against him, thrusting her hips and spreading her legs to give him access.

That was all the urging he needed. Or so she thought. He moved between her legs and she clutched his buttocks, pulling him toward her. "Tony, I want you now," she whispered. But he didn't enter her.

The warm, solid weight of him pressed against her as he stretched over her and kissed her with a hunger that made her heart pound even harder. She wrapped her long legs around him, wanting him more with each second that ticked past. Never before had she wanted to make love as much as she did now.

"Tony," she whispered again, the rest of her words smothered by his mouth covering hers and his tongue entwining with hers.

How could she want him so much? She couldn't answer her own question, she just knew she did. She ached for him, her pulse pounding. "Tony, I can't keep waiting…"

"Yes, you can and it'll be better than ever," he said. He laved her breasts, teasing her nipples between his teeth, and she felt a tug between her legs. All the while, his hands caressed her, binding them in one night of love-making that she would always remember. Though this night could not be repeated, she knew this was the time to make memories she'd carry with her forever.

"I want you now," she finally gasped, tugging him closer.

He stepped off the bed to open a night table drawer and then he watched her, his eyes burning her, as he stood beside the bed to slowly put on the condom.

As she caressed his thigh, her hips shifted slightly in anticipation. She wished he would hurry. Then, he knelt between her legs, his eyes still on hers, as he finally entered her. She wrapped her legs around him again, caressing his smooth, muscled back and hard buttocks, as he slowly thrust into her. She cried out, arching to meet him, wanting him to move with her to give her release for all the tension that coiled tightly in her.

Hot and hard, his manhood filled her, moving slowly, driving her to greater need as she clung to him and moved beneath him in perfect sync.

"Now," she cried, running her hands over his muscled thighs. He obeyed her, and her hips moved faster, her head thrashing as she was lost in the throes of passion, until finally he gave one last thrust, deep and hard, and she cried out. Arching under him, her fingers raking his back, her hips thrusting against him, she found that elusive release and he followed her, bursting within her.

"Tony," she cried.

"Ah, darlin'…" He ground out the words through clenched teeth as his body continued to move over hers.

Finally, satiated, they stilled.

"You're fantastic in every way," he whispered, kissing her temple lightly, trailing light kisses down her cheek and sighing as he lowered his weight carefully onto her.

Gasping for breath, she clung to him while her heartbeat and breathing returned to normal. Tony rolled to his side. He kept her with him, his legs entwined with hers.

"I don't want to let you go."

"You don't have to right now. I want to stay here in your arms, against you. Tony, this has been a wonderful, once-in-a-lifetime night."

"I agree," he said, hugging her lightly and kissing her forehead. "Our lives have changed."

"Not really. It may not ever again be as bad or as hateful, but tonight doesn't really change what we'll face tomorrow. My water problems, you telling me what I should or should not do, not to mention the next thing that'll come up between us."

There was silence while he toyed with locks of her hair. It seemed to her that many minutes went by until he finally spoke. "There's one question I'd like you to answer. Is water what was behind your high bid tonight? You wanted something from me, Lindsay, and I haven't heard one word about what it is."

Three

At his question, she felt her very core stiffen. She didn't want to get into that with him lying beside her and her wrapped in his arms. She didn't want to say anything that would upset him and break the spell that had been woven around them.

"We'll talk about that tomorrow. Tonight is special, Tony. I want to keep it magical until the sun rises and brings the reality of our regular lives back to us. Is that okay with you?"

"Sure, because I have plans for the rest of this magical night. Big plans."

"I do hope they involve me and your sexy body and your wild kisses."

"My sexy body and wild kisses? Wow. Definitely back to my plans for tonight," he said, leaning down to kiss her again. In minutes he propped his head on his hand to look at her again.

She couldn't tell from his eyes what he was thinking. "What?" she asked him.

He toyed with a strand of her hair as he answered. "At this moment I can't imagine ever returning to the way we were. All I'll have to do is remember tonight. All of it, darlin'."

"You better stop calling me darlin' when we go back to real life."

"I can call you that if I want."

"I suspect you won't really want to, but it's very nice tonight under the circumstances."

He smiled at her. "As you said, this is a magical night. One giant surprise after another. And deep down, I know you're right. We'll go back to our ordinary lives and our usual fights, except maybe they won't be quite so bad. After tonight I'll listen, I'll try to cooperate with you and maybe even do what you want."

She couldn't hold back a laugh. "Like hell you will!"

He chuckled, a deep throaty sound that she could feel in her hand as it lay on his muscled chest. Her fingers traced the solid muscles in his shoulders, chest and arms. Occasionally, she would feel the rough line of a scar. His daily outdoor work not only showed in the strength of his fit body but in his scars, as well.

He pulled her close against his side. "Do you have to go home tomorrow? I hope not. I want to stay right here."

"I suppose I don't, until late afternoon. I'll need to be home early Monday morning," she answered, thinking more about his flat stomach, hard with muscles and dusted with hair, over which she ran her fingers.

"Good. I have plans and they involve staying right here and not talking to anyone except each other."

"I have to check out of the hotel tomorrow by noon,

though. That room was paid for by the auction board."
She drew another circle slowly on his stomach.

"I'll call and have tomorrow night put on my card, so
you can get your things whenever you're ready," he said,
rolling over and stretching out his long arm to retrieve
his phone. "What hotel?"

"I can do that."

"Don't argue. We're not going to disagree with each
other this weekend."

She smiled as she told him the name of her hotel and
watched him get the number on his phone. Once again she
thought his take-charge attitude was delightful when he
focused on her. When he finished and she had the room
for another night, he turned to take her into his arms again.

"Thanks, Tony. That was nice of you," she said, running her fingers over the dark stubble on his jaw. "I have
to say, I didn't know I could ever be quite so fascinated
by a cowboy's body."

"I guarantee you, I'm totally fascinated by a cowgirl's
body," he said, trailing his fingers lightly over her breasts.
Even though she had a sheet pulled up over her, she felt
his feathery caresses, and her rapidly heating body responded to them.

"A beautiful blonde cowgirl," he continued, as his eyes
seemed to feast on her. "I want you here with me as long
as possible."

She felt the same way and had no desire to get up and
leave him. Though her heart wished the night could go
on forever, she couldn't get her head around the fact that
she was in Tony Milan's bed. "My family would never
believe we're together tonight. No one would."

"All those people who heard what you paid for a night
with me will believe it."

She laughed. "I suppose you're right." She rolled over

and sat up slightly to look down at him. "You're really amazing, you know that? Tonight is astonishing. I never dreamed it would be like this."

"I promise you that I didn't, either." His face took on a sheepish look. "When I stepped out on that auction stage earlier, I didn't really think anyone would bid for me."

"Now that is ridiculous."

"I'm just a cowboy."

"A cowboy named Milan—a name that's well known in these parts. And a very wealthy rancher," she remarked. "With all the ranches and businesses owned by your family, I think you could count on someone bidding for an evening with you."

"Who bid against you? I couldn't see either one of you because of the lights in my eyes, not until you stood to come to the stage and a spotlight picked you out. As soon as I laid eyes on you, my attitude about the evening did an immediate reversal."

She smiled at him. "I don't know who bid against me. There were people from Dallas and Lubbock there, and from other places, as well. Probably one of your old girlfriends who wasn't ready to say goodbye," she said.

"Let's not discuss my old girlfriends," he said through a grin. "I'd much rather talk about you anyway. I still say if you'd wear a dress to town, you'd have a slew of guys asking you out."

"I don't want a 'slew' of locals asking me out, thank you very much."

"Why not? There are nice guys out there."

"Sure there are, but they're ranchers and cowboys. I don't want to go out with ranchers or cowboys."

"You could've fooled me. You paid a small fortune to go out with a rancher tonight, in case you've forgotten."

"I won't ever forget you," she said, hoping she kept

her voice light, but a shiver slithered down her spine because she suspected she had spoken the absolute truth. This had turned into the best night of her life because of Tony. He'd charmed her, seduced her and become the most appealing man she had ever known—as long as she didn't think about him as a rancher.

He didn't let the subject drop. Instead, he questioned her. "Why don't you want to go out with ranchers or cowboys? We're nice guys."

"I know you guys are nice. It's just that—" She stopped, hesitating to tell him the truth. But Tony deserved an answer to his question. "I'm a ranch owner, remember? I'm not a party girl out for fun. I'm also not a sweetie who'll go dancing and come home and cook and have a family and kiss a cowboy goodbye every morning while he goes out to work and listen politely to him at night while he tells me bits and pieces about what he had to do at work. Even worse, I don't want to fall for another rancher and have him tell me how to run my ranch."

"I should have guessed. Two bosses can't run a ranch."

"Not my ranch," she said.

"If you don't marry a rancher or a cowboy, the guy is going to want to move you to the city."

"Now you're beginning to get the picture—the complete picture—of why I never wear dresses. I can't imagine marrying a city guy, either, so there you are." She gave a nod of her head, then shrugged. "I have a nice life. I have my nephew, Scotty, who stays with me a lot, and soon there will be another baby in Mike's family."

"But, Lindsay, you were meant for marriage in so many ways. I hope some guy comes along and sweeps you off your feet and you can't say no. Rancher or city guy."

She giggled. "My, oh, my. Is this a sideways proposal?"

He grinned. "You know better than that. We're doing

well together tonight, but for a lifetime...? Would you want that?"

She studied him, knowing she had to make light of his question, but another shiver ran down her spine and she couldn't explain why. She squeezed his biceps. "Mmm, you do make good husband material. You have all your teeth and they look in good shape and you're healthy and strong and light on your feet. And you're incredibly sexy." She gave an exaggerated sigh. "Given our past and probably our future, I think I have to answer...no."

"Incredibly sexy? Oh, darlin', come here." He drew her closer, but she resisted and placed her hand against his chest.

"Whoa, cowboy. Don't let that compliment go to your head...or other parts," she said, and he grinned.

"I told you our future will not be like our past."

She had to agree. "I don't think it will, either."

"Right now I want to relish the present. How about a soak in the tub?"

"A splendid idea," she said, already eager to be naked in the water with him.

He stood and picked her up. She yelped in surprise as she slid her arm around his neck. "I never dreamed you could be so much fun or so charming."

"I promise you, I have to say the same about you. And, to boot, you're breathtakingly beautiful and hot and sexy. I guarantee that sentiment will not end when morning comes," he added with an intent look that made her heart skip a beat.

He carried her to a huge two-room bathroom. One room held plants, mirrors, two chaise longues with a glass-topped iron table between them, plus dressing tables, a shower and an oversize sunken Jacuzzi tub.

Soon they were soaking in a tub of swirling hot water while she sat between his legs, leaning back against him.

"Tony, this is decadent. It feels wonderful."

"I suspect you're referring to the hot water and not my naked body pressed against yours. Right?"

"I won't answer that question."

"An even better choice than I expected from you. Also, I seem to remember a short time ago hearing you say something about my sexy body and wild kisses," he whispered, fondling her breasts as he kissed her nape.

"That I did and I meant it," she concurred, running her hands over his strong legs.

In no time, desire overwhelmed her, and their playful moment transformed. She turned to sit astride him. Placing her hands on both sides of his face, she leaned forward to kiss him, long and thoroughly, her hair falling over his shoulders. He was ready to love her again, too—she felt it. His hands caressed her breasts, then slid down over her torso to her inner thigh. His fingers glided higher, stroking her intimately until she closed her eyes and clung to him, her hips moving as he loved her.

"Tony, you need protection," she said, her eyes flying open.

"So I do," he said, reaching behind him for his terry robe on the footstool. He took a condom out of the pocket and, in seconds, he was sheathed and ready. He pulled her close again, lifting her so he could enter her in one smooth stroke. She locked her legs around him and lowered herself onto his hard shaft.

Her climax came fast, as if they hadn't made love earlier, and she achieved another before Tony reached his. When he was sated, he watched her with hooded eyes and she wondered what he thought.

She picked up a towel to dry herself, her gaze running

over broad shoulders that glistened with drops of water. "I'll see you in bed," she said, leaning close to kiss him. His arm snaked out to wrap around her neck.

"I want to keep you right here in my arms," he said between kisses. Damp locks of his hair clung to his forehead and he felt warm and wet.

"I'll see you in bed," she repeated with amusement. "You're insatiable. When do you run out of energy?"

"With you, I hope never."

She laughed, snatching up another towel to wrap around herself as she got out of the tub and headed to bed.

She felt as if she was having an out-of-body experience. The night continued to shock her—Tony continued to shock her. She couldn't believe he'd given her the best sex of her life, three bone-shattering orgasms—and the night wasn't over yet.

She walked into a big closet and looked at his clothes so neatly hanging. Boots were lined in rows. She found what she wanted—a navy terry robe—and she pulled it on, belting it around her waist.

She climbed into bed, detecting a faint scent of Tony's aftershave, wondering how long it would be before he joined her.

In minutes he walked through the door and her heart skipped a beat. With a navy towel knotted around his waist, he oozed sex appeal as he crossed the room.

"I couldn't wait to be with you. You look more gorgeous than ever," he said, discarding his towel and scooting beneath the sheet. "Want a drink? Something to eat? Music and dancing?"

She laughed out loud. "You've got to be kidding. Relax, Tony. Sit back and enjoy the moment." She sobered and ran her fingers over his smooth jaw. "You shaved."

"Just for you." Turning on his side, he pulled her close against him. "This is better. I like your hair down best."

"I rarely wear it that way, but I'll keep that in mind."

"No, you won't. You'll forget." He ran his fingers through the damp locks. "You know you never gave me an answer to my invitation to go to dinner next Friday night."

She was silent, mulling over his question. She had wanted to accept instantly when he had asked her the first time, but reluctance had filled her. It still did. "I think when we go back to our real lives, you'll wish you hadn't asked me."

"Not so."

"Call me next week and ask me again if you still want to go out. I don't think you will."

"Darlin', if I didn't want you to go, I wouldn't ask you."

"Just call me next week."

He gave her a long look and she wondered what was running through his mind. Had their mild clash reminded him of the big fights they'd had? From the shuttered look that had come to his eyes, she suspected it had. She didn't want any such intrusion on this night. She scooted close against him. "In the meantime, I intend to keep you happy with me," she said, hoping for a sultry voice.

The shuttered look was replaced by blatant desire, and she guessed she had succeeded in making things right between them again. When he turned to kiss her, she was certain she had.

It was midafternoon the next day when she walked out of the shower. Wearing the navy robe again, she roamed through his sprawling condo into a big kitchen that had an adjoining sitting room with a fireplace.

Exploring the refrigerator and his freezer, she saw

some drinks, a few covered dishes and an assortment of berries. She had leaned down to look at the lower shelves when Tony's arms circled her waist to draw her back against him. He nuzzled her neck.

"I know what I want," he said.

She turned to wrap her arms around his neck. He wore another thick navy robe that fell open over his broad chest.

Aware their idyll was about to end, she kissed him passionately. She dreaded stepping back into reality, where she would have to wrangle with him again.

He released her. "Hold that thought and let me put something in the oven so I can feed us."

"At last…food," she said, clutching her heart and batting her eyelashes dramatically at him. When she licked her lips slowly as she watched him remove the covered casserole dish from the fridge and nudge the door closed, he placed the dish on the counter and turned to draw her into his arms.

"You were going to get fed until you did that," he said in a husky voice, pulling her close.

"Did what?"

"You know what," he said, leaning closer to kiss her, a hungry kiss that ignited fires more swiftly than ever.

In minutes she wriggled out of his grasp. "I think we should eat. Whatever I did, I won't do again. How can I help?"

He was breathing hard, looking down, and she realized the top of her robe was pulled apart enough to reveal her breasts. She closed the robe more tightly. "As I was saying, what can I do to help?"

He seemed to not even hear her, but in seconds he looked up. "If you want to eat, I suggest you go sit over there on the sofa and talk to me while I get something heated up. If you stay within arm's reach, I'm reaching."

She smiled and left him alone, watching him put the dish into the oven and get plates, pour juice, wash berries. Her gaze raked over him. He was a gorgeous man. Sexy, strong, successful. Why hadn't some woman snatched him up already? As far as she knew from local gossip, there had never been a long-term girlfriend. Just a trail of girlfriends who'd come and gone. Apparently, he didn't go in for serious affairs.

"Tony, you really should let me help you. I feel silly sitting here doing nothing except watching you work."

"This isn't hard work. You stay where you are so I'm not too distracted to get breakfast on the table."

"I do that to you? Distract you?"

"Lindsay," he said in a threatening tone, "do you want breakfast or do you want to go back to bed?"

She laughed. "Breakfast. I'm famished. And I'll help any way I can."

"You know what you can do, so do it," he said.

"Yes, sir," she answered demurely, teasing him. When his gaze raked over her, she became aware of the top of her robe gaping open enough to give a another glimpse of her breasts and the lower half of her robe falling open over her crossed legs. She closed her robe and belted it tightly, glancing up to find him still watching her.

"Show's over," she said.

He nodded and turned to finish preparing the meal.

After a breakfast of egg-and-bacon casserole and fruit, he turned on music as they cleared the table, and took her wrist. "Stop working and come dance with me," he said, moving to a familiar lively rock number.

Unable to resist him, she danced with him, aware as

she did that her robe gaped below her waist, revealing her legs all the way to her thighs.

Next a ballad came on and he drew her into his arms to slow dance. He was aroused, ready to make love again. His arms tightened around her and he shifted closer to kiss her. Dimly she was aware they had stopped dancing.

His hand trailed down between them to untie her robe while he continued kissing her. When she reached out to do the same, his belt was tightly knotted and she needed his help, but soon both robes were open. He shoved them aside, pulling her naked body against his.

Her soft moan was a mixture of pleasure and desire as he kissed her and picked her up to carry her back to bed.

It was almost two hours later when he held her close beside him in bed and rolled over to look at her. He wound his fingers in the long strands of her hair, toying with her locks.

"I know you have to go home soon," he said. "I think it's time we get to the reason behind this weekend and your incredible bid for me at the auction. You paid a mind-boggling sum to get my attention, so now you have it. What's behind this? What did you want me to agree to do?"

Tony looked into her big eyes that were the color of blue crystal. His gaze went to her mouth and he wanted to kiss her again. He stifled the urge, difficult as it was. Their time together had been fabulous, a dream, but it would end shortly and they would go back to their regular lives. How much would it change because of the auction? For a moment a memory flashed in his mind of the second and most direct encounter they had, when a big tree on her property fell during a storm in the night. It had fallen on his fence, taking it down and also smashing one of his trucks, which had stalled in the rainstorm.

One of the men had called to tell him. When he drove out to view the damage, she was already there with a crew working to cut up the fallen tree and haul it away. She held a chain saw and had a battered straw hat on her head with a long braid hanging over her shoulder. He'd known her all his life but rarely paid any attention to her. He knew she was two years younger than he was, but right then he thought she looked five years younger. The noise of chain saws was loud, the ground spongy from the rain when he stepped out of his truck.

Even though she had to pay for the damage because it was her tree, he'd tried to curb his anger that she hadn't called him first. She saw him and walked over.

"My tree fell in the storm. Sorry about the damage. But I'm insured."

"Did you call your agent?"

"No, I will. I want to get the fence up as soon as possible so I don't lose any livestock."

"Lindsay, that's my fence and I'll fix it. You should have called me. Your insurance should cover the damages when a tree falls on something, but only if you have notified your company. They would have sent someone out to see what happened, take pictures and write a report. Now the tree is back on your property, cut up as we speak, and I doubt if you can collect anything."

She had looked surprised. "I haven't had a tree fall on anything before. I'll check with my insurance company, and I'll pay you for the damage."

"Stop cutting up the tree. I'm going to call and see if my adjustor wants to come out anyway."

She'd frowned but agreed.

"And leave the fence alone. It's my fence and I'll get it replaced today."

She had scowled at him. "Today?"

"This morning," he said. "As soon as we can. If you have livestock grazing here, move them. Don't let them in this pasture. That's simple enough," he said, wondering if she knew how to run that ranch of hers.

"I know that," she snapped.

"Leave the fence to me. Stop cutting up and hauling away the tree. I'll get someone out here to look this over," he repeated, suspecting she was stubborn enough to keep cutting up the tree.

She had clamped her mouth closed as her blue eyes flashed. "Anything else you want to tell me to do?" she snapped, and his temper rose a notch.

"Probably a lot, but I'm not going to," he answered evenly.

"Why was your truck parked right by my property?"

He had been annoyed by her question, though he tried to hang on to his temper. "It was on my property and we can park the truck wherever we want on this side of that fence. If you want to know, one of the men was headed back in the storm and checking to see if the fences were okay. He'd been driving through high water in several low places and the truck quit running here. Unfortunately, near your tree."

She'd been silent a moment as if thinking about what he had said. "I know it was my tree on your truck. My word should be good enough for the insurance."

Impatiently, he shook his head. "No, it's not good enough. Next time, remember to call your adjustor before you do anything else. You may have a hard time collecting."

He remembered her raising her chin defiantly and he'd

wondered if she would argue, but then she looked around and seemed lost in thought until she turned back to him. "That isn't a new truck. Get three estimates in Verity for the repairs and I'll cover the lowest bidder's charges."

"Look, I can't get that kind of damage fixed in Verity. At least not at three different places and you know it. The truck will be totaled."

"I'm not buying you a brand-new truck."

"Tell your guys to stop working and then go home, Lindsay, and call your insurance company. They'll tell you what to do next."

Her cheeks had grown red and fire had flashed in her eyes, but he hadn't cared if his instructions made her angry. She had already annoyed the hell out of him.

Yes, Lindsay Calhoun had that unique ability to boil his blood.

Right now, though, as he reined his thoughts back to the present and looked down at her naked body, she had the ability to heat his blood in a different way.

Tony pushed aside the past to gaze into her big blue eyes. He didn't expect what they'd had this weekend to last much longer because the real world was settling back into their lives.

Last night he hadn't cared what she wanted from him. He'd been totally focused on her as he adjusted to his new discoveries about her. Now, though, curiosity reared its ugly head and he wanted to learn her purpose behind the evening.

"You should know what I want to talk about," she said, scooting to sit up in bed and lean back against pillows, pulling the sheet demurely high and tucking it beneath her arms. Her pale yellow hair spilled over her shoulders. She looked tousled, warm and soft, and he wanted to wrap his arms around her and kiss her again, but he refrained. It was time he heard her out and learned what was so important to her that she would pay several thousand dollars just to get his attention.

"Two things, Tony," she said, and he sighed, trying to be quiet and listen, to be patient and talk to her calmly. He had already given her the solution to her water problem, but she didn't believe him. He could deal with this in a civilized manner, but underneath all her sex appeal, breathtaking beauty and their dream weekend, there still was the real woman who was mule-stubborn and did not take advice well.

Lindsay was all he avoided in women—stubborn, far too serious and constantly stirring conflict.

The irony of the fact that she was now sharing his bed was not lost on him. But he ignored it as he focused on her.

She continued her explanation. "First and foremost I hope that we have some sort of truce where we can be civil to each other, with no tempers flaring."

"I'd say we can be mighty civil to each other. You should have some of your money's worth there," he said, caressing her throat, letting his fingers drift down lightly over her breast.

"I hope so," she said solemnly.

"I'm willing," he said. "So continue."

She squared her shoulders and fussed with the sheet. Then she cleared her throat and spoke. "My wells are running dry and I figured you've replaced your old pumps with bigger ones that are drawing on the aquifer and depleting my groundwater. I can get bigger pumps, too, but that might take water from other neighbors and I don't want to do that."

He held up his hand. "I told you, Lindsay, I do not have bigger pumps."

"Well, for some reason, my water is dwindling away to almost nothing."

"It's a record drought," he said, as if having to explain the obvious to a child.

"I've asked Cal Thompson and he doesn't have bigger pumps. Neither does Wendell Holmes. I figured it was you."

"It is not. According to the weather experts, this is the worst drought in these parts in the past almost sixty years—before you and I were born, much less before we became owners of neighboring ranches. I told you the solution to my problem. You can do the same. Just dig deeper wells and you'll have much more water. Then when it rains, the aquifer will fill back up again. If you don't want to dig deeper, buy water and have it piped in. That's what Wendell is doing."

She stared at him thoughtfully in silence for several minutes. It was difficult to keep his attention on her water worries while she sat beside him in bed, naked, with only a sheet pulled up beneath her arms. He couldn't resist reaching out to caress her throat again, letting his hand slide down and slip beneath the sheet to caress her bare breasts. It took an effort to sit quietly and wait when all he wanted to do was take her in his arms and kiss her thoroughly. Well, that wasn't all he wanted to do.

The instant his fingers brushed her nipple, he saw a flicker in her eyes.

"You really had them dug deeper?"

Thinking more about her soft skin and where his fingers wanted to go, he hung on to his patience. "Yes, I did. When we get home, come over anytime and I'll show you my old pumps."

When she merely nodded, he felt a streak of impatience with her for being so stubborn. She didn't seem convinced he was telling the truth, and he suspected she wasn't going to take his advice. With every passing minute he could see her sliding back into her serious, stubborn self, stirring up conflict unnecessarily. Lindsay seemed to thrive on conflict. Except for last night. For that brief time she had been sexy, appealing, cooperative and wonderful. Now they were drifting back to reality and he had to hang on to his patience once again.

"I might do that."

As his gaze ran over her, it was difficult to think about anything else except how sexy she was and how the minutes were running out on this brief truce. She looked incredibly enticing with her bare shoulders and just the beginning of luscious curves revealed above the top of the sheet. How could she be this appealing and he had never noticed? He knew his answer, but it still amazed him that he hadn't had a clue about her beauty. In the past, once she started arguing he couldn't see beyond his anger. He saw now.

He was unable to resist trailing his fingers lightly over her alluring bare shoulder, looking so soft and smooth. If his life depended on it, he couldn't stop touching her or looking at her. He wanted to pull away the sheet, place her in his lap and kiss her senseless. They were wasting their last few moments together talking about the drought, when he had other things he wanted to do.

He leaned forward to brush a kiss on that perfect shoulder.

"Tony, you're not even listening," she snapped, her voice taking on the stubborn note he had heard her use too many times. Right now, he didn't care, because he knew how to end her annoyance.

He trailed kisses to her throat and up to her ear while his hands traveled over her, pulling the sheet down as they set out in exploration. Suddenly, she pushed him down and moved over him to sit astride him. She had tossed aside the sheet completely and was naked. It still startled him to realize what a sexy body she had.

"This weekend has opened possibilities I never thought of when I was bidding," she said in a throaty voice while her hands played over his chest.

He cupped her full breasts, their softness sending his temperature soaring. He was fully aroused, hard and ready and wanting her as if they hadn't made love ever.

"I'll leave you with memories that will torment you," she whispered, leaning down to shower kisses over his chest.

He sighed as she moved down his body, her hand stroking his thick rod as she trailed kisses over his abdomen and lower. When she reached his erection, he groaned.

He relished her ministrations, but he didn't want their last time to be like this. He wanted to be inside her. In one smooth motion he rolled her over so he was on top. His mouth covered hers in a demanding, possessive kiss at the same time that he grabbed a condom from the bedside table.

In seconds he entered her, taking her hard and fast while she locked her legs around him and rocked wildly against him in return.

He wanted to bring her to more than one climax, as he'd done before, but this time was too unbridled, too untamed. The second he sent her flying over the edge of an orgasm, he joined her, reaching the stars together on a hell of a ride.

When they slowed and their breathing became regular, he stayed inside her, too exhausted to move. Finally he kissed her lips and said softly, "You can't imagine how beautiful and sexy I think you are."

A smile lit up her eyes, though it did not grace her mouth. "I hope so. I don't want you to forget this weekend," she whispered.

He gazed into her eyes and doubted if he ever would.

This time with her had been special, but now they would be going back to their real lives. While they should be more neighborly in the future, they were still the same people, with the same personalities. Lindsay was not his type—she was way too serious for him and far too stubborn. He suspected today would be goodbye.

He pulled out of her and rolled over.

"I should get ready to go home," she said.

He turned to her. "I'll fly you home if you want to have someone pick up your car. Or I can take you home when I go."

She shook her head. "Thank you, but I'll drive home. I'd better get in the shower now. It's time," she said.

He caught her arm and she pulled up a sheet to cover herself while she paused getting out of bed.

"Lindsay, more water is a poor return on your money. For your bid and for this weekend, you should get a whole lake of water in return."

To his surprise she smiled, standing to wrap the sheet around herself in toga fashion. She walked to the other side of the bed to put her arms around his neck. When she did, he placed his hands on her tiny waist, wanting to kiss her instead of listening to whatever she had to say.

"Maybe not such a poor return," she said in the throaty voice that conjured up images of them in bed together. "We've made some inroads on our fighting that will make a huge change in our relationship. At least the fights in the future might not be so bitter."

He grinned. "We'll see how long we can both hold on to our tempers. All I have to do is remember you like this," he said, leaning down to kiss her lightly as he ran his hands over her back.

"I need to shower," she said, stepping away from him.

"Shucks. I hoped I was irresistible," he drawled, and she smiled.

"You are, Tony. Far too much," she said as she walked away from him, picking up the navy bathrobe on her way to the shower.

After her last statement he was tempted to catch up with her and kiss her again. He wanted to hold her, to see how truly irresistible he could be. But they were getting ready to go home and return to their regular lives and there would be no lovemaking in their future. With a sigh he pulled out some fresh clothes and went down the hall to another bathroom.

All the time she showered, Lindsay wondered how much this weekend would change how they treated each other at home. Tony was still Tony, telling her what to do. She hadn't said anything to him, but she wanted to check his pumps by herself. She wouldn't put it past him to be bluffing with his invitation to come look. After all, he was a Milan.

One of her earliest memories had been her grandmother telling her to never trust a Milan. Could she trust Tony now?

The Tony she had just been with for the past twenty hours was a man she would trust with her life. That thought startled her; it was completely at odds with how she'd been raised. Then again... Had her grandmother just been passing down family opinions that could have gone back generations?

Thirty minutes later, dressed and ready to go, Lindsay joined Tony in the living room. He came to his feet when she entered, his gaze sweeping over her, making her tingle. To her surprise, reluctance to see the weekend end filled her. After all, she and Tony had always known it wouldn't—couldn't—last.

Even in jeans, boots and a navy Western shirt, Tony looked sexy and handsome. A short while ago, as they'd talked about ranching, she'd felt the old annoyance with him for telling her what she should do. Now, simply looking at him made her heart beat faster.

She looked down at the red dress she'd worn last night and wore again now. "I have to go back to my hotel in this. It's four in the afternoon, so I may turn heads," she said, forcing a grin that never made it fully to her lips.

He crossed the room to place his hands on her shoulders. "Lindsay, in that dress, you'll turn heads any hour of the day or night. You're gorgeous." He reached out to play with her hair, which fell about her shoulders. "I like your hair down."

For some reason she hadn't put it up when she got ready. She couldn't say why.

"Thank you. I'm ready to go. You know what the drive is like back to the ranch. Are you going home today?" She knew he was driving her to her hotel, but wasn't sure where he was headed after that.

"No, I have an appointment in Dallas in the morning. Otherwise, I would have pushed harder to go home together."

"I see." She gave one nod. "Well, now we go back to our real lives and the real world. But it was a wonderful, magical weekend that I never, ever expected."

"My sentiments exactly," he said. "I don't want you

to go. I don't want this to end, but I know it has to and it won't be the same."

"Afraid not," she agreed with him. "I'm ready. Shall we go?"

"Yes. But how about one last kiss?" He took her in his arms and he kissed her, hard, as if his kiss was sealing a bond that had been established between them this weekend. His lips were making sure that she would never forget his lovemaking, even though she knew it wouldn't happen again.

She kissed him in kind, wanting just as much to make certain he couldn't forget her, either.

He raised his head. "How about a picture of the two of us to commemorate the occasion?" he asked, pulling out his phone. "Do you know how few selfies I've taken? I think one—with a friend and my horse at a rodeo."

She laughed. "I rank right up there with your horse. Wow."

He grinned as he held out the phone and took the shot, then he showed it to her. "You're gorgeous, Lindsay."

"Look at that picture the next time you think about dumping trash on the entrance to my ranch."

He shook his head. "I'm still telling you that I did not do any such thing. You might have annoyed someone else, you know."

Startled, she studied him. "You really mean that?"

"I really mean it."

"If you didn't do it, then I owe you an apology," she said, still staring at him. But, even if she had accused him of something he didn't do, there was bound to have been things he did do. And he still had those take-charge ways that drove her nuts. Besides, he liked to play the field and never get serious. No, Tony was not for her.

"One picture, Lindsay, just of you, so I can look and

remember. Okay?" he asked, stepping away and taking her picture as she placed her hand on her hip and smiled.

"We have to go. I need to get home," she said, shouldering a delicate, jeweled purse that matched the straps on her dress.

"Sure thing," he said, taking her arm to walk her out to the car. As she slid onto the passenger seat, her skirt fell open and she glanced up to see him looking at her legs. She tucked her skirt around her while he closed the door and walked around to his side of the car.

He was quiet on the ride to the hotel, and so was she. As he drew up to the front entrance a short while later, he stepped out and talked to a valet, then came around to escort her into the lobby. "I'm glad you were the high bidder. But I don't want to say goodbye."

"We both know the weekend is over. Really over. Reality sets in now, Tony. As we've already agreed, it might be a little better than it was."

He nodded. "You take care."

"You, too. Thanks for a weekend that was worth my bid."

"That'll go to my head. I didn't dream I could bring such a price." He smiled as he stepped away. "Goodbye," he said, turning and walking out of the hotel.

She stood watching him, unable to understand the feelings of sadness and loss as he walked away.

Four

When he vanished from sight, she turned to go to her room to change to jeans and get her things to drive back to her real life at her ranch. She wished she had gotten a selfie for herself and then she laughed at herself. If she had, at the first ornery thing he did, she would have erased it. And she didn't expect one weekend to change Tony's alpha-male ways or his flitting from woman to woman.

Even if he changed, which couldn't happen, she didn't care to break her rule about avoiding entanglements with cowboys and ranchers. Tony would be the last man on earth she would want to fall in love with because it would be disaster for each of them from the first minute. They were both ranchers, with clear ideas of how they wanted to run things and opposing ideas on most everything. Life with Tony would be a continual battle. Unless he retired and just stayed in the bedroom. That thought made her laugh out loud as she drove all alone in her car, heading west out of Dallas and back to her ranch.

Midmorning on Tuesday as Tony sat at his ranch desk and worked at his computer, trying to find Texas water sources, his phone rang and he answered to hear his brother Wyatt.

"I thought I better call and see if you survived Saturday night. I heard you didn't come home until Monday evening."

"Keane, my foreman, always knows how to get hold of me. You didn't know I was worth so much money, did you?" Tony asked.

Wyatt laughed. "You brought in a fortune at the auction. And it was all for a good cause, so thanks. You really contributed, but don't let it go to your head. Even though this is bound to bring another slew of admiring females into your life."

Tony hadn't thought of that. "Maybe, but there's one thing I do know. I will never bet with you on saddle bronc riding events again."

Wyatt gave a belly laugh. "How'd the date with Lindsay go, bro? I was worried what she might want to do with you. I gotta tell you, I had no idea she could look like she did."

Tony recalled the blonde beauty who was such a surprise. "Lindsay's looks sent me into shock, and once I caught sight of that red dress, the evening instantly improved. But you shouldn't worry. We did fine together."

"I figured her looks would smooth things over. Don't know if you know yet, but the two of you are all the gossip in Verity and in the sheriff's office. I've been asked more than a few questions. I think around my office, they're waiting for a report from me about how the evening went."

"Civilized. That's what you tell them. We just set aside our differences—for charity."

"I'll bet you did," Wyatt said, and Tony could hear the amusement in his brother's voice. "No way in hell would you fight with someone who looked like she did Saturday night. And she must have wanted something from you badly to pay that kind of money."

"Yeah, she wants more water."

"Don't we all. She should know you can't help her out there. No rain in the forecast, either. Hang on a sec, Tony." Wyatt put him on hold while he consulted with one of his deputies. When he returned, he was back on what appeared to be his favorite subject. "Like I was saying, some people will never look at Lindsay the same way. Those who didn't see her at the auction are curious as hell. I don't know why she keeps those looks hidden."

"She's not interested in dating cowboys or ranchers. She doesn't want anyone telling her how to run her ranch. You can figure that one out."

"Definitely. I was shocked to see who had won the bid," Wyatt remarked drily.

Tony would agree with that. "We had a good time Saturday night, but she's still Lindsay, all stubborn and serious. But we did agree to ease off the fights from now on."

"Thank heaven for that one. My life will get a hell of a lot more peaceful. Call when you come to town."

"Sure, Wyatt."

After he hung up, he stared at the phone, thinking about Lindsay, and he was tempted to pick up the phone and call her. Then reason reared its head. Beneath all that beauty, he reminded himself, she was still the stubborn, obstreperous woman she had always been. She was as wise to avoid ranchers as they were to avoid her. She was not his type. Still…that weekend with her had been the sexiest in his life, and she had been the sexiest woman he'd ever been with.

He had to shake his head to get rid of the images that flooded his mind. The two of them in bed, in the Jacuzzi… No, he had to leave things alone. The weekend was over and it wouldn't happen again.

Breathing a sigh, he turned to the ledger he needed to work on and tried to forget her and the steamy memories of their weekend.

The next few days slipped by without a cloud in the bight blue sky, the drought growing more severe as water dwindled in the creeks and riverbeds and strong, hot winds warmed the parched earth. Lindsay threw herself into work, trying to forget the weekend with Tony, but she was unable to do so. It surprised her how much she thought about him. Even worse, she finally admitted to herself that she missed seeing him. She gritted her teeth at the thought. She didn't want to miss Tony. She didn't want him or the weekend they'd had to be important. Her reactions to him continually shocked her.

All her adult life she had avoided going out with men who would want to tell her how to run her ranch. She had managed, until Tony. That was the road straight to disaster. She didn't want to marry a take-charge male— and a Milan, to boot!—and then fight over running everything. There was no way she would be in agreement on everything or turn her ranch over to someone else to run. She shook her head, knowing she needn't worry. Tony wouldn't ever get close to proposing to her. He wasn't going to propose to any woman. He was not even the type of person she wanted to go out with again, and she was certain he felt the same way about her.

It was done. They were done. It was that simple.

Turning back to work, she forced him out of her mind. Soon she wouldn't even think about him.

But that resolve didn't stop her from mulling over his property. That afternoon when she drove her pickup along the boundary between her ranch and Tony's, she stopped, switched off the engine, got binoculars and climbed up on her pickup to find out if she was close enough to see his pump on the water well nearest her land.

It was visible in the distance, but she couldn't tell whether it was old or new. Damn. Time was running out for her.

How much longer could she go without rain?

Her other neighbors were buying water and having it piped or shipped in.

Tony had told her to come look at his pumps. If he still had the old pumps and he had dug deeper—if he was telling the truth—then that would be the best thing for her to do. She frowned. Why did it rankle so much to do what he told her to do?

As she looked at his land, she couldn't keep from moving her binoculars in a wide swing, curious whether Tony worked in the area. She didn't see him and she hated to admit to herself that she was disappointed. She missed his company. Now she was sorry she hadn't accepted his dinner invitation for Friday night, instead telling him to call her this week if he still wanted to take her out again. She hadn't expected to hear from him and so far, she had been right. It was Thursday and he hadn't called, so he must have had second thoughts when he got home.

She hated to admit that she was disappointed, but she told herself it was for the best. Still, she couldn't stop the memories… She remembered being in his arms, his kisses, his blue-green eyes that darkened to the color of a stormy sea when he was in the throes of passion. How could he be so handsome and so sexy? Maybe it had been the tux. Or his naked body that was male perfection. Or his—

Her ringing phone cut off that steamy train of thought. Shaking her head as she wiped her brow, she yanked her cell out of her pocket expecting Abe, her foreman, but the caller ID read T. Milan. Her heart missed a beat as she stared at the phone until the next ring jolted her out of her surprise. She said hello and heard Tony's deep voice.

"How are you?" he asked politely, and suddenly she was suspicious of why he was calling, but at the same time, she was happy to hear his voice.

"I'm fine. Actually, I'm at our boundary line and looking at your closest well trying to see your pump."

"Hey, are you really? I'm not far. Stay where you are and I'll join you and give you a closer look."

She laughed. "You don't need to."

"Of course I don't need to, but I'm already headed that way, so don't drive off."

"I wouldn't think of it."

"Oh, I almost forgot. I called to ask about dinner tomorrow night."

So he hadn't had second thoughts after all. She couldn't stop the smile from spreading across her lips.

"How about something simpler than last weekend?" he continued before he had her answer. "Like Marty's Roadhouse? I know it's two counties away, but if we go anywhere around here, you'll be besieged by cowboys wanting to take you out. Also, we'll be the top of the list for local gossip."

"I don't want either to happen."

"We'll do a little two-steppin' and eat some barbecue and discuss what you can do to get water."

She should say no. They could talk about water on the phone or when he arrived in a few minutes. Common sense told her to decline. But then she thought about dancing with him. If she just had some self-discipline and had him bring her home after dinner, an evening with him couldn't hurt. "That would be good," she said.

"Great. I'll pick you up at six. We'll have a good time dancing."

She heard a motor. "I think I hear you approaching."

"You do. Stay where you are."

"See you in seconds," she said, and broke the connection. Amused, she pulled on leather gloves and parted strands of barbed wire that formed the fence that divided their property. She had been climbing through or over barbed wire since she was little. She straightened to watch him approach.

He drove up in a red pickup, stopped and jumped down. As he came into view, she saw that he wore a light blue long-sleeved shirt with the sleeves rolled up, tight jeans, boots and a black broad-brimmed hat.

She knew she was going against good sense getting involved any more deeply with Tony. So why did her entire body tingle at the sight of him?

"You look great," Tony said as he approached her and reached out to tug her braid. "I never realized how good you look in jeans."

She laughed. "Until last weekend, I never realized you could look at me without getting annoyed."

Grinning, his gaze roamed down her legs again and every inch of her felt his eyes on her. "Oh, darlin', those jeans do fit you. I just should have taken a second look." He looked into her eyes and her breath caught. How could he cause such a reaction in her now? She had known him all her life and until last weekend she'd never once had this kind of response to him just saying hello.

"I'm glad you said yes to tomorrow night," he said, the amusement fading from his expression.

Her smile vanished when his did. "Tony, we're probably doing something we shouldn't. You and I have no future with each other in a social way."

He didn't argue with her and, instead, continued to stare at her. He shrugged and stepped closer to run his finger along her cheek. The feathery touch sizzled and she had to draw a deep breath and resist walking into his arms.

"It's just a fun Friday night, Lindsay. Surely we can do that just one more time."

She knew the more time she spent with him, the more she could get hurt. Tony would not change, and neither would she. At the next problem to come up between them, he would be telling her what to do and she would be angry with him all over again. She needed to stay rooted in reality for the good of her ranch, because she couldn't afford to be sidetracked by him. "Come on," he urged. "We'll have a good time dancing. Marty's on Friday night is fun."

"Until the fights break out."

"That doesn't happen often and if it does, we'll get out of there. I have no intention of spending any part of my night in a brawl."

"So it's two-stepping and eating."

He caught her braid in his hand again as he gazed into her eyes. "Plus some kissing."

She drew a deep breath, wanting him to lean closer and kiss her now yet knowing at the same time that she shouldn't want any such thing.

His phone rang and he looked at it. "I have to go, so let's look at the pumps another time. I have an appointment, but I thought as long as I was close, I'd come say hello. Tomorrow night can't come soon enough." He looked at her as if he still had something he wanted to say. Silence settled between them and she wondered what it was and what was keeping him from saying it.

"I've missed being with you," he finally said. He placed his hands on her shoulders, and an odd expression came over his face. "You seem shorter."

She laughed. "I am. I'm not in my high heels like last weekend."

"Oh, yeah," he said, still staring at her. "But you weren't always wearing heels last weekend," he added in a low voice. "Oh, dang," he said, on a ragged exhale. "I shouldn't, but I'm going to anyway." Pulling her closer, he kissed her.

Her heart thudded and she couldn't catch her breath. His kiss was thorough and sexy, making her heart race. And she responded to it instantly.

When he released her, he was breathing hard. "I have to go. I'll see you tomorrow night at six. Leave your hair down so I can see if it looks as good as I think it did last weekend." As she laughed, he grinned while he placed his hands on her waist to pick her up and set her on the other side of the fence. She remembered how easily he'd carried her in his arms Saturday night. He went back to his pickup in long strides, climbed in, waved and drove away.

Her lips still tingled as she stood there staring after him in a daze. "I should have said no," she whispered to herself. "I should not be going out with him. He's still Tony, all alpha male, a man I've always fought with."

Each hour she spent with him only meant more trouble. She knew that as well as she knew her own name. But she'd already accepted, and besides, it was just dinner and dancing, in a place with lots of people. And talking about water. Far from romantic. She wasn't going back to his ranch afterward. Their evening together would be meaningless.

So why couldn't she wait for tomorrow night?

Lindsay studied herself in the mirror while her two Australian shepherd dogs lay nearby on the floor. It was ten to six; Tony would be here any minute. Time for a last check in the mirror. She'd brushed her hair, curled it slightly in long, spiral curls and finally tied it behind her head with a blue silk scarf. She wore a black Resistol, a denim blouse with bling, washed jeans with bling on the hip pockets and her fancy black hand-tooled boots.

She turned to her dogs and each raised his head.

"I promise you, Tony Milan will not be invited inside tonight. When he comes to the door, don't bark at him and don't bite him."

Both animals thumped their tails as she patted their heads and left the room. The dogs followed her to the front room, where she could watch the drive.

In minutes she heard Tony's pickup approach the house. Hurrying to the door, she turned to tell the dogs to sit. As soon as they did, she opened the door. The sight of Tony took her breath away, just as it had when she had seen him yesterday. His black hat, long-sleeved black Western shirt, tight jeans and black boots made him look 100 percent gorgeous cowboy.

She kept a smile on her face as he approached, even as she silently reassured herself there was no way an attraction between them could possibly develop into anything meaningful. With Tony that was impossible and she was certain he felt the same way. As the dogs barked, she gave them commands that caused them to stop, and they came forward quietly to meet Tony, who patted their heads.

"Hi, cowboy," she said.

"Oh, yeah, you don't go out with cowboys. Well, consider this a business dinner," he said, his eyes twinkling.

"Of course. And business kisses."

"Who said one word about kisses?" he asked, his voice lowering a notch as he placed his hand on the jamb over her head. While she looked up at him, her pulse raced.

"I thought there might be a few kisses as well as dinner."

"We could just skip dinner and go inside and you can show me your bedroom."

She smiled and tapped his chest. "What finesse. I think not. You promised dancing and barbecue."

"Whatever the beautiful lady wants," he said, sounding serious, as if he had stopped joking and flirting. She wanted to step into his arms and kiss him. Then she remembered Tony had broken more than a couple of hearts with his "love 'em and leave 'em" ways.

"Let me turn on the alarm, lock up and we can go," she said in a breathless voice that she hoped he wouldn't notice.

"Sure thing." As she moved back, his eyes raked her body. "Each time I see you, you look fantastic."

"Thank you." She said goodbye to the dogs, who now sat near his feet. "You must have a way with dogs. They don't usually take to strangers."

"Women, children and dogs," Tony said.

"I suppose I have to agree on the women and dogs because that's definitely proven. I don't know about children."

"They love me, too," he said with humor in his voice. "Ask your nephew, Scotty."

Smiling, she switched on the alarm and stepped out with him, hearing the lock click.

He linked her arm in his and they walked to his red pickup.

"Allow me," he said as he held the door for her. She climbed in, aware of his constant scrutiny.

"I do love tight jeans," he said, closing the door behind her.

Laughing, she watched him walk around the pickup, feeling excitement mount as she looked forward to being with him again.

"Some of my family has called me to ask about our evening. My guess is that yours has called you," she said, turning toward him as much as her seat belt allowed. She could hardly believe she was sitting here next to him. Her anticipation of this night with him had built all day.

There still was no danger of it becoming a habit for either of them, just one more night—only a few hours of dancing and talking and, maybe, kisses at her door. As they turned on the road toward the county highway, she gripped his arm. "Tony, look over there in the trees. That's a wolf."

Tony followed the direction of her hand and looked toward a stand of scrub oaks. He didn't see any animal. "I don't see anything and there are no wolves in Texas."

"There's one on my ranch. Look."

She was insistent, so he slowed and backed up, stretching his arm over the back of the seat as he reversed the car around the curve. He saw a furry gray animal at the edge of the trees.

"That has to be a coyote," he said. "It looks like a wolf, but it's not. There aren't any in Texas."

"It's too big and furry to be a coyote," she said. As they

watched, the animal turned and disappeared into the darkness of the trees.

"That animal didn't really look like a dog," Tony said, putting the car in gear and continuing to drive. "Well, we've always got wild animals around here. My money's on a coyote."

"It's a gray wolf. They have them now in New Mexico, and a wolf doesn't know state boundaries. They could easily roam into Texas and probably already have. That was only a matter of time. Remember, there's an old legend around these parts about a gray wolf roaming West Texas and anyone who tames him will have one wish granted."

Tony glanced at her with an exaggerated leer. "I know what my wish would be," he said, his gaze sweeping over her.

She laughed. "You lusty man. You've got no chance of taming it. You'd have to catch the wolf first." She returned to her earlier topic. "About our families…"

"Yeah," Tony said. "Wyatt called me Tuesday morning and said we're the hot topic in Verity."

"Imagine that. Me—the hot topic in Verity. Well, let them talk. It'll die down soon because there won't be enough to talk about."

He cast a glance at her. "I'll bet some new guys have asked you out since last Saturday night."

"They have," she said, "but I turned each one down. A couple were at the auction and a couple heard about the auction," she said, having no intention of telling him six guys who saw her Saturday night had asked her out and three who had simply heard about the auction had called and one more had dropped by the ranch.

"All ranchers, I suppose."

"Ranchers, cowboys and an auctioneer from Fort Worth. No way will I get involved with any of them."

"I can understand that, except you're with me tonight."

She smiled. "Maybe you've moved into the classification of an old friend. Besides, there's no danger of involvement for either one of us. I figure this for our last time together."

"You're probably right," he said.

"You can dance, you're fun, and after last weekend, we're civil to each other. I'm sure we'll have a good time."

"I agree about the good time. I can't wait to get you on the dance floor."

"Also, I want something from you."

He shot her a quick glance and then his attention went back to the road. "What can I do for you?" he asked evenly, but his voice had changed, taken on the all-business tone that she was more familiar with.

"I'm trying to see if I can finagle an invitation to your ranch."

He smiled. "Darlin', I thought you'd never ask! I'll take you home with me tonight."

"Cool it, cowboy. I just want to take you up on your earlier offers to look at one of your water pumps."

His smile disappeared and she wondered if he wanted to turn around now and take her home. "Sure, Lindsay. Tell me when you want to come."

His voice had turned solemn and a muscle now worked in his jaw. She knew she was annoying him, but she wanted to see for herself if he still had his old water pumps.

"Thanks, Tony. I appreciate your offer. You told me to come look."

"So I did," he answered, and then he became silent as they drove on the empty road.

After they reached the county road, he glanced at her

once again. "Lindsay, if that's what you wanted tonight, and why you accepted, do you still want to go?"

"But, Tony," she said in a sultry voice, "that wasn't the sole purpose of accepting your offer to go dancing tonight." She ran her fingers lightly along his thigh. "I also remember how much fun and sexy you can be."

She received another one of his glances and saw him inhale deeply. "Then I'm glad you're here, darlin'. That makes the evening much better. 'Fun and sexy,' huh? I'll try to live up to that description."

She laughed. "I'm sure you will," she said.

Flirting with him made the drive seem shorter, and he flirted in return, causing her to forget about water pumps.

When they reached the roadside honky-tonk, loud music greeted them outside the log building. Inside, they found a booth in the dark, crowded room that held a few local people she knew but more that she didn't.

As soon as they had two beers on the table, Tony asked her to dance. The band, made up of a fiddler, drummer and piano player, had couples doing a lively two-step. As they stepped into the group, Tony held her hands, staying close beside her as they circled the room, and then he turned her, so she danced backward as he led. His gaze locked with hers. Desire was evident in the depths of his eyes as he watched her while they danced. She had his full attention and she tingled beneath his gaze and forgot about her problems.

They danced past midnight and after they returned to their table, he leaned closer. "Ready to leave? We can't talk in here anyway."

When she nodded, he stood, waiting as she slid out of the booth to walk out with him. The air was warm outside, the music fading as they climbed into his pickup.

Light from the dash highlighted his prominent cheekbones, but his eyes were in shadow. The ambience reminded her of their night together, when the dim light of his condo bedroom had shielded his eyes from her view. The memories stirred her as she recalled making love with him. She had tried to avoid thinking about him all week, yet here she was with him. This was crazy. She had to get over Tony, forget him and go on with her life. No way did she want to think about their lovemaking or give him a hint that she would ever want to make love to him again.

As they approached her ranch house, lights blazed from it. "Looks like you have a house filled with people."

"I leave it that way. I don't like to come home to a dark, empty house. And I leave some lights for the dogs," she explained. "Drive around to the back door. It'll be easier for me."

He drove through her wrought iron gates, which closed automatically, and did as she instructed. "I can tell you a better way to avoid a dark, empty house. Come home with me." He unbuckled his seat belt and turned to her. "My house will be neither dark nor empty, and I promise you some fun."

She smiled at him, able to see his eyes now; their blue depths seemed to sparkle even in the darkness. "Thanks, but I belong here. Besides, we agreed on the parameters for tonight."

"It's temptation. You're temptation, Lindsay. Beyond my wildest imaginings," he said, leaning forward to unlock her seat belt. As he did, his lips nuzzled her throat while his fingers caressed her nape. Then he turned to get out of the truck and strode around to open her door for her.

He draped his arm across her shoulders as they walked to her door. "Tonight was fun. I could dance with you for hours. There are a lot of things I could do with you for hours."

Her insides tightened and heated, but she forced a grin. "Is playing chess one of them?" she asked, trying to lighten the moment and get his mind off making love.

"No, chess is not what I had in mind at all," he said as he stopped and turned her to face him in the yard under the darkness of a big oak. As he slipped his arm around her waist, her heart thudded. He leaned close to trail kisses on her neck, her ear. "No, what I want to do is hold you close, kiss you until you melt," he said in a deep, husky voice.

His words worked the same magic on her as his lips and hands. Her knees felt weak and she wanted his mouth on hers. Forgetting all her intentions to keep the evening light, she slipped her arm around his neck and raised her mouth for his kiss.

"Why do I find you so damn irresistible?" she asked.

The moment his mouth touched hers, her heart thudded out of control. More than anything she wanted a night with him, wanted to ask him in, but she intended to stick with her promise to herself to say goodbye to him at her door. He deepened the kiss, his tongue stroking hers, slowly and sensually, and she could barely remember what promise she was thinking about. He was aroused, ready to make love, and she, too, ached to take him to her bedroom and have another night like before.

She didn't know how long they had kissed when she finally looked up at him. She had no idea where her next words came from. "I better go in now."

He stared at her, his hot gaze filled with desire that wrapped itself around her and held her in its spell. Stepping out of its heat, she turned to walk onto her porch. Reluctantly he followed.

When they entered the house, the dogs greeted them. She turned them into the fenced yard, closed the door and faced him.

Though he didn't ask for one, she wanted to give him an explanation.

"Tony, we both agreed last weekend was an anomaly. As special as it was, it's over and we need to leave it over. I don't want an affair and I don't think you do, either. With our families intermarried, we would complicate our lives. We're not really all that compatible anyway. I'm too serious for you and you're too much a playboy for me. If I have an affair, I want it long-term, with commitment. You're not the type for that."

"Don't second-guess me, Lindsay. You're incredibly desirable."

"Do you really want us to get deeply involved?"

He inhaled and gazed at her while seconds ticked past.

"I think that's an answer," she said, "and I agree with it."

"There will never be a time when I can look at you and honestly say I don't want you. I—" He stopped when she placed her fingers against his lips.

"Shh. Don't say things that you don't really know."

Kissing her fingers before she took them away, he nodded as he released a breath. "Okay, so we say good-night now. But I'm not going without a goodbye kiss."

He reached out to take off her hat and toss it onto a nearby chair along with his. "Hats get in the way sometimes," he said as he pulled loose the silk scarf that held her hair behind her head and dropped it into her hat. She shook her head and her hair swung across her shoulders to frame her face.

"You're beautiful, Lindsay," he whispered before his mouth covered hers. He kissed her hard, a passionate kiss that tempted her to throw away common sense and invite him upstairs for one more fabulous night.

She felt his arousal, knew he was as ready to make love as she.

But suddenly, before she could speak, he released her. "Good night, Lindsay. If I don't go right now, I won't go at all. I know what you really want is for me to leave." Before she could move, he turned and hurried out the door.

She fled to her bedroom before she called him to come back. Her heart pounded and she ached with longing for him. How could she feel this way about Tony? A Milan, and her nemesis for so many years?

She had to get beyond this heart-pounding reaction she had to him. She couldn't afford to see him again because each time bound her more closely to him.

He had walked out of her life tonight and there wasn't any reason for him to come back into it. At least not in the immediate future. Things would always happen that would cause them to see each other, but her usual encounters with Tony had been only three or four times a year.

When she had asked him if she could come to his ranch and look at one of his pumps, the question had made him angry. Would he be even angrier if she actually went to his ranch? He probably would, but she was going anyway to see for herself whether he had been truthful. It had been ingrained in her by her family not to trust a Milan and she found it difficult to trust Tony on ranch matters.

And personal matters? After last weekend, she might have to answer that question differently.

She lay across the bed, the lights out, and as thoughts of Tony swirled in her mind, she knew she'd never sleep tonight. Not when she was wishing she were with him, in his arms, naked beside him. Would he sleep? Knowing him, she figured he'd sleep like a bear in winter.

She closed her eyes against the tears that stung them. Tony was out of her life—where he should be. There was no way they had any future as a couple. She'd accomplished all she'd set out to do that night at the bachelor auction. She'd bid on him to butter him up, to make him more amenable. At least that seemed to have worked. With any luck, the fights had stopped or at least changed to simple quarrels. If that had happened, it all would have been worthwhile.

There'd be no more calls from Tony after tonight. The thought swept her with a sense of loss. She shook her head as if she could shake away the feeling. How long would it take her life to get back to normal?

Five

He hadn't been ready to tell her goodbye tonight. The whole time he'd cruised down the driveway he'd watched her house in the rearview mirror, fighting the urge to turn around.

If he let himself, Tony could envision the scene clearly. He'd stop sharply, his tires spewing dirt and gravel as he spun around and gunned his engine. When he pulled up at her back porch, she'd be there throwing open the door, and she'd run to him just as he stepped out of the truck. He'd pick her up in his arms and carry her back into her house, right up to her bedroom. They wouldn't say a word to each other; they wouldn't need to. They'd simply make love. And it would be amazing.

A nice image, he had to admit. But one that wouldn't happen.

Instead, he drove the pickup onto the county road toward his own ranch.

He couldn't help but feel tense, and not just sexually.

He'd been looking forward to this night with Lindsay, and to say it hadn't ended the way he'd hoped would be an understatement. But she was right. They had no future. And Lindsay wasn't the type of woman to have an affair without a future.

And she was too serious, just as she said.

Not to mention the whole business with her wanting to see his water pumps. Damn, she still didn't believe that he hadn't installed bigger pumps to steal her water. She wanted to see it with her own two eyes. Because he was a Milan, no doubt, and Milans never told the truth!

He banged the palm of his hand on the steering wheel. He needed to forget her.

As he drove along the darkened road, he turned on the radio, but the guy who sang—some guy who'd won one of those ubiquitous TV reality shows—strummed a soulful guitar and sang about the cute filly he was pining for. Tony didn't want to hear it. He shut it off. He had enough of his own problems with his own cute filly. A spirited one, at that.

He had to let out a laugh at the thought of Lindsay knowing he had referred to her as a filly. She'd probably take out her shotgun and fill him with buckshot.

The drive home seemed endless, but by the time he pulled onto the long driveway up to his ranch house, he knew what he had to do. He had to forget everything about Lindsay Calhoun, starting with last Saturday night. From the moment he'd seen her in that red dress all the way to tonight. As sexy, as enticing, as appealing as Lindsay was, she wasn't the woman for him. They could never be together. She was commitment with a capital *C*, and that was one thing he couldn't—wouldn't—ever be willing to give.

He entered the house and went up to bed, not even bothering to turn on a light.

* * *

She hadn't bothered to turn on the light.

For some reason, that thought struck her as she woke up. She remembered running up to her room, in the dark, after Tony left, and throwing herself on the bed, sad and uncharacteristically near tears. She thought she'd never sleep tonight, but apparently she had.

She felt beside her and at her feet, but the dogs weren't in their usual position. Then she remembered. She'd let them out when she got home and then forgotten about them. They'd probably gone over to the bunkhouse for the night.

She sat up, glancing at the clock on her bedside table to see it was after three in the morning. A long, sad howl sent chills down her spine and she ran to the window to look out. Another sad howl filled the night.

Moonlight splashed over open spaces and something moved. Chills ran down her spine again as she saw the wolf standing at the edge of a grove of trees. As she watched, it threw back its head and howled again.

She shivered. For the first time since being on the ranch, she felt alone and didn't like it. She wished she had kept the dogs with her and hoped no one at the bunkhouse turned them out, because she didn't want them tangling with a wolf. She also hoped no one at the bunkhouse got his gun. The men were good shots. If they wanted to kill the wolf, they would surely succeed. She grabbed her phone to call her foreman, thought about it and decided it would be ridiculous to wake him. When morning came, she would talk to Abe about the four-legged intruder.

Another lonely howl caused a fresh batch of shivers to crawl up her spine. Impulsively, telling herself she shouldn't, she called the one person she thought of.

She felt silly when Tony answered, and she suddenly

wished she hadn't called him. But she'd awakened him and she had to explain why.

"Sorry, Tony. I know I woke you."

"Lindsay? Are you okay?" he asked, in a surprisingly clear, alert voice.

"I'm fine, Tony." Now that she had him on the phone she couldn't seem to tell him about the wolf. What did she expect him to do about it?

"Okay then, darlin', what's on your mind at…3:17 a.m.?"

"I feel really silly now."

"Lindsay, you didn't call me in the middle of the night to tell me you feel silly."

"The wolf/coyote/dog—except it looks like a wolf—is howling near my bedroom. I can see it and the animal sounds hurt."

"All animals sound hurt when they howl. So? I know you're a crack shot even with that big .45 you own. Take him out and go back to sleep."

"A gunshot would wake everyone on the ranch and create an uproar. Anyway, I can't kill him. Or her. He or she sounds pitiful and eerie, and for the first time since I've owned the ranch I don't like being here alone."

"I'm coming over."

"No, Tony. I just wanted to hear your voice. Don't get up and come over."

"I can be there in a few minutes."

"Stay in bed," she said, hearing another long howl and looking at the animal standing half in the moonlight and half in shadow. "I feel sorry for it. It sounds hurt and lonesome."

"I'll be over in a flash. I can really take your mind off the wolf, howls or no howls."

She smiled and sat back in the chair by the window.

"You're succeeding right now and you just stay home. We'll both be better off."

She didn't want a repeat of the scene they'd endured only hours ago at her back door. Watching him walk away was hard enough then; she couldn't go through seeing him—and losing him—again.

"That may be true for you, but if I come over, I would definitely be better off."

Despite herself, she laughed softly. "You make me feel so much better. But I still think you should stay home."

"Lindsay, I'm already pulling on my jeans."

"Don't. I really mean it. I feel better now and I can go back to sleep, and I know you can roll over and go to sleep the minute your head is on the pillow." She refused to picture him taking off his jeans and getting back into bed, shirtless and sexy.

"Fine," he said. "The guys will take care of the animal for you and, hereafter, you won't have to listen to it howl again."

"I don't know why, but I feel sorry for it. Unless it kills some of the livestock, I'd hate for them to shoot it."

"Well, this is a change. You're usually pretty damn tough and I know you've shot plenty of wildlife."

"Now how would you know that?"

"The guys talk. And I remember a few marksmanship competitions over the years. Come to think of it, you haven't participated in any in a long time."

"Nope. It doesn't seem to matter any longer. When I first got the ranch, I felt I had to prove that I could handle running the place and a few other things. I don't feel that way any longer."

"I would think not. Half the ranchers around here call you about their animals."

"Not really half, but a few have," she said. She settled

back in the chair to talk, forgetting about everything but the sound of his voice, soothing and smooth as it settled around her in the darkness. It was an hour later when they finally said goodbye and she went to bed. That's when she realized the howls had stopped long ago, but she hadn't actually noticed when, thanks to Tony.

As the next week passed, Lindsay tried to keep busy and struggled to stop thinking about Tony, but that was impossible. She heard nothing from him for eight more days, but, instead of forgetting about him—something she once could easily do—she thought about him constantly, to the point where she had been distracted at work.

It was Thursday, in the middle of a hot, dry afternoon, after she'd helped move steers to another pasture, when her phone rang and she saw it was Tony. She pulled her truck off the road into the shade of an oak and opened the windows.

"It's Tony. I thought it was time to see if you want to come look at the pumps on my water wells."

She was surprised, to say the least. Even though he'd offered, she'd never really expected him to have her over to his ranch—because she still figured he had installed new and bigger pumps. She glanced at her watch. "Give me about two hours and I'll be there. Tell everyone I'm coming so they don't send me away if they see me."

"Nobody's going to send you away and my foreman knows I was going to call you. Come on over. See you in two hours," he said, and ended the connection.

She looked at her phone for seconds, as if she could see Tony. Was he up to some trickery to convince her that he still had his old pumps and had just dug deeper?

She would never tell Tony, but she had already started checking into having her wells dug deeper, and Tony had been right. If she went deeper, there was still water in the aquifer, and when the rains finally came, that depleted water would be replenished and everything would be like it was.

She had already told the men she was headed home, so she started her truck and drove back to her house to shower. She changed into washed jeans, boots and a short-sleeved blue cotton shirt. She knew Tony liked her hair down and not fastened, but she was back at home and she didn't care to change her appearance, so she braided her hair and got her wide-brimmed black hat.

She hadn't been to Tony's ranch house even though she had seen pictures of it on the web, along with a map of his ranch land. As she approached, she looked at the sprawling two-story ranch house that appeared even larger than hers. A porch ran across the front and a wide circle drive joined a walk leading to the front porch.

Flower beds surrounded the house with rock and cactus gardens, plants well adapted to the drought that usually hit West Texas. As she approached, Tony crossed his porch, coming to meet her, his long legs covering the distance. His hair was combed and he had on a clean short-sleeved blue-and-red-plaid shirt, tucked into his jeans. She smiled, happy to see him again.

Tony opened the door of her truck and watched her step out.

"Oh, lady, you do look great," he said, his gaze sweeping over her and making her tingle and momentarily forget why she was here.

"And hello to you. Thank you."

"You've never been to my home, have you?"

"Nope, I haven't. And you haven't been in mine, yet. Not really," she amended, as she thought about last week and how he'd barely made it through her back door before he left.

"Well, I hope to remedy that soon," he said.

"We'll see."

They stepped into an entry foyer that held a full-length mahogany mirror, two hat racks, hooks for coats, shelves that housed several pairs of boots. Stepping through the hallway, they came to a huge kitchen with state-of-the-art-equipment and luxurious dark wood cabinetry. The adjoining family room held a stone fireplace, a big-screen television, a game table, as well as a desk with two computers and other electronic devices.

"All the comforts of home, huh?" she asked. "It's a marvelous home."

"I suspect you have one to match," he remarked.

"Odd that we've never been in each other's houses in all the years we've known each other," she said.

"There's a lot we didn't do in all the years we've known each other," he said, setting her nerves on edge. "C'mon, I'll show you more."

They walked down a wide hall with Western paintings and beautiful tapestries that surprised her. The hall held finely crafted furniture, double front doors where floor-to-ceiling windows let in light and offered a grand view of the front of his property.

"Very beautiful, Tony. And a little surprising."

"You probably pictured me in a log cabin with brass spittoons and bawdy paintings," he said grinning.

She smiled. "Not that extreme, just maybe a little more rustic than this. After all, you're a rancher at heart. This fancy home could belong to a Chicago stockbroker."

He shrugged. "It's comfortable, what I like and a haven when I come home."

"That I understand." She followed him as he directed her down another hallway.

"I don't really know much about you as a person," she

said when he stopped outside a closed door. "Just as an annoyance in my life—until this month," she said.

"I'm glad you added that last part. Here, Lindsay," he said, ushering her into a suite with a sitting room that held floor-to-ceiling windows affording a panoramic view of a terrace and fields beyond it where horses grazed. "Here's my living room. Want to see my bedroom next?"

Smiling at him, she shook her head. "I think we're skirting the edge of temptation too much as it is. Thanks, I'll pass."

"Okay, then, on to the study."

They went down the hall to another room, as elegant as the last, with leather furniture, oils on the walls, heavy shelves and polished cherrywood floors.

As she looked around, he said, "We can finish the tour later." He glanced out the window. "Because I want you to see one of the pumps before the sun goes down."

"Good idea," she said. She wanted to see it in daylight, too, because if it really was his old pump, it would have rust.

"I'm ready."

He placed a hand on the small of her back. "So am I," he said in the husky tone he'd had when making love.

She stepped back. "You're not helping the situation. We agreed that we were not pursuing…" She searched but couldn't find the word she wanted. "Not pursuing this," she said, "any further." She tried to sound forceful, but her words sounded hollow, even to herself.

Tony must have thought so, too, because he said nothing. He merely stepped close and placed his hands on her waist. Her breathing became shallow and erratic as his steady gaze met her eyes and then lowered to her mouth.

Dimly the thought nagged at her that it had been a

mistake to come here, but she wanted to see if he had been truthful with her.

She couldn't step away or protest. She saw the desire in the blue-green depths of his eyes and her mouth went dry. She wanted his kiss just one more time.

He leaned down to kiss her, a hot, possessive kiss that made her feel he wanted her with all his being. Her heart pounded as she wrapped her arms around his neck and kissed him back, once again trying to make him remember this moment and be as conflicted as she was.

Her world spun away, lost in Tony's kisses that set her ablaze. She felt his hands drifting up her back, then moving forward to lightly caress her breasts.

"Tony," she whispered, unable to tell him to stop, yet knowing they should.

She caught his wrists and leaned back. "This isn't why I came," she whispered, and then stepped away. "Water well pump, remember?" she asked, unable to get any firmness in her voice.

"When you're ready, we'll go," he said. He stood so close that her heart pounded and it took all the willpower she had to move away.

"We both have to do better than this tonight."

"I intend to do a lot better," he said, teasing and leering at her, causing her to laugh.

"You're hopeless and headed for trouble, and you're taking me with you." She smoothed down her shirt and stood tall. "I'm ready to look at that pump now."

"One thing—in case you think I might have one old pump for moments like this and the rest are new, I'll let you select which one we go see," he said. She went with him to his desk, a massive cherry table. He opened a drawer and pulled out a map, which he unfolded. "This is a map of the ranch with the water wells circled in yellow. You can select one. If you want to look at all of them, we can."

She gave him a searching look. "I'm beginning to believe you and feel really foolish."

"This is why you came. Pick the wells, Lindsay," he instructed.

She looked again and pointed to one the shortest distance from the house.

"Is that all? I want you totally satisfied when you go home." He said the last words in the tone of voice he used when he was flirting with her. He was back to sexy innuendos, which kept her thinking about his kisses and lovemaking.

"Tony, you've got to stop that," she said, unable to suppress another laugh. He grinned and took her arm.

"I don't think you really want me to. You say those words, but your body, your eyes, your voice are giving you away, darlin'."

"Time to go, Tony," she said, trying to resist him, the sensible thing to do.

They drove to the well and she could see the rust on the pump from yards away. She turned to place her hand on his arm. "Tony, I'm sorry. I've misjudged you and accused you of things you didn't do."

He turned to face her. "You don't want to see another well?"

She shook her head, "No. I apologize."

"Apology accepted."

"I've already taken your advice and called to see about digging my wells deeper."

"Good. C'mon, let's go home and have some juicy steaks."

She knew she should say no, but she couldn't. She

had been wrong about him—he had been telling her the truth all along.

She thought of all the times she had been told not to trust a Milan. Her grandmother had practically drummed it into her head. But her brother had married Tony's sister and trusted her fully. Shouldn't she have learned anything from Jake?

They rode back in silence, but when they stepped into his kitchen, she had to apologize again. She felt that bad.

"Tony, again, I'm so sorry. I—"

He turned to her and put his hands on her waist. "Don't worry about it, it doesn't matter now. This is all that matters."

He tilted her chin up, and she saw the flicker in his eyes and knew when the moment changed. He drew her into his embrace and kissed her, holding her tightly and kissing her thoroughly until she was breathless. With a moan of pleasure, she slipped her arm around his neck and another around his waist to hold him tightly, wanting his kiss in spite of all her intentions of resisting him.

When he released her, he smiled. "That's better," he said. "Let's have a drink and I'll start the steaks."

Though she knew she should go home for a quiet dinner alone, she nodded instead. She tingled from his kiss and wanted more. Each kiss was a threat to her heart and she promised herself she would stop seeing him after this evening. It was just one more night.

She drew a deep breath as her throat went dry. "We weren't going to do this."

"So we're together three times instead of two. Seeing each other will end and we both know it, so what does tonight hurt?" he asked.

"You make it sound like something silly for me to protest."

"You know I want you to stay. It won't be a big deal, Lindsay."

With her heart drumming, she watched him walk to a bar. Who would have thought it? A cowboy who could turn her world upside down, who had become the sexiest, most handsome man she had ever known. How could Tony have become important to her, able to set her heart pounding just by walking into a room where she was?

What seemed worse, the more she knew him, the better she liked him and the more she thought of him. That realization scared her. She didn't want to respect him, admire him and like him. He was still Tony, who had to run everything all the time. Physically, she was intensely attracted to him, but it was beginning to spill over into other aspects of their lives and that scared her.

Never in her life had she been attracted to someone who could put her way of life at risk—until now.

To protect her own lifestyle, she had to make tonight the last time she would socialize with him. She had to break off seeing him before her life was in shambles and her heart broken.

Could she adhere to that…or was it too late?

Six

He wasn't in the kitchen when she came back from freshening up in the powder room. Where had he gone?

She saw a column of gray smoke spiraling skyward and followed it to the glassed-in sitting room where she saw him outside at a grill. When she went out, he turned to smile at her. Tall, lean and strong, he kept her heart racing. His blue-eyed gaze drifted over her and she could see his approval.

"The steak smells wonderful," she said.

"Thanks. We have tossed salad and twice-baked potatoes, too."

"When did you fix all that? Twice-baked potatoes? You planned this?"

"No. I have Gwynne, a cook who has gone home now. She fixes dinners and leaves them for me. The potatoes were frozen and easy to thaw and heat. She lives in her own place here on the ranch and cooks five days a week."

"And what do you do the other two days?"

"Eat alone," he said.

"I can imagine," she remarked, thinking of women she knew he had taken out.

He chuckled as he turned to look at the steaks.

The terrace was broad, running across the back of the house and along the bright blue swimming pool that looked so inviting.

"What do you want to drink? Iced tea, wine, cold beer, martini—you name what you'd like."

"With a drive home tonight, I think iced tea is a good choice."

"I'll get you that, but I'd be happy to drive you home tonight."

"I'll take the tea," she answered, smiling at him, wanting to accept his offer, wanting to stay all night, but determined to do what she should.

In minutes he brought her a tall glass of tea and he held a cold beer. "Shall we sit where I can keep an eye on the steaks?"

All the time they talked, she was aware of him sitting close. His hand rested on her shoulder, rubbing it lightly, or on her nape, his warm fingers drifting in feathery caresses, all small touches that were heightening desire. Was it going to be easy to forget the times spent with him? Was she going to miss him or think about him when they parted for good? She knew the answers to both questions. What she was uncertain about was whether she could resist him.

Soon they sat down to eat in his cool, informal dining area.

"Once again, I'm surprised and impressed. You're quite a cook, Tony. The steaks are delicious."

"Thank you. Our own beef and my own cooking. Ta-da."

When she laughed, he shook his head.

"I need to make an improvement," he said, reaching out to unfasten one more button of her shirt and push it open to reveal her lush curves. His warm fingers brushed her lightly and she drew a sharp breath, longing for his touch.

She hoped what she wanted didn't show. She could barely eat. All she wanted was to be in his arms. In some part of her mind she wondered if he had an ulterior motive for inviting her to see the pumps.

He turned on the charm during dinner, smiling and telling her stories about his family and funny incidents when he started as a rancher. They sat for hours after they finished their steaks, laughing and talking over coffee, until she realized the sun had gone down a long time ago. She stood. "It's getting late, Tony. I should go home." She picked up her plate. Instantly Tony took her dish from her hands.

"None of that. Gwynne will be here in the morning and will take care of it."

"So then I should be going," she said, trying to stick to what she felt she should do.

Placing his hands on her shoulders, making her tingle in anticipation, he turned her to face him.

"Don't go home tonight, Lindsay. You have choices— you can sleep downstairs alone or upstairs with me, but stay. I don't want you to drive back tonight."

"Tony," she said, her heart drumming as she looked into his blue-green eyes, "you know I should go. We've talked about this."

He stepped closer to wrap his arms around her and kiss her. When she knew she was on the verge of agreeing to stay, she stepped out of his embrace.

"I have to go home," she said breathlessly.

He nodded and watched as she straightened her blouse and turned for the door.

Draping his arm across her shoulders, he walked her to her pickup.

"I know you're doing what's sensible. We have different lifestyles. Even so, I don't want you to go."

"I have to," she said and turned to climb into her pickup.

She smiled at him. "Thanks for dinner and for showing me your water pump."

"Sure. I'll call you," he said, and closed the pickup door.

He stood on the driveway watching her as she drove away. She glanced several times at the rearview mirror and he still stood watching. Then she rounded a curve and he was gone from view.

She trembled with longing, wanting to stay, telling herself over and over that she was doing the right thing and the smart thing. She had no future with Tony. Far from it, he would be a threat to her and her ranch. Why didn't that knowledge make her feel better?

She tried to stop thinking about his kisses, the laughs they had shared. What she was doing was for the best. She missed him, but she was not brokenhearted after an affair that Tony had ended, something she wanted to avoid with all her being.

The auction had been worth the money if she got friendliness and cooperation from him. She knew he would never stop telling her what she should do, but they could have a more neighborly relationship. In a week she would probably feel differently about him if she stopped seeing him and talking to him.

Tony stood a few minutes after Lindsay drove out of sight. Longing for her tore at him and was impossible for him to ignore.

How could he have so much fun with her now, find her

so desirable when not long ago they were at each other's throats over every issue?

He knew the answer to his question. She was the sexiest, best-looking, most fun woman he had ever known. The realization still shook him.

Feeling empty, he stared at the road, wishing she would turn around and come back. Back into his arms and into his bed tonight.

He shouldn't miss her—he had never missed a woman this much or given one this much thought when he wasn't with her.

Of all the women in Texas, why did it have to be Lindsay who had turned his life topsy-turvy?

With a long sigh, he turned to go inside, knowing he wouldn't be able to stop thinking about her or sleep peacefully tonight.

As he walked back to his house, he saw a light in one of the barns. On impulse, to avoid being alone, he changed direction and strolled to the barn, where he found Keane nailing up more shelves in the tack room.

"I wondered who was working. Need help?"

"Yep. In a minute. I need a break. If you have time, four hands will be better than two trying to get these shelves in place," Keane said as he sat on a crate.

Tony sat on a bale of hay and stretched out his legs. "Lindsay just left and she's happy about my water pumps. She is going to look into doing the same, as we have to get water."

"She can be a nice lady. Good for neighbors to get along."

"It should be more peaceful. I hope it lasts, because she still can be her stubborn self."

"She's not so bad, but you know that now. The people who work for her like her."

"For a time it will probably be better between us."

"I'd bet money on that one," Keane remarked drily. "She's a strong woman who knows what she wants."

"Amen to that. Actually, I don't think we'll see any more of each other in the future."

"Maybe so. You'll work it out, I'm sure."

Tony focused on his foreman because it sounded as if Keane was trying to hold back laughter. "Ready to get back to work?" Tony asked, standing because he wanted to end the conversation about his private life.

"Sure. You can hold one of these boards in place for me."

Silently, Tony followed directions from Keane, but his thoughts drifted to Lindsay. He didn't want to go back to his empty house. He missed her and didn't want to think about her staying or having her in his arms in his bed tonight.

Once Keane stopped to look at him.

"What?"

"You're getting ready to hammer that board in and it's in the wrong place."

Startled, Tony looked at the narrow board he held in his hands. "Sorry," he said, adjusting it as he felt his face heat. He had been lost in thoughts about Lindsay. He made an effort to stop thinking about her and focus on the job at hand.

Tony managed to keep his thoughts on the task and, in minutes, Keane stepped back to look at his completed shelves.

"With your help, we're through," Keane said. "Thanks, boss. That went quickly. I'll put away the tools."

"I'll help," Tony stated, acting quickly. In minutes they parted, Keane for his house and Tony walking back to his, which was dark and empty.

He stepped inside, locked the door and went to the kitchen to get a beer. He carried it out to the patio to sit and gaze at the pool, gardens and fountain while he thought about Lindsay.

He had to get her out of his thoughts. They had no future together and neither one wanted a future together. It still amazed him how much she was in his thoughts.

"Goodbye, Lindsay," he said aloud, as if he could get her out of his thoughts that way. He didn't expect to see her again soon. He tried to ignore the pang that caused.

Lindsay stood in front of the calendar the next morning counting the days. Once and again. No matter how many times she counted it, the results were the same. She had missed her period by almost a couple of weeks now, and that had never happened before. Common sense said there could be a host of reasons and she should give it more time. But could she be pregnant? Tony had taken precautions, but there was always a chance. She knew the statistics.

Anxiety washed over her with the force of a tidal wave, and she pulled out her desk chair to sit down.

After a few minutes, she reminded herself that women were late all the time without it meaning they were pregnant and she should give it a few more days. No sense worrying needlessly. She simply put it out of her mind and got ready for work.

But when the next two days passed with no change, she had to get a home pregnancy test. She couldn't get it in Verity or any town in the surrounding counties where she knew nearly everyone.

She was having Tony's baby. She knew it. Shock buffeted her. How could she deal with it?

She was going to have to figure out how to deal with

it. She picked up her phone to send a text to her foreman. *Something's come up. I'll call later.*

In a minute she received a reply: *Okay.* She put her head in her hands. If only she could undo everything and go back to the way she and Tony had been before the auction. She didn't want to be pregnant with Tony's baby. She'd always thought someday she would marry and have a family. Now she was going to have the family without the marriage.

She didn't want Tony to know yet. She had to have plans in place so he couldn't take over.

She ran her hands through her hair. She wasn't ready for this. Tony would want to be part of his child's life, and he would take charge and tell her what to do the moment he learned she was carrying his baby.

Telling her how to run her ranch would be nothing compared to telling her how to raise a baby.

Their baby.

A Milan baby.

A Milan baby fathered by a man she could never marry.

But their families would want them to marry. Hers would pressure her, just as his would pressure him. She knew he was the family type who would think they should marry for this baby's sake. She would have a bigger fight with Tony than she had ever had before. Running two big ranches and raising a baby together. They wouldn't have a battle—they'd have a war! She put her head in her hands to cry, something she rarely did. How would she cope with this? For once in her life she felt overwhelmed.

For a few minutes as she cried, she let go, swamped by a looming disaster. She raised her head and her gaze fell on a picture of her nephew she had taken when Scotty was two. He was laughing, sitting astride a big horse and holding the reins. She loved the picture and she loved Scotty with all her heart and had always hoped she would have a little boy just like him.

She sat up, dried her eyes and stared at Scotty's picture, pulling it close. She was going to have a baby and maybe her child would be as wonderful as Scotty. And her family would stand by her. She had no doubts about that.

She had always avoided dating ranchers until Tony. When she bought a night with him at the auction, she had not expected to fall into bed with him or to even want to see him again.

She should have stuck to her rule of not dating a rancher, no matter the circumstances. But it had never once occurred to her that she could be attracted to Tony, not until she had seen him in that tux, looking so sexy, those eyes that could convey enough desire to melt her.

Logic said to make a doctor's appointment and have her pregnancy verified by a lab and a professional. She could get a home kit, but she wanted a doctor's results to be certain. That was step one. Telling Tony would be step two and the one that she could not cope with thinking about now.

Why had she ever bid for him in the damn auction? No undoing that night now, but it was coming back to haunt her. She needed to plan and to find a good doctor. She couldn't go to a doctor in Verity or anywhere around the area. Texas might not even be big enough. She didn't want word getting to Tony until she was ready to tell him herself. She should fly to a big city, like Tulsa or Albuquerque, but she didn't know any doctors there. She thought about Savannah, Mike's pregnant wife who was from Arkansas.

If Savannah gave her an Arkansas doctor's name, she

could drive to Dallas and then fly to Arkansas without anyone else in the family knowing where she had gone or why. As she thought about her older brother, Mike, she wanted to talk to him and to Savannah. Because of Scotty, she had gotten where she felt close to Mike, and now that he had married Savannah, they would be the ones to talk to about her situation. Savannah had never intended to become pregnant and when her ex-fiancé in Arkansas found out, he had been hateful and hadn't wanted his baby. Lindsay sighed. At least she would never have to worry about that with Tony. It would be just the opposite with Tony. He would want this baby in his life all the time.

Madison, Jake's wife, was expecting, too. That would help soften Jake's attitude about her situation. And Jake liked Tony. Her brothers liked him and their wives did, too. She had been the sole member of her generation to fight him. In fact, it was the older generations of Calhouns that didn't like the Milans. She had heard Destiny talk about her grandmother's intense dislike of Milans. Maybe that had eased up now that Wyatt and Destiny were married, as well as Jake and Madison.

She had always been close to all her brothers, particularly Josh when they were young, so Josh and Abby would give her support. Abby had a heart of gold and would be as kind as Josh.

Looking again at the calendar, she picked up her phone and called Savannah and in minutes made arrangements to see her.

By noon she was showered and dressed. She studied herself in the mirror, turning first one way and then another, knowing it was ridiculous to expect to see any change yet. Her cell phone rang. When she saw it was Tony, she ignored the call.

* * *

Smiling, Savannah opened the back door. "Come in. Mike is out on the ranch somewhere and you said not to call him, so I didn't. Scotty is napping."

"I'll make this short, Savannah. I wanted to talk to just you. Not Mike. And not Scotty right now."

"Sure. Come in," Savannah said, stepping back out of the way and shaking her blond hair away from her face. "Want a cool drink?" Savannah asked.

"Ice water would be fine, and you sit and let me get it and whatever you want to drink. I know this kitchen almost as well as my own."

"I'm a little clumsy, but I'm not feeble. I can get us glasses of water," Savannah said as she turned to wash her hands and get down glasses. Lindsay's gaze ran over Savannah's navy T-shirt and jeans. She knew Savannah's baby was due in October, which was only weeks away now that it was already the first day of September. Savannah's round belly didn't look big enough to deliver in another month. "You don't look very pregnant."

"I feel very, very pregnant. And believe me, there's no such thing as not very pregnant."

Lindsay laughed politely, but she still couldn't cope with the prospect of being pregnant or joke about it. Each time she thought about it, she also wondered how she would ever tell Tony. She had no answer to that one.

In minutes they had glasses of water and sat in the family room. Savannah gazed at her. "I heard you and Tony got along fine on your auction date. And you've been out with him since."

"I suppose it's impossible to keep our going out together private as long as we go out in Texas."

"I don't imagine you can. Both of you know many

people," Savannah said. She sipped her water. "Are you okay, Lindsay?" she asked finally.

"I don't know. That's why I think you're the one to talk to. I do need to keep this secret awhile and I thought about you being from Little Rock. I need to see an obstetrician without my family or anyone else around here knowing except you and Mike. Savannah, I think I'm pregnant with Tony's baby."

"Oh, my word," Savannah said, her blue eyes growing wide. "I know that's a shock."

"It is a shock that I haven't adjusted to, but I want it officially confirmed."

"Maybe you're worrying needlessly."

"I don't think so. I feel it to my bones."

"Oh, my. It'll be better than what I went through, although it led me to Mike. With Tony, it'll be good. He'll marry you, Lindsay. It's obvious you have made peace with each other. And the whole Calhoun family loves Tony. And he's so good to Scotty. Scotty is crazy about Tony even though they don't see each other often."

"I can't imagine Tony wanting to marry me and I don't want to marry Tony. I don't want to marry any rancher. Until Tony, I've never even dated one. Marriage to one would be a perpetual clash because I want to run my ranch my own way and I don't want some other rancher telling me to change the way I do things. And Tony is a take-charge person."

"Oh, dear." Savannah frowned. "You might have a problem."

"I have a big problem."

"Are you sure you're pregnant?"

"About ninety-nine percent, but that's why I want your doctor's name. I should see a doctor before I get Tony all stirred up. Other than you and Mike, I don't want anyone else to know I even suspect I'm pregnant until I verify it. Then I can tell Tony. I haven't even tried a home pregnancy test yet because I'll have to drive so far to get away from everyone I know, but I'm going today." She shook her head. "Even though I know what the outcome will be."

"Let me call my doctor's office and introduce you, then you can get on and make an appointment. Until you have a home test and the lab tests and have a doctor confirm your condition, you don't know for sure. You may not even be pregnant and may be worrying for nothing."

"Hopefully not, but if I had to bet, I'd bet the ranch that I am."

Savannah's eyes widened. "You mean that?"

Lindsay shrugged. "You get a feeling for things, you know?"

"Mike says you have a knack for knowing things and a touch that's just right. He's impressed by your abilities."

"That's nice. He hasn't mentioned that to me."

Savannah laughed. "You're his little sister. He probably doesn't realize he hasn't told you." She stood up. "Let me make that call before Scotty is up or Mike comes home. This doctor is so good about working people into his schedule."

Within the next thirty minutes Lindsay had an appointment in Little Rock on Thursday.

She sat again to face Savannah. "I really thank you for this. That was very nice."

"I'm glad to help. I only hope Mike doesn't suspect anything."

"Savannah, I don't want you to have to keep secrets from Mike. Just make it clear that you two are the only ones I'm telling at this point."

"I can wait a bit to tell Mike. He'll understand."

"You really don't need to, but thanks. I better go."

They walked to the door. "Take care of yourself," Savannah said. "Call me after you see the doctor. I'm your sister-in-law, and I'm also your friend. I can give you my doctor's name in Dallas, too." They gazed at each other and Savannah reached out to hug Lindsay.

"Thanks, Savannah. You're really good for Mike and good for our family."

"He and Scotty and the Calhouns are wonderful for me, too. Take care of yourself."

"I will," Lindsay said, and hurried to her pickup to drive home.

Thursday she drove to Dallas and flew to Little Rock to go to the doctor's office. She was thankful no one would know or question what she was doing or where she was going. The only person who came close was Abe, who had worked for her family since he was seventeen. She saw the questions in his eyes, but he didn't voice them.

The only thing that indicated his feelings was when she told him goodbye.

"Lindsay, if you want me to do anything, let me know," he said, looking intently at her, and she was certain he knew she had something she was hiding.

"Thanks. I will. I'm all right," she answered, looking into his light brown eyes. "I have my phone and if I need anything, I'll call. I'll be back tomorrow about noon."

"Sure," he said. He settled his brown hat on his head, nodded and headed back to the barn as she climbed into her pickup to drive to Dallas.

Now as she got out of the cab in front of the obstetrician's office, she felt her heart start to pound and her palms sweat.

But that anxiety was nothing to what she felt when she came out.

She felt so stressed she had to stop on the sidewalk. She stood staring and not seeing anything in front of her. Hot September sunshine blazed overhead, but chills skidded up her spine. She had known for the past two weeks that she was pregnant, but to have it confirmed by a home pregnancy test and now, to hear it officially announced by a physician after a lab test made it real.

How was she ever going to tell Tony?

Seven

Tony threw himself into work, coming home nights to an empty house that he had never felt alone in before. Constantly, he remembered Lindsay in his arms, and he wanted to talk to her or see her again. Every time he reached for the phone, he stopped, reminding himself she wanted them to break off seeing each other and he should, too, because it was inevitable.

In spite of logic, he missed seeing her. He knew from one of the men who worked for him that she had gone to Dallas and he wondered why and what she was doing there. He would get over her soon because he knew as well as she did, in spite of their truce, they were still the same people and she remained stubborn as ever. It was just a matter of time before there was another conflict between them, something she seemed to thrive on. Though common sense told him that he was better off without her, he missed her in a way he wouldn't have thought possible.

He woke up on Friday morning and she was still on his mind. He knew time would take care of this longing for her, but right now memories of her wouldn't stop coming.

He rose and got ready for a first-thing-in-the-morning meeting with Keane, who had problems with one of their trucks.

Tony stood on his porch with his foreman, who had his hat pushed far enough back on his head to reveal a pale strip on his forehead where his hat always shaded him. His tangled, curly brown hair framed his face. He was shorter than Tony, slightly stocky and the most capable ranch hand Tony had ever had.

"Keane, I heard an animal howling last night. I've seen it before on Lindsay's ranch," he said, remembering the eerie howls that had been so forlorn and sounded like an injured animal. As he had listened, he understood why the howls had unnerved Lindsay and caused her to call. They'd been jarring in the night, even to him. He'd finally got up and retrieved a rifle, switching off yard lights and stepping out on his dark porch. He'd seen it plainly in the moonlight, but he'd paused as he lifted his rifle, remembering Lindsay's request that the animal not be put down. He'd lowered his rifle and walked back inside to lock up, put away his rifle and go back to bed.

"It might be a dog," he told Keane now. "Might be a coyote. Lindsay thinks it's a wolf and she doesn't want it put down unless it starts killing livestock. Pass the word to leave it alone unless it kills something and until we know it isn't a big dog."

"Sure. Have you seen it?"

"Yes. It's big, has black and gray shaggy fur and, frankly, it does resemble a wolf, but I can't imagine it is."

Keane had a faint smile. "You know that old legend."

"If I thought that were possible, which I don't, I'd try to catch and tame the critter and I'd wish for rain."

"Amen to that one," Keane said, glancing at the sky. "Still none in the forecast. No break in the heat, either—over a hundred today. When it does rain, the ground will soak up water like a sponge. It'll just disappear. We need a month of rains."

"Right. Well, I'll see about replacing that truck," Tony said, and turned to go.

While Tony worked all day alongside the men, keeping his hands busy, he couldn't keep his mind from returning to Lindsay.

On second thought, he told himself, maybe he should tame that wolf and wish for amnesia. That might be the only way he'd forget her.

Feeling torn, miserable and caught in an uncustomary inability to make a decision, Lindsay stared at her dinner. She didn't want to eat but knew she should. Her thoughts were constantly on Tony. It seemed with each day she dreaded telling him about the baby more and more. She had to before she began to show and word got back to him. But when?

First she needed to go see Scotty, to hold him and think about having her own little baby, and then she needed to talk to Mike who would probably be a bulwark in the storm that would eventually rage around her. She didn't want to hide behind her brother from Tony, but Mike would take a levelheaded view of the situation and he and Savannah would support her in what she wanted to do.

Maybe she just needed to take Tony's call, go out with him and tell him the news. Get it over with and move on with her life and planning for her baby. Maybe Tony would back off and leave her alone.

She knew better than to expect that to happen. Mr. Take-Charge would dominate her life when she told him. Each time she thought of that happening, she was filled with dread.

She played with different scenarios in her mind: telling him soon, waiting four or five months to tell him or not saying a word until she had to. Like maybe when the baby was born.

As she headed to her house Friday afternoon, she was wrapped in worries and indecision and through it all, though she hated to admit it to herself, she missed Tony. She was so tired she paid little attention to her familiar surroundings until she steered her pickup toward the back of her house and saw a truck near the back gate. Frowning, she glanced at the house and saw Mike seated on the porch with his feet propped on the rail while he whittled.

She didn't know whether to be happy or annoyed with him and wondered whether Savannah had made him come.

As Lindsay parked behind his pickup and stepped out, Mike rose to his feet and put his knife away, along with whatever he had been whittling while he waited at the top of the steps. "What are you doing here?" she asked as she walked up the steps.

"Waiting to see if you need a big brother's hug," he said.

His kindness shook her and she walked into his arms. "I do," she whispered.

He hugged her, then stepped away to smile. "Let's go inside where we can talk and it's not a hundred degrees in the shade."

She tried to smile. "You mean where I can cry without

someone seeing me," she said, unlocking the door and leading the way. "Want a beer?"

"I'd like one, but not if it's going to make you want one."

"No. No problem there. I'll drink ice water." When they had drinks and were seated in the cool family room that overlooked the porch, patio and swimming pool, she sat facing him.

He had hung his hat on a hook in the entry hall and he raked his fingers through his hair. "Savannah said that you gave her permission to tell me." Mike leaned forward to place his elbows on his knees. "Here comes some brotherly advice and words of infinite wisdom."

She smiled. "There are moments I'm truly glad you're my big brother."

"I'm happy to hear that," he said. "There are moments I'm truly glad you're my little sis," he said, smiling at her. "Lindsay, don't forget for one minute that you have three brothers and three sisters-in-law who will support you in every way we can."

Tears threatened and she wiped her eyes. "Look at me, Mike. Do you know how few times in my life I've cried?"

"Chalk it up to hormone changes," he said. "I just want you to always remember you have our support and you can call me or Savannah anytime you want."

"Thanks. That means a lot," she said, meaning it with all her heart.

"Next thing—if being pregnant gets you down, just think of Scotty. You shower him with love and he seems to be a huge joy to you. He loves you and I know you love him. A baby in your life will be great."

"I know that and I do love Scotty beyond measure. He's adorable and I feel so close to him."

"He's a good kid. And he's going to love your baby. I

can promise you that. I'll let you tell Scotty when you're ready because he is very excited over Savannah's baby. He'll go into orbit over yours."

She smiled. "Maybe not so much if I have a girl."

"Oh, yes, he will. You wait and see. So now the next thing I want to mention, even if you don't want to hear it, is Tony. He's a good guy. I like Tony, and all the guys who work for him like him. All your brothers and sisters-in-law like him."

"I know that."

"Obviously, the two of you can get along. You were seeing each other after the auction."

"Does everyone in the state know we were going out together?"

"C'mon, Lindsay. All the Calhoun ranches and Milan ranches and the people that work on them—cleaning staff, cooks, cowboys—you think they don't get around and see who is leaving a ranch and who is entering one? Or talk about who they saw when they're out? The grapevine is alive and well in these parts. You and Tony were discreet about it, but your whole family probably knows you dated. Anyway, cut him some slack. He'll be shocked, but he's going to welcome this baby like I would, and you know it."

"Maybe that's what worries me. Tony is a take-charge guy."

Mike grinned. "I'm considering the source of that statement. Now, one last thing—would you like me to tell Mom and Dad before you talk to them?"

She thought about her parents and closed her eyes. She rubbed her hands together and looked at Mike. "Will Dad threaten Tony if he doesn't marry me? I haven't even wanted to think about dealing with our parents and, thank heavens, they're in California and have their own lives."

"Get some plans made before you tackle telling them. Tony's the one who has the difficult parents. Listen, all the rest of us will stand by you and between you and our folks. Mom will just have hysterics and faint."

Lindsay smiled and relaxed slightly. "Sounds ridiculous, but I think that might be exactly what she'll do. I've resisted her tears and hysterics plenty of times."

"The rest of us just hide from her. You're the brave one," he said, grinning. "Frankly, I don't think you'll have any pressure from our parents. They have their own lives, and I think when we grew up they let us go."

"I'm grateful for that. Tony is the person who worries me."

"You two will work it out." Mike squeezed her shoulder gently. He finished his beer and stood. "I've said what I wanted to say. I'll go home now. We're there for you—call in the middle of the night if you need us. You and Tony will work this out because you both love your families and you each will love this baby with all your hearts. You'll see."

"So when did you get to be such a counselor?" she said. Mike hadn't mentioned it, but she wondered if he or her other brothers would pressure her to marry Tony. "You know, even if we can be civil, Tony may not propose."

"There will probably be more than one pot for bets on that one," Mike remarked drily as they walked to the back door. Before they stepped outside, she closed her hand around his wrist.

"Thanks. Your advice might be a bit misguided, but your intentions are wonderful. You have cheered me up and I don't feel quite so alone."

"Lindsay, you should know your family well enough to know how very un-alone you are. Jake would be right here if you need him, or Josh. Tony's family will be the same." He stepped out on the porch, then resumed his talk. "There'll be plenty of kids on both sides of the family for your little one to bond with and to grow up with. Tony's sister, Madison, is pregnant. His brother Nick has a son, Cody, who is Scotty's age. I'll have another baby before yours is born. It'll be great." He reached out and gave her another hug.

"If only the father wasn't so take-charge and so stubborn."

"Said the kettle about the pot. You two are exactly alike in some ways and you're a strong enough woman to deal with most any man." He put his hat back on and made for the steps, then turned to her again. "Jake and Josh and I can go beat him up for you if you want."

"Mike, don't you dare!" He grinned and she saw he was teasing her. "Mike, shame on you, and I fell for it when I should know better."

"I made you smile," he said, sounding satisfied. "I gotta run, sis."

Lindsay followed him to his pickup. "Thanks for coming. I'll call Savannah and thank her. I liked her doctor—he was very nice, cheerful and kind. Now that I know for certain I'm pregnant, I'll have to find one around here. Savannah has one in Dallas she likes, so I'll probably get that name from her."

"When the time comes, you can stay at my house in Dallas if you want. If you stay on the ranch, you'll be a long way from your doctor and hospital."

"Thanks. We'll see."

"If you stay here, I guess it's a consolation that everyone on the place can probably deliver a baby."

"That's definitely not what I have in mind," she said

while she stood in the hot sun with her hands on her hips and stared at him.

"Call me and I'll do it." Grinning, he jumped into the truck and revved the engine.

"You're a wonderful brother, but you're not delivering my baby."

"For that matter, Tony can. He's good at delivering calves."

"Enough of you planning my life. How did I get tangled up with so many bossy men?"

"I think we're called alpha males," Mike corrected.

"Not in my view. I'll see you soon. Thanks for coming over."

"Sure." He smiled at her. "See you soon," he said, pulling along the driveway to head back to his ranch.

Smiling, she waved, but as the pickup drove out of sight leaving a plume of dust behind, her smile faded. None of Mike's cheerful advice or reminders of what a good guy Tony was changed the fact that Tony ran everything he could in his daily life. He was commanding, decisive, a Mr. Do-It-My-Way. Even as she enumerated those attributes, she felt a pain in her chest because she missed him. She ignored the feeling, certain it soon would stop haunting her and disappear forever.

She could tell him now, or she could tell him later. She was in for a fight and she felt it coming any which way she looked at her future.

Eight

Lost in thought, she walked into the house, mulling over how and when she would tell Tony.

By midnight she wasn't any closer to a solution. She sat in her darkened bedroom, looking out over her ranch and wondering what course of action she should follow. When the baby came, she would face more decisions. Stay home and take care of her baby all day or hire a nanny and go back to ranch work?

Eventually, she figured, that's probably what she would do, but she wanted to be home with her baby those first few months no matter what she decided to do later. Would she have to buy a house in Verity to secure a nanny or would she be able to find someone to live on the ranch? But maybe she was jumping the gun. First, she needed to find a doctor and have the baby.

She rubbed her forehead and thought about Mike's offer of his Dallas house in her ninth month. Tony might have some issue with that, being that he had a place in Dallas, too.

Tony. Mentioning his name made her remember he hadn't called her the past few days. Did he know she had been away from the ranch? She guessed he probably did, but he also knew she always had her phone. Had she heard the last from him until she contacted him?

On top of her worries and her woes, she missed Tony. He was too many wonderful things to suddenly have him disappear from her life and not feel his absence. She missed his energy, his optimism, his charm, his sexy ways. She didn't want to admit it, but a considerable amount of joy and excitement had gone out of her life. She dreamed about him at night, thought about him constantly during the day. Did Tony miss her at all?

The following Friday Tony climbed from his pickup after a long day. He'd helped some of his men clear a field. He was hot and dirty. He wanted a shower and a steak and he wanted to spend the evening with Lindsay. Since she hadn't taken his calls or answered his texts, he'd interpreted that as a sign she wanted to be left alone and he'd stopped calling. But that didn't stop him from wanting her.

He changed and went to his gym to work off the pent-up anxiety he felt from thinking about her. Exercising helped, as did swimming laps in his pool. But when he lay back in the pool, Lindsay invaded his thoughts once again. It was ridiculous, he told himself. If he didn't hear from her by next week, he promised himself he'd go out and forget all about her.

He swam laps until he couldn't stand to swim one more. Climbing out, he went in to shower and change, then work on taxes and his records. Later, he lay in the darkness, wanting sleep to come, hoping it was not another night of dreams filled with Lindsay.

During the night, he woke to hear a long, piercing howl. Stepping out of bed, he walked onto his balcony and gazed into the night. After a few minutes, another howl cut through the night. This one seemed to come from somewhere close to the barn nearest to his house.

Returning to his room, he pulled on his clothes and got a rifle. He went outside again to sit and wait, but the howls had stopped. He sat thinking about Lindsay, remembering times together, until he noticed the sky was getting lighter. It was dawn, so he went inside to shower and dress for the day.

After he had breakfast, he headed to the barn. Curious to see if he could find any signs of an animal, he knelt down and searched. But it was unlikely he'd find tracks in the hard, baked earth, so he rose and walked along slowly, studying the ground and turning a corner where thick bushes grew. He heard the faintest whine and froze for a minute. Then he moved slowly and cautiously toward the bushes, stopping instantly when he looked into a pair of brown eyes.

For a startled moment he thought it was a wolf, but then his gaze ran over the animal and he realized it was a big, furry gray-and-black male dog and it was hurt.

As the dog whimpered, Tony moved slowly, holding out his hand, wishing he had brought a piece of meat or something to offer. He spoke softly to the animal and knelt beside him. The dog tried to raise its head but lay back, watching him and giving one thump of its tail.

"Hey, boy," Tony said, speaking softly. "You're hurt." He saw the coat, tangled and matted with blood. One front leg and one hind leg each had bloody gashes. Tony pulled out his phone to call Keane.

* * *

Two hours later the dog was awake again, sedatives wearing off. Cleaned and bandaged, he lay in a stall in the barn on a blanket that had been tossed over hay spread on the floor. The barn was air-conditioned and comfortable.

Keane had helped Tony with the dog and, later, Doc Williams had stopped by. Now Tony was alone, sitting on the blanket by the dog and scratching its ears. He pulled out his phone and called Lindsay.

Warmth heated him at the sound of her voice. "I'm glad you answered."

"I've been in Dallas," she said, a cautious note in her voice that he'd never heard before.

He let her answer go without comment even though her phone had also been in Dallas. "Remember the howls and the coyote/wolf/dog?"

"Yes," she said, curiosity filling her voice so she sounded more like herself.

"He's in my barn. He was hurt, with lots of cuts. He may resemble a wolf, but he's actually just a big, furry gray dog that has been hurt. I thought you'd want to know."

"Oh, Tony, will he be all right?"

"Yes. Doc Williams has taken care of him. When the sedative completely wears off, he'll get a little steak. He's had some water. I held his head and sort of spoon-fed it to him. Want to come visit my patient?"

There was a pause. "Yes, I'll be there soon. Thanks for calling me. I'm headed to my pickup. By the way, how did you catch him?"

"I didn't catch him. He woke me in the night and when dawn came, I found him by the barn lying in the bushes where it was shady."

"I never thought about going to look for him. His

howling just gave me the creeps. But I'm so glad you rescued him. And it's a dog, huh?"

"Definitely. Mixed breed and looks like a wolf, but it's domesticated."

"It's wonderful that you saved him." He picked up the emotion in her voice.

"Well, well, Miss Tough Rancher is a real softie for dogs? How about men? Men named Tony?"

She laughed. "Maybe dogs."

He didn't press the point. He needed to slow down and just be happy that she'd taken his call. He brought the conversation back to the dog at his side. "Well, our patient already looks much better. Keane has a nice touch, and Doc said we did a good job. He said the dog has wounds from a fight. He's not sick, but Doc said he would stop by again and check on him."

"You're a good guy, Tony."

"I'm glad I can impress you," he said, brushing the dog's head as he talked. Despite his resolve, his eagerness to see Lindsay grew by the second. "We'll let you name him, Lindsay. Doc said no one had inquired about a lost dog that fit this one's description, and I've checked some ads and I don't see anything. I think he's homeless."

"I hope not any longer," she said breathlessly. "I hope you give him a home."

"We'll see how he fits in with the other dogs the guys keep on the ranch. I don't know what he's been fighting, but if he fights my dogs, I can't keep him."

"If you don't keep him, let me know." He heard her fumbling on the other end of the line, then she said, "I gotta go so I can drive."

"I'm in the first barn. Come on in."

"See you soon," she said and ended the call.

Putting away his phone, Tony smiled at the dog. He

was happy because Lindsay would soon be at his ranch. "Lindsay is coming to see you," he told the animal. "I hope she loves you and keeps coming to see you. Don't look too well too soon, okay, boy?"

The dog thumped its tail a few times. "I'll feed you in a while. Doc said to wait. Lindsay's going to love you and you're going to love her. Maybe you'll end up at her house and then I can come see you. Just be nice to all the ranch dogs. That's all that's required."

Big brown eyes looked up at him as the dog thumped his tail. Tony petted the dog's head gently, talking to it softly until he heard a motor. "Here she comes. Be a very nice dog now."

A pickup door slammed and Lindsay rushed in to stop in front of the stall. She had her hair in her usual braid and was in jeans and a blue T-shirt. She looked wonderful, and he fought the urge to get up, put his arms around her and kiss her.

"Hi, Tony. Oh, my, look at this beautiful dog," she said, coming into the stall to sit on the floor by Tony and reach out slowly to hold her hand in front of the dog, a treat in her palm.

He thumped his tail and raised his head slightly. His tongue licked out to take the treat.

"Oh, Tony, I'm so glad you didn't put him down. But he's all bandaged. Is he hurt badly?"

"Doc said he may limp. Other than that, he should heal just fine," Tony said, watching Lindsay instead of the dog. She smelled wonderful and she looked great. He still wanted to pull her into his arms and kiss her, but he knew that wasn't what she would want.

She placed her hand on the dog's head to pet him and he slowly thumped his tail.

"He has to get well. Thank you for calling me and

thanks for taking care of him. I think he's wonderful. Look at him. He's so sweet."

"You don't know if he's sweet yet. Remember, he still has the lingering effects of sedatives."

"He's sweet. You'll see. Look at those beautiful eyes."

"I am," Tony said, and she turned to look at him as he met her gaze.

She shook her head. "That's what I thought. You're not thinking about the dog."

"No, I'm not. It's good to see you."

She didn't respond to his statement. Instead, she teased him. "You know, if he had been a gray wolf, you could have had a wish granted, according to legend. As it is, you just became the owner of a stray dog."

"If I could have a wish, I'd wish that you'd go out with me tonight. But I guess, for the good of all, I would wish for rain this week."

"Doesn't matter. That was just a legend and he is just a dog." She petted him and Tony watched her. He couldn't help wishing those gentle hands were on his body, caressing him. But while her touch stilled the dog, it had aroused him.

"So," he prodded, "will you go out with me tonight?"

She turned to look at him solemnly, a slight frown on her brow, and he feared her answer. Then the frown disappeared and she nodded. "Tony, we need to talk," she said, suddenly sounding serious, as if she had something difficult to discuss. After her hesitation, she nodded again. "Yes. Tonight will be a big thank-you for rescuing this dog and giving him a home."

"Great. Let's go someplace fancy in Fort Worth. Someplace to dance, to talk and have a good time and super food, and then you can come back here and we'll see how our patient is doing."

Again he received a solemn look that puzzled him. "I don't know about coming back here, but we'll go out." Then, as if a thought just struck her, she asked, "But what about the dog? When you leave, he won't leave, will he?"

"I'll shut him in here where it's air-conditioned and he can be comfortable. In his condition, he can't get out. He'll have water and by that time I will have fed him something, so he should be all right."

"Do you want me to stay with him today?"

"Lindsay, I'm guessing you have a lot of things to do today."

She shrugged. "I suppose so, but I just don't want him to get up and go."

"He won't. I promise you."

She leaned down to croon to the dog and scratch behind his ears, and Tony took the opportunity to run his gaze over her. He didn't know if it was his imagination or just knowing what was beneath the clothes she wore, but she looked better than she used to with her braid, her old hat and jeans. Or was it because he hadn't seen her for a while and it was good to be with her again?

After a short time, she leaned back. "I need to get home, but I had to come see him."

They both stood and left the stall. While the dog raised its head, Tony closed the stall door and walked with Lindsay outside. "I'm glad you're going with me tonight. How about six so we have time to get to Fort Worth? I'll be glad to see you."

She smiled, but despite her acceptance of his dinner date, he sensed something off about her. Something had changed. There was a reluctance about her.

He tried to tease her out of her funk. "Still no fights between us, darlin'," he said quietly. "I'd say we've done well."

"Yes, we have, Tony. I hope it lasts," she said, and he had an even stronger feeling that something bothered her.

"Lindsay, come back into the barn for a minute."

She walked with him into the cool barn and turned to look at him with curiosity in her expression. "What's on your mind?"

"I wanted some privacy for us. Is anything wrong?"

Something flickered in her eyes and her cheeks became pink. "Not really. I just want to talk tonight."

He gazed into her eyes and wondered if he should probe more deeply. Then he figured they could talk tonight. But he couldn't let her go without doing one thing. When he stepped closer to place his hands on her shoulders, he felt her stiffen slightly. He studied her and then slipped his arm around her waist to kiss her.

"Tony, I should—" His lips on hers ended her talk.

For a moment she was resistant. Then all her stiffness vanished as she put her arms around his neck and returned his kiss passionately, a blazing kiss that meant whatever her problem was, she still couldn't cool the blazing sexual attraction between them.

When she stepped away, he let her go. She was breathing as hard as he was and they looked at each other a moment. Her blue eyes seemed clouded with worry. Turning away, she rushed out to her pickup.

"I need to get home, Tony. See you tonight," she called over her shoulder.

He hurried to watch her while she started the pickup. Gravely, she glanced at him and then drove away.

He stared after her. Something had definitely changed since the last time they were together. He didn't know what it was, unless she was trying not to tell him that she didn't care to go out with him again or receive phone calls from him. But knowing her as he did, he was certain she would have just said it.

That day was inevitable and he probably shouldn't have called her, but he knew she would want to see the dog. Oh, who was he kidding? He'd called because he wanted to see her. The dog was just an excuse. As much as he told himself to leave her alone and forget her, he couldn't stay away. His body seemed to crave her, the way a starving man craves food. Maybe tonight would be different, he told himself. Maybe tonight the reluctance and resistance he'd sensed in her would disappear. He could only hope.

He retrieved his hat and headed to his pickup to catch up with Keane and see how they were coming on clearing the land for the new pond.

But as he drove, he couldn't stop the niggling feeling that something big was going to happen tonight. Something sure as hell was wrong with Lindsay and he could only wonder what.

Lindsay spent the rest of the day at her house. Part of the time she helped her cook, Rosalee. Part of the time she was shut in her room deciding what to wear and how to tell Tony about her pregnancy.

She had wanted to wait, make her own decisions, but she couldn't go back to the carefree, happy times when she was with him after the auction. She had decided to tell him immediately and face dealing with him. It would come sooner or later and she wanted the battle over and done.

She wanted to look her best when she told him. When he was dazzled by her, Tony was much more cooperative. Take the night of the auction, for example. But then, that night she'd had surprise on her side. Oh, she had a surprise this time, all right. One that might make him faint.

Rummaging in her closet, she selected a black dress she had bought on impulse when she had been shopping in Dallas. She had never worn it, just because no occasion had arisen, but tonight should be one.

She yanked off her jeans to try on the dress. Before she pulled it on, she stopped to look at herself in the mirror. Even though it was too soon for physical changes, she couldn't keep from looking for them. It was satisfying to see she looked as slim as ever. Change was inevitable, but she hoped it didn't show really early. She wanted to keep working on the ranch, and if any of the guys noticed and realized, word would get to Abe. He would insist she stop and if she didn't, he'd probably talk to her brothers about it.

By five in the afternoon Rosalee had finished and left for the weekend. Lindsay had bathed and still worked to fix her hair, planning to leave it down in long spiral curls around her face.

As the time drew closer for Tony to arrive, her nerves became more raw. She dreaded talking to him, knowing all the peace between them would go up in flames tonight and they would each have to make a big effort to be civil and work out how they would deal with their new situation. Most of the changes would be in her life, but Tony would have adjustments and decisions, too. And their dates, their lovemaking, the fun they'd had—all that was over. It wasn't something she expected to get back in her life.

Feeling she had reached a point where her appearance was the best she could do, she went to the front window to watch for him coming up the drive. After a moment she stepped out on her porch to sit in a wooden rocker. In spite of the hot weather, she was chilled. Mounting dread about revealing her pregnancy to Tony enveloped her. She could anticipate his reactions and she suspected battles with him would fill the coming weeks. Underneath that dread was an undercurrent of anticipation, because she would finally be with him again.

When his sports car came into view, her pulse jumped. He might be bossy, but he still was the most charming, exciting, sexy man she had ever known. She went inside to take one more look at herself in the mirror, then stood waiting for the doorbell. Was she about to face her biggest struggle ever with Tony?

As Tony drove up the driveway to Lindsay's ranch house, his eagerness to see her grew. He'd been nervous all day to find out what disturbed her but, right now, knowing he'd see her in minutes, he couldn't help hoping for another hot, sexy night of lovemaking.

Never in his life had he been deeply involved in a serious relationship and he knew he wouldn't start now with Lindsay. They were just too different. Even so, at the moment he wanted to be with her; he missed talking to her and seeing her. He feared their tenuous relationship might be close to termination right now, but he intended to enjoy tonight to the fullest.

When the door swung open, his heart thudded and for seconds all he did was stare.

Lindsay wore another pair of stiletto heels with thin sexy straps crossing her slender feet, which matched her black sleeveless dress. Her plunging vee neckline revved his pulse another notch. Her straight, short skirt revealed her legs for him to view. Had she left her hair falling freely around her face to please him? Probably not, but he'd enjoy it anyway.

"You look gorgeous, Lindsay," he said. He was breathless, his voice deeper. "That black dress is killer on you."

She smiled at him, but it wasn't the wholehearted smile he had received before. "You've never been in my house. Come on in and look around."

He stepped in and the second he inhaled her perfume, he wanted to hold her and kiss her and forget about going out to dinner or eating anything for hours. He could cancel the reservations in Fort Worth and stay right here beside her.

He walked alongside her through a short hallway that opened out into a wide hall with a spiral staircase to the next floor. Above, a beamed ceiling was three stories high with skylights that let light pour into the house.

On either side of the stairs, the house opened up into spacious areas defined only by columns, furniture groupings and area rugs. The open rooms, high ceilings and lots of glass made the already large house seem twice as big.

"Like many other things about you, your house surprises me," he said. "It's beautiful, but not what I ever expected. I pictured you in a house more Western, but not the way you pictured mine would be. Just leather furniture and Western scenes in the paintings and traditional Western decor." He strolled into a living area he'd glimpsed from the hall and noticed a second-floor balcony extending over the length of one side of the room and the French period pieces upholstered in elegant silks and antique satins.

"Now I can picture you in your house," he said. "At least in part of it."

He turned to find her staring at him intently with a slight frown. Her expression jolted him. Just as he'd feared, something was very wrong and he didn't have a clue what it was.

"Lindsay, what's the problem?" he asked, unfastening the one button on his jacket and slipping out of it. He placed it on a chair. "Looks as if we need to talk."

As she wound her fingers together, her knuckles whitened. He took her hands in his.

"The weight of the world might as well be on your shoulders. Whatever is bothering you can't be that bad." He bent his knees so he could look directly into her eyes. Silently, he studied her.

"Before we talk, I think it would be wise to cancel our dinner reservation. I debated just telling you to come over for dinner, but I thought I might not have the courage to talk to you tonight—"

"Damn, Lindsay, what the hell? Is it—"

"Don't start guessing. Cancel the dinner reservation. My cook was here today and I had her leave us a casserole if either of us feels like eating later."

Watching her, he pulled out his phone, looked down and sent a short text. He put away his phone.

"I think you might like a drink. I'll get you a beer," she said.

Mystified, he stared after her. Whatever this was, the problem disturbed her a hell of a lot more than any other she'd encountered while he'd known her. From the way she was acting, it seemed even catastrophic.

Was it the ranch? Did she have to sell it? If she did, she wouldn't have any trouble telling him. Nor could it involve anyone in her family; he didn't think she would hesitate letting him know that.

He knew she had gone to Dallas recently. He also realized she had another life away from her ranch. Was it someone else? Did she have a lover in Dallas? No, she wouldn't have stayed with Tony if there'd been anyone else.

So why did she go to Dallas? Did she have some illness and need a big-city doctor?

She looked as healthy as anyone could hope to be, even though that was no indication of how she might feel or why she would have to see a doctor. The thought that Lindsay was sick was like a punch to his middle. What was wrong and how serious was it? Was it incurable? That question almost buckled his knees.

He watched her behind the bar fixing their drinks and went to join her. The more he thought about it, the more convinced he was that she had gone to Dallas because of a medical problem. She knew when she told him he'd need a drink.

What the hell could be so wrong that she knew ahead of time and it involved him enough for her to expect him to be upset?

His knees did almost cave on that one. He sat on the nearest bar stool while he stared without seeing anything and his head spun.

One possibility occurred to him and he knew in every inch of his being that he guessed correctly. Taking deep breaths, he looked up to see her coming around the bar with a glass of ice water for herself and a whiskey on the rocks for him.

"I thought you might prefer this," she said, handing him his drink. She frowned. "Tony, you look white as a sheet."

"You're pregnant, aren't you? You're carrying my baby."

Nine

"How did you find out?"

He closed his eyes. "Wow," he whispered. "I just figured it out. I tried to think of reasons for you to go to Dallas. And reasons for the big change in you since the way you were with me before you went to Dallas. And when you offered to get a drink for me, I realized it had to involve me, too. There was only one thing I could think of." He reached for the drink she held out. "I think I need that whiskey now."

He downed it in one swallow and set down an empty glass. "I'm in shock. You're going to have to give me a minute to digest this bit of news," he said. "You've had time to think about it a little."

He sat there staring at the floor but not seeing anything, just thinking about the changes coming in his life—changes that would be monumental.

He would be a father. Lindsay would have his child.

He was so dazed he knew he couldn't even fathom the changes that would downright transform his life. He couldn't even try.

There would be no financial worries for either one of them, so he could cross that concern off his list. But there was one giant problem—and only one solution.

He pulled himself together as best he could and stood up to take her hand.

"Lindsay, marry me."

His words didn't have the desired effect. Instead, he watched a transformation come over her and he had a sinking feeling a proposal wasn't what she wanted. Once again her stubbornness surfaced. He could see that in the set to her jaw and the fire in her eyes. Annoyance filled him as it always had. From the start he had known she always stirred up conflict, and this was no exception.

"Tony, that's a knee-jerk reaction. You take some time and think this through. I'm financially well-fixed, so that's not a consideration. I have a big, supportive family, so I'll have all the help I need. The biggest reason I can't marry you is that we are basically not compatible." Before he could make a point, she added, "You're bossy and arrogant and you want to take charge of every situation—which is exactly what you're doing right now. I don't want you telling me what to do."

Impatience stabbed him. Every issue was a conflict with her. Why did he think for one second this wouldn't be? She was, as always, her usual stubborn self. But then his gaze roamed over her and for an instant he forgot everything. She was stunning. Even steeped in worry, when he looked at her, she took his breath away.

"Lindsay, stop and think and consider my proposal. Don't answer now. It's the logical solution for a lot of reasons, plus we get along great in some ways."

With a slight frown, she started to answer, and he placed his finger on her soft lips. "Shh. Don't answer me now—give my proposal time and think of all the positive reasons to do this. We can be compatible, we have these big families that have drawn close and we'll be thrown together constantly. All you're thinking about right now is that I'm a rancher and how I run my ranch. Just think of all the things in our lives and give my offer consideration." He walked behind the bar to pour another drink. He stood there, not saying a word, sipping the whiskey while she was quiet. He suspected she was getting her argument lined up.

Shock still reverberated in him. Of all people—Lindsay would have his baby.

Everything fell into place—why she didn't want to see him, why she was so somber. He walked to the window with his back to Lindsay and the room and stared outside. His entire life was about to change drastically. After a few moments he turned around to find her still standing where he had left her. She looked at him but said nothing.

His mind reeled with questions. He gave one voice. "When did you find out?"

She told him. "As soon as I realized I was late, I had a feeling. I went to a doctor and had the lab work done. I wanted to confirm it before I told you."

He nodded. "This is something I thought would never happen—an unplanned pregnancy. I know you thought the same thing."

They lapsed into silence again as he contemplated the changes coming in his life. Fatherhood. Coming fast and unexpected.

"Did you get a doctor in Dallas? I assume that's why you went."

"No. I know too many people there. I called Savannah

and got an appointment with her doctor in Little Rock. I didn't want word to get back to you until I could tell you myself. I didn't think about you guessing correctly."

"Well, you'll have to find a doc closer than Little Rock," he remarked drily. "Damn."

"I will. I just couldn't take a chance going to any big Texas city where I could have run into someone I know."

Another silence fell and he was thankful again that she was giving him a chance to adjust to his new status before they talked very much.

"There are a few things I think we can decide tonight."

As he stared at her, he thought, *Here we go*. She sat at the edge of a pale antique satin sofa and crossed her legs. Long, beautiful legs—the best pair of legs he had ever seen. As he looked at her, he noted that her blond hair was like a halo around her head. In almost every respect, he knew this woman would be the best mother possible for his child. He just hadn't planned on fatherhood so soon. And he and Lindsay were not in love. She didn't like ranchers. He didn't like her stubborn streak, her knack for constantly living in conflict.

"We should keep this between us for a little longer, if possible," he said, "until we make some major decisions about the future."

She nodded. "When people hear I'm expecting a baby, I'm going to get questions."

"That's fine with me. Whatever you want. You said Savannah knows and, I'm assuming, Mike. Who else?"

"Besides you, no one else. Believe me, Mike and Savannah know how to keep quiet."

"Good. It's better for both of us to keep it quiet for now," he repeated. "You don't show at all and I doubt if you will for another month. That gives us time." He became silent, his thoughts swirling in his head. Like a mantra, one statement kept reverberating in his mind. Lindsay was pregnant with his baby.

His gaze swept over her again. She was the most beautiful woman he had ever known. And the sexiest. He remembered their lovemaking, which was never out of his thoughts long. Marriage to her would have big pluses, if her stubbornness didn't overshadow the rest.

She'd had a bit of time to think about this and adjust to the prospect of being pregnant, so she might have already made decisions about the future. He'd better come out of shock and plan what they should do.

Minutes ticked past while he tried to sort through the jumble of thoughts, possibilities and outcomes. Finally, her voice broke the silence.

"I never thought this would be a problem I'd have," she said, gazing up at him. Her blue eyes were wide and clear.

"There's a simple solution I've already given you." She directed a steady look at him and he could feel the battles looming between them. "Lindsay, we're going to have a baby," he said. "You know I'll love this baby with all my heart."

"I know you will," she replied.

"Did the doctor tell you an approximate due date?"

"Next May."

"Then we should have that wedding soon," he said, and her eyes flared.

"I'll do what I feel I have to do," she said, the old tension coming between them again. He could feel the first stir of his own anger over her answer. Trying to curb it, reminding himself of the huge upheaval this would cause in her life, he crossed the space between them to draw her to her feet and place his hands on her shoulders. She stiffened.

He could feel barriers coming up between them. Anger

plagued him over her stubborn refusal to cooperate, which showed in her body language as well as her facial expression.

But who was he kidding? In spite of the problems and differences between them, he still wanted her—in his arms, in his bed. The minute he touched her, that familiar desire flared up in every part of him, and if he wasn't mistaken, he caught the same response in her.

Unable to resist any longer, he pulled her into his arms to kiss her hard and passionately. For an instant she pushed against him, but he couldn't step away if he wanted to, and in seconds, her arm went around his neck and she surrendered to his kiss. It was all the invitation he needed.

In one motion he peeled away her black dress while he continued to kiss her. When her bra was gone, he caressed her breasts, kissing first one and then the other. Her moans and soft breaths encouraged him to take her. He paused only long enough to strip off his clothes. Then, naked and hard, he picked her up and lowered her onto the sofa. Without a second's hesitation he entered her in one smooth thrust. She was ready for him. Hard and fast, they moved together. Quickly, desperately, she clutched him to her as she climaxed with him, her cries muted by his frantic kisses. They both gasped for breath as wave after wave of ecstasy washed over them.

For Tony, though it was fast and furious, this was the best lovemaking he'd ever had. He leaned back to tell her as much till he saw the look in her eyes. He'd expected a contented haze; instead, he found a storm brewing in their blue depths.

She stared at him and he could feel her anger rising again.

Instead of lashing out, she simply pushed him off her.

"I'm going to shower, Tony. I'll be back shortly," she said, still breathless. She yanked up her clothes and left.

He watched her walk away and wondered if he could ever get her to listen and cooperate or if they were at an impasse. Gathering his clothes, he went to find a bathroom and dress. As he did, his thoughts were on Lindsay. Would she even talk to him when she came back?

He returned to wait and soon she entered the room. As always, she made his heart beat faster. "You look gorgeous."

She had changed from her dress and wore a white linen blouse and white slacks with white high-heeled sandals and she still looked good enough to model.

"Thank you," she said in a dismissive manner, as if she barely heard what he had said. "Tony, I think our evening is over. I don't feel like dinner together."

He tried to curb the flash of anger that returned. Stubborn, stubborn woman who wanted life her way and her way only.

He wouldn't leave, not without reiterating his proposal. "Lindsay, the logical thing is for us to get married. Think about it tonight."

"I will," she said, but from the way she replied, with anger in her voice, he suspected the next time he saw her, he would get only arguments about marrying.

She raised her chin. "Do you really think we can get along in day-to-day living?"

They stared at each other and he felt the palpable clash of wills.

"See. I proved my point," she said. "Frankly, Tony, I'm trying to hang on to my temper. I really would like to scream at you for getting me pregnant, except I know full well that I had as much part in that happening as you did."

"Thank you for that one." At least she was rational. "Lindsay, I just see one solution and I hope you'll come to the same conclusion."

"We irritate each other."

"Sometimes, but we can get past the problems. I know now that beneath the tough rancher is a stunning, sexy woman who can simply melt me."

"Tony," she said impatiently, "whatever we found compatible in the past few weeks since the night of the auction… it's gone. That's over."

"Not altogether," he remarked drily. "We found it again less than an hour ago."

Anger flashed in her expression. She closed her mouth tightly while she glared at him.

"I know we need to work this out," she said after a few minutes of silence. "I just can't be the same person with you that I was."

"Don't stop communicating. I won't be cut off from my child. I want this baby in my life and I feel strongly that, if possible, a baby needs both a mom and a dad. That isn't always feasible, but in this case, it damn sure is, Lindsay," he said, trying to keep his temper.

Again, he got a glacial stare. "I know it, Tony. We both caused this and I agree that we both need to be in our baby's life. But don't pressure me," she snapped.

"Dammit, Lindsay. Before you make any decisions, stop and think about our baby. I'll talk to you later." He walked out before he lost it with her.

He slammed the door and hurried to his car, then drove away. Had she already closed her mind to his proposal?

Lindsay felt as if all the frustration and anger building in her since realizing she was pregnant had finally burst and she couldn't act as if nothing had changed between them.

His controlling personality had surfaced in a big way tonight—a glimpse of what she would live with if she even considered his proposal. She couldn't imagine being married to him and taking orders from him every day.

She hadn't been able to resist his kisses, succumbing to sex, but afterward she regretted the intimacy. Sure, there was no doubt they were sexually compatible but, as she'd said many times, sex wasn't everything. Outside the bedroom, she couldn't live with him.

She had wanted him to leave. She wanted to tell him goodbye and not see him again until she worked things out for her future.

One thing her feelings were certain about was that she was not going to marry Tony. That would be disastrous for both of them.

Just as she'd expected, he had tried to take over her life tonight. In marriage he would take over her ranch, tell her what to do on a daily basis. Besides, they weren't in love.

She could imagine Tony wanting to put both ranches together with him running everything while she stayed home to raise their child. That wasn't going to happen.

In spite of her irritation with him, when she looked at the sofa, she saw Tony there, his marvelous, strong body, his vitality, his sexy lovemaking that still now made a tremor run through her. But it was over.

Though she was too upset to sleep, she got ready for bed and sat in a chair in the dark, her eyes adjusting to the moonlight that spilled into her bedroom.

Knowing she should go to bed but certain she would just stare into the darkness and sleep would still escape her, she sat where she was until she finally fell asleep in her chair.

When she crawled into bed, it was almost four in the morning. As soon as her head touched the pillow, memories of better moments with Tony bombarded her. Then she thought about tonight with him and felt her anger return.

The next day she sent a text to Abe that she couldn't work. She needed to tell him about her pregnancy, but she had to get a grip on her emotions. When she talked to Abe, she had to be able to tell him that she had decided to turn the daily running of the ranch over to him, and she had to be able to say it without tears. She loved her ranch, working on it, raising her horses, dealing with livestock and making decisions. Her land was beautiful to her, spreading endlessly to a blue horizon with gorgeous sunrises and sunsets. Tony wasn't going to marry and take that away from her.

She had been nauseated after breakfast this morning and she wondered if that was something she would have every morning. She needed to find a Dallas doctor, as well as decide where she would live in her ninth month.

Three days later she still hadn't told Abe anything except that she couldn't work. Soon he would come to see about her, but she dreaded telling him. He could keep it quiet, that she could count on. But him knowing just made it more real.

She tried to do some of her paperwork, but she couldn't keep her mind on it. There was no call from Tony, but that didn't surprise her. What did surprise her was how much she missed him.

She sat staring into space and thinking about Tony. If she wouldn't marry him, would it hurt when he married later? Would she be able to watch him go out of her life except when it was necessary to see him because of their child?

She hadn't considered that before and it hurt to think of Tony marrying someone else. If the thought of Tony marrying hurt, how much did she really care for him? Could she be in love with him?

No way she could be in love with him. He was too authoritative, too opinionated, so certain he was always right. There was a point where all her affection and his appeal came to a stop.

They would have their lives tied together for years to come, but going out with each other the way they had been had ended. She saw that clearly and felt it was for the best. Just as swiftly, she felt a pang at the thought of not going out with him, of not making love to him. Startled, she shook her head. Life with Tony was over and that was the way she wanted it. She would stop missing him soon.

And what about Tony? He might want out of seeing her just as much. He had been in shock last night. The proposal had been a knee-jerk reaction. Now that he was home to think things through alone, his conclusions about the future might have changed.

The idea made her feel even more forlorn, as if she were losing someone important. As the day passed, she tried unsuccessfully to shake the feeling of loss. How long would it be before she stopped missing him?

Ten

As each day passed, Tony tried to adjust to the situation. Without thinking, too often he reached for his phone to call Lindsay only to stop himself. He'd reminded himself how mulish she could be. But that didn't stop him from missing her.

Friday afternoon, the second of October, when he returned from work he saw Lindsay's pickup on his drive.

His heart jumped and he sped up his steps, all tiredness leaving him instantly. Lindsay stepped out of her pickup and his breath caught in his throat. She wore tight jeans, a clinging red T-shirt with a vee neckline. Her hair was in the usual braid and she had a wide-brimmed brown hat on her head. She looked great to him and his pulse raced as eagerness to talk to her made him walk even faster.

"Hi," he said as he approached, smiling.

She gave him a fleeting smile and he drew a deep

breath because she kept a wall between them. He could feel her coolness toward him and knew there was a specific reason for her visit.

"Come in, Lindsay."

"No, I just thought I'd stop in and talk in person instead of on the phone, but this won't take long. Now that my waist is getting a bit bigger—"

He looked down at her and wondered if she could even be one inch larger. "You don't look it."

"I feel it. Anyway, as I was saying, now that I'm getting bigger, I want to tell my family that I'm pregnant and I want to tell Abe and the guys."

"Lindsay, have you even thought about our baby?"

Her eyes narrowed and her cheeks flushed. He was certain she would start yelling at him any minute. He struggled to keep his temper.

"Yes, I have," she said. "I still don't want to marry you. You would want to take charge of every detail of my life and of our child's upbringing. Hell, no, I'm not marrying you."

"You're so damn stubborn, you'd mess up your own life."

"It still is my 'own life.' Are you okay with telling our families? I'll just tell them that we're working out our plans. They'll accept what I tell them."

"That's probably a good idea, because you need to get a doctor and word has a way of spreading, especially when it's about babies. I'll tell my family, too. And Keane and the guys. And I'll tell all of them I asked you to marry me and you said no—but that opens you up to some pressure."

"No more than I'll get anyway." She opened the door to her pickup. "Thanks, Tony. We got that settled."

He put his hand on her door and blocked her way from climbing in.

"It doesn't have to be this way."

"I don't see how things can be any other way," she said. He dropped his hand and held the door for her while she climbed in.

"Bye," he said as he closed the door, feeling as if this was a real and lasting farewell. That any intimacy or closeness they'd shared—the laughter and joy and steamy sex—all of it was over. Stepping away, he rested his hands on his hips as he watched her drive away, heading back to the county road to go home to her ranch. As her pickup widened the distance between them, he knew he would always remember the day she drove out of his life. He didn't think they would ever be close again. A cloud of gloom, along with his anger, settled on him as he entered the house.

The following week, Tony saw he had a text from his sister, Madison; she wanted to come see him. With a sigh he sent her a text in return.

Yes, you can come see me. Tonight's fine. Tomorrow morning is fine. Take your pick or suggest a time.

They had finally settled on early Saturday. He waited on the porch because it was a cool, sunny morning.

He watched Madison come up the walk. Her brown hair was in a ponytail. She wore jeans and a tan cotton shirt that was not tucked into her jeans. In spite of hiding her waist, it was obvious she was months along in her pregnancy. He placed his arm around her shoulders to give her a brief hug, then led her inside the house. "Haven't seen you in a while. I have breakfast ready. Or anything else you'd like."

"I've had breakfast. I'll just have a glass of ice water. It's a beautiful morning and what is even more wonderful is that rain is predicted next week—they give it a twenty-percent chance."

"If it actually happens, I'm going out to just stand in it. Might take a picture of it since it's been so long since I've seen any."

She smiled. "Is Gwynne here?"

"Not on Saturday. How are you feeling?"

"Fine. Just bigger by the day." She faced him, her green eyes sparkling. "Tony, congratulations. I've talked to you on the phone, but I wanted to tell you in person. I'm so happy for you and Lindsay. I know you have things to work out, but you will. A baby is so wonderful."

"Thanks, Madison. It's sort of a mixed blessing at this point in my life."

"It's an enormous blessing. And our babies will not be so far apart in age," she said, rubbing her stomach lightly.

"I can't think that far ahead," he remarked drily. "I'm just getting accustomed to this becoming-a-dad business."

She laughed and accepted the glass of water as he handed it to her. "I'll carry your coffee, Tony," she said as he helped himself to scrambled eggs from a pan on his stove. He added a piece of ham and picked up a slice of toast.

"I'm set. It's beautiful outside. Let's sit on the porch."

As soon as they were seated at a glass-topped iron table, he sipped his coffee and sat in silence, certain she had a mission.

"Tony, any chance you want some sisterly advice?"

"Actually, no," he said, smiling at her, "but since this drive to visit me was unprecedented and a little difficult for you under the circumstances, I'm sure I'm going to get some."

"I'm just concerned. And Jake is concerned about his sister. She's hurting, and I came to see for myself how you're faring."

"I'm faring fine," he said, startled to hear about Lindsay. He'd figured she had gotten on with her life and wasn't giving much thought to him. He knew she had stopped working with the men.

"Mike Calhoun's wife is expecting her baby this month, which is exciting. We'll have the three new babies, plus Cody and Scotty. Our families are growing and I think it's exciting and wonderful."

He smiled at her. "At the moment, you're in love with Jake, having his baby, and the whole world looks rosy to you," he said, studying her and realizing she looked happier and prettier than ever before.

"You're right," she agreed. "Are you okay?"

"I'm absolutely fine. And you're looking good yourself. I think marriage and motherhood really suit you."

"I'm happy, Tony. So happy with Jake," she said.

"Our dad should have stayed out of your lives and not deceived you about Jake, as well as driving him away," Tony said quietly. "I don't know how you can ever forgive him. Dad and I have butted heads since I was able to talk back to him. I paid for it, but I never got along with him the way Wyatt and Nick did."

"Wyatt is quiet and peaceful. Nick's the politician who's going to please the world and he started by pleasing Dad. And I always, well, until high school, did what he wanted. I never dreamed he would interfere in my life the way he did." Her frown disappeared and she smiled. "That's over. Jake and I are married, having a baby and I'm happier than I ever dreamed possible." Impulsively, she reached out to squeeze her brother's hand. "I hope you find that with Lindsay, Tony. You can't imagine how wonderful marriage can be."

He laughed. "I do believe you're in love, sis. That's good. You and Jake deserve all the happiness in the world. I'm amazed Jake hasn't punched Dad out."

"Jake isn't going to hit an elderly man, much less hit my father."

"He has a right to."

"Whatever," she said, flipping back her hair. "Anyway, I'm glad to hear you're okay. I just wanted to see for myself. I'm excited our babies will be fairly close in age. December and May aren't really far apart after the first year or two."

"Madison, you didn't drive out here to tell me how thrilled you are about our babies being close in age. You could have done that on the phone."

"Well, I more or less did. And to see if you're okay."

"I'm quite okay. But what's wrong with Lindsay?"

"I think she's just unhappy."

"Well, Jake should realize that being pregnant has put a big crimp in her lifestyle. For corn's sake, look how she's always lived—like one of the guys. Suddenly, she's a woman and her body has limitations because of her pregnancy. She's not accustomed to that, didn't expect it and evidently is having difficulty adjusting to it."

"Just be nice to her, Tony. It's a big change and for Lindsay, without a husband, without planning for a baby, changing her entire life and future is an enormous upheaval."

"She'll adjust. And she could have a husband if she wanted," he said, unable to keep the bitterness out of his voice. "She turned me down absolutely. Lindsay will handle this just like she handles everything else—in full control."

"You think a lot of her, don't you?" Madison asked.

"Sure, I do. Every rancher in the area does. She's capable and intelligent."

"You didn't take her out because she's capable and intelligent."

He laughed. "No, she can be fun and pretty."

"Lindsay has the looks of a model when she wants to. I saw her at the auction. Anyway, you be nice to her. She needs you now."

"I'll be nice to Lindsay," he said with amusement. "Though I don't think she needs me or wants to see me or talk to me."

Madison sat quietly so long that he turned to look at her. "What?" he asked.

She stood. "I've seen that you're doing fine. I don't want to pry into your life with Lindsay. I just want you to know that I'm excited about your baby. I should go home now."

"That was a short visit, but I'm glad you came. Madison, let me know when Mike's baby is born. I might not hear about it."

"Lindsay will tell you," she said.

"Lindsay isn't going to tell me one damn thing."

Madison looked startled and stared at him intently.

"We don't speak, we don't see each other. It'll have to change later, but that's the way she wants it now."

"Sorry to hear that. I'll tell you about Mike and Savannah." She gave him a hug, then leaned away to look intently at him again. "Be patient with Lindsay. This is a giant change for both of you."

"Sure," he answered, knowing his sister meant well. He stood on the porch and watched her drive away, his thoughts on Lindsay. Lindsay was unhappy? She did what she wanted to do.

And how unhappy was she? It had to be a lot to worry Jake enough to get Madison to drive out and talk to him. He wished Lindsay's unhappiness was because she missed him, but he knew better. She was probably unhappy with him and unhappy she had to change her lifestyle.

He carried his dishes into his empty house. As he passed his landline, he stared at the phone, tempted to pick it up and call Lindsay to just talk. He missed her and every time he realized that he missed her, it surprised him.

How important had she become to him?

He couldn't answer his own question.

The next week he threw himself into work, going to the corral to ride some of the unbroken horses at night with a few of the men who worked for him, just keeping busy. But none of it stopped the moments of longing for Lindsay.

Nights were long and unpleasant. He had always fallen into bed and been asleep instantly, sleeping soundly until early morning. Not anymore. His nights were filled with memories of Lindsay, dreams about her, moments of missing her.

The weekends were worse because he had no one he wanted to go out with. He missed her and the longing to see her intensified instead of diminished, until he finally sat up in bed one night, tossed back the covers and walked out on his porch.

The gray dog was still recovering, but better. The bandages were gone and his hair, where they'd had to shave it away to work on his cuts, was growing out again. He had gained weight and his coat was shiny now. Tony kept it brushed so it wasn't a tangle.

Tony let him stay at the house with him. The dog

seemed a faint tie to Lindsay, and Tony enjoyed having him around. When he went to the porch, the dog followed him, sitting with his head on Tony's knee while Tony scratched his ears. "Maybe I should invite her over to see you," he said to the dog, who wagged his bushy tail.

Tony sat quietly while he thought about Lindsay. He thought about her constantly each day. Was he in love with her and hadn't realized it when it happened?

If he was, he didn't know where it could lead. She was as stubborn as ever, refusing to give an inch, while she had accused him of being too take-charge and bossy. Plus, he was a rancher—the kind of man she said she would never marry.

He sat in the dark and mulled over his feelings for Lindsay and the problems between them.

Madison had said Lindsay was unhappy. Was their parting a cause of her unhappiness? Could he ever get past her stubborn nature? He had some of the time. His heartbeat quickened at the thought of getting past their problems. Could he think before he told her what she should do?

Could he live without her?

Was he in love with her?

Staring into the dark, he realized he was. He wanted her in his life. Lindsay would be a challenge, but if he loved her, he would cope with her. But could he get her to consider working with another rancher? That wasn't impossible. He worked with them all the time and for that matter, she did, too.

Suddenly feeling better, he wanted to call her and he wanted to be with her. One thing he knew for certain: he didn't want to lose her. Someone would come along and marry her and, at the thought, he felt as if he had been punched in his heart.

He needed to get her a ring and tell her how he felt and propose—for real this time. He had fallen in love with her and hadn't even recognized the depth of his own feelings.

He remembered her call at three in the morning when the dog was howling. It was about four o'clock now. What would happen if he called her, told her he had to see her? Could he get her to listen to him and go out with him?

Or was she out of his life no matter what he felt for her?

Lindsay sat up and shook her hair back away from her face. She stared into the dark bedroom as she clutched the phone. "Tony?" she asked, sounding more alert. "It's four in the morning. What's wrong?"

"Lindsay, I need to see you. Let me pick you up for dinner tonight."

She frowned at the phone. "You called at 4:00 a.m. to ask me to dinner?"

"You called at three to tell me a dog was howling. Will you have dinner with me? We need to talk."

She couldn't imagine what the urgency was, but her heartbeat quickened because she missed him and she wanted to be with him.

"Yes, I'll go to dinner with you. But you do know I'm pregnant and need my sleep, right?"

"I figured four is close enough to when you'll get up anyway. And can't you go back to sleep?"

"Yes," she said, but she wondered whether she would or not.

"Me, too, darling'," he said, and a warm fuzziness filled her. She hadn't heard that endearment in too long and it made it worth the wake-up call. "How about I pick you up at six?" he asked.

"That's fine," she said, curious what was on his mind.

"See you then," he said, and was gone.

She settled in bed, turning toward the windows so she could look at the bright moonlight outside. White cumulus clouds drifted rapidly across the black sky. She missed Tony more than she would have believed possible. She missed him every day and thought about him constantly and got lost in memories too often each day.

When had Tony become so important to her? At first she'd thought she would forget him as the days passed. Instead, each day she missed him and thought of him more.

She hadn't faced the question that hovered in her mind. Was she in love with him? Had she fallen in love with a man who would always want to run her life, their child rearing and her ranch? All indications said she had. She didn't know his feelings for sure, but she knew he hadn't been in love with her when she last saw him.

Tony had been so many good things—energetic, sexy, positive and upbeat, full of fun and life. She knew he was a good rancher. And she knew he was a take-charge person. Could she cope with having him back in her life? And on a larger scale? She couldn't answer her own question. The only solid answer she could give was that she had been miserable without him. She didn't want to tell him goodbye and watch him marry another woman while she raised his child.

This time without Tony had been the unhappiest stretch in her life. Excitement coursed through her at the thought of seeing him again. What was so urgent that he had to see her tonight? She hoped it was to get back together. She didn't know how they could, but she was ready to try.

She climbed out of bed, moving restlessly to a chair to think about Tony. She was guessing he wanted to see her because he missed her, too. But what if he had another reason—like a permanent parting of the ways?

That possibility filled her with concern. It couldn't happen now, she told herself, not when she finally realized she wanted him back in her life with all her being.

He still might propose to her again, even if he didn't love her. If he did, was she willing to accept that and hope she could win his love over time?

She ran her hand across her flat stomach. Their baby needed them. Could they set aside their monumental differences and give love a chance?

There was love on her part. She was ready to admit it now. She was in love with Tony, alpha male or not. She had gotten herself into this situation by bidding on him at the auction, and now she was in deep, over her head.

Would she tell him that she was in love? Or keep it from him until he declared feelings of love for her? She didn't see how she could keep from revealing her love to him. At the thought of seeing him tonight, what she most wanted was to throw herself into his arms when she opened her door. Now that she knew she would see him and had finally admitted that she was deeply in love, she ached to be with him and hoped with all her heart he might have missed her or, better yet, be as in love as she was.

She glanced at her clock and saw it was almost five. In just over twelve hours she would be with him and get an answer to the question that plagued her. What did Tony feel for her?

Only time would tell.

By six that night she had even more questions. As she left her room, she turned for one more look in the mirror. She wore a deep blue sleeveless dress with a low-cut back, a hem that ended above her knees and high heels. She had left her hair falling freely because Tony liked that best.

Downstairs, promptly at six she watched him step out of his black sports car and come up her front drive, and her breath rushed from her lungs. He looked handsome, filled with vitality. He also looked like a Texas rancher in his white Stetson, his black boots, black Western-cut trousers and a pale blue, long-sleeved cotton shirt that was open at the throat. She longed to throw herself into his embrace, but she restrained herself, opening the front door and smiling.

His blue-green eyes filled with desire that revved up her heartbeat. "Darlin', you look gorgeous," he said, his gaze moving over her slowly, a tantalizing perusal that set her pulse pounding. "You look more fantastic than ever. I'd say that pregnancy becomes you."

"Thank you. I'd say prospective fatherhood becomes you, because you're a sexy hunk, Tony Milan." As she spoke she was unable to keep from letting her gaze skim over him, wanting more than ever to be in his arms and kiss him.

"Lindsay," he said.

She looked up to meet his hungry gaze and her heart thudded at the heat and desire she saw there. He stepped inside and closed the door. She didn't have to throw herself into Tony's arms. He drew her into them and kissed her.

Her heart slammed against her ribs and she clung to him to kiss him in return. "Tony, I've missed you," she whispered breathlessly between kisses.

"I'm not doing any of this the way I planned," he said, between showering her with kisses.

Looking into his eyes, she felt a physical impact that

heated her insides. It seemed months instead of weeks since she last saw him.

He kissed her and she closed her eyes again, holding him tightly while her heart pounded.

"I might not let you go this time," he whispered. He showered kisses on her and finally picked her up, carrying her as he kissed her. "We were going to my house, but I think that's temporarily on hold. This is far too urgent," he said. "Lindsay, I've really missed you."

Clutching his shoulders, she kissed him slowly and thoroughly. "I've missed you."

He took the stairs two at a time, hurrying to the big bed in her room.

It was covered with dresses, lacy underwear, bits and pieces of clothing that she had tried on earlier.

He yanked back the cover and all of the clothing flew off. He turned to kiss her, his fingers trembling as he drew the zipper of her dress down while she twisted free the buttons of his shirt. She couldn't wait to show him how much she loved him.

Over an hour later, she lay wrapped in his arms beside him in bed while he lightly combed her hair away from her face with his fingers and showered feathery kisses on her temple and cheeks.

"I think we were going to my place for dinner," he whispered, nuzzling her neck and kissing her throat so lightly.

"We still can if you want or I can find something here to feed you."

"I had plans and I wanted to show you the dog."

She sat up so fast he rolled away slightly. "The dog? You didn't tell me. Is he okay?"

"He's more than okay," Tony said, smiling as he pulled

her back against his shoulder and held her close. "Lindsay, I've missed you, darlin', more than I thought possible and I've thought about my feelings for you."

She focused on him, her heart beginning to drum, and she could barely catch her breath upon hearing his words. He gazed into her eyes and looked at her intently. "Lindsay, I love you."

"Oh, Tony," she gasped, wrapping her arms around his neck to kiss him and hold him tightly. "I'm in love with you. I didn't want to be in love with a rancher, absolutely not the controlling type, which you are. I tried not to be. We're misfits, you and I—two ranchers. I know you think I'm too stubborn and maybe I am. Am I babbling?" she asked. Without pausing for breath or for his answer, she continued. "I've been miserable without you in my life. You're too take-charge. We'll clash and it won't be any more peaceful in the future than it was in the past—"

"Damn, Lindsay," he said, and kissed her, stopping her chatter. She clung to him, kissing him, pouring out the love that she felt along with joy and relief over his declaration.

Suddenly, she leaned away to look at him, framing his face with her hands. "You really, really love me?"

"I really, really love you. Lindsay, will you marry me?" he asked, holding her close against him with one arm wrapped around her waist.

Her heart thudded. "Yes," she gasped. "Oh, yes, Tony. We'll fight, but we'll be in love."

"We might not fight," he whispered. "We may learn to negotiate." She heard the laughter in his voice. He wrapped his fingers in her hair and tugged lightly so she had to look at him. Startled, her eyes flew wide as she looked up at him.

"Will you marry me?" he repeated.

"Yes, I will," she answered.

"Then I'm the happiest man in the world tonight," he said. "I don't care about the differences and I can cope with you and you can cope with me. You'll get used to this rancher, darlin'. You may not get used to my take-charge ways, but we'll work things out because I promise to try to keep you happy. I promise to shower you with love so you won't ever regret marrying an alpha male cowboy."

"Shh, Tony. Stop making wild promises you can't keep," she said, laughing, trailing light kisses over his face. "I love you, cowboy. I love you with all my heart."

He kissed her, a kiss of joy and promise, a kiss that melted her heart and ignited desire again, and soon she was lost in passion.

It was almost ten when she sat with him in her tub while hot water swirled around them and he held her close between his legs as she leaned back against him.

"Hungry? I was going to cook steaks."

"I hadn't thought about it," she said. "I don't know about hunger, but I'm shriveling up from being in this hot water so long."

He chuckled, cupping her full breasts in his hands to caress her. "Not too shriveled," he said. "We'll get out, dry and go eat something. I know you have something in this house and if you don't, we'll head to my place." With big splashes, he stood, pulling her up with him and helping her step out of the tub. He picked up a towel and began slow, light strokes to dry her.

She caught the towel, wrapping it around herself and picking up another folded one to hand to him. "If you keep doing that, we'll end up in bed again. I'll dry my-self and you do the same, then get dressed and I'll meet you downstairs. I'm getting hungry and for some reason, I can't skip meals like I used to be able to."

Nodding, he grinned. "Not as much fun, but I'll cooperate."

When he met her downstairs in her kitchen, she already had a casserole heating and in minutes it was on the table. His fingers closed on her wrist and she looked up at him, startled.

"Darlin', I had this evening planned and it hasn't gone the way I expected from the moment you opened the door. But I came prepared for whatever happened." He reached into a pocket, pulled out a small folded bit of tissue paper tied with a tiny strip of blue ribbon. "This is for you, Lindsay."

Surprised, she looked up at him, giving him a searching look, and then she took it to tug free the bow and open the paper carefully, her heart drumming as she did. She looked at a dazzling ring. "Oh, Tony," she gasped, thrilled to look at the ring he had for her. It was a huge, emerald-cut diamond, surrounded by sapphires and diamonds with more diamonds scattered on the gold band.

He took it from her and held her hand. "One more time, the way I should have done it the first time. Lindsay Calhoun, will you marry me?"

"Oh, yes," she replied, laughing. "Yes." She threw her arms around him after he slipped the ring on her finger. Wrapping her arms around his neck, she kissed him and he held her tightly, kissing her in return.

When they finally stopped, he took her hand to walk to the table. "Lindsay, you need to eat. Let's sit and eat and talk about when we'll have a wedding. I hope we can agree on a date soon. Very, very soon."

He held her chair and then sat facing her. She could

barely think about eating because of the excitement and joy churning in her.

"Tony, I've missed you so and I realized I've been in love with you for a long time. I don't know how marriage will work with the two of us, but I can't wait to try."

"You'll be you and I'll still be me. We're in love, so we'll work it out." He grinned and picked up her hand to brush kisses over her knuckles. "I love you, darlin'. Back to the date. Lindsay, let's get married soon. Really soon.

She stared at him and then nodded. "In that, we're in agreement. The sooner the better for so many reasons, not the least of which is I love you with all my heart."

His eyes took on the greenish hue that she recognized from moments of intense emotion or passion. He held her hand and, without taking his gaze from hers, lifted it to his lips to brush more kisses lightly over it.

"Lindsay, I love you and I always will."

"Even if we fight?"

"Even if we fight. But I don't think we really will." He wagged his brows and grinned. "Well, maybe sometimes."

"Now, do you want a surprise?" she asked.

"I think my entire life will be filled with surprises. What's this one, darlin'?"

"It's early, and I'll have an ultrasound later this month, but my doctor thinks I may be having twins."

Stunned, he stared at her. "Twins?" He got up and walked around the table to reach down and draw her to her feet to kiss her hard. When he released her, he grinned. "Lindsay, why do I think my whole life will be like this night? One shock and one change after another."

"You know it won't be that way all the time."

"Get a calendar and let's have this wedding this month."

"Savannah's baby is due this month, but I'd like to

have the wedding soon, too. I've waited as long as I want to wait without you in my life. I don't ever want to go without you again," she said, holding him tightly.

He slipped his hand behind her head and leaned close to kiss her, a long kiss that made her want to be in his arms again and forget wedding plans.

"Tony," she whispered.

"Go get a calendar or I'll get my phone and we'll look at my calendar."

"I have one here." She turned to open a cabinet and came back with a calendar.

With it on the table between them, they discussed dates while they ate.

"After dinner we can call our parents and then start calling our siblings."

"Tony, I love you and I'm so happy."

"I'll show you how I feel in a little while," he said, smiling at her.

Her phone played a tune and she got up to answer it. "Sorry. Anyone calling at this hour has to have a good reason."

"Or a wrong number," he remarked, pulling the calendar close.

She picked up her phone and listened before turning to come back to the table. "That was Mike. Savannah went into labor and they didn't make it to Dallas. She delivered a little girl in the Verity hospital." She couldn't stop the smile that lit up her face. "Wyatt met him at the hospital to get Scotty. He said he texted me earlier, but he didn't hear back. He wants me to come to the hospital to see their baby. Mike sounds incredibly happy."

Tony pulled his chair close beside her. "Sit for a minute and let's pick a date so we can tell everyone and you can show them your ring."

"I don't want to detract from the baby," she said.

He gave her a look. "You're not going to. Babies are wonderful. We're probably not going to surprise anyone. We'll just announce it before we tell everyone goodbye. I didn't intend to walk in and say 'look at us,'" he said.

"You win," she said, smiling at him. "I can't keep it quiet anyway. Well, now we don't have to worry about our wedding interfering with Savannah having her baby."

Tony took her hand. "Lindsay, I want you to have a big wedding, the one you always dreamed of as a little girl. This is once in a lifetime. You won't do it again, I guarantee it."

She gazed at him and then turned to kiss him lightly. "Sometimes you're a very nice man even when you're bossy."

He smiled at her. "Don't sound so surprised." He tapped the calendar. "Pick a date so we can go see your new niece and the happy family."

Eleven

On the first Saturday in November, Lindsay stood in the foyer of the Dallas church watching Scotty walk down the aisle. Dressed in a black tux with black cowboy boots and his hair neatly combed, he was doing just as he had been told. He scattered rose petals along the aisle and took his place at the front by his dad.

Milans and Calhouns were present in abundance. Tony's best man was his older brother Wyatt. Tony had said they would kill the old feud between Calhouns and Milans, so along with his two brothers, he had asked her brothers to be groomsmen and all three accepted. Scotty stood in front of his dad and both of them looked pleased.

Lindsay had asked Savannah if she felt up to being matron of honor. After thanking her, Savannah had declined because of her new baby girl, Caitlin. Lindsay then asked Josh's new wife, Abby, and she accepted instantly, seeming grateful that Lindsay had thought of her. Madison had declined to be a bridesmaid because she was almost into the eighth month of her pregnancy.

"It's time," the wedding planner said, smoothing the train to Lindsay's white satin dress and checking her veil. She smiled at Lindsay as her dad took her arm.

"Lindsay, I wish you all the happiness possible," he said to her as they walked down the long aisle.

"Thanks, Dad," she replied. She looked at Tony in his black tux and best black boots and her heart beat faster with joy. She loved him with all her heart. It seemed like a miracle, something she once thought impossible.

When she joined him at the end of the aisle and met his gaze, she lost all awareness of their families and friends. The big Dallas church was filled, but she could see only Tony.

She repeated her vows, meaning every word, feeling as if there would be enough love between them to carry them through any kind of adversity, even the kind they stirred up themselves.

It seemed a long ceremony, but finally they were pronounced husband and wife. Above a fanfare of trumpets, an organ, and applause from the audience, thunder boomed as they rushed up the aisle.

"Wow," Tony said, glancing over his shoulder at double glass doors. "Is that really thunder?"

"Rain on our wedding day—"

"We had sunshine this morning and rain would be the best possible thing next to being alone with you within the hour."

"Rain is more likely to happen than that," she replied, laughing. "Look how dark it is outside," she said, turning to stare.

"Dare I hope?" Tony replied. "How long will this reception take?"

"Tony, you've asked me that half a dozen times. Hours. It will take hours for me to dance with all the Milan and Calhoun men who are going to ask me to dance because it's the courteous thing to do, much less all the guys who work for me that are here and will be polite and ask me to dance."

"They're not asking because they're polite. This is probably the first time they've seen you look like this and they're having the same kind of reaction I did the night of the auction," he remarked.

"I hope not." A bolt of lightning streaked in a brilliant flash, followed by thunder that rattled windows. Tony grabbed her hand. "C'mere," he said, stepping outside and drawing her beside him as he inhaled deeply.

"Smell that," he said. "And look at the trees. We have an east wind. It's going to rain. Hallelujah!" He yanked her to him to kiss her hard, and for a few minutes she forgot everything else until the first big drop hit her.

"Ki-yi-yippie-ki-ay!" Tony yelled, turning his face up to feel the rain.

"Celebrate inside." She grabbed his hand. "Let's go around where we're supposed to or everyone will be out here and we'll have a mob scene."

They rushed through an empty hall and Tony pulled her into an empty room and closed the door. "Just one more kiss," he said.

"Oh, no. You'll mess us both up for pictures. You have to wait. Come on, Tony," she said, wiggling away and stepping through the door into the hall, smiling and looking away.

"We're coming," she called. "Hurry, Tony."

He stepped out. "Yes, Miss Bossy." He looked down the hall. "Who were you talking to? I don't see a soul.

You made that up to get me out here," he accused, shaking his head but still smiling.

"Come on," she said, laughing and hurrying along the empty hall.

When they passed double glass doors, Tony pulled her to a stop. "Look at that," he said in awe, giving another whoop of joy while she clapped.

"Tony, rain! Finally."

"Just pray it lasts for a week," he said. "What a fantastic wedding gift—rain. Buckets and buckets of rain."

"Reception, remember?" she said, tugging on his hand.

Over an hour later, Tony took her into his arms for their first dance as husband and wife. "Lindsay, you're the most beautiful bride ever. You look even more stunning than the night of the auction," he said, meaning every word. He knew as long as he lived, he would never forget looking at her as she walked down the aisle to marry him.

"Tony, I'm so happy. I didn't think I could ever be this happy."

"Hang on to that as long as you can. I'll try to always make you happy, darlin'."

"Don't make wild promises."

"I'm not. I want you happy. I love you," he said, his arm tightening slightly around her waist as he held her. "Thanks again for agreeing to move into my house. My offer still stands—anytime you want me to build a new house for us, it's fine with me."

She smiled. "I think your house is wonderful," she said. "We'll see, but right now, it looks quite suitable. As long as you love me and you're in my bed at night, what more could I ask for?"

"I wish I could dance you out the door, through that pouring rain, into the limo and off to that bed right now."

"You can't do that. We have to stay and be sociable before we leave for New York."

"I hope you're still happy with going to New York for a few days."

"Very happy. After our babies are born, we can go to Paris and Italy, but I don't want that big a trip right now while I'm pregnant."

"It's your choice, darlin'." He held her close, inhaling the faint scent of her perfume. He just wanted to make her happy because she made him happier than he had ever been in his life.

"Lindsay, we still haven't told anyone we're expecting twins."

"It's just been confirmed and it's still early in my pregnancy. I want to wait a bit. We have time."

"We'll do it however you want," he said, and her blue eyes twinkled.

"I love it when you say that and I hope I hear it millions of times."

He grinned. "I'll try. That's the best I can do, just promise to try. Something I'm trying to resist doing is going out and standing in the rain. I may succumb to that one before we leave."

"Don't you dare. A soggy tux would be dreadful."

"Soggy from rainwater would be dreadful? I beg to differ."

She laughed. "Tony, life is a blast and I intend to enjoy being married to you."

"I'll keep reminding you of that. I'm going to wish I recorded it to play again."

"You still think we're going to fight. I don't think so. You're doing a great job so far of keeping me happy."

He laughed. "You can't imagine how badly I want to get you out of here and all to myself," he said.

"I'll see what I can do about that. Maybe I can hurry things up a bit."

"Darlin', you do know how to please a man."

She felt as if she'd danced with every cowboy in Texas when Mike stepped up to ask her to dance. She smiled at her brother as they danced away.

"Caitlin is a beautiful baby, Mike,"

He grinned. "Thank you. I agree. You look beautiful, too, Lindsay."

"Thank you."

"And happy. I'm glad. Tony's a good guy."

"I agree with you on that one. Savannah said Caitlin is a quiet baby."

"She is and she's a little doll. Someone's holding her constantly. When Mom and Dad arrived, they stayed with us last weekend instead of their usual hotel stay."

"Our mother?"

"Yes, she did. She thinks Caitlin is adorable."

"I'm so glad. She looks like Savannah, even as tiny as she is."

"I agree. I see Jake watching us, so I'm sure he's going to want to dance with you next. I talked to Abe. He's happy for you and he'll run the place just fine while you're gone. I told him if he needs me, call."

"That was nice, thanks," she said. "I've never been away like this."

"It's time you did, Lindsay, and time you got a life of your own. You don't have to get out there and work like one of the boys."

She laughed. "I think those days may be over. Being a mama sounds like a big responsibility."

He smiled at her and danced her toward the sideline. "I'll give you to Jake. You have so many guys who will want to dance with you that you and Tony will never get away."

"Thanks, Mike," she said, planting a kiss on his cheek as they halted and Jake stepped up to take her hand.

Mike was almost right. By the time she'd danced with all the Milans and Calhouns and talked to each of their guests, it was hours later. Finally they made it out of their reception hall.

For just a moment Tony stopped, standing in a downpour and laughing, dancing a jig until she grabbed his wrist and tugged.

They rushed to the waiting limo and fell laughing onto the seat as their chauffeur closed the door.

"The drought will lessen now and your brother told me rain is predicted for the next three days," Tony said, pulling her to him to kiss her before she could answer.

When she pushed him away she laughed as she shook her head. "You're incredibly sexy and appealing, but that wet tux is going to ruin my wedding dress."

"It's rainwater. Do you really care?"

As she shook her head, she laughed until he drew her close to kiss her again.

Tony had a private plane waiting at the airport, but it was the wee hours of the morning when he finally carried her over the threshold into the New York penthouse suite he had reserved for their honeymoon. Standing her on her feet, he pushed away her short charcoal jacket and wrapped his arms around her.

"I love you, Lindsay. I don't think I can ever tell you enough. All I can do is try to show you. I've waited all day for this moment when we would be alone together."

Wrapping her arms around his neck, she smiled at him.

"Mrs. Anthony Milan! It's a whole new life for me. Tony, once again, I am happier than I ever dreamed possible."

His smile vanished as he held her and began to unfasten the buttons down the back of her navy dress. "I hope so and I want to always make you happy, Lindsay. You've filled a huge void in my life. I want to be with you, to love you, to have a family with you. I need you, darlin'."

She tightened her arms around his neck to pull his head down and kiss him. He held her close against him, their hearts beating together.

Joy filled her. She had never known as much contentment as she had found with Tony, and so much excitement as they looked forward to their babies. She couldn't wait to start her new life, a life shared with the man she loved with all her heart—the one rancher in the whole world she could love.

* * * * *

"What happened last night—"

"Will happen again," Braden finished. "The pace we set is up to you, but the end result is inevitable."

Zara shifted to face him. "I need this job."

"I assumed so, that's why I hired you." *Well, one of the reasons.* "And the job has nothing to do with what's going on between us."

"Nothing is going on," she all but yelled. "Nothing can go on. Not while I'm working for you."

"Fine. You're fired."

Zara glared at him. "That's ridiculous."

"I always get what I want, Zara."

"And you're that desperate for a bedmate?"

Leaning forward, his fingertips found the side of her face, stroking down to her neck where she trembled. "No. Just you."

"Why?" she whispered.

"Why not?" he retorted.

His hand came up to cup the side of her face. He stroked her lip as his other hand cupped the back of her head. A soft sigh escaped her.

"You're not thinking work right now, are you? You're concentrating on my touch, on how you want more."

"What are you doing to me?"

"Proving a point."

* * *

Trapped with the Tycoon
is part of the Mafia Moguls series:
For this tight-knit mob family,
going legitimate leads to love!

TRAPPED WITH THE TYCOON

BY
JULES BENNETT

First Published in Great Britain 2016
By Mills & Boon, an imprint of HarperCollins*Publishers*
1 London Bridge Street, London, SE1 9GF

© 2016 Jules Bennett

ISBN: 978-0-263-91845-8

51-0116

Our policy is to use papers that are natural, renewable and recyclable products and made from wood grown in sustainable forests.The logging and manufacturing processes conform to the legal environmental regulations of the country of origin.

Printed and bound in Spain
by CPI, Barcelona

Award-winning author **Jules Bennett** is no stranger to romance—she met her husband when she was only fourteen. After dating through high school, the two married. He encouraged her to chase her dream of becoming an author. Jules has now published nearly thirty novels. She and her husband are living their own happily-ever-after while raising two girls. Jules loves to hear from readers through her website, www.julesbennett.com, her Facebook fan page or on Twitter.

When I proposed a mafia series for
Mills & Boon Desire, I had no idea how
it would go over with my editor. But when
Stacy Boyd's face lit up with excitement,
I knew we were on the same page… literally.

This book is for you, Stacy!

One

The second her ex's fingers closed around her arm, Zara Perkins jerked from the firm grasp. "I'm not dancing, I'm working."

Having Shane Chapman show up at the biggest job she'd ever taken on for the most prestigious family she'd ever worked for was just her luck. She prided herself on her business, on doing everything in her power to make her clients' parties the event they hired her for. And Shane could ruin it all.

"You're such a tease," he mocked, the whiskey on his breath repugnant. "I saw you looking at me."

Sure, with disdain when she realized he was in attendance. She'd rather walk barefoot over shards of glass than let his arms wrap around her. Zara prayed Shane would go away. This was a new job, a job she desperately needed. The last thing she wanted to do was have to defend a man she had the misfortune of dating a few times.

"Dance with me."

The low, demanding words sent shivers through her body. Zara knew without turning around who would be behind her…her new employer and rumored-to-be corrupt business mogul Braden O'Shea.

With Shane directly in front of her and Braden behind her, Zara was literally stuck in the exact predicament she didn't want to be in on her first big night of working for the O'Sheas. But right now, she was bracketed by two powerful men. One she wanted nothing to do with and the other set her heart racing as only a mysterious, intriguing man could do. The few times she'd been in his office had been a bit difficult to concentrate. Braden O'Shea exuded authority, control and sex appeal.

Humiliation flooded her at the idea that Braden had to intervene. She was here in a professional capacity. Having her ex confront her was not exactly showcasing the reputation she'd worked so hard to build, and coming off as anything less than professional could be career suicide.

Shane glared over her shoulder, silently telling Braden precisely what he thought of the interruption, but before Zara could say a word to either man, Braden took hold of her arm and pulled her to the dance area in the ballroom of his lavish, historical home.

Instantly she was plastered against the oldest of the O'Shea siblings…not a difficult position to find herself in, actually. She had often appreciated the visual of his broad, sexy body wrapped in the finest of black suits with black shirt and no tie. But being up close and personal, breathing in what was undoubtedly expensive, masculine cologne that had her eyes fluttering closed as she inhaled, was another level of torture entirely.

The man exuded sex appeal, but he was her new boss, and she needed this job for the prestige and the insanely large paycheck. This was her first official event with this prominent family after being officially hired a few months ago. Screwups…screwing of *any* kind…was not allowed.

So, no sex thoughts. None. Okay, maybe later when she was alone.

"I really need to be working."

A little protest was in order, wasn't it? Even if sliding against Braden felt like some sort of foreplay in itself, she was the events coordinator for this party. Dancing with the host and boss was a major professional no-no, even if they'd always gotten along well with each other before tonight. There'd always been some ridiculous magnetic energy between them that she'd never experienced before but refused to explore.

Braden's dark gaze studied her, his mouth unsmiling. "With a dress like that, you should be dancing."

The sexual undertone wasn't lost on her. She'd thrown on her go-to black dress with a low V in the back and front, long sleeves, with the hem stopping at her knees. The dress was simple, yet made a statement. Hiding her curves wasn't an option unless she wore a muumuu. Besides, this was the best dress she'd found in her boxes of belongings since she hadn't unpacked from her move…three months ago. Because unpacking meant settling in, making roots.

"You're not paying me to dance," she told him, though she made no motion to step out of his powerful embrace. Her mind told her this wasn't professional, but her stubborn body wasn't getting that memo. "I'm positive this isn't professional to ignore my position here."

"You're on break."

With one large hand at the small of her back and the other gripping hers, Braden led her in a dance to an old classic. Crystal chandeliers suspended from the ceiling, illuminating the polished wood floor in a kaleidoscope of colors. The wall of French doors leading to the patio gave the room an even larger feel. The O'Sheas were known for their lavish parties, and now that she was in the ballroom, she could see why. Who had an actual ballroom in their house?

Other couples swirled around them, but with few words

and those dark, mesmerizing eyes, this man captured her undivided attention. She needed to get back control over this situation because even though Braden insisted she was taking a break, she wasn't paid to socialize. She was given an insane amount of money to make this annual party an even bigger success than the last one, and she'd heard a rumor the last events coordinator for the O'Sheas was fired in the most humiliating of circumstances. She couldn't afford slipups.

Or crazy exes.

"I could've handled him," she told Braden. "Shane was just…"

"I'm not talking about another man when I have a beautiful woman in my arms."

Okay, yeah, that definitely crossed the professional threshold. Each word he spoke dripped with charm, authority… desire. He held his feelings back, remained in control at all times. From what she'd seen, he was calculating, powerful and the aura of mystery surrounding him was even more alluring and sexy.

But, no. She'd just ended things with one powerful, controlling man. She was fine being single and focusing on her year-old business. Her goal was to be the company all major names turned to when needing a party planned or hosting a special event. Having the O'Sheas was a huge leap in the right direction. No matter the rumors surrounding their, well, less-than-legal operations behind the front of their world-renowned auction house, the O'Sheas had connections she could only dream of. She hoped this event led to new clients.

"If you keep scowling, I'm going to think you prefer Shane's company," Braden stated, breaking into her thoughts. "Or maybe I interrupted a lover's quarrel?"

Zara nearly recoiled. "No. Definitely not a lover's quarrel."

Had Braden overheard what Shane had said? Heat flooded her cheeks. She'd dated Shane briefly and had broken things off with him weeks ago, yet the man was relentless in trying to get her attention again. When they'd gone on only a few dates, he'd started getting a bit too controlling for her comfort. Thankfully she hadn't slept with him.

Still, he'd made a point to tell her how fast he could ruin her business. Did he honestly think that would make her give him another chance? Threats were *so* not the way to a woman's heart.

She wasn't one to back down without a fight, but she was realistic, and Shane did have money and connections. She shivered at the severity of his words.

"Cold?" Braden asked.

Braden's hand drifted up, his fingertips grazed across her bare skin just above the dip in her material.

With the heat in his eyes, there was no way she could claim a chill. The firmness of his body moved perfectly with hers; that friction alone could cause a woman to go up in flames.

"Mr. O'Shea—"

"Braden."

Zara swallowed. "Fine. Braden," she corrected, forcing herself to hold his heavy-lidded stare. "I really should check on the drinks—"

"Taken care of."

"The hors d'oeuvres—"

"Are fine."

He spun her toward the edge of the dance floor, closer to one set of French doors leading out on to the patio. Snow swirled around outside; a storm for later tonight was in the forecast. February in Boston could be treacherous and unpredictable.

"You've done a remarkable job with this evening," he told her. "I'm impressed."

She couldn't suppress the smile. "I'm relieved to hear that. I love my job and want all of my clients happy. Still, dancing when I should be working isn't something I make a habit of."

His thumb continued to lightly stroke the bare skin on her back. The man was potent, sparking arousal without even trying. Or maybe he *was* trying and he was so stellar at being charming, she couldn't tell.

It took her a moment to realize that Braden had maneuvered her into a corner. With his back to the dancers, he shielded her completely with those broad shoulders and pinned her with that dark, mesmerizing gaze. "I heard what he said to you."

Zara froze, took a deep breath and chose her next words carefully. "I assure you I would never let anyone or anything affect my ability to work. Shane is—"

"Not going to bother you again," he assured her with a promising yet menacing tone. Braden's eyes darted over her body, touching her just the same as his talented fingertips had done mere moments ago.

No. No, no, no. Hadn't she already scolded herself for having lustful thoughts? He was her boss, for pity's sake. No matter how intriguing Braden O'Shea was, she had no room for sex in her life right now. No wonder she was grouchy.

"Storm is kicking up." Braden nodded over her shoulder toward the floor-to-ceiling window. "Do you live far?"

"Maybe twenty minutes away."

"If you need to leave—"

"No." Zara shook her head, holding a hand up to stop him. "I've lived in Boston my entire life. Snow doesn't bother me. Besides, I would never leave an event early."

Braden studied her a moment before nodding. "I'm happy to hear that, but I don't want you driving on these roads. My driver will make sure you get home."

"There's no need for that."

Braden leaned in, just enough for her to feel his breath on her cheek. "Let's not waste time arguing when we should be dancing."

Snaking an arm around her waist, he pulled her against his body once again. Apparently her break wasn't over. Good thing, because she wasn't quite ready to leave the luxury of brushing against his taut body.

Her curves were killer from a visual standpoint, but to have them beneath his hands was damn near crippling. Braden knew she was a sexy woman, but he hadn't expected this sizzling attraction. He had a plan and he needed to stay focused. Those damn curves momentarily threw him off his game.

Zara in her elegant black cocktail dress with a plunging neckline showcasing the swell of her breasts was absolutely stunning, eye-catching and causing him to lose focus on the true intent of this party.

Which was why he hadn't missed the encounter when one of his most hated enemies sidled up next to the woman Braden had been gazing at off and on earlier in the evening. A flash of jealousy had speared him. Ridiculous, since Zara was merely the events coordinator…and that job had not come about by chance. Braden had purposely chosen her. He needed to get closer, close enough to gain access into her personal, private life and into her home. His family's heritage could be hidden in her house, and she'd have no clue if she stumbled upon the items.

Nothing could keep him from fulfilling his deathbed promise to his dad.

Braden was all for adding in a little seduction on his way to gaining everything he'd ever wanted. Pillow talk always loosened the tongue, and if Zara could tell him everything he needed to know, then he wouldn't have to break any laws…at least where she was concerned. He'd be a fool to turn that combination down and there was no way he could ignore how her body moved so perfectly against his. He also hadn't missed how her breath had caught the second he'd touched her exposed back. He had to admit, just to himself, the innocent touch had twisted something in him, as well. Arousal was a strong, overwhelming emotion, and one he had to keep control over.

For now, he needed to remember he was the head of the family and as the leader, he had a duty to fulfill. Flirting, seducing and even a little extracurricular activities were fine, so long as he kept his eye on the target.

Tonight O'Shea's Auction House was celebrating not only being a prominent, world-renowned auction house for over eighty years, but also the opening of two more satellite locations in Atlanta and Miami, thanks to his brother, Mac, who had moved down to Miami to oversee the properties.

Boston would always be home to the main store, Braden's store, now that his father was gone. And now that Braden was fully in charge, there were going to be some changes. This family had to move toward being legit. The stress and pressure Braden had seen his father go through wasn't something Braden wanted for his future. The massive heart attack that stole Patrick O'Shea's life wasn't brought on by leading a normal, worry-free life.

Braden had a five-year plan. Surely in that time they could remove themselves from any illegal ties and slowly sever those bonds. The killings had to stop. That was the first order of business, but tonight, after seeing Shane manhandle Zara, Braden was almost ready to go back on his vow.

Death was nothing new to him. He'd witnessed his father give a kill order multiple times for reasons he'd always justified. Braden may not have always agreed with his father's ways, but his father was an effective businessman and well respected.

Zara's deep chocolate eyes shifted around the room before landing back on him. "Your brother is coming this way."

Braden didn't turn, didn't relinquish his hold on Zara.

The music continued, guests around them danced and chatted, but Braden paid them no mind.

"We need to talk," Mac stated.

Braden stopped dancing but didn't let go of Zara as he threw Mac a glance over his shoulder. "I'll meet you in the study in five minutes."

"Now."

Braden resisted the urge to curse. He prided himself on control. "Five minutes," he said, before turning back and focusing solely on Zara.

He picked up right where they'd left off dancing. He could still feel Mac behind him, so Braden maneuvered his partner toward the edge of the dance floor. Zara was his for now, and sharing their time wasn't an option.

"You can go talk to him." Zara smiled, a deep dimple winking back at him. The innocence of the dimple and the sex appeal of that dress were polar opposite. "I should be working anyway, you know."

He *was* paying her to work, but that didn't mean he didn't like the feel of her in his arms, against him. There would be time for more later. He'd make sure of it. Gaining her trust on a personal level would lead him exactly where he needed to be.

Gliding his fingertips over her exposed back one last time, Braden stepped away from Zara and tipped his head. "I'll find you when I'm done with Mac. If you have any more problems with Shane, you come straight to me."

Zara nodded, clasping her hands in front of her and searching the room as if trying to get a location on the man in question. "I'll be fine. Go talk to your brother, and thank you for the dance. I have to get back to work."

Braden closed the space between them, picked up her hand and kissed her delicate knuckles. "I should be thanking you."

Her mouth parted as she let out a slight gasp when his lips grazed her hand. Yes, enticing her would be no problem at all. He'd been waiting on the right opportunity, the moment he could get the greatest impact out of this game of seduction.

First things first, he had to see what the issue was with his younger brother. Braden excused himself and went in search of Mac.

The entire O'Shea family had come for the party despite the bad weather predictions for the Boston area, including cousins from Boston and down the East Coast, his brother, sister and Ryker.

What kind of celebration would this be for the O'Sheas if the whole Irish clan didn't attend? Mac would be overseeing the southern locations, a job he was all too eager to take over and to get out of the cold winters for, especially since his best friend, Jenna, had moved to Miami about a year ago.

Once in the study, Braden closed the door behind him and crossed the polished wood floors. Mac leaned against the old mahogany desk, swirling bourbon around in his tumbler. Braden knew it was bourbon without even asking because the O'Sheas were simple men with simple needs—power, good bourbon and women. The order varied depending on the circumstance.

"You need to calm down," Mac commanded. "That murderous look in your eyes is scaring our guests."

"I'm calm." To prove it, Braden flashed a smile. "See?"

Mac shook his head. "Listen, I know you hate Shane Chapman. We all do. He's a lying prick. But, whatever his personal—"

"He's harassing Zara."

Braden stopped short just before he reached his brother and crossed his arms over his chest. Shane Chapman was the bane of the O'Sheas' existence. A few years ago, he'd attempted to hire the auction house to acquire an heirloom illegally. Braden had made a valiant effort to get it, spending more time and money than he really should've, but to no avail.

Viewing it as a deliberate slight, Shane had attempted to blackmail the O'Sheas. His laughable threats were quickly taken care of by means nobody discussed. Shane was lucky he was still breathing because that had been during the Patrick O'Shea reign.

Shane was only at this party for one reason—the whole "keep your friends close and your enemies closer" wasn't just a clever saying.

"Keep your eye on him," Braden went on. "This can't interfere with the plans. If Shane needs to go…"

Mac nodded. "I'll let Ryker know."

Ryker. The O'Sheas' right-hand man, who may as well have been born into the family. Instead, he'd been unofficially adopted as a rebellious preteen, and he'd been with them since.

But damn it, Braden didn't want blood on his hands. He wanted to concentrate on retrieving the heirlooms and relics their auction house was officially known for. They had an elite list of clients, and word of mouth always brought more on board. The timeless pieces the O'Sheas uncovered all over the world kept their business thriving. Several pieces were "discovered" by less-than-legal means, but they were paid hefty sums to be discreet. Smuggling in items with legal loads for big auctions was easy to do.

"I think your approach to Zara isn't the smartest." Mac sipped his bourbon. "You're coming on too strong and not focusing."

Braden narrowed his gaze. "That's a pretty bold statement coming from the man who has a woman in every major city."

Mac eyed him over the glass. "We're not talking about me. Unless you'd like me to seduce the beautiful party planner."

"Keep your damn hands off her."

Why was he suddenly so territorial? Braden had no claims on Zara.

But he'd held her, felt her against him and seen a thread of vulnerability when Zara had been looking at Shane. He refused to see any woman harassed or mistreated.

His sister, Laney, was currently dating some schmuck, who could be demeaning at times. Yet another issue Braden would deal with now that he was in charge. No way in hell would he allow his baby sister to be belittled by anyone. Ever.

"Leave Zara to me, and you concentrate on your new locations," Braden told his brother. "Is that all you needed?"

Mac finished off his drink, setting his tumbler down on the desk. "For now. I'll keep an eye on Shane. Ryker will be a last resort. I know you want to move in a different direction, but Shane can't interfere. We're too close to finding those scrolls."

Braden nodded and headed back out to the party. Those scrolls, all nine of them, were centuries old and held immense power over Braden's family. He wanted them back, and at one time, during the Great Depression, they'd been in the home Zara currently lived in. Supposedly they'd been stored in a trunk that had been sold decades ago. Unfortunately, the trunk had been recently tracked down but as the scrolls hadn't been inside, they were back to square one with Zara's house as the last known location.

Just as Braden cleared the wide opening leading to the ballroom, he spotted Shane standing over Zara. She shook her head and started to turn when Shane's hand whipped out and gripped her bicep, jerking her back to his chest.

Braden didn't care about moving stealthily through the crowd. He felt Mac right behind him as he charged forward. His brother always had his back.

"Remove your hand from Miss Perkins's arm." Braden didn't try to mask the rage in his tone. He waited a beat, but Shane still held tight and kept his back to Braden. "Remove your hand or I won't need to get my security team. I'll throw your ass out myself."

Over his shoulder, Braden heard Mac telling someone, most likely one of their employees, to have security on standby. Braden knew Mac was only looking out for everyone's best interest, but Braden could only see red right now. Thankfully, Shane had backed Zara into a corner, and the guests were still milling about, oblivious to the action.

Shane threw a glance over his shoulder. "This doesn't concern you. Zara and I have a little unfinished business. Just a lover's spat."

The look on her face told Braden there wasn't anything unfinished here and this sure as hell wasn't a lover's spat—she'd told him as much earlier.

Zara's wide, dark eyes held his. Even though she had her chin tipped up in defiance, her lips thinned in anger, there was a spark of fear in those eyes, and Braden wouldn't tolerate Shane one more second.

Braden grabbed on to Shane's wrist, applying pressure in the exact spot to cause maximum pain. "Take your damn hand off her. Now."

Shane gave Zara's arm a shove. "You can't keep avoiding me," he told her, rubbing his wrist where Braden had squeezed. "Next time I call, you better answer or I'll come by your office. I doubt you want that."

Just as Shane turned, Braden blocked his exit. "If you ever touch her or any woman that way again and I hear of it, you'll wish for death. Feel me?"

Shane hesitated a second before he laughed, slapping Braden on the shoulder. "You're Patrick O'Shea's son, right down to the threats. And here I thought you were too good to get your hands dirty."

Even though the bastard had touched Braden, he wasn't about to take the bait Shane dangled in front of him. Flexing his fists, Braden was more than ready to hit Shane, but he knew deep down he wasn't like his father.

Braden had never ordered anyone to be killed, had always said he wouldn't. Right now, though, he was reconsidering that promise he'd made to himself.

"There's a first time for everything," he promised just as two security men in black suits came to show Shane the door.

They didn't put their hands on him, as that would've caused even more of a scene, but they did flank either side of the nuisance and walk him toward the closest exit. People around him stared for only a moment before going back to their conversations. Nearly everyone knew to mind their business if they wanted to remain in the O'Sheas' tight circle.

As soon as Shane was gone, Braden went back in with Zara.

"You okay here?" Mac whispered behind him.

With a nod, Braden wrapped his arm around Zara's waist. "We're fine. Cover for me." He silently led her to the small sitting room off the ballroom and closed the door behind him before turning to face Zara. She rubbed her arm, and it took all of Braden's willpower not to rush back out and follow through on his need to punch Shane.

Braden gently took Zara's other arm, trying to ignore the brush of his knuckles against the side of her breast, and guided her toward one of the leather club chairs.

Flicking on the light on the accent table by the chair, Braden squatted down in front of her.

"Braden—"

He held up his hand, cutting her off. "Let me see your arm."

"I'm fine. I really need to get back to work. I'm sorry I caused a scene."

"Either pull your sleeve up or pull the shoulder down so I can see."

Zara hesitated a moment, then pulled the material off her shoulder, exposing creamy white skin and a royal blue strap from her bra. She shrugged enough to pull her arm up a bit.

Rage bubbled within Braden at the sight of blue finger-print-shaped bruises already forming on her flawless skin. "I should've knocked him out."

Slowly, Braden eased the material back over her arm and shoulder. Her eyes held his and her body trembled as she placed her hand over his, halting his movement.

"I'm fine," she assured him again. "I really need to get back to work. I appreciate what you did, though."

He hadn't realized how close he'd gotten until he felt her soft breath on his cheek. He glanced up to her, his eyes darting down to her lips.

"My motives aren't always so selfless."

The corner of her mouth quirked. "Whatever your motives are, they were effective."

He leaned in closer, close enough that barely a breath could pass between their lips. "I'm always effective."

Two

Effective. Thorough. Protective. So many adjectives could be used to describe Braden O'Shea. Yet he'd come to her defense without question earlier when Shane had snapped.

Zara nestled deeper into her coat as the heat from Braden's SUV hit her. This dress had been such a good idea when she'd been inside. Now that the snow was near blizzard-like conditions, not so much. She'd had to swap her sexy heels for snow boots, which she'd packed with her once she'd seen the forecast. So now the allure of her favorite LBD was lost thanks to the thick, rubber-soled, sensible shoes.

"When you said you'd have your driver bring me home, I didn't know you were the driver." She glanced over, taking in his profile illuminated from the glowing dash lights. In the dark, Braden seemed even more mysterious, more enigmatic.

"After the incident with Shane, I'm not placing your safety in anyone else's hands." He gripped the wheel as the tires slid, then gained traction again. "I wouldn't want you driving in this mess anyway. I heard a couple at the party say the forecasters mentioned feet instead of inches."

Zara's breath caught in her throat as Braden carefully maneuvered around a slick corner with skill. The back end fishtailed before he righted the vehicle. They'd only passed two other cars since leaving his historic Beacon Hill mansion.

"I'm so sorry about this," she told him, once the car was on a straight path and she could focus on breathing normally. "I should've left when you suggested it earlier because of the bad weather. Then Shane wouldn't have been a problem, and you wouldn't be out in this mess."

"Shane will be a problem until he meets his match." Braden flashed her a wicked grin that looked even more ominous due to the minimal lighting. There was also the veiled implication that Braden was the perfect match for Shane. "As for the weather, don't worry about it. This storm came on faster than I thought, and I have nothing else to do tonight."

"Hopefully the guests all made it home okay," she said, voicing her thoughts. The caterers had left around the same time she did, so hopefully they were safe, too. "They left over an hour ago, so maybe it wasn't too bad then."

She'd stayed behind to clean up and make sure the place was just as it had been before she'd entered—as she did with every event. All part of the party-planning business. Still, there would be a few people left from the cleaning service. She hoped they all got home okay, as well.

"You live alone?"

Braden's question sliced through the quiet. As if she could actually forget she was this close to the world's sexiest man. Then again, she didn't know every man in the world, but she'd still put Braden O'Shea and his sultry eyes and broad frame against anyone.

"Yes. I actually just moved into my grandmother's home three months ago. She'd just passed away, and I'm the only relative she had left."

"Sorry about your loss." In a move that surprised her, Braden reached across the console and squeezed her hand in a gesture of comfort before easing back. She didn't take him for the comforting type, but she knew in her heart his words and his touch were sincere.

"My father has been gone six months," he went on, his tone understanding. "On one hand, it seems like yesterday. On the other, I feel like I'm going to wake up from a nightmare and he'll be fine. None of us had a clue his heart was so bad."

Zara swallowed. She knew that nightmare-versus-reality feeling all too well. In the midst of her fantasizing over Braden, she'd not figured in the fact this man was still vulnerable, still suffering from a loss just as big as her own. Great, she'd not only been unprofessional tonight, she'd also been heartless.

"It's rough." For the first time since her grandmother's passing, Zara felt comfortable opening up to someone. Shane certainly hadn't been consoling in the few times they'd dated…another red flag where he'd been concerned. "Living in her home feels strange. I remember sleeping over there when I was little, but now it just seems so much larger, so empty."

Zara had never been afraid to live alone, but in a house this size, she was a little creeped out at night—the old ghost rumors didn't help, either. Perhaps once she rid the house of some of the antiques and actually unpacked her own things, that would help the place feel more like home. But she wasn't to that point yet. Removing her grandmother's favorite things just didn't seem right yet. And unpacking… Definitely not something Zara was comfortable with. A shrink would have a blast digging inside her mind over the reasons Zara had a fear of commitment even when it came to a house.

Red-and-blue flashing lights lit up behind them. Braden threw a glance in the mirror, his jaw clenched as he maneuvered cautiously to the side of the road.

Zara tensed, gripping her coat even tighter. What was wrong? They certainly hadn't been speeding. The rumors about the O'Sheas having illegal operations going flooded her mind. She didn't know whether the myth was true or false and it wasn't her place to judge, but she couldn't help but wonder. All she knew was they were powerful and they were paying her well. Oh, and Braden was the sexiest man she'd ever laid eyes, or hands, on.

Braden glanced at her. "Don't say anything."

Stunned, Zara nodded. What would she say?

Braden put his window down as the officer approached. "Evening, Officer."

The trooper leaned down and looked into the car. "The roads are at a level two now, and they're getting ready to up that to a three. Are you folks out because of an emergency?"

"No, sir. I'm giving my employee a ride home because I didn't think it was safe for her to be out alone."

The officer's eyes scanned over Zara, and she offered a slight smile.

"How far away is her house?"

"Just right up the street," Braden said, pointing. Zara had given him directions before they'd started out, and they were actually only a few houses away from hers.

"I suggest you plan on staying put once you drop her off. Any drivers caught out once the level three goes into effect will be ticketed," the officer stated. "I'll follow you to make sure you get there all right."

The full impact of the trooper's words hit Zara fast. Braden had to stay put? As in...stay the night? At her house? A ball of nerves quickly formed in her stomach. Her boss was spending the night? Her boss, whom she found utterly sexy and nearly irresistible, and there was already crackling sexual tension charging between them? Sure, this would be no problem at all.

"Thank you, Officer," Braden replied "We appreciate that."

Braden rolled his window up as the officer went back to his car. Silence filled the vehicle, and the weight of what was about to happen settled between them.

Zara risked a glance at Braden, but he didn't seem affected one bit. He kept his eyes forward, occasionally checking his mirrors as he pulled right into her drive. The cop gave a honk as he passed on by. Braden maneuvered the SUV around the slight curve that led to the detached garage around back.

Once he parked and killed the engine, Zara couldn't take the tension another second. She unfastened and turned to face him.

"I'm so sorry," she started. "Had I known you'd have to stay, I wouldn't have let you bring me home."

Braden threw her a lopsided smile. "No reason to be sorry. I don't mind spending the night with a beautiful woman."

Braden was well aware of his power. Hell, everyone who'd ever heard the name O'Shea knew the authority this family possessed. They even had a few of the local cops and federal agents in their back pockets…which had kept them out of the proverbial hot water more than once.

But even Braden couldn't have planned the timing of this snowstorm better, or the condition of the roads. Under different circumstances, he probably would've chanced driving back home regardless of the officer's warning. Wouldn't be the first time he'd gone against the law. But why would he want to leave? A forced stay at Zara's home was the green light he'd been waiting for, and it had come so much sooner than he'd ever intended. No way in hell was he leaving now. Not when this sexual chemistry between them had skyrocketed since he'd held her in his arms.

As he pulled his vehicle up to the garage, the streetlights went out. He cursed under his breath as the entire street was plunged into black. "Looks like the power went."

"Great," Zara muttered. "I don't have a generator. But I do have some heat that isn't electric. I've only used those gas logs once in my bedroom, and I've never tried to light the ones in the living room. Guess I'll have to figure it out in the dark."

Braden didn't know what got his blood pumping more: the fact he'd be able to fulfill his father's dying request and search this house, or the fact he'd be all alone in the dark with his sexy new employee.

He pulled to a stop by her back door. "Stay there. I'll come around to help you in."

He didn't wait for her to agree as he hopped out into the freezing temps to round the hood, using his phone to light a path. Even though he was still wearing his suit from the party, he'd thought ahead and changed from his dress shoes to his boots.

Jerking on the frozen handle, Braden opened the passenger door and took Zara's gloved hand as he settled his arm around her waist. The second she slid down from her seat, her body fell flush against his—well, as flush as it could be with the layers between them. Zara tipped her face up to his. Snow drifted onto her long, dark lashes, framing those rich chocolate eyes. Her unpainted mouth practically begged for affection as flakes melted against pale pink skin.

Damn it. That punch of lust to the gut was going to get him in trouble if he wasn't careful. He had a goal, and Zara was merely a stepping-stone. Harsh as that sounded, he had to remain fixed on the objective his late father had been adamant about—finding the family's lost heirlooms. Braden was near positive they were hidden somewhere inside Zara's house…a house that used to be in his family up until they lost everything in the Great Depression.

"You know, I can walk," she laughed, holding up her heels. "I swapped shoes, so I'm good."

"Maybe I'm holding on to you so *I* don't go down," he

retorted as he closed the door behind her and locked his vehicle. "I'll hold the light so you can get your keys out."

He kept an arm around her as they made fresh tracks to her back door. The snow was already well past their ankles, and the fat flakes continued to fall.

Zara pulled a set of keys from her coat pocket and gestured him into the house ahead of her. Once inside, she turned to the keypad and attempted to reset the alarm. With a shrug, Zara said, "Habit to come in and enter my code. Guess that's out, too."

Braden ran his light over the room, noticing how spacious the kitchen was and the wide, arched doorway leading into the living area. More light would be nice, now that he was actually inside. Somewhere his father was laughing at the irony of Braden finally getting in…and not being able to see a damn thing. But a power outage wasn't going to stop him from making use of this opportunity.

"Do you have flashlights and candles?" he asked, bringing his light back around but careful to keep it from shining in her eyes.

"I know where my candles are, but I'm not sure about the flashlights. I've only been here a few months. I haven't actually unpacked everything, yet." Zara removed her coat and hung it by the back door. "Let me hang your coat up since you're staying."

Braden removed his coat and started to hand it over when Zara reached out, her hand connecting with his cheek. "Oh, sorry. I didn't mean to punch you."

Braden welcomed the impact, as her fist caused no damage but reminded him that he needed to focus. "I'm fine," he stated as he maneuvered out of his coat while holding his light. "It's hard to see, so I'd say we'll be bumping into each other."

Not that he was complaining about the prospect of randomly brushing against her. Braden actually welcomed the friction. So long as he kept his goal in the forefront of his mind, bumping into Zara was definitely not a hardship.

"I know I have a candle in here and one on the coffee table in the living room. The matches are in the drawer beside the sink." She placed his coat on a hook beside hers. "I should try to figure out these gas logs in the living room first with the light of your phone."

She eased past him, her feet shuffling along the floor. Braden held his light over to where she was heading. Pulling open a drawer, Zara grabbed a box of matches before coming back to him.

She started forward but stopped. "You better stay close so you don't bump anything. I have several boxes in each room that are left from the move."

Stay close? No problem at all. Braden slid his hand around the dip in her waist and gave her a light squeeze as he leaned down to whisper in her ear. "How's this?"

Beneath his touch, her body trembled. Just the reaction he'd wanted…except now he was on the verge of trembling, too, because damn, she smelled so amazingly good and her silky hair tickled his lips. Wait, wasn't he the one who was supposed to be seducing? She wasn't even trying, and she nearly had him begging.

"Well, maybe not that close," she murmured as she attempted to put distance between them.

He moved with her, keeping their contact light so as not to freak her out right off the bat. Let her get used to his touch, his nearness. He planned on getting a whole lot closer.

"You realize this isn't a good idea?" she asked.

"Lighting the logs is the best idea. It's going to get colder in here if the electricity doesn't come back on."

Her soft laugh filled the darkness. "You know what I mean. I work for you."

"I'm aware of your position." With his hand on her waist,

Braden held his phone toward the living room. "I know we need to get heat in here, and if it's not with the logs, then we'll have to use a more…primal method."

Zara slowly started forward. "Acting on any desire because of the circumstances is a bad, bad idea for both of us."

"I've forgotten nothing, Zara." He allowed his body to move with hers, making sure to stay close. "Why don't we work on keeping warm and finding more sources of light? Then we can discuss the circumstances and what's going on between us."

Zara threw him a look over her shoulder. "We can settle this right now. I need this job and even if I was attracted to you—"

"Which you are."

"*If* I was," she countered in a louder tone to cut him off. "I wouldn't risk sleeping with you and damaging our working relationship."

He could barely make out her face in the darkness, and his light was facing ahead. But the way her body slightly leaned against his, the way she continued to tremble beneath his touch told him that her little speech was as much for her as it was for him. A slight obstacle but nothing he couldn't handle.

At first he'd been all about searching her home, and he still was, but there was no reason a little seducing couldn't come into play. He was an expert multitasker, and having Zara plus finding his family's heirlooms would be the icing on the proverbial cake.

After a fun romp and hopefully discovering his family's scrolls, Braden would be on his way, and she'd never even have to know his true intentions. Nobody would get hurt, and everything about this situation was legal. See? He did have a moral side, after all.

She could deny wanting him, but he was a master at lying and recognized that trait in others. So, let her think what she wanted…he knew the truth, and he'd completely use her attraction to his advantage.

"Fair enough," he told her. "I'll not mention it again."

That didn't mean he wouldn't touch her or seduce her with his actions. The darkness provided the perfect setting for seduction, but it could make it a bit harder to snoop. Granted, the darkness could also provide him the cover he needed to look without being seen.

So, as far as he understood, the nine scrolls, which had been in his family since his ancestor transcribed them from Shakespeare himself, were last known to be in this house. The history ran deep with his Irish family, and the precious scrolls were lost in the chaos of the fall of the O'Sheas during the 1930s. The trunk that had been recovered from this home after the Depression had shown up empty, so it only made sense the scrolls were here…somewhere.

Decades had passed, and Braden's family had attempted to purchase the property, but Zara's family had owned it since the O'Sheas lost it and they were adamant about not being bought.

Several attempts were made by Braden's father to purchase the place, but the efforts were always blocked. Eventually Patrick opted to go about things the illegal way. Ryker had even broken in a couple of times when Zara's grandmother had been alive. The old lady had been sharp, and Ryker had been forced to dodge the cops, but they were still left empty-handed. Patrick O'Shea had even mentioned waiting until the elderly lady passed and trying again to purchase the property, but Patrick had passed before Zara's grandmother.

So, Braden would get the job done himself. Failure was not an option, and buying the place wasn't necessary at this point.

Would the scrolls be somewhere obvious? Doubtful, or someone would've found them by now, and if those scrolls *had* been found, they would've made headlines around the world. His ancestor, a monk, had transcribed original works, supposedly plays that never came to be.

Zara sank to her knees in front of the fireplace. "Shine that light a little closer."

He did as requested, waiting while she fidgeted with getting the pilot light going.

"Need help?" he offered.

"Damn it." She sat back on her heels and shook her head. "This one isn't working. It was always causing Gram issues, but I'd assumed it was fixed. I know the unit in my bedroom works fine because I've used it."

Braden shouldn't delight in the fact her bedroom had gas heat and nowhere else in the house seemed to, but he was a guy, and, well, he couldn't help himself.

"Then maybe we should find those flashlights and more candles and head upstairs."

Zara threw him a look over her shoulder as she came to her feet and turned to fully face him. "Get that gleam out of your eye. I'm on to you."

Not yet she wasn't.

"What gleam?" he asked. "It's dark, so how can you see anything?"

"Oh, I can see enough and this can't get any more awkward than it already is."

"I'm not feeling awkward at all." He focused back on her eyes and offered a smile. "Are you?"

"Damn it, you know I am. Even if this—" she gestured between them "—wasn't making me nervous, you're my first overnight guest in this house."

Surprised, Braden shifted. "You mean Shane—damn. None of my business."

Zara crossed her arms over her chest. "After rescuing me tonight, I'd say this is your business. Shane never stayed here. We were dating when my grandmother passed, but he wasn't there for me much during that time. That's when I started reevaluating our relationship."

A pity Braden couldn't have gotten away with punching Shane in the face, but he hadn't wanted to cause any more of a scene at his home during the party. This was his first appearance as head of the family; he needed to hold tight to that power, that control.

What man wasn't there for his woman during a difficult time? Shane had always been a bit of a stuffed shirt, a man who probably polished his cuff links and didn't even know how to pleasure a woman properly. Braden knew for damn sure when he got Zara into bed, he'd know exactly what to do to her, with her and for her.

Seduction hadn't been a key factor in his grand scheme, but he wasn't looking the gift horse in the mouth. He couldn't deny the attraction, and why should he ignore such a strong pull?

"I don't want to talk about Shane." Zara maneuvered around him. "Let's go find the flashlights. I suppose you'll have to sleep in my room, but that is not an invitation to any other activity."

"I'll be a perfect gentleman." He'd have her begging before the night was over. "You won't have to worry about a thing." Except that he'd be snooping through her house once she fell asleep, and he'd be stealing back what was rightfully his.

Braden shone his light toward the steps and watched her head up. Like a predator after his prey, he followed those swaying hips snug in that killer dress. If he were totally honest with himself, he'd admit that Zara had the upper hand here. Even though she had no idea why she'd been hired and why he was so eager to be in her home, she had completely taken him by surprise with her professionalism, her kick-ass attitude and her sliver of vulnerability. She'd worked his party with a smile on her face and a firm hand where her assistants were concerned, all the while trying to keep Shane silenced and take on the difficult situation herself.

He tamped down his frustration. No personal emotions were allowed to creep in on his plan. A fling was all he'd allow.

He was on a mission, and Zara was in the crosshairs.

Three

Zara stepped into her bedroom, even more aware of the crackling intimacy. The intense stare Braden had offered, the way his eyes had darted to her lips more than once… she wasn't naive and she wasn't afraid of the rumors of him being such a bad boy.

Although he'd felt very bad in a delicious way when he'd been dancing with her earlier.

However, she was fully aware that he was her boss and no matter how much she ached for him to make a move, she knew anything beyond a professional relationship would be a mistake. Besides, she couldn't commit herself to anything other than a physical relationship with any man, so that definitely left Braden O'Shea out.

Zara suppressed a laugh as they stood just inside her bedroom. Yes, this was totally professional, especially since she had a stack of bras on her dresser she'd yet to put away. Thankfully he hadn't shone the light there yet. At least the unpacked boxes were lining her walk-in closet, so that was helpful.

"My room is the only one with a king bed, but I can sleep on the chaise and you can have the bed."

Her face flushed. Why had she said anything about a bed? Why talk about the elephant in the room? She'd been so worried about this situation becoming awkward, but she was the one making it worse. Clearly Braden wasn't nervous. And why should he be? He was well aware of how jittery she was, which only proved he held the upper hand here.

"I just meant that you're a big guy and you'd be more comfortable in my bed—er, a bigger bed." *Great, Zara. Keep babbling. When one foot goes in the mouth, throw the other one in, as well.*

Braden leaned against the door frame to her bedroom. With his light facing outward, she couldn't read the expression on his face.

"I'm making you nervous."

Clearly she wasn't convincing him that she was confident. "No… Maybe a little."

That low, rich laugh filled the bedroom, enveloping her in an awareness of just how intimate this situation was going to get, whether she wanted to admit it or not.

"Chemistry and attraction can often be misinterpreted as nerves."

Zara couldn't help but laugh. "Get off the attraction. I'm your employee, and your bold statements make this awkward."

"I see no reason not to be bold." He shifted, closing the gap slightly between them. "But I've promised not to bring up the matter again, so let's just focus on staying warm. It's late, and we both need sleep."

Really? He was just going to leave it at that? Maybe he was going to hold true to his word. Zara was almost disappointed, but she shouldn't be. Braden had to be strong, because if he continued to make remarks or advances, she didn't know how long her self-control would hold out.

Hopefully the roads would be better tomorrow, and Braden could go home. Then this would all be a memory, and they would move on with their working relationship. Because that's what they should do, right? He had another party coming up in a few months, and since she'd been hired as the O'Sheas' permanent events coordinator, she had to keep her mind focused on her career.

"I'll hold the light," he told her. "Let's get these logs on."

After the logs were on and heat started filling the room, then they went in search of more flashlights, and Zara grabbed her cell. She had almost a full battery and she hoped it held out until the electricity came back on. If need be, she could always charge it in his car if the electricity stayed off too long.

Unfortunately, the snow was still coming down just as fierce as it had been, and with the roads being a hazard, Zara had no doubt it would be a while before crews could work on the lines.

Mother Nature clearly had it out for her. First the roads, now the electricity. Throw in some darkness and watch that sexual tension skyrocket and blow their clothes off.

Zara cringed. No. The clothes had to stay on. They were her only shield of defense because she'd already imagined her boss naked, and if he actually took that suit off, she would not be responsible for her actions.

Once back in her bedroom, Braden closed the door to keep the heat in. Zara had lit a candle and sat it on her nightstand. The flickering, warm glow sent the room to a level of romance that had no business being here.

And then the fact that she was still wearing her black dress hit her. Great. So much for keeping all the clothes on.

"Um, I'm going to have to change." She hated how her tone sounded apologetic. This was her house, damn it. "I don't have anything to offer you unless you can fit in a pair of small sweatpants and one of my T-shirts."

"I'll be fine. Go, get out of that dress."

Those words combined with that sexy tone of his had her sighing. He'd promised not to mention sex, but the man practically oozed it with every action, every word.

"Can you wait in the hall for a second?" she asked.

Taking his own flashlight, Braden stepped out and closed the door behind him.

Zara quickly shoved her bras into her drawer and whipped her snug dress over her head. She peeled off her stockings and tossed them into a drawer, too. She really wanted to lose the bra, but she couldn't get that comfortable with her sexy guest.

As she pulled on a pair of leggings and an oversize sweatshirt, Zara truly wished she'd met Braden under different circumstances. Maybe then they could explore this attraction, but she couldn't risk intimacy when she needed this job, this recognition too much. She'd only had her grandmother, and now she was gone. There was no husband, no other family to fall back on if her financial world crumbled. Her company was only a year old, and being tied to the O'Sheas would launch her into a new territory of clientele.

Yes, the rumors of O'Shea's Auction House being the front for illegal activity had been abuzz for years—decades, even—but the mystery surrounding the family only kept people more intrigued, so Zara would gladly ride the coattails of their popularity.

After sliding on a pair of fuzzy socks and pulling her hair into a ponytail, Zara opened the door. Braden was texting but glanced up at her and slid his phone back into his pocket.

"I had to check in with the security team. I try to keep them updated on my whereabouts."

"Oh, you don't have to explain yourself."

"You look…different."

With a shrug, Zara glanced down to her outfit. "This is me in my downtime. I'm pretty laid-back."

Why did the room seem so much smaller when he came back in from the hallway? Why did he have such a presence about him that demanded attention? And how the hell did she act? What was the proper protocol for bringing your billionaire boss to your house and then having him spend the night? Milk and cookies? Bourbon and a cigar? She honestly didn't know the man on a personal level.

Zara's cell vibrated on her dresser. With the screen facing down, she didn't see the caller before she picked it up and automatically slid her finger over the screen.

"Hello?"

"Hey, I wanted to make sure you made it home okay."

"Shane."

Zara's eyes darted to Braden. In the dim light she could see his narrowed gaze, his jaw clenched.

"I know I acted like a jerk earlier, but I want another chance with you and I was worried about you getting home in this storm."

Were his words slurring?

"Shane, it's nearly one in the morning. Are you drunk?"

He must've shifted, because there was the slightest bit of static coming through the phone before he continued. "I miss you, Zara."

She turned her back to Braden and rubbed her forehead. "I got home safe. Thanks for checking, but we really are over, Shane. Good night."

"Don't hang up." Now his voice rose, as if the real Shane was emerging. "You're selfish, you know that? I'm trying to talk to you, and you're already dismissing me. We were good together, you know it."

"No, we weren't, and I'm done with—"

Suddenly the phone was ripped from her hand. Zara whirled around as Braden hit the end button and then turned the phone off.

"You won't explain yourself to him."

Zara sighed. Damn it, why did he have to be right? "He's not been this persistent until the past week or so. I'm not sure why he wants to get back together so bad, but I swear he won't affect my work with you."

Braden closed the gap between them and stared down at her. The darkness slashing over half his face made him seem even more menacing, more intriguing.

"I don't give a damn about that. I know you're a professional. But I'm not going to stand here and listen to you defend yourself to an asshole who doesn't deserve you."

"Wow." Zara crossed her arms and tried to process Braden's words, his angry tone. "Um…thanks."

Unsure what to do next, Zara glanced around the room. "I guess I'll just grab a blanket and pillow and lie down. I'm pretty beat."

The strain of the evening had seriously taken its toll on her, and all she wanted to do was crawl on to her chaise and fall dead asleep. Okay, maybe that wasn't all she wanted to do, but doing her boss was out of the question.

By the time she'd gotten situated on the chaise, she glanced to her bed where Braden sat on the edge staring in her direction.

"What?"

"Are you going to be comfortable? I didn't expect to take your bed."

Seeing him there, knowing her sheets would smell like him long after he was gone, was just another layer of arousal she didn't need.

"I'm perfectly comfortable. You're the one still in a suit."

With a soft laugh, he shook his head. In moments, he had his jacket off and was in the process of unbuttoning his shirt.

"Uh, wait. Are you undressing? Because—"

"Zara." His hands froze on the buttons. "I'm just taking my shirt off."

Just taking his shirt off. *To which he will no doubt ex-*

pose a chest she'll want to stare at. With the light from the gas fireplace and the candle on the nightstand, she could see perfectly fine.

And yup. He'd taken his black dress shirt off and revealed an amazingly sculpted chest, smattered with dark hair and...was that ink on his arm?

"You're staring," he said without looking up at her. "You're going to make me blush."

Zara laughed. "I highly doubt you blush, let alone over a woman looking at you." Because why deny the fact she had been? She'd been caught, but she didn't care. The man was worth a good, long stare. "Good night, Braden."

Her damn floral scent mocked him as he lay on top of her plush comforter. With his hands laced behind his head, Braden stared up at the ceiling watching the orange flickering glow from the candle. He wouldn't get any sleep tonight. Besides the fact he had every intention of getting back up to check out the house after Zara had gone to sleep, how the hell could he actually rest when the object of his desire was lying only feet away?

He hadn't expected to actually want her with such a passion and fierceness. Damn it. He knew he'd been attracted, but he'd passed being attracted long ago. Now he had a need so deeply embedded within him, he was going to go mad if he didn't have her.

Zara had been knockout gorgeous in that black dress and those sexy heels earlier at his party. But seeing her in such a simple, natural way, with hair up and sweats on, had Braden questioning why the hell he wasn't coercing her into this giant bed. He could have her clothes off in record time, despite what she'd said about mixing business and pleasure. The allure was there—the chemistry was hot enough to scorch them.

But he had a mission. One that couldn't be forgotten just because he'd been sidetracked by this unexpected quest for Zara. He needed to focus. Sex was one thing, a marvelous thing actually, but she'd put up a defensive wall. He was alone in the house he'd been wanting in for quite some time. So why the hell was he lying here focused on what was denied to him instead of formulating a plan of where he'd search once she was fully asleep?

Braden suppressed a groan as he rolled to his side. He needed to start this process, so he could be ready to get the hell out when the roads cleared.

The scrolls had to be in this house. They had to be; he refused to believe any different. But at the same time, he had to be realistic. His family had lost this house and everything in it during the Great Depression—a little fact Zara most likely didn't know.

In the decades that had passed, who's to say someone hadn't found the scrolls, moved them to another location and kept the secret to themselves?

A gnawing pit formed in his stomach. What if someone had found them and thought they were trash?

No, the scrolls were supposedly rolled up in small tubes. Nine different tubes for the nine works. They were somewhere, and Braden wasn't going to leave this house until he'd searched every inch of it.

He thought of the built-in bookcases in the living room he'd spotted earlier when he'd ran his phone light over the room. He'd tried to be casual about it, no reason to raise a red flag with Zara, because, as of right now, she was totally unsuspecting and completely worried about being alone with him.

Since she'd walked into his office for the job, he knew he wanted her in his bed. No reason he couldn't enjoy a little recreational activity and search at the same time. Besides, getting Zara to open up to him may be the angle they'd needed all along, even if Ryker just wanted to break in and be done with it.

No way in hell was Ryker getting close to Zara. He was

mysterious at best, terrifying at worst. And women loved that mysterious side. He had no intention of Zara being one of those women. Zara was all Braden's…for now.

Braden knew full well what Ryker did for the family. Ever since Ryker had come to be friends with Braden and Mac in grade school, their father had taken Ryker in as another son. By the time they were out of high school, Ryker was just another member of the family. The Black Sheep was too benign a term when referring to the man who did all the dirty work.

Braden stared across to Zara and realized she was looking right back at him. This was ridiculous. They were adults acting like horny teens trying to get a mental feel for what the other one was thinking.

"You're supposed to be asleep," he told her. "Do you need your bed back?"

The image of Zara in her bed wasn't new. He didn't need to say the words aloud to conjure up a vivid image. He'd already had her in bed several times in his mind.

"I can't sleep."

He knew a cure for insomnia.

"It's too quiet," she continued. "I usually sleep with a fan because I can't handle the silence at night."

Interesting. Braden bent his elbow and rested his head on his palm. "Are you afraid to stay here alone?"

"Not really. It's just my old place was so much smaller, and this house has always had that creepy factor, you know? It's old, it creaks and groans. Then there's the rumor it's haunted." She laughed. "I guess when I'm alone with my thoughts, I let my imagination run wild."

"It's not unusual for these old homes to have some ghost story. They're either based off some truth people believe, or they make for a good resale value for those seeking adventure."

"Yeah, well, I'm not up for an adventure and I don't believe in ghosts."

Braden found he liked hearing her talk. He liked how soft her voice was, how it carried through the darkness and hit him straight with a shot of arousal. So he wanted to keep her talking.

"Since we both can't sleep, why don't you tell me the ghost story?"

He saw her lick her lips as she clutched the blanket near her chest. Thanks to the dim lighting, Braden found her even more alluring. Sleep wasn't even a priority.

"It's silly, actually. Apparently there was a young couple in love, and supposedly the man went off to the army and never returned. There are stories he died in the war, stories he fell in love with another. Who knows? She went on to marry, but the rumor is you can still hear her crying."

Braden knew that story all too well. Considering this house had been in his family at the time Zara was referring to. And the woman was his great-great...several greats, grandmother. He'd always heard the story that the man who went to the army was actually her husband and he'd been killed. She'd remarried, had children but, supposedly, never got over her first love. A tragic story, a romantic one for those who were into that sort of thing...and his Irish family most definitely was.

"But, if I ever hear a woman crying in this house, it will take me one giant leap to get out of here," Zara went on with a light laugh. "An intruder I can handle. A ghost, not so much. At least a real person I can shoot."

The more she talked, the more Braden found he didn't like her in this big house alone. But, if she had a firearm, at least she could defend herself.

What if Shane showed up? The man obviously called her drunk, and, on a good night with clear roads, what would stop him from just coming over, forcing his way in? And now that she worked for Braden, Shane would see that as a betrayal. The man was that egotistical and warped.

"But I'm not sure a woman would be crying over a man

if she was married to another," Zara went on as she shifted beneath her covers. "I mean, I can't imagine loving one man, let alone falling in love twice. Or maybe she'd just married the second guy so she wasn't lonely. I'll never be that desperate."

Braden thought to his parents. They'd been in love, they'd raised a family and they'd had a bond that Braden wanted to have someday. His mother passed when Braden had been a pre-teen, and the car accident that claimed her had an impact on the entire family. They became stronger, more unified than before because they realized just how short life was.

Not now, but one day he'd have a family of his own. First, though, he'd have those scrolls back in his family's possession and steer his family right. He refused to bring a family into his life when there were enemies, people who used loved ones as a weakness to exploit.

"You've never been in love? Never knew people in love?" he asked, easing up to rest his back against the headboard.

"I've never seen love firsthand, no." Zara turned onto her back, lacing her hands on top of the blanket. "My grandmother loved me and I loved her, but as far as a man and woman... I'm not sure true love exists. Have you been in love?"

Even though he'd removed everything but his pants, heat enveloped Braden. Granted, it could be because he was in the company of a woman he wanted more than his next breath, but honestly, the logs were doing a great job, and with the door closed, the thick air was starting to become too much.

"Would you mind if I turned the logs down a bit?" he asked.

"Nice way to dodge my question." She jumped up from the chaise and threw him a smile. "I'll turn them down. It is getting a bit warm in here."

Braden watched her move across the room. In her black, body-hugging dress she'd been a knockout, but in her sweat-

shirt and leggings with her hair in a ponytail, she almost
seemed…innocent, vulnerable.

Damn it, he didn't want to see her that way. He didn't
want this to become personal with emotions getting in the
way of his quest to get her in his bed and search for the
scrolls.

And when the hell had he officially added her to his list
of must-haves?

Somewhere between dancing with her and settling in
for their sleepover.

As she started back to the chaise, she gestured toward
him. "If you're hot, you can, um…you can take your pants
off. I won't look. I mean, I don't want this to be uncomfortable for either of us, but I want you to be… Sorry, I'm
rambling. Go ahead, take your pants off. I'll turn around."

She was killing him. Slowly, surely, killing him.

But the lady said he could remove his pants. So remove
them he would.

Four

Just as Braden unzipped and started to lower his pants, Zara cried out in pain, followed quickly by words that would've made his mama blush.

With pants hanging open, Braden carefully crossed the space. "What is it?"

"Banged the side of my ankle on this damn chaise," she said through gritted teeth. "Stupid scrolled legs on this thing."

Without thinking, Braden dropped to his knees before her. His hands ran down the leg closest to the chaise, gently roaming over her tight, knit pants.

When she hissed, he pulled back and glanced up. The light was even dimmer now that she'd turned the logs down, but the miniscule candle flickered just enough of a glow for him to make out those heavy lids and the desire that stared back at him.

Keeping his eyes locked on to hers, Braden slid his fingers around her slender ankle once again. "Does this hurt?"

"Just tender."

Trailing his fingertips to another spot, he asked, "How about here?"

"No."

Weighing his next movement, Braden moved his hand on up to her calf. Zara sucked in a breath, and he knew it was for a whole other reason. Gliding over the back of her knee, he curled his hands around her thigh as he shifted closer to her. With his other hand, he slid beneath the hem of her sweatshirt to grip her waist. Satiny skin met his palm, and he'd swear she trembled and broke out in goose bumps right that second.

"Braden," she murmured.

"Relax."

Ironic he was telling her to relax when his own body was strung tighter than a coil ready to spring into action.

"This isn't appropriate," she whispered. If her tone had held any conviction whatsoever, he would've stopped, but with the way she'd panted his name, with the way her hips slightly tilted toward him, he wasn't about to ignore what her body was so obviously telling him.

He continued to allow his hands the freedom to roam as he came to his feet, pulling her with him. With one hand settled on her hip and one just beneath her shirt, he watched as Zara stared up at him, her eyes locked on to his. He refused to break the connection, didn't want to sever the intensity of this moment.

That warm skin begged for his touch, and it was all Braden could do not to jerk this shirt up and over her head so he could fully appreciate the woman. The seduction of Zara would have to be slow, romantic and all about her. He could handle that order because right now he wanted to feel her, wanted to have her come apart.

The second he encountered silk over her breast, he wasted no time in reaching around and unfastening her bra. Now that she was freed of the restraint, he cupped both breasts in his palms and watched with utter satisfaction as her lids drifted closed, as a groan escaped from her lips.

Why did she have to feel so amazing? Why was he fighting taking what he wanted instead of giving her full pleasure? This had to be about Zara, about seduction.

Braden slid one hand down to the top of her pants. Zara's eyes snapped open. She scrambled from beneath his touch. Her eyes darted away as she righted her clothes. Damn it, he'd pushed her too far when he couldn't control his hormones.

"This can't happen," she stated, her voice shaky. "We— I…"

"Don't say you're sorry," he told her as she jerked her sweatshirt down as if she was trying to erase what had just occurred. "We're adults, and dancing around the attraction wasn't going to last for long. I've been wanting to touch you since you walked into my office."

Zara's hands came up to her face. "I can't believe I did that. I just let you…" She dropped her hands and waved them in the air. "I let you…"

"Yes?" he asked, trying not to smile as she struggled.

"Is this how you treat all your new employees?"

Braden reached for her arms, pulling her flush against his body. "I've never in my life slept with an employee."

"We haven't slept together," she retorted.

"Yet."

Her gasp had him laughing, but he didn't release her. "You're so sure of yourself, aren't you? I'm not easy, Braden. I don't want you to even think that for a minute. I shouldn't have let this go so far."

"Zara, if I thought you were easy, I wouldn't waste my time trying. I look for the challenge, the chase, the risk in everything."

Now she laughed as she shook her head. Her hands were trapped between their bodies. "You're already talking about sleeping with me and you've not even kissed me. I'd say that's—"

His lips slammed on to hers. Hadn't kissed her? Was she complaining?

For one troubling moment, Braden worried she'd push him away, but after her hesitancy, she finally opened up and accepted what he was giving.

Her hands flattened against his chest as he coaxed her mouth open and tipped her head. Kissing Zara was just another total-body experience he hadn't anticipated. Kisses were either good or bad. With Zara, they were arousing, a stepping-stone for more and a promise of all the passion she kept hidden away.

If he wasn't careful, he'd start craving more of her touches, more of her soft moans, because damn it, the woman got into a man's system and…

No. Hell, no. She was not getting into his system. Nobody was penetrating that until he was damn good and ready.

Braden had to force himself to step back, to put some distance between their heated bodies.

"There. Now you've been kissed." He licked his own lips, needing to taste her again. "If you're feeling cheated on anything else, I can oblige."

Her eyes widened as she trailed her gaze down his bare chest. "N-no. You've obliged enough."

Braden smiled. "Then we both need to get some sleep."

As if he hadn't just had her body trembling against his seconds ago, he turned and sat back on her bed. Zara hadn't moved from her spot next to the chaise.

"Is your ankle okay?"

"My ankle?" She glanced down. "Oh, yeah. It's sore, but fine. Um…good night."

He watched as she slowly sank down onto her makeshift bed. He could practically hear her thinking and he knew full well she was replaying how far she'd let him go. Hell, he was, too, but he had to push that aside and keep his eye on the main reason he was here and not how close he'd been to getting her to explode in his arms.

"Don't overthink this, Zara." She continued to lie there, looking up at the ceiling. "Get some sleep."

Because the sooner she fell asleep, the quicker he could start looking through the house.

How could the man just fall asleep? Seriously? Braden acted as if this was no big deal, as if he'd patted her on the head and sent her off to bed like an obedient lover.

And the longer she lay here, the more she was wondering how she'd lost control of that situation so fast. Oh, yeah. He'd touched her. That was it. The man touched her, looked at her with those piercing eyes, and she'd been helpless. For the briefest of moments she'd forgotten all about her job, the fact her boss had his hands beneath her shirt and was working his way into her pants. Thankfully, she'd come to her senses before they'd crossed a point of no return. She needed this job, even more than she needed a one-night stand.

Braden O'Shea was a powerful man, and she was not immune to his allure. Yet she'd told herself over and over this evening how she couldn't get intimate with him, no matter how much she wanted to. She couldn't risk losing this job because she was a sad cliché and slept with her boss. How tacky was that? She prided herself on being a professional, yet the man who'd written her a colossal check was snoozing in her bed.

Whatever his secret for flipping the horny switch, she'd like to know because she was still just as turned on as before she'd put the brakes on.

She'd never known a man who was so giving, but then she hadn't known many men like Braden O'Shea. Something told her he was quite different than any other guy she'd dated.

Zara nearly groaned as she tugged on her blanket and rolled over. Dated? She and Braden were far from dating.

He'd given her a few minutes of toe-curling excitement, and that was all. He was stuck in her house thanks to Mother Nature's fury, and that was the extent of their personal relationship.

From here on out, no more touching, no more kissing. Though she had to admit that kiss had been nearly as potent as the touching.

What would morning bring? The questions whirled around in her head. Would he act as if nothing happened? Would he be able to leave, or would he be stuck here for another night? Zara wished he weren't her boss, wished this powerful, sexy man were stuck in her house under different circumstances, but the fact was he was helping to pay her bills. And without the prestige of working for him, it would take her a lot longer to get the recognition she needed for her new company.

She wasn't worried about his questionable reputation. The O'Sheas were legends, and despite the rumors surrounding Braden's father's dealings, Zara had only heard praise about Braden. He may be tough when needed, he may even show off his brute force like he had with Shane, but none of that made him a bad guy. And the way her body was still thrumming, Zara felt Braden was indeed a very good guy.

No matter what her common sense was telling her now, Zara couldn't help but want more. Not being able to touch Braden at all left her feeling somewhat cheated. Those broad shoulders, those lean hips…a man with a body like that surely knew how to use it in the most effective ways.

Gripping her blanket beneath her chin, Zara tried not to think about the man who lay just behind her, in her bed, shirtless. She tried not to think of how he'd looked at her when he'd been kneeling on the floor. She tried to keep her body from tingling even more at the fantasy of how they'd be if she crawled in between those sheets with him.

Her best hope now would be to fall asleep and dream, because having the real thing was simply out of the question.

Braden padded from the bedroom. It had taken Zara over an hour to fall asleep. She'd tossed and turned, letting out soft little moans every now and then, and there wasn't a doubt in Braden's mind she was just as sexually frustrated as he was.

Zara was one of the most passionate women he'd ever met. And when she let her guard down...purely erotic. Knowing she was lying over there restless nearly had him forgetting the plan to search the house tonight and instead dragging her back up to her own bed and finishing what they both wanted.

But she'd finally dozed off, if the subtle snoring was any indication. Braden threw one more look her way as he gently closed the door behind him. The logs were keeping the room plenty warm, because this hallway was flat-out chilly. The temperature must have really dropped outside for the inside to get so cold, so fast. At least he'd put his shirt and socks back on, so that was a minor help.

With his phone in his pocket, Braden flicked on the small flashlight that had been on Zara's bedside table. He swung it back and forth down the hallway, finally deciding to venture into the rooms toward the end where he'd never been before.

He'd seen the layout of the home several times. The floor plan was ingrained into his mind, the blueprints locked away in his home office, but seeing the rooms firsthand was entirely different. He knew there was a third floor, but right now he was going to focus on the bedrooms that sat empty. Every inch of this home could be a hiding spot, and Braden had to start somewhere. Sticking close to Zara was the smartest move right now.

There was something eerie about an old house that was pitch-black with the sounds of whirling winds and creaking. But fear never entered Braden's mind. Nothing scared him, except the prospect of not finding these scrolls. His father had wanted them back in the family's possession, but once Patrick had passed away six months ago, Braden knew this endeavor now fell to him. That, and strategically severing the ties to an underbelly of the city he wanted nothing to do with.

Nearly a decade ago, his father had supposedly ordered a prominent businessman to be taken out, along with the man's assistant. That dangerous rumor kept filtering around, but if Braden could pull this family around, point them in the right direction, perhaps such whispered speculations would be put to rest.

Everything would take time. This was a business Braden learned to be patient in. Effective, forceful and controlling, but patient.

He'd never ordered any killings, prayed to God he never had to. Transitioning was difficult, but Braden had to. He had to secure a future for the family he eventually wanted, but at the same time fulfill his father's dying wishes.

As he entered the last bedroom, he stood in the doorway and moved his light around, familiarizing himself with the furniture layout. More built-in bookcases. Nice charm to add to each room, but a pain in the ass for someone on a scavenger hunt.

Ryker had mentioned searching the obvious places, but Braden was here now and wanted to see everything for himself firsthand.

Braden slid the flashlight beneath his arm so he could use both hands to shift books and knickknacks around on the shelves. So far no hidden door, no secret hole hidden behind a panel. Nothing. But he wasn't discouraged. Getting into this house was one of the biggest hurdles, and here he was. Now he just needed to be patient, because the scrolls were here. They had to be.

The irony that his family unofficially dealt in retrieving stolen relics and heirlooms, and they couldn't even get back their own possessions, was not lost on him. Granted, they technically stole back the items, but those words would never come out of his mouth, and Ryker was the guy who did all the dirty work. So in a sense, Braden never saw how the items were taken back. So long as it was done correctly and satisfied clients all over the globe, the details didn't matter. The auction house gave them the front they needed to play modern-day Robin Hood, but the rumors around the family gave them that edge that helped them with their tough, hard-ass image.

Generations of corruption would be hard to move past, but Braden was determined. The art dealings would continue, and there was no harm in taking back what was rightfully due to those who had lost heirlooms, as long as it didn't require any violence. But any more than lying and stealing had to cease…sooner rather than later.

Ryker wasn't too keen on Braden's new, somewhat lilywhite direction, but Braden wasn't asking for permission. He was in charge now, and Ryker would have to understand that any sort of bloodshed was a thing of the past.

Which reminded him, he needed to check in with their right-hand man who was currently in London looking for a rare piece of art that needed to be returned to a client in Paris during the next auction.

By the time he'd finished the two large bedrooms at the end of the hall, Braden was no closer than when he'd started. Sleep was going to have to happen because his eyes were burning, and most likely it was nearly morning at this point. He couldn't help but wonder what all the unpacked boxes were, though. He'd seen a few in her kitchen, several in the living room, and with her closet door open, he'd spotted a good amount stacked in there. Hadn't she said she'd lived here for a few months?

Those unpacked boxes held so much potential, but how many were hers and how many were already here for years?

Using his flashlight to head back to the bedroom, Braden

flicked it off as soon as he reached the doorway. The second he stepped inside, warmth surrounded him. Zara lay on her side, her hand tucked beneath her cheek, her ponytail now in disarray as hair draped over her forehead and down the side of her face.

Slipping back out of his shirt, he sat on the edge of the bed, unable to take his eyes off the sleeping beauty. He had tried to keep his hands off her. Okay, he could've tried harder, but damn it, something about her made him want to get closer to her in the most primal way possible.

He knew she was a sexy, take-charge woman. The fact she was a businesswoman, career-driven and independent, was a definite turn-on. But after dancing with her and seeing that flash of vulnerability in her eyes when Shane had entered the picture, Braden felt even more territorial…and not in the typical employee/employer way. There was no way he could not step into her life.

Braden slid between the sheets and refused to acknowledge the arousal threatening to keep him awake. He needed sleep because when morning came, he fully intended to continue his quest for the scrolls, and he sure as hell planned on more seducing. Multitasking had never been this sweet.

Five

Zara stared at her cabinets and sighed. Was it appropriate to offer your millionaire boss a s'mores Pop-Tart or a cherry one for breakfast? Because that was the extent of her options. Well, she had other flavors because she was a junk-food junkie, and Pop-Tarts were her drug of choice.

He'd still been asleep when she'd slipped from the warm room. Now she stood shivering in her kitchen and wondering when the electricity would be restored. The snow was still coming down in big, fat flakes, and there was no sign of any cars in sight.

Grabbing three different varieties of breakfast pastries, Zara spun on her fuzzy socks and raced back up the steps. Mercy, it had gotten cold in here. When she eased open the door, Braden was shifting around on her bed, sheets slipping down a bit. His glorious chest looked even better with daylight streaking through the window. Granted, it had also looked spectacular on display with the fire flickering last night.

With boxes of food under one arm, she gently closed the door behind her, but Braden's eyes instantly popped open and zeroed in on her. Suddenly she was pinned in place. That piercing gaze penetrated her across the room. Such a potent man to be able to hold such power over someone without even saying a word.

Slowly, he sat up. The sheet fell to his waist, giving up an even more tantalizing view of all that tan skin with dark hair covering his chest. Dark ink curved over one shoulder, and Zara found herself wanting to trace the lines of that tat. With her tongue.

Down, girl.

"Breakfast," she said. "I hope you like Pop-Tarts."

His brows drew in. "I can honestly say I've never had one."

Of course he hadn't. Not only was he a bajillionaire, he had the body of a sculpted god. Someone who looked like that wouldn't fill themselves with the finer junkie things in life.

"Well, you're in for a treat." She crossed the room, trying to ignore the fact that she looked like a hot mess after last night. "I'm a connoisseur of all things unhealthy and amazingly tasty."

She sat the boxes on the trunk at the end of her bed and opened each one. She tried to focus on anything other than the fact he still hadn't reached for his shirt. Was he going to spend their entire time half naked? So this is what the saying "both a blessing and a curse" meant.

"I have s'mores, cherry and chocolate." She glanced back up as he slid from the bed and came to stand beside her. "Take whatever you want. I have plenty more downstairs."

He eyed the boxes as if he truly had no clue what to choose. "I'm a chocolate lover, so the cherry is out. Should I go all in for the s'mores?"

Zara smiled. "They're the best, in my opinion."

She handed him a foil package and grabbed one for herself before heading over to stand near the logs. She needed to keep a bit of distance, because if the shirtless thing wasn't enough to make her want a replay of last night, the fact that he had sheet marks—*her* sheets—on his arm and face and he smelled musky and sexy was more than enough to have her near begging. And Zara wouldn't beg for any man, especially one who wrote her checks.

"You can have all you want, though." She was babbling. Nerves did that to a woman. "I forgot the drinks. I'm sure the fridge kept things cold, but I'll need to—"

"Zara. Breathe." Braden's hand gripped her shoulder. She hadn't even heard him come up behind her. "I'm making you nervous again."

Swallowing, she turned to face him. Holding his heavy-lidded gaze, Zara tried not to look at the sheet mark on his cheek. A minor imperfection that made this man seem so… normal.

"I'm not nervous," she said, defensively. "Why would I be nervous? I mean, just because you… I…last night…and now your shirt is still off, so I'm not sure what to do or how to act. I've never had a man here, let alone my boss. So this whole morning-after thing is different, not that we did anything to discuss the typical morning after…"

Closing her eyes, Zara let out a sigh. She shook her head to clear her thoughts before looking back up to Braden. "I'm rambling. This is just a bit awkward for me, and I didn't want to make a total fool of myself, but I'm doing just that."

Braden took the package from her hands and tore it open. After pulling out a Pop-Tart, he held it up to her.

"Why don't you eat?" he suggested. "I'm not worried about what happened last night, but if you want to run through it again, that's fine with me. Maybe we can discuss how much farther I wanted to go."

"No, we shouldn't." Zara took the pastry he held up to her. "Maybe we should just check on the road conditions instead of reliving anything."

Braden laughed as he tore open his own package. "Whatever you want. I'm at your mercy here."

Did every word that came out of his mouth have to drip with sex appeal? Was he trying to torment her further? Because if this was him putting forth no effort to torture her, she'd hate to see when he actually turned on the charm.

Zara didn't want to think about staying in this room with him for another day. If she didn't get out of here, her hormones may explode.

They ate their gourmet breakfast, and Braden muttered something about them being amazing before he went and grabbed a different flavor. Traditional chocolate this time. While he had round two, Zara went to dig out her old boots. She was going to have to get the frozen food outside and put it into the snow to stay cold. There was no other way, not if she wanted to salvage her groceries.

After she shoved her fuzzy-socked feet into her boots, Zara headed for the door. "I'll be right back."

Braden swallowed his last bite and crumbled his foil in his hand. "Where are you going?"

"I'm going to run downstairs and get the food from the freezer and fridge and set it out in the snow. It will stay cold there. I don't know what else to do with it."

Crossing to the bed, Braden reached for his shirt and shrugged into it. "I'll help."

"You don't have to. I've got it."

Ignoring her, he buttoned each button with quick, precise movements. "What else do I have to do?"

Keep that potent, sexually charged body away from hers? Stay in the warm room while she went outside and cooled off?

Zara knew she wasn't going to win this argument, so she turned and headed from the room. Braden closed the bedroom door behind them. The cooler air in the hallway slid right through Zara, helping her to focus on something other than the man who pretended like make out sessions were passed out each night before bedtime like a hug good-night.

Should her body still be humming, given they hadn't even gotten to the good part? Seriously?

As soon as she went into the kitchen, she turned to Braden, only he wasn't there. Zara backtracked a couple steps to find him in the living room staring at the built-in bookcases.

"This house has a lot of the same old-Boston charm mine does," he told her without turning around. "The trim on the top of these cabinets, the detailed edging. It's all so rare to find in homes these days. I appreciate when properties have been taken care of."

"I imagine you see quite a variety of homes with various decor in your line of work."

Throwing her a glance over his shoulder, he nodded. "I've seen million-dollar homes that were polished to perfection, every single thing in them brand-new. But it's the old houses that really pull me in. Mac is more the guy who wants all things shiny and new."

Zara crossed her arms to ward off the chill. The only vibe she'd gotten of the younger O'Shea brother was that he was a player. And with his looks and charm, she could totally see women batting their lashes and dropping their panties.

Braden ran a fingertip over a small glass church her grandmother had loved. "He's working on the opening of our Miami location. That fast-paced lifestyle and the warmer climate are also more his speed."

"You guys are quite opposite, then."

"Except when it comes to business," Braden amended as he moved to another shelf and carefully adjusted a pewter picture frame holding a picture of Zara as a child. "We see eye to eye on all things regarding the auction house."

"I've always hated that picture," Zara stated with a laugh. "My grandmother took that on my first trip to the beach.

I was eleven and had just entered that awkward stage girls go through."

Turning to face her, Braden crossed his arms and offered a slight grin. "Whatever phase you went through, you've more than made up for it."

Zara shivered at his smooth words. Apparently this smooth talker liked a woman with curves.

"You didn't go to a beach until you were eleven?" he asked, moving right on.

Oh, no. She didn't want to get into her childhood. Granted, the first decade of her life wasn't terrible, but there certainly were no family vacations, no fun beach pictures or pictures of any kind, really. Her parents had been rich, beyond rich, but they couldn't buy affection. They'd tried. Zara had more toys, more nannies than any one child needed or deserved.

When her parents had died, Zara had been numb. She hadn't even known how to feel, how to react. How did a child respond to losing the two people who were supposed to love her more than anything, yet had never said the words aloud? They'd shown her in ways, material ways, but that was the only way they knew how to express themselves.

That money she'd always thought her parents possessed was suddenly gone. Her parents' overspending had finally caught up with them, and Zara was paying the price. Apparently her parents owed everybody and their brother thousands, if not hundreds of thousands. Zara's grandmother had maneuvered funds, had borrowed against this house and had paid off every last debt her parents had left. Now the money was gone after all the debts were paid.

Just another reason Zara was determined to succeed in her business. She wanted to make her grandmother proud, even if she wasn't here to physically see Zara's triumph. She didn't want to have to sell this house that had been in her family since the Depression. Her grandmother had loved this place, and Zara wanted that last piece of family to hold on to.

"Zara?" Braden took a cautious step toward her, then another. "Where did you go?"

Zara shook her head. "Nowhere worth traveling to again. Let's get this food outside and get back upstairs. I'm freezing."

Just as she turned, Braden curled his fingers around her arm. With a glance from his hand to his eyes, Zara thought she saw a flash of something other than the desire she'd seen previously. Those piercing eyes were now filled with concern, and Zara didn't want him to be concerned for her. Having compassion was just another level of intimacy she couldn't afford to slide into with this man. It would be all too easy to lean on someone, and she'd not been raised to be dependent on others.

Zara didn't want to identify the feelings coursing through her, not when her emotions were already on edge and her body hummed even louder each time he neared, let alone touched her.

"Come on, Braden." She forced a wide smile and nodded toward the kitchen. "Let's get this done."

He looked as if he wanted to say more, but finally he nodded and released her. Maybe if they could focus on food, not freezing to death and no conversations involving personal issues, they'd get through this blizzard without any more sensual encounters or touching.

As she plucked her coat from the peg by the back door, Zara nearly laughed at her delusional thought. No way could she pretend Braden being here was just like having a friend over. Where he'd gripped her arm seconds ago was still tingling, and in a very short time, she'd find herself back upstairs, closed off in her bedroom with a man who made her ache for things she had no business wanting.

"That's all of it." Milk, eggs, cheese, frozen pizzas, meat and other groceries were tucked down into the snow to keep them from going bad. "Let's get back inside before my toes fall off."

Even though she had her fuzzy socks on under her rubber boots, her toes were going numb.

Braden held up a hand. "Wait," he whispered. "Did you hear that?"

Zara stilled. All she heard was silence because no cars were out. It was as if the rest of the world had ceased to exist, leaving only her and the boss she'd dreamed of last night.

"I don't hear anything," she told him, shoving that fantasy aside. "You have to be freezing. Come on."

He still wore his suit and the dress coat from the party. At least she could bulk up in warm layers. No way was he not freezing out here.

"Wait a second." His eyes searched the ground near her house. Slowly, he took a step, then another. "Go on inside if you don't want to wait, but I heard a cat."

A cat? She didn't own a cat. Compassion was not in her genetic makeup, so she'd spared all animals and sworn to never own one. She wouldn't have the first clue what to do if left in charge of a living, breathing thing.

Just as she reached for the door handle, Braden crouched down. Zara gasped when he pulled a snow-covered kitten up in his gloved hands. Instantly he cradled the animal to his chest and swiped the snow off its back.

Braden took cautious steps toward the back door, keeping the kitten tucked firmly just inside his coat. Zara realized his intentions immediately.

"You're bringing that inside?"

His eyes went from the gray bundle to her. "Yes. He'll freeze to death out here. He's wet and shivering."

Zara glanced around. "Where's the mom? Aren't animals made to live outside? They have fur on."

His brows shot up. "You have a coat on, too. Do you want to stay out here and see if you survive?"

Swallowing, she shook her head. "Um…so what do we do once it's inside?"

Braden tipped his head to the side. "You've never had a pet, have you?"

"Never."

Braden's sharp gaze softened. "Let's talk inside. This little guy needs warmth, and so do we."

Zara opened the back door and ushered Braden in ahead of her. Once they had their coats and boots off, Braden started searching her cabinets. He seemed to be satisfied with the box of crackers he'd found.

"Grab a bowl of water and let's get back upstairs where it's warm."

Without waiting on her, he took the box and the kitten and disappeared. Okay, so he'd basically ordered her around in her own home and that was after bringing in a stray animal.

Was badass Braden O'Shea brought to his knees over a little bundle of fur? Zara nearly laughed as she pulled out a shallow bowl and filled it with water. By the time she got upstairs, Braden was sitting on the edge of the bed, the kitten at his side, as he peeled off his socks. His feet were red and had to be absolutely freezing.

"These got soaked," he told her. "The snow went right into my boots."

"Let me have those." Placing the water on the floor at the foot of the bed, Zara reached out and took the soaked, icy socks.

"My pants are wet, too."

Her eyes darted up to his. That smirk on his face had her shaking her head. "Oh, no. Don't even think of stripping. You can roll the pant legs up and come sit by the fire."

His big hand stroked over the cat as the damp animal snuggled deeper into her cream duvet. "You're no fun at all."

"Oh, I'm loads of fun. I'm an events coordinator. I get paid to be fun."

After she laid his socks by the gas logs, which she cranked

up because she was still shivering, she turned back to see Braden feeding the kitten small bites of a cracker. For a second she just stood there and stared. She'd not met many men like Braden, hard and powerful on one hand, soft and compassionate on the other.

"You're staring," he stated without looking up.

She remained where she was because the sight of him on her bed being so…adorable was not something she'd planned on. She'd had a hard enough time resisting him when he'd been flat-out sexy. Now that an adorable factor had slipped right in, she was losing what little control she had left.

How would she handle another night with this man?

Six

So now Zara was not only nervous around him, she was nervous over a cat. This woman had so many complex layers, and damn if he didn't want to peel back each one.

"I'm going to take my pants off if you keep looking at me like that," he threatened. He didn't know what was going through her mind, but he couldn't handle her looking at him as if he was some savior or something.

"I'm just trying to figure you out."

His hand stilled on the kitten's boney back. "Don't," he told her, meeting her gaze across the room. "That's not an area you want to go to."

Zara crossed to the chaise and shoved her blanket aside before taking a seat and curling her feet beneath her. "Oh, I think maybe I do want to go there. What makes a rumored bad boy go all soft with a kitten?"

"I wouldn't have left any animal out in this. Would you?"

He needed to turn the topic of conversation back to her. Nothing good would come from her digging into his private life, but he wanted to know more and more about hers. Suddenly, finding out more intimate details had less to do with the scrolls…not that finding those weren't still his top priority.

"Honestly, if I'd been alone, I wouldn't have known what to do. I guess maybe I would've brought it in, but I seriously thought animals were made to be outside."

Braden reached into the sleeve of crackers for another and broke off a piece for the kitten. "Why no pets growing up?"

He watched from the corner of his eye as she toyed with the edge of her sweatshirt a moment before speaking. She was either nervous or contemplating how much to tell— most likely a little of both. Fine by him. He would wait.

"My parents weren't the most affectionate," she started slowly, as if finding the right way to describe her mom and dad was difficult. "To be honest, I never asked for a pet. I figured they'd say no, so I didn't bother."

When the kitten turned away and stretched before nestling deeper into the covers, Braden set the crackers on the nightstand before shifting on the bed to face her.

"Were they affectionate to you?" he asked, wondering why he was allowing himself this line of questioning. Seduction was one thing, but finding out about her childhood was a whole other level he didn't need to get into in order to do the job he came to do.

"It doesn't matter."

Suddenly it did. Braden came to his feet and padded over to join her on the narrow chaise. Easing a knee up on to the cushion, he turned sideways.

"Were you abused?" he asked, almost afraid of the answer. "Is that why you had such a strong connection with your grandmother?"

"Oh, no." Zara shook her head. "I wasn't abused. There were and are kids who have worse lives. I guess I've just always felt sorry for myself because of all the things I think I missed out on. But, they gave me a nice house, toys, camps in the summer."

"Family vacations?" he asked.

"Um…no. They went on trips and cruises while I was away at camp. When they traveled during the school year, I would stay with my grandmother." A sad smile spread across her face. "To be honest, those were the best times of my childhood. I loved spending time here. Gram would make up a scavenger hunt, and I'd spend hours exploring all these old rooms and hideout areas."

"Hideouts?" he asked. Damn, he felt like a jerk for listening to her, caring what she was actually saying and now turning it around to benefit his plan. Still, the end result would be the same. He would find those scrolls, and Zara was going to have to inadvertently help. "I know my house is old and has secret areas. I assume this one does, too?"

Zara smiled and tipped her head to meet his gaze. "Yeah. There's a hidden door beneath the stairs. It actually takes you into the den at the back of the house. In the basement there's a couple of hidden rooms, but they're so narrow, they're more like closets."

He wanted to check those areas out right this second, but he had to remain motionless and let her continue. Once she was asleep he'd be able to continue his quest. Those secret rooms she'd mentioned weren't on the blueprints he'd seen, and his father had never mentioned them, so he had to assume no one had checked there, either.

"My grandmother always told me how much she loved me," Zara went on, her voice almost a whisper as if she were talking to herself. "She always told me how I was her biggest treasure. I didn't get that until recently. I look at all the antiques in this old house, pieces I know are worth a lot of money. But to know she valued me even more…"

Braden continued to watch her battle her emotions, trying to remain strong and hold back. He admired her strength, her dignity and pride.

Slowly, Braden was sinking into her world—a world he never intended to be a part of. If he could somehow get away with taking back the scrolls, maybe they could see where this attraction led.

Damn it. All this secret snooping was supposed to be Ryker's area. Braden and Mac were more the powerhouse guys who ran everything smoothly and kept a few cops and federal agents on their payroll to keep their reputation clean.

"I'm sorry." Zara let out a soft laugh. "I didn't mean to get all nostalgic and sentimental on you."

Braden reached out, placing a hand on her knee. Her body stilled beneath his as her eyes widened. "Don't apologize for talking to me. We're more than employee/employer at this point."

Zara's actions betrayed her as her gaze darted to his mouth, then back up. She may have been stiff beneath his touch, but she couldn't hold back her emotions. Those striking eyes gave everything away.

She pulled in a deep breath. "What happened last night—"

"Wasn't nearly enough," he finished. "The pace we set is up to you, but the end result is inevitable."

Zara shifted her knee and turned to face him, mirroring him. His hand fell away, but he stretched his arm along the back of the chaise as he waited for her to offer up some excuse as to why they shouldn't explore this chemistry.

"I need this job."

He smiled. "And you were the best candidate, that's why I hired you." *Well, one of the reasons.* "Your job has nothing to do with what's going on between us."

"Nothing is going on," she all but yelled, throwing her arms wide. "Nothing can go on. Not while I'm working for you."

Braden shrugged. "Fine. You're fired."

Zara tipped her head, glaring at him from beneath heavy lids. "That's ridiculous."

"I always get what I want, Zara."

"And you're that desperate for a bedmate?"

Leaning forward, his fingertips found the side of her face, stroking down to her neck where she trembled. "No. Just you."

"Why?" she whispered.

"Why not?" he retorted.

The pulse beneath his hand jumped as he leaned in a bit closer. Her warm breath tickled him, the flare in her eyes motivated him and her parted lips begged him.

His other hand came up to cup the side of her face. His thumb stroked over her full bottom lip. Never once did she take her eyes off his, and while the power appeared to be completely his right now, this woman, who had him in unexpected knots, could flip that role at any moment and bring him to his knees. And the fact that she had no clue about her control over him made her even sexier.

He continued to stroke her lip as his other hand slid around to cup the back of her head. His fingers threaded through her hair, massaging as he went. A soft sigh escaped her, and Braden's entire body tightened in response.

"You're not thinking work right now, are you?" he whispered against her lips. "You're concentrating on my touch, on how you want more."

"What are you doing to me?" she asked as her lids lowered.

"Proving a point."

Her tongue darted out to lick her lips, brushing against his thumb, instantly flipping that control. His completely snapped with that simple move.

Braden captured her mouth beneath his, not caring for finesse or gentleness. There was only so much a man could handle. Zara's hands came up and fisted the front of his shirt as she moaned…music to his ears.

Tipping his head slightly, Braden changed the angle of the kiss. When Zara leaned into him, he wanted to drag her into his lap and speed this process along. So he did.

Gripping her around the waist, without breaking the kiss, Braden shifted to sit forward as he placed her over his lap.

Instantly her legs straddled his thighs, and her hands slid up over his shoulders as the heated kiss continued. Braden hadn't wanted a woman this bad in a long time…maybe never. Zara was sexy, yes, but there was more to her than anything superficial, and he wanted more. He wanted all she would give.

His hands slid beneath the hem of her sweatshirt. That smooth skin beneath his palms could make any man beg. He was near that point. Who knew he'd actually find a weakness in his life? He prided himself on being strong, being in control.

Just as his thumbs brushed the silk on her bra, Zara jerked back, pushing against his shoulders.

"Wait," she gasped. "We—we can't do this."

Scrambling off his lap, she held her fingers to her lips and closed her eyes. Was she trying to keep that sensation a while longer? Was she still tasting him? Braden waited. She was seriously battling with herself.

"Kissing me like that…" Zara sighed, dropped her arms and looked him in the eyes. "I can't want this, Braden. Don't you understand?"

Relaxed against the back cushion, Braden eyed her, letting her stand above him, giving her the upper hand here. A smart businessman knew when to pull back on the reins in order to get ahead.

"Why are you denying yourself?" he asked. "If the job wasn't a factor, what other excuse would you use?"

He'd hit a mark. Her chin when up a notch, her eyes narrowed. "I'm not making excuses. Nothing would've happened between us at all had you not been stuck here. The next time I would've seen you would've been at the party you're throwing in five weeks for all of your employees."

Braden laughed, shaking his head.

"Now you're laughing at me?" she asked, crossing her arms.

Slowly coming to his feet, Braden crossed to her, not a

bit surprised when she didn't back up, but tipped her head back to continue to glare.

"I'm laughing at the fact you think we wouldn't have seen each other." He tucked a portion of her hair behind her ear, purposely trailing his fingertips down her cheek. "Zara, I would've found reasons to see you. The fact I'm stuck here only provided me the opportunity I needed to seduce you properly."

Silence settled between them seconds before Zara moaned and threw her arms out to her sides as she spun toward the logs and went to stand before them. "Your ego is something I hadn't taken into account. Maybe you've forgotten I just ended a relationship with a man who thought he could control me, thought he was in charge."

Braden stared at her back, deciding to let that jab about Shane roll off him. He knew he wasn't anything like that bastard. She knew it, too.

"I didn't say I wanted a relationship," he corrected. "And I know you well enough after hearing about your childhood to say you don't, either."

Zara whirled around, her dark hair flying about her shoulders. "You think you know me? Because I gave you a small portion of my life?"

"So you do want a relationship?"

"Stop twisting my words."

Why was he purposely getting under her skin? This wasn't part of his plan, but seeing Zara worked up and verbally sparring with her was more of a turn-on than he'd thought. He needed to steer things back to where she felt in control, where she felt as if he was less of a threat. He knew she wanted him, she knew it, too, stubborn woman. But for now he'd let this moment pass. The ultimate goal was still pressing, and he had work to do.

"Why don't you show me those secret rooms?" he asked, pleased when her eyes widened.

"What?"

"Those rooms. They sound cool, and I'd like to see them."

Her eyes darted to the kitten, still sleeping on the bed. "What about him?"

Braden walked over, scooped the kitten into his arm and motioned toward the door. "All set."

"It's cold in the rest of the house."

He quirked a brow. "You want to stay in here and keep dancing around the sexual tension?"

She moved to the door so fast, Braden couldn't stop laughing. Finally he was getting somewhere. He may not be getting her into his bed, but he was seeing these illusive rooms and perhaps he'd find something, anything, to hint at the scrolls. When all was said and done, and this freak blizzard was over, he'd have all his wishes fulfilled.

Seven

Zara gripped the neck of her sweatshirt as she came down the wide staircase. Trying to hold it up just a bit more to ward off the chill helped.

Eerie quiet settled throughout the house. Who knew darkness had a tone? She could hear Braden's breathing, his every step, every brush of his clothing. Every single thing he did made her even more aware of his presence.

What the hell had she been thinking kissing him back like that? Straddling his lap and practically crawling all over his body? Part of her was mortified she'd acted like that, but on the other hand, he'd been right there with her. He'd been the one to instigate every heated occurrence. But no more. If he touched her, she'd have to walk away. Even if she had to step out into the cold hall or bundle up and sleep in a chilly spare bedroom, she couldn't let him kiss her again.

Because she feared the next kiss would lead to clothes falling off and them tumbling into bed.

With the mid-morning sun shining in the windows, enough

light filtered through to make this encounter not seem so intimate.

She led him to the den and eased the door open. "This room was never used by my grandmother. She usually just put books in here. I think I'm the only one who ever came in here, and that was just because I wanted to get to the secret passageway. As a kid, that was the coolest thing in the world to me."

"Did you ever have friends over?" he asked as he stepped into the room with her. "This house would've made the greatest backdrop for hide-and-seek."

"I had a few friends sleep over," she admitted. "Looking back now, I only brought friends here. My parents wouldn't have gone for me inviting them to our house. They were always going to some party, throwing a party or worried about their next travel venture."

Braden loathed her parents. Why bring a child into this world if you didn't intend on caring for said child? He admitted he wanted kids, when the time was right. Having them now would be ridiculous because he didn't have the time to devote to them. And children needed structure, needed family and a bond that provided security.

Zara was a strong woman, but he could see the vulnerability, the brokenness of her childhood still affecting her today.

Stepping around him, she pulled the flashlight from beneath her arm. "Follow me."

One of the built-in bookcases had a small latch. Zara jerked once, twice, and finally the hinges creaked open. As she flicked on the light and angled the beam into the darkness, Braden's heart kicked up. He desperately wanted to find what he came for, though realistically he figured things wouldn't be that easy.

The kitten purred against Braden's chest. He'd never owned a cat, but he loved animals. His sister would be so happy to take in another stray. She was the proverbial cat lady, though she'd never own up to the term. Laney would take this kitten in with a squeal of delight. He could already envision her snuggling the thing.

Braden stepped into the narrow hallway behind Zara. "Don't worry if that door closes behind you. We can't get trapped in here. I guess whoever owned this before my grandmother had a latch installed on both ends of the tunnel. My guess is someone got locked in, so they learned their lesson."

Locked in a dark place with Zara…not too far off the mark of how they'd spent last night. And not a bad predicament to be in.

The kitten perked up at Zara's voice and leaped out of Braden's arms. The little thing moved so fast, Braden worried he'd hurt himself, but when the kitten slid against Zara's ankles, he figured the animal was just fine.

Zara's flashlight held steady on the stray. "What is he doing?"

With a laugh, Braden continued to watch the cat seeking affection. "Looks like he wants to be friends."

"I have enough friends," she muttered and tried to take a step. When she tripped over the kitten, Braden held out a hand to steady her. "Will she stop trying to be an ankle bracelet anytime soon?"

"If you pick her up," Braden stated. "Cats have a tendency to cling to one person. You may be the chosen one."

With the light casting enough of a glow, Braden saw her eyes widen. "You're kidding."

"Nope."

Reluctantly, Zara plucked up the kitten, held her in a bit of an awkward way, but the little fur ball didn't seem to mind. Braden felt it best not to mention the obvious that the cat seemed to love Zara. Best move on to the point of this tour.

"Is this just a hallway?" he asked, trying to look on the

walls for any compartments or doors…hell, anything that would be a clue as to where he could search.

"It opens up into a little room before letting you out into the kitchen."

Zara let out a grunt, the flashlight bobbed and Braden used his free arm to reach out as she tumbled forward. His arm banded around her waist, his hand connected with her breast as he supported her from falling. Thankfully the kitten was snuggled tight, and Zara had a good grip on the oblivious little thing.

When Zara fell back against him, he didn't relinquish his hold. How could he when she felt too perfect with her body flush against his?

"Thanks," she whispered. "I forgot there's a bit of a dip in the floor right there."

"Are you all right?" he asked.

She nodded, her hair tickling the side of his face. "Um… you can let me go."

Her body arched, betraying her words. He couldn't stop himself. His thumb slid back and forth across her breast before he reluctantly released her. He wanted her aching for him, for his touch. If he kept pushing, she'd completely close off, and he'd look like more of a jerk that what he was. But keeping her body on high alert, having her wonder about what would happen next between them would inevitably have her in his bed. Well, technically her bed.

She said nothing as she continued on, slower this time. Finally they came to the room she'd mentioned, which wasn't more than a walk-in closet in size. Her light darted around, and she gasped. His eyes followed the beam and landed on a little yellow chair; a book lay open, cover up to hold the page. Zara turned and handed him the kitten.

"I used to sneak in here to read." She moved forward and picked up the book, flipping it over in her hand. With a laugh, she laid it back down. "This was one of my favorites."

Braden crossed the space and glanced down to the book.

He couldn't see the title, but the embracing couple on the cover told him all he needed to know.

"You read romance as a kid?"

"I was a teenager and curious," she said. Even in the dim light he could see her chin pop up a notch. "Maybe I wanted to know what all that love stuff was about, because when I was sixteen I thought I'd found love. Turns out I found a guy who'd made a bet with his buddies on who would take my virginity."

That entire statement told him more about her than she'd ever willingly reveal. She was bitter, she'd been used. She was raised by parents who were never affectionate, and other than her grandmother, she didn't have anyone she could depend on in her life.

Coming from a large Irish family, Braden had no clue what that felt like. Granted he'd never fallen in love, but he believed it existed. He'd witnessed it firsthand from his parents. While he'd had so many levels of love, Zara had emptiness.

"So you would sneak in here and read dirty books?" he asked.

"They weren't dirty. They were sweet, and now that I know how life really is, I see why they're labeled as fiction."

Yeah. Definitely bitter.

He scanned the rest of the area. There were a few empty shelves along one wall, a door on the other and absolutely nothing of use for him in here. Except for the bundles of information he'd just gathered on Zara.

"That concludes the tour," she stated. "Not as exciting as you thought, right?"

Braden shifted the kitten to his other arm, careful not to wake him. "Oh, I wouldn't say that. I got to cop a feel. I wouldn't call this venture a total loss."

For a second she said nothing, then she reached out and smacked his shoulder. "You're a smart-ass."

Braden wanted to see that smile she offered. He craved

it. Knowing he pulled her from those past thoughts with his snarky comment and put her in the here and now with a laugh was exactly his intent.

"Why don't you show me the other hidden rooms, and I'll see what other smooth moves I can come up with?" he suggested, which earned him a light right to the face. Squinting, he shielded his eyes with his free hand. "All right, I promise to be on my best behavior."

Turning away, Zara pushed open the door to the kitchen. "You'll have to do better than that," she muttered.

Nothing. He'd not found a damn thing that indicated where the scrolls were. He didn't even know if they were all together at this point. At one time there were nine, stored in the infamous trunk that now sat in his office as if to mock him on a daily basis. They could be long gone, but Braden refused to give into that line of thinking, because if they were gone, he had absolutely nowhere to look. They had to be here.

Before they'd headed back up to the bedroom, Zara had stepped out the back door and plucked some cheese and fruit out of the snow. She pulled a loaf of bread from the cabinet and got a few bottles of water.

Now they were sitting in the floor in front of the fire having a gourmet lunch while the kitten roamed around the room. Occasionally he would come back, rub against Zara as if to make sure she was still there, then he'd roam a little more.

"Is he going to pee on my things?" she asked, popping a grape into her mouth.

Braden shrugged. "Maybe, but I found a box in your kitchen and brought it up. Put a towel or something over there and he'll be very happy. Cats love boxes."

"Really?"

Nodding, he tore off another hunk of cheese. "Trust me on this. Granted, he's still a kitten, so he'll stick close to us, or you as the case may be, but once he gets comfortable here, that box will be his new home."

Zara stared as the kitten snuck beneath her bed. "I'd rather he find a new home."

"Aww, now don't be like that with your new best friend."

By the time they'd devoured the assortment, Zara leaned back and stretched her arms high above her head, pulling her sweatshirt up just enough to draw his gaze down to her creamy skin and the slight roll over the band of her pants.

"I wish the electricity would come back on," she stated, dropping her arms, oblivious to the knots in his gut. "I have so much work to do. My laptop may only have a couple hours left of charge."

"What are you working on?"

"I have an event scheduled for a client in four weeks. I need to adjust some things on the spreadsheets and set up another schedule for an event I'm working on for a bridal party." Zara started picking up the garbage and bundling it all in the empty bread sack. "Plenty of work to do with no Wi-Fi, but I'm going to get backed up if I can't get some emails done in the next few days."

Braden listened to her talk of the event scheduled a week before his next party. Zara was efficient, and the passion for her work came through in her tone. She definitely was career driven, but was that all there was to her life? He'd not heard her mention friends and he knew there was no boyfriend. He'd never met a woman who remained so closed off on a personal level.

"Why don't you work?" he suggested. "I'm going to head to my car, charge my phone and turn it on to make some calls."

He needed to check in with Ryker to see if he'd located the missing art piece in London. Then he needed to see if Mac was stuck at the main house, most likely since Mac's flight back to Miami would've been canceled with this weather. Braden would have to call his sister, too, because…

well, he worried about her even though she hated her older brothers fussing over her.

Hopping to her feet, Zara nodded. "Yeah. I need to do something. I'm not one to sit still and do nothing. After I draft my emails I'm grabbing a shower."

"With cold water?" he asked.

She smiled down at him. "I have a gas hot water heater."

His eyes raked over her body, and the very last thing he needed was an image of her naked, soapy and wet body with only a thin door separating them.

Rising to stand before her, he took the trash from her hands and headed for the bedroom door. "I'll be in my car for a while. I'll throw this away on my way out."

He left the room before he would give into temptation and join her in the shower. He needed to let Mac know that, so far, nothing had turned up. This house was damn big, but the secret hidey-holes were literally bare, save for the yellow chair and romance novel.

After throwing away the trash and bundling up, Braden tried to get through the mounds of snow to his car. There was no way to get there without soaking his feet once again because the snow was up to his knees; but he needed to check in, and once the engine warmed up, he could put the heater on full blast.

Most likely his battery would've been fine to talk inside the warm house, but he couldn't risk Zara overhearing his conversations.

Powering up his phone as he slid behind the wheel and tried to ignore his freezing wet feet, Braden watched as seven texts popped up on his screen. Mac had sent two, and the other five were from a frantic Laney asking if he was all right.

He decided to call her first because an angry woman, especially an angry Irish woman who happened to be his sister, was not someone he wanted on his bad side.

"You better be in a ditch with little cell service," she answered.

Braden laughed. "Not quite in a ditch, but I'm stuck at a friend's house and the electricity is out."

"What friend?" she asked, skepticism dripping from her voice.

"You don't know her."

"Her? So you're shacking up and can't return my texts? I had you lying in a ditch bleeding and with the roads closed, and no one saw you and you'd died all alone."

Braden pinched the bridge of his nose and sighed. "I assure you, I'm fine, and I'm not shacking up. To be honest, I'd feel better if I was."

Laney laughed. "Whoever she is, I want to meet her. Someone has you in knots. I like her already."

He wasn't in knots. Really, he was completely knot free and in total control. Just because he'd had to physically remove himself from the house since Zara was going to shower didn't mean he couldn't keep his wits about him.

"I'm at Zara's, okay?" He tried to keep his tone level so she didn't read any more into what he was saying. "I was worried about the roads, so I offered her a ride home. On the way, I got pulled over by a deputy and was informed there's a level two snow emergency on the roads and I was to stay put. So here I am."

"Aww, poor baby. Stuck in a house with a beautiful woman. Don't think I didn't see you two dancing at the party. And great job getting into the house, by the way. If I didn't know better, I'd think you had some weather god on your payroll, as well."

"Yeah, I've turned up nothing. But I'm not done yet. I'm hoping to loosen Zara up enough to get her talking. She may not even realize she knows something useful."

"You sound crankier than usual," Laney mocked. "No scrolls, no sex. I hope you're not acting like a bear toward your hostess."

Cranking the heat up, Braden dropped his head back against the seat. "Now that you know I'm alive and sexually frustrated, can we be done with this call?"

Laney laughed even harder. "Only because I love you am I letting you off the hook. Don't think I won't be discussing this with Mac."

"I've no doubt you'll do so as soon as we hang up," he muttered. "Are you okay? You're home?"

"I'm fine. Carter stayed over last night, which was a good thing because I couldn't get my generator started."

Well, at least Carter was good for one thing, but Braden still considered Laney's boyfriend a prick.

Braden bit his tongue, because if Carter kept treating his sister as if she should be thanking him for a relationship, Braden was going to step in. He'd seen too many times how Carter would act as if he was doing Laney a favor by being with her. He'd even hinted once that she'd be lonely without him. No way in hell would Delaney O'Shea be lonely. She was gorgeous, she was successful and she was a member of the most powerful family in Boston. They were never alone.

He said his goodbyes before he said something that would drive a wedge between them. He'd much rather deal with Carter on his own terms. But, at least the guy had been there during the storm, and his sister was safe. Braden would keep that in mind when he actually confronted him…and that day was coming sooner rather than later.

Braden turned the heat down, now that he was thawed out and his feet weren't so chilled. He quickly dialed Mac, only to get his voice mail.

"Hey, man. I'm stuck at Zara's house, little cell service. I'll call back when I can, but nothing has been found yet."

He disconnected the call and stared back at the house. He wondered just how long he'd have to sit out here to avoid seeing her glowing, damp body from the shower all under the pretense of letting his phone charge. He had plenty of charge to go back in, but he figured he'd let it fill up.

He needed to keep a little distance from her because he was having a hard enough time controlling this ache. He didn't like the unfamiliar need that seemed to grow stronger with each passing moment.

No need in going back in just yet, because he knew without a doubt that once he saw Zara partially nude again, there would be nothing holding him back.

Eight

Feeling refreshed after her shower, Zara found another pair of sweats and fuzzy socks. More armor to fight off the sexy man with seduction on the brain.

Okay, fine. Sex was on her mind, too, but she couldn't let herself settle too far into that part of her brain because, honestly, the sex she'd had with guys in the past had just been…meh. And she wasn't about to risk her job on some mediocre moment. Besides, if they had sex now, what if he was stuck here for two more days? Seriously. Talk about a new level of awkward. Added to that, would he expect a replay? Was he a one-and-done man?

Zara groaned as she took out her frustrations by towel-drying her hair. Why was she overanalyzing this? She wasn't shedding her fleece, no matter what tricky moves he put on her.

Zara hung her towel on the knob of her closet door. No way was she going back out to the bathroom. While the water had been nice and hot, the room itself was an icebox. There was no master bath in this house, but the bathroom was right outside her bedroom door. Still, given she was damp and her hair was still drying, that would make for one cold walk.

Grabbing her brush from the dresser, she took a seat on her bed and crossed her legs as she pulled her hair over her shoulder and started working out the tangles at the bottom.

That kitten darted out from beneath her bed, and Zara just knew that thing was making a litter box out of the space. Once again the bundle of fur slid against Zara's ankles and feet, purring as he went. Even though she'd never had an animal, she honestly didn't mind that it was in her house. She may not have a clue how to care for a pet, but she didn't want the thing outside freezing to death. Okay, and maybe she kind of liked knowing something was looking to her for care and support. She didn't necessarily love it, but she had a kernel of like.

The bedroom door opened as Braden came sliding back in. Immediately he went to the fire and peeled off his wet socks once again. Zara sighed, tapping the brush against her thigh.

"Why don't you go hop in the shower and warm up your feet? And when you're done, I'll give you a pair of my socks. They're small, but they're warm and dry." When he didn't say anything, he merely turned and stared at her, she went on. "Maybe stop going outside. Whatever you need, I can go. I at least have taller boots."

Raking a hand through his hair, Braden strode back out the door. Apparently he was taking her up on the shower. But what had happened in the time he'd walked out until now? He seemed quiet, wouldn't quite look her in the eyes. Something was wrong.

The O'Sheas were mysterious and closed off, so she'd never know. But she didn't want him upset or angry. It was freezing, they were stuck. Oh, yeah, and sexually frustrated. That made for a nice combo.

While he was gone, Zara got an idea and snuck out to the kitchen. Finding exactly what she needed, she raced back up to the bedroom. The shower was still running, so she had time to set up. Apparently he'd found towels and was making himself at home. Granted, all she had were floral specialty soaps, but she'd not exactly prepared for male guests.

Zara moved the chaise back closer to the wall to open up the middle of the floor. She settled down, crossing her legs and had the necessary items in front of her just as Braden came back in...wearing only a towel.

"You've got to be kidding me," she muttered.

Without a word, he crossed the room and laid his clothes out in front of the fire. "Unlike you, I don't have the luxury of throwing on different clothes. I've been wearing these since yesterday morning."

She glanced over and seriously wished she hadn't. Were those...yeah. He was a black boxer brief man. No tighty-whities for this alpha male...and seeing his underwear made it crystal clear he was commando beneath that terry cloth.

Braden cleared his throat, and she realized he'd turned and was staring at her. Great. Way to really hold her ground about not getting intimate when she's caught staring at the man's underwear.

"What's this?" he asked, motioning down to her stash.

She ignored the items she'd brought up from the kitchen and continued to stare up at him as if having a conversation wearing only a towel were perfectly normal.

"So you're going to be like this until your clothes dry?" She motioned with her finger up and down his body.

Clutching one side of the towel over one very muscular, very exposed thigh, Braden shrugged. "I can lose the towel, but I thought you'd be more comfortable like this."

Zara rolled her eyes. The man was proving to be impossible to resist, and she truly didn't know how much longer she could hold out.

"I'm comfortable with your clothes on," she muttered. "Anyway, I thought we could play cards, and since I'm not one to gamble, I brought up pretzel sticks we can use instead."

He quirked a brow. "You play poker?"

Zara laughed. "You didn't know my grandmother. That woman could outwit the best of the best when it came to seven-card stud. She taught me how to play when I was still learning how to write my name."

Braden quirked his brow, then headed over to the chaise and pulled off the blanket she used to sleep with. He wrapped it around his waist and sank to the floor in front of her.

That bare chest with dark hair and just a bit of ink showing over his shoulder held her captive, and she would have to concentrate on this game if she wanted to control her urge to rip that blanket and towel from his deliciously sculpted body.

"Can you play?" she asked, pulling the cards from the box.

Piercing eyes held hers. "I can play whatever game you want."

Of course he could, and he could make everything sound sexual with that low, intense tone that had her stomach doing flips.

When she offered the cards to him to shuffle, he waved a hand. "Ladies first."

Shuffling them with quick, precise movements, Zara finally felt comfortable. Cards was something she could handle, something she could somewhat control. A hobby of hers from long ago, she hadn't played for a while, but she needed the distraction, and there was only so much they could do stuck in this room.

"What's the ante?" he asked, tearing open the bag of pretzels.

"Your choice."

"Ten."

Zara dealt their first hand while he counted out twenty pretzel sticks for each of them. As soon as she laid down the door card, she smiled when his was lower than hers.

"Your bet," she told him.

He smirked. "I'm aware of the rules."

"Just making sure you know you're dealing with a professional."

There. Maybe if she kept throwing verbiage out like that, he wouldn't be so determined to cross territory they could never return from.

Braden raised the bet, but Zara didn't think he had anything worth raising for. She'd call him on his bluff. He had a poker face, that was for sure. No doubt he'd used that same straight, stoic look in the business world. As the oldest son of the late Patrick O'Shea, Braden had big shoes to fill, and being the powerful man he was, he'd have no problem at all, Zara knew.

By the time the last card was dealt, Zara was looking at a full house with aces on top. Not the best hand, but still better than whatever he was lying about.

"I'll raise you," she told him, throwing in three more sticks.

When he flipped his cards over, Zara gripped her cards and simply stared. Seriously? She'd dealt him a flush? There hadn't been a gleam in his eye one time during the entire game, and she'd thought he'd been bluffing.

Narrowing her eyes, she tossed her cards down as he raked in his pretzels. The kitten chose that time to dart over and walk right through the cards and the pretzels as if he owned the place. He swatted at a pretzel and kept swatting it until he was moving too close to the logs. There was a screen around the fireplace, more for looks, but she still didn't want the little guy rubbing against it and singeing his fur.

Zara reached out, stretching to grab hold of him and his

pretzel, then deposited him on the other side of her away from the heat.

"I believe it's my deal," Braden stated with a smirk. "Hold tight. We're about to take this to a whole new level."

She tipped her head in a silent question.

"We're playing for answers now," he told her as he reached down, grabbed a pretzel and popped it into his mouth. "Whoever wins the hand can ask the other player anything, and they have to answer."

Still eyeing him skeptically, Zara asked, "Just questions? No touching, no clichéd strip poker?"

Shuffling the cards, he smiled. "I'll touch and strip if you want. Hell, that can even be one of your questions. Up to you, so ask what you want."

Mercy, the man was incorrigible, and she was finding that she loved every second of his quick wit, his flirty side and the fact he made no secret that he wanted her.

Thankfully, she won the next hand with a pair of kings, beating out his jacks. Zara reached to push the cards back in order to shuffle them as she pondered her question.

Staring down at the cards as they shuffled and fell into place, she asked, "If you believe in marriage and family so much, why are you still single?"

That sexy laugh filled the room. "I'm so glad you didn't ask something as boring as my favorite color or movie."

Risking a glance, she looked him in the eye. Okay, fine, her eyes may have lingered a little longer on his bare chest, but they eventually hit his eyes, where she saw amusement staring back at her.

"Well?" she asked, raising her brows as she started dealing.

"Haven't found the right one."

He studied his cards, offering nothing else with his response. Zara gritted her teeth. If he was going to be vague, then so could she when the time came…though she didn't intend to lose.

As she stared at her cards, though, a pit grew in her stomach. Unless she was dealt something spectacular in the next round, she was going to be answering a question, and she was almost afraid to see what he'd come up with.

The second he realized he won, he dropped a question she definitely hadn't expected.

"Why do you choose assholes to date? Because of commitment issues?"

Zara refused to be rattled. "That's two questions, so your round is disqualified."

Just as she reached for the cards, Braden's hand covered hers. As if knowing he was naked beneath that blanket weren't enough to sizzle her mind, his warm touch only added fuel to the proverbial fire.

"I'm not disqualified." Gently squeezing her hand, he turned her palm over and laced their fingers, holding their joined hands up between them. "Tell me why you only date jerks."

"How do you know I date jerks?"

His thumb stroked hers as he spoke, as if the man were trying to put her under a spell. Too late. He'd done that the moment she'd walked into his office months ago. But once he'd held her at the party, once he'd shown a more personal side, she'd turned a corner and she wasn't sure she could ever get back.

"Who did you date before Shane?" he asked.

Zara stared at him for a second before laughing. Damn. That came out sounding nervous. She wasn't nervous. Just because he was holding her hand, looking at her as if he cared and asking about her love life. Why should any of that worry her?

And even as much as all of that worried her, it was the desire, the lust staring back at her that had her stomach in knots.

"You're asking way too many questions," she whispered.

"Your silence tells me all I need to know." Inching closer,

he set the cards between them and kept his eyes locked on to hers. "You don't like commitment because your parents weren't loving or affectionate. You didn't get the attention a child deserves. Now as an adult you're dating jerks because you know you won't get attached. Same reason you haven't unpacked, if I'm guessing right. You can't even commit to this house."

Zara jerked her hand back. "Whatever you're trying to prove, stop. You don't know me well enough to analyze me."

Coming to her feet, she smoothed her hair back from her face. "I'm done playing."

Before she could turn away, Braden slowly rose. That predator look in his eyes as he closed the space between them held her firmly in place. The fact he could be so menacing, so arousing while holding on to a bulky comforter at his waist with one hand proved just how far she'd fallen from her initial mind-set. She was crumbling right at this man's feet.

And the more her resolve deteriorated, the more she wondered, why was she holding back? He'd pegged her perfectly when he said she wasn't looking for any commitment. First, she didn't have time with her business soaking up her life. Second, well, she just didn't want to. She wouldn't have any idea how. Since she'd signed on with the O'Sheas, she'd seen the close-knit family they were. A piece of her wondered what a connection that strong would be like. Leaning on someone else, expecting support was too much of a risk. But she didn't need a man.

He'd made it clear he didn't want a commitment, though. Once the roads cleared he'd be gone, and whatever happened here would stay right here. Braden wasn't one to talk, of that she was sure. Her reputation wouldn't be tarnished, she wouldn't be known as the woman who slept with her clients or her boss. Honestly, what was holding her back?

From the look in Braden's eyes, he wasn't looking for a walk down the aisle…just a walk to the bed.

Nine

Braden didn't know what changed, but the look of determination and stubbornness was wiped clean. Now Zara stared back at him with passion blazing in those striking eyes. She didn't step forward to meet him, but she no longer looked as if she wanted to flee the room.

As he stood within touching distance, Braden took in the rapid pulse at the base of her throat, her shallow breathing and wide eyes. She wasn't thinking how angry she was now.

"You're not running," he muttered, delighting in the fact she tipped her head up to look at him instead of backing up. Braden reached out, tucking her hair behind her ear and sliding his fingertip along her jawline. "Why is that, Zara?"

"Because this is my house, and I'm not afraid of you."

For such a petite woman, he was impressed. He intimidated men twice her size, yet this woman wasn't backing down. He admired her—more than he should, because all he wanted from her on a personal level was right here and right now. The scroll business had no place in this bedroom.

"Or maybe you're finally giving in," he stated, raking his finger over her bottom lip. "Maybe you see that we're both adults, we're stuck here together and this attraction isn't going away."

Her chin tipped up a notch. "Maybe I am."

Braden smiled at her bold statement. How could he not find her charming and sexy and confident all rolled into one perfect package?

Wait. Perfect? No. Nobody was perfect, but she was perfect for him right at this moment.

In all of his thirty-five years, Braden had been taught to take chances to get what he wanted. There was no greater time to test that theory than right now.

Braden dropped the comforter and the towel. Both fell to his feet without a sound. The light coming through the plantation shutters gave enough for her to see that he was completely ready for her.

"You have all the control now," he told her. "Whatever you want to do from this point on is your call. You can humiliate me and reject me, you can quit your job and claim I'm just like the jerks you dated, or you can start stripping out of those clothes and join me by the fire so I can show you exactly how much I want you."

He didn't wait on her response. Braden stepped out of the mess of comforter and tugged the blanket toward the fireplace. As he spread it out, he thought for sure he heard her shifting behind him. She wouldn't deny him or herself. That longing look in her eyes, the way she was speechless and flushed were all telling signs of what she was afraid to admit aloud.

He stilled when her hand settled on his shoulder blade. Slowly, as if to drive him completely out of his mind, she started trailing her fingers over his bare skin. She was tracing his ink, and he wasn't about to turn around and stop her no matter how much he wanted to see her, touch her. He meant it when he'd told her she was in control.

Even though he only wanted something physical from Zara, he still wasn't about to prove to her that he was like the other men she wasted time with. He would put her needs first, let her know she mattered here and what was about to happen didn't have to be ugly.

"Why did you get this?" she asked as she continued to trace the pattern. "I always wonder why people choose certain images to mark their skin for life."

On this he could at least tell her the truth. "It's a symbol that has deep meaning to my family. It dates back to the sixteenth century."

"It's beautiful," she whispered.

He couldn't wait another second. Braden turned, causing her hand to fall away, but the loss of her touch was made up for with the sight of her standing before him completely bare, completely giving and completely trusting.

"We need to set some rules," she told him.

Braden snaked an arm out around her waist and pulled her flush against his body. From chest to knee they touched, and there was no way in hell he was going to start in on some ridiculous conversation now.

"To hell with the rules."

He crushed her mouth beneath his. Zara stiffened for a second. Then, as if she couldn't deny herself anymore, she wrapped her arms around him and returned the kiss. Her passion came alive, bursting on to the scene in ways he hadn't experienced before.

She matched his desire, raising the bar to a level all her own, and Braden was the one who was nearly brought to his knees. He allowed his hands to roam over her, wanting to memorize the feel of her body, wanting her to get used to his touch because he planned on doing a whole lot more.

Braden eased back from the kiss, ignoring her protested groan which turned into a moan when his mouth traveled down the column of her throat and continued lower.

She gripped his hair as he palmed her breasts. Arching

her back, she silently offered herself up to him. Braden's lips covered her breast as he lowered her to the floor. He couldn't get enough of her, not her gasps, not her kisses, not her touch. He wanted it all, and willpower and trying to hold back were going to be a struggle.

"Do you have protection?" she asked.

Braden froze. Considering he'd only come here in his party attire, he hadn't planned on getting lucky that night. Damn it.

A smile spread across her face. "Go to my nightstand."

Thankful she was prepared, Braden made a mad dash to the drawer and found what he needed. Also thankfully, the cat stayed out of sight.

By the time he'd stepped back to the comforter, Zara was practically on display. Her arms on either side of her head, hair fanning out all around her. But it was those eyes that watched him so cautiously that made something twist in his gut. She may be trusting him with her body, but she was still not letting him in.

That fact should have given him a sense of relief, considering he was technically using her, but it didn't. He didn't want to just be some prick who proved to her that all guys were jerks.

But when she reached her arms out to him in a silent invitation to join her, there was no way in hell he could deny her or himself. Consequences be damned. Yes, this started with the scrolls, but the moment she'd walked into his office he'd wanted her, and he refused to feel guilty now. Allowing feelings to override what he was literally aching for would just leave a void that only Zara could fill.

Braden reached for her hand and settled down beside her, propping himself up on one elbow. While he wanted to devour her all at once, he also wanted to take his time, because this was a one-time thing and he wanted to savor every single second.

Trailing his hand up and down her abdomen, watching her muscles contract beneath his touch and hearing her swift intake of breath, had him appreciating the fact he was practicing that self-control now. He had a limited supply of it and was using it all up on her, on this moment.

Braden watched her, studied her. He wanted to know what she liked, what she responded to. The moment his hand started trailing down her stomach, her lids fluttered closed, her legs shifted in response and he was damn near crawling out of his skin.

As his fingers found her most intimate spot, he captured her lips, swallowing her moan. Zara's arms wrapped around his neck, her hands sliding up into his hair, holding him still…as if he would be anywhere else.

Braden eased back, enough to get protection in place, before he settled between her legs.

"Don't look away," he commanded. "Your eyes are only for me."

Why the hell did he want her to be so focused on him? Why did he have that overwhelming primal feeling to keep her all to himself?

Because he was selfish. Plain and simple and for right now, Zara was his. He wanted to leave an imprint in her mind of this moment and have her compare every single man to him. He wanted to ruin her for others…and if he thought too much about that, he would scare the hell out of himself.

Braden pushed all other thoughts aside as he joined their bodies. When her eyes closed, he shifted to his elbows, using his hands to frame her face as his lips hovered over hers.

"Only me, Zara."

When he started to move, she held on to his shoulders, keeping her gaze on his. "Braden," she whispered.

Hearing his name on her lips as he filled her only exacerbated this unwanted emotional ache.

The second her body started pumping against his, her

face flushed, and Braden slid his mouth over hers, pushing her even further. Her fingertips dug into his shoulders as her body tensed. Braden lifted his head, wanting to watch her as she peaked. With Zara's head thrown back, a sheen of sweat covering her face and neck, Braden couldn't resist gliding his lips over her heated skin as she came undone around him. As he gripped her hips and tasted the saltiness of her skin, his own body started to rise.

Her trembling slowed, and Braden rested his forehead against hers. "Zara," he whispered, wanting her name to be the one he cried out, needing her to know he was fully aware of the woman he was with, that she mattered.

Before he could delve into that too much, his control broke. Braden covered her lips with his, wanting to join them in all possible ways. Her tongue met his as he shattered. Wave after wave washed over him, leaving only one thought, one thing that mattered at that moment…and it wasn't his family or the scrolls.

It was Zara.

Zara didn't do regrets, and there was no way she was going to start now. How could she when her body had lit up and was still tingling? Was tingle even the proper verb? She couldn't pinpoint what her body was doing, but the thrill that kept pulsing through her had everything to do with the man whose body still covered hers. Those long, lean legs rubbed against hers, the coarseness of his hair tickling her, sending new sensations throughout.

Part of her wanted to get out from under him, to get dressed and go on like nothing happened. He was her boss, for crying out loud, and she'd been so clichéd as to sleep with him.

But the other part, the part of her that was still lit up with passion, wanted to lie just like this wearing nothing but the weight of a powerful man.

"I can hear you thinking." Braden's warm breath tickled her ear. He eased up, propping himself on his elbows on either side of her face. "Maybe you need a replay so you can relax."

There was no way she could replay anything that just happened because then she'd want more. She'd want him. Sex was one thing, but wants were an entirely different matter she couldn't afford right now...and not with this man.

Zara pushed on his shoulders and slid out from under him. "No replays," she told him as she gathered her clothes. She tried like hell to not think about the fact she was walking around naked in front of her boss, but after what they'd just done...

"Already running, Zara?"

She risked a glance over and wished she hadn't. With a wrist dangling over one bent knee and his other hand holding is body upright, Braden's intense gaze pinned her in place. She clutched her sweats to her chest as if she could use them as some sort of defense against feelings. Damn emotional womanly feelings. Why did this have to be the man to stir something within her?

"I'm not running," she said. "I'm getting dressed and checking on the cat that's probably peed all over my floor."

"The cat is fine, and there's no rush to get dressed." He came to his feet and crossed the space between them. Just like he had before they'd gotten intimate. Only this time, Zara backed up.

"Braden." She held up a hand, thankful when he stopped. "I don't regret what just happened, it was amazing, but we can't do that again."

"If you're going to pull the whole boss/employer card, we're past that." His kissable mouth quirked.

"Yes, we are," she agreed. "But we're done. Nothing more can come of this."

There. She'd had a fling, she wasn't having regrets and now they could move on.

Crossing his arms over his broad chest as if he hadn't

a care in the world, Braden shrugged. "I'd had the same thought, but then I decided that wasn't right. Why should we deny ourselves what brings us pleasure?"

Zara listened to him, processed the justification, but in the end, she knew she'd get hurt because Braden was the type of man she could fall for…if she would ever let herself fall. One and done was the only way she could justify this encounter.

"It's best if we stop here and try to live with each other until you are able to leave."

The muscle ticked in his jaw, and Zara wanted to take back her words, ignore all the warning bells going off in her head and wrap her arms around him and have him give her that replay he'd suggested.

"I'll do what you want, Zara." He stepped closer, so close she could see the flecks of black in his deep brown eyes. "I'll honor your wishes, but that doesn't mean I'll stop trying to convince you that we were good together, and now that we know all about each other's bodies, we could be even better."

Those promising words delivered by a low, sexy tone did not help her cause. She clutched her clothes and watched as he wrapped up in that damn comforter again. He picked his cell up from the accent table and threw her a smile.

"I'm going to call the sheriff's department and see when travel is expected to resume."

And he walked out the door. Now the cat darted from beneath the bed and slid across the hardwood, bumping into her feet, but Zara remained frozen in place, still naked, still holding on to her clothes.

Still wanting him just as much, if not more than she had before they were intimate.

What had she gotten herself into? Because now she had a sense of what it meant to belong, just an inkling of how powerful a bond with someone else could be.

Ten

"You've got to be missing something," Mac stated.

Yeah, common sense.

"I've searched the hidden areas," Braden explained for the third time. But Mac was understandably frustrated, as was Braden.

He felt utterly foolish with this damn comforter as he stood at the base of the steps. He watched the landing for any sign of Zara, but she was most likely still up in her room replaying everything that had just happened between them.

"I'm telling you, if they're here, they're well hidden."

Mac's sigh carried through the phone. "Maybe her grandmother sold some things before she died. Hell, I don't know. Put more pressure on Zara. We need this, Braden."

Yeah, like he wasn't aware of that. "I'm doing what I can. Pressuring Zara will only make red flags go up."

"Is she suspicious of you?"

"No."

How could she be? He'd snooped either in plain sight of

her or when she'd been sleeping. And the fact that he still needed to do more searching and his time was running out only irritated him even more because, while he wanted to find the scrolls, he wanted to go back upstairs and talk Zara into spending the entire day in bed.

"Damn," Mac muttered. "Tell me you're not actually falling for this woman."

Braden gripped the wad of comforter and sank down on to the bottom step. "I'm not."

"You don't sound convincing."

Braden gritted his teeth. "I'm not trying to convince you, so drop it."

"Keep me posted when you can," Mac said. "I changed my flight to next week. Obviously with the weather I'm not getting back to Miami anytime soon. And Ryker is stuck in London. He had a slight run-in with the cops."

Braden rubbed his forehead and cracked his neck. "Define a slight run-in."

"No charges were filed and the art is now in our possession. The rest of the details can wait."

"There will be no backlash on us?"

"It's taken care of," Mac promised.

At least one thing was going their way for now, but Braden wasn't giving up on his hunt for the scrolls. And he wasn't giving up on this need that only Zara could fill. He'd thought for sure she would be out of his system, but she was in deeper than ever.

"I'll text you if I find out anything," he told Mac. "Hopefully I'll be home by tomorrow."

"Don't come back without the scrolls."

Braden disconnected the call just as he heard Zara behind him. Jerking to his feet, he replayed the conversation he'd just had with Mac and was positive he hadn't said anything to give himself away.

She descended the stairs and barely threw him a glance.

"I'm just grabbing a notebook from the office. Do you want me to take any food back up?"

She continued by him without even stopping. So she wanted to put this awkward wedge between them? He could work with that. He could handle anything she wanted to throw his way.

"I'm fine. I'm going to head up and check on my clothes."

He didn't wait for her to turn around or reply. Shuffling back upstairs, Braden was eager to get out of this makeshift skirt because he was going to have to revoke his man card if he didn't get back into pants soon.

Once he was dressed, they needed to talk. Zara was closing back in on herself, and there was no way he was going to let that happen. He may not be the man in her life, but he wasn't about to let her think that her feelings, her emotions meant nothing. Whatever pricks had taken her to bed in the past had let her think less of herself. Most likely they'd been selfish, too, and Braden refused to be lumped with those guys.

Regardless of what happened after he left this house, he wanted Zara to know her self-worth.

Braden placed the comforter back on the bed, smoothing out the edges, and pulled on his boxer briefs. They were damp but better than nothing. His pants were still wet, so he turned them and placed them even closer to the fire.

He'd called one of his contacts at the sheriff's department before calling his brother. Apparently the road crews were working around the clock, but with the layer of ice beneath the snow, there wasn't much chance of getting out within the next two days because the temperatures were still hovering below zero.

Perfect opportunity for him to keep up his search and prove to Zara that they were good together in bed. He wasn't asking for her hand in marriage; he just wanted to enjoy her company while he was here, and who knew, maybe after he left.

He chuckled at the fact he was strutting around her room in his underwear. She may not find the matter funny at all, but it was. Braden was snooping like Ryker and seducing like Mac…a position he never thought he'd find himself in as head of the family.

As he took a seat on the bed and sent off a quick text to Ryker, the cat rubbed against Braden's ankle. Reaching down, Braden lifted the fur ball on to the bed and started stroking his back.

The kitten let out a soft purr and flopped over on to his back. Braden continued to show affection, and his mind started drifting. He had no clue what he expected from Zara. Somewhere along the way he'd gone from wanting to use her, to wanting the hell out of her, to wondering more about her and wanting to uncover those complex layers she kept so guarded.

But he couldn't let himself get too involved. He wasn't ready to start looking for "the one." What he felt for Zara had nothing to do with forever and everything to do with right now. When she'd actually let go, let him close, he'd seen a woman with pent-up passion. All of that desire she kept locked away was a shame. She deserved to be…

What? Used? Because that's where he was right at this point. He was using her and justifying it by saying they had a physical connection. But damn it, he'd never denied himself anything before and he wasn't about to start now. He still wanted Zara, but she deserved more than a man who wanted her in bed and to technically steal from her.

The bedroom door swung open, and Zara came in juggling an oversize box. Braden leaped off the bed and crossed the room, taking the box from her hold.

"Let me have it," he said when she hesitated to let go. "You carried this up the steps when I could've done it." Once he set the box down at the end of the bed, he turned back to Zara. "You should've asked for help."

Her eyes took in his body, and he couldn't help the instant male reaction. "Zara—"

Those heavy-lidded eyes snapped up to his. "You have got to put clothes on."

"If I thought you really wanted me to, if you weren't just looking at me like you wanted me again, I would throw on those damp things and put you at ease."

She stared for a moment before a bubble of laughter escaped her. "At ease? That's the last thing you're trying to do here."

When she tried to step around him, Braden moved to block her. His hands gripped her shoulders, and he tipped his head down to look her in the eye.

"You're even more withdrawn than you were before we slept together. Care to tell me what's going through your mind?"

Those bright eyes darted to his, then to the bed where the kitten lay stretched out. "I'm just trying to keep this from getting too awkward. Okay? We need to go back to boss/employee."

Braden released her, took a step back and nodded. "That doesn't mean I wouldn't have helped you with the box."

For now he let the subject drop, but he wasn't leaving anytime soon, and no doubt they'd revisit their status again. Whether he had clothes on or not, she was strung so damn tight no matter how he looked. And now that he'd had her in every way, he wanted her again. So much for getting her out of his system.

"What's in the box? I thought you were going down for a notebook."

She maneuvered around him and pulled on the folded flaps until they sprang open with a puff of dust. Coughing and waving her hand in front of her face, Zara turned to face him. "I've been putting off going through some of my grandmother's things. They've been boxed up for a while. Long before her death, she wanted to downsize, so she started packing things away and putting them in a storage unit. I only had them brought back so I didn't have to keep paying the unit fee. This house is more than big enough to hold all her things. I have no clue what all she's put away and I've been too busy to look through them. I figure now would be a good time since I'm stuck here. Maybe after I go through her stuff, I will start unpacking my own."

Braden heard every word, but he focused on the fact her grandmother had boxes packed away, and now they were back in the house. These boxes wouldn't have been in here during the search Ryker did. Did he dare hope he could uncover the scrolls that were somewhere so simple as packed away in a box?

Braden leaned forward, glancing into the box. "I can get the other boxes and bring them up here for you."

Zara knelt down on her knees and started sorting through the newspaper-wrapped goods. "They're actually down in the basement. And let me just say, if you think the first floor is cold, that basement is frigid."

Braden laughed, more out of his own anxiety and nerves over the potential in the basement, but Zara relaxed at his actions. "Tell you what, I'll go down and bring up more. You start going through this box."

She crossed her arms and rubbed them, most likely trying to get rid of the chill from being downstairs. "I hate to have you do that. I can get them later."

No way in hell was he backing down on this, not when everything his family had wanted could be right within his reach. "Which boxes am I looking for? Are they all needing to come up?"

"Now who's stubborn?" she asked, lifting her brows and smiling. "Fine, you can get them. They're on the far wall. I believe there's about five more. All the others are mine, but they're under the steps."

Braden nodded and barely resisted the urge to rush out

the door. Then he remembered he was wearing only his underwear.

Zara glanced up at him; her gaze roaming over his body only heated him even more, making him want to put those boxes on hold and give into that look of desire staring back at him.

"You're going to freeze your important parts off if you don't put something on."

His inflated ego took control as Braden propped his hands on his hips and grinned down at her. "Worried about my parts?"

"You'll be needing them again."

He continued to stare until her face flushed.

"With someone else, I mean. Not with me," she quickly added. "I just meant… Wipe that smug look off your face and put your damn pants on."

Laughing, Braden went over to check, and sure enough his pants were nearly dry except for the damp waistband. He could handle that. After dressing, he glanced at the items she was pulling out of the current box. So far just a few old pieces of pottery. Not the scrolls.

Maybe they were hidden in the basement. Maybe they were in the boxes he was about to bring up…not before he searched through them, though.

And if that was the case, if he did indeed find the centuries old treasures, he could finally give back to his family what they'd been searching for.

He could also pursue Zara with his full concentration, because the way she'd been looking at him moments ago— yeah, she wasn't over whatever they'd started, and he'd barely scratched the surface of all he wanted to do with her.

As soon as Braden was out the door, Zara blew out a breath. Mercy, but that man strutting around in his black boxer briefs was a sight to behold. He could easily put models to shame with that broad chest, those lean hips and those muscles…she'd felt every single one of them, and if she were totally honest, she wanted to again.

No matter what she told herself, no matter the common sense that normally kept her grounded, all she could think of was how amazing Braden would be if they actually took advantage of this situation and stayed in bed exploring each other.

But what would happen once the roads cleared and Braden went home? She'd work his party in a few weeks, and they'd be professional…sure. How could she watch him from across the room, knowing full well what an attentive lover he was while she should be focusing on the hors d'oeuvres and making sure the Riesling fountain kept flowing?

Zara closed her eyes and willed herself to gain some sort of control over her emotions before he came back. She needed to concentrate on sorting through these boxes. Who knew, with all of the antiques and treasures her grandmother hung on to, maybe Braden would be interested in some pieces for the auction house.

There. When he came back, they would focus on work and not the fact they were going to spend another night together. Granted, it didn't matter whether it was night or not—they'd had sex in the middle of the day.

Day sex. That was new for Zara. Not that she had some big grand arsenal of partners and experiences, but she'd always been a night, dark room, vanilla type. Maybe that's why she wanted to explore more with Braden. He'd awakened something in her, and she wasn't sure she could ignore it now. What else could he show her? Braden O'Shea was a full-body experience, that was for sure.

Zara shook her head, hoping to clear some of these crazy thoughts. She reached into the box and pulled out another paper-covered object. As she unwrapped the oblong container, she wondered what could be in this tube she'd never seen before.

Zara set the paper to the side and concentrated on the silver caps on each end. She pulled on one, then the other. Either they didn't open or they were seriously stuck. Whatever was in there was extremely light. She shook the tube, but nothing rattled.

"I forgot a flash—"

Zara turned toward the door just as Braden's eyes zeroed in on the container she held.

"Don't touch that." One second he was by the door, the next he was kneeling at her side, taking the tube from her hands. "Did you look inside?"

Stunned at his reaction, Zara stared at him and shook her head. "The caps are stuck."

He ran his hands over the outer shell as if he was dealing with the most precious of gems. She'd never seen this side of him. She could sit here completely naked, and he'd not even notice she was in the room. For a man who was hell-bent on seduction and succeeding rather well at it, he was completely focused on this container.

Which made her wonder, what the hell was in that tube, and why was he so mesmerized with it?

Eleven

Braden had no idea if he was actually holding one of the coveted scrolls. All he knew was he wanted to get inside this tube now, but he didn't want to break anything or cause damage. This container was old, not as old as the scrolls themselves, but he had no idea what they would be stored in at this point. And with the way the caps were so secured, they'd obviously been in place a while. Which only added to that layer of hope.

Holding on to the tube, he glanced toward the box. "Anymore like this in there?"

Zara reached in but only brought out a wrapped vase that was rather valuable with familiar etching. He'd worry about the other treasures later, because if he was truly holding a scroll that dated back to the time of Shakespeare, that meant the others could be in the boxes in the basement.

Braden lifted the tube and pulled gently on one of the caps again. It was sealed good and tight. While he was maneuvering as cautiously as he could, Zara got up and went out the door. He had no clue where she was going or what she was doing; all he knew was he needed to get in this compartment right now.

Both ends were good and stuck, and all he could think of was how fast he could search the other boxes for more tubes and how quick he could get Ryker to look into this. Something akin to elation flooded him as he gripped this container. Could he have found what his father hadn't been able to? Could he finally bring these back to the O'Shea family? As head of the family, he felt the pressure to do what his father hadn't been able to.

His family prided themselves on their business, yet they hadn't been able to relocate their own inheritance after decades of trying. All the frustration and anger and stomps on their pride may finally be coming to an end.

They'd hunted down so many false leads over the years, but now Braden wanted to focus on the last point of origin. This house held the answers; he just had to know where to look, and he may have struck gold.

Braden held on to the tube and stepped into the cool hallway. Where had she gone? He called her name, waiting to hear her reply. Silence greeted him, but then she appeared at the top of the stairs with the kitten beneath her arm. Even though the little guy nestled against her, Zara still didn't look comfortable with her new friend.

Maybe Laney shouldn't get this kitten, after all. Perhaps Zara needed this bonding experience to get her to open up, to not be afraid of any type of a relationship. Animals had that effect on people.

"What were you doing?" he asked.

"You left the door open, and he darted out." She stopped before him and held the cat out to his chest. "You were too preoccupied with whatever is in that cylinder and didn't see him run out the door."

Braden winced at the harshness of her tone and knew he needed to come up with a quick cover so she didn't get too suspicious. He'd never expected her to be around when he found something of interest, so holding back his emotions hadn't crossed his mind.

"Sorry. Occupational hazard. Old treasures get the best of me."

She quirked a brow as if she wanted to argue, but didn't say a word as she brushed by him and went into the bedroom. Braden followed, closing the door and placing the cat back down on the rug. He immediately went to the paper and packaging beside the box and started swatting and playing.

"Did you get that open?" she asked, pointing to the tube.

"No." He needed to be careful how he approached this. The last thing he needed was for Zara to distrust him. "I'd like to have Ryker look, if you don't mind."

She shifted slightly, and her brows drew in. "Ryker is a friend of yours?"

"He's more than a friend." How did he even explain Ryker? Ryker was more of an experience than a person. The man was a force to be reckoned with. He butted heads with Braden more often than not, but the man was loyal to a fault. "If anyone can get into this and not do any damage to the container, it would be him."

Zara stared at him before her eyes darted to the tube in his hand. "What do you think is in there that's so important? It felt empty to me."

A paper wouldn't weigh much, and if this was indeed one of his family's scrolls, Braden wanted it to be opened without Zara present. Waiting to get this to Ryker would be a true test of self-control, but Braden had come this far; he wasn't about to destroy the tube by breaking it to get in.

"Old documents could be hidden," he told her. "You never know what you can find stored away. We've uncovered some pretty important things from all over the world when people thought containers were empty."

"I don't care if you take it to look in, but you'll let me know what's inside, right?"

"Of course." He refused to feel guilty about lying to her face. If the scroll was indeed inside, it would be of no use to her.

Well, she could sell it for a ridiculous amount of money, but the worth to the O'Sheas was invaluable. Braden was so hyped up on adrenaline with the possibilities, he could hardly stand still. He needed to contact Mac.

Braden set the tube on the side table by the door and pulled his cell from his pocket. He quickly shot Mac a text that he'd found an old tube, but couldn't confirm the contents.

"I'm going to head back downstairs." Braden glanced around the room, searching for the flashlight. "I'll get those other boxes."

"I'd like to talk to you about selling some pieces." Zara had taken a seat back on the floor and was wrapping items back up and placing them in the box. "I'm not sure how that works or even if you'd be interested for the auction house, but…"

She was back to being nervous. And to be honest, he was a bit nervous, too, because he had no clue how to proceed from here. He'd never been in this position before. Sex with women was something he'd always enjoyed, yet he'd never gotten emotionally attached. Casual relationships worked fine, but in his line of work, getting too close to someone was difficult. One day he wanted a family, but he truly had to find the right woman who would fit into his life…first he had to steer the business into a bit more legit territory.

But he kept feeling this pull toward Zara, a pull he'd not experienced with any other woman.

So why Zara? Why now? Did it all stem from needing to gain trust? He'd never had to rely on someone like this before. He'd never placed himself at the mercy of needing anyone; he purposely didn't leave himself vulnerable.

"I can look through whatever you want," he replied. "If

we agree on certain items, you have a few options we can go over."

She nodded, and the tension in her shoulders seemed to lessen as her body relaxed. "Good. I hate getting rid of her things, but at the same time, I can't keep everything."

Braden knew that ache, that need to hang on to possessions of lost loved ones. He'd still not gone through his father's belongings and he wasn't sure when he'd be ready to face that daunting task. Mac and Laney weren't ready, either. Thankfully, they were all there for each other because family meant everything to the O'Sheas. They clung to each other in times of trial. Ryker may be a hard-ass, but the man was just as much family as any blood relative, and he'd grieved right along with the rest of them after Patrick's death.

"Let me get those boxes, and we can spend the day looking through them and deciding where to go from there." When she smiled up at him, Braden had to ignore that punch of lust to the gut. She was trusting him…and he was betraying her. "Be right back."

Before he could be swept under by those mesmerizing eyes, he snatched the flashlight off the bed and headed back to the basement. Right now he needed to focus on what they would uncover, on how this could possibly end his family's hunt for what was rightfully theirs. He couldn't think how Zara was slowly getting under his skin, how she was softening toward him and opening and driving him out of his ever-loving mind.

Because if he started letting Zara have control over his mind, she'd start silently taking control over other aspects of his life. And he couldn't afford to be sidetracked right now. Not when he was so close to getting everything he'd ever wanted.

Zara ran her fingers over the pewter picture frame. "I remember this picture sitting by her bed."

The black-and-white photo of a young, newly married couple stared back at her. Her grandparents on their wedding day, standing outside the courthouse because they hadn't wanted to wait for a big ceremony in a church. They'd fallen in love and hadn't wanted to spend another minute apart.

Tears pricked Zara's eyes. "Sorry," she said, smiling as she blinked back the moisture. "I get a little sentimental when it comes to my gram."

Sitting with his back against the headboard on the bed, Braden stretched his legs out as he stared down at her. Zara sat on the floor, legs crossed, looking through yet another box. Every now and then she'd pass a piece up to him to get his opinion on selling, but now she'd found a box of photos.

Braden extended his hand toward the picture, so Zara passed it over. "My grandfather was the love of her life. She never quite got over his death, even though she lived without him for nearly twenty years."

Braden studied the picture, then glanced back down to her. "And you still don't believe in true love?"

Zara rolled her eyes and swiped at the tear that escaped. "I believe my grandparents found it, but my parents sure as hell didn't. They were more concerned with making money and traveling than they were with love or family."

Propping the photo up on the nightstand, Braden adjusted it so it faced at just the right angle. "Love exists, Zara. If you want it, you just have to wait until it finds you."

Zara had always been sure that if she ever heard a man mention love, she'd run fast and far because he only wanted something from her.

This wasn't like any scenario she'd planned in her mind. For one thing, Braden wasn't professing his love by any means. Second, even if he was, he couldn't use her for anything. He was an O'Shea. One of the most powerful families in Boston and known around the world. There was nothing he could gain from getting involved with her.

"You're unlike any man I've ever met," she told him, trying not to think too hard about how amazing he looked taking up so much space in her bed. "I don't know many men who are so open at discussing love and relationships, let alone a man who claims he's wanting a wife and marriage."

"Family is everything to me. I want kids and a wife." He shrugged as if the explanation were so simple and not to be questioned. "When I find the woman for me, I'll do anything in my power to keep her safe and to make sure that she knows she's loved at all times. My woman will never question where I stand."

The more he spoke, the more stern he became. Zara knew without a doubt that he believed love existed, and she also believed there would be one woman who would come along, capture his attention and live happily ever after because she truly didn't think Braden failed at anything he set his mind to.

"Well, there is one lucky lady in your future."

Zara pushed off the floor and scooted the box to the wall. Turning, she scanned the other unopened boxes and finally decided on one that wasn't marked. Grabbing it, she took a seat at the foot of the bed on the opposite side. She faced Braden and pulled the lid off the box. Breath caught in her throat as she reached in and ran her hand over the silky yarn. Slowly, she pulled the crochet item from the box.

Zara smiled as she laid the bright red throw across her lap. "I remember when she made this," Zara murmured, running her fingers across the tight weave. "She'd asked me what color she should make, and I told her red. I remember thinking she was such a lively woman, brown or gray wouldn't do. When she was finished, she held it up and wrapped it around my shoulders. I was sitting on the couch doing homework."

Zara pulled the piece up to her face and inhaled. That familiar vanilla scent she associated with her grandmother hit her hard. A vice gripped her heart as she willed back the emotions. The bed dipped just slightly before a hand settled on her bent knee.

"It's hard losing someone you love, someone you've depended on."

His soft words washed over her, offering comfort when she really had no one else. How pathetic had her life become that she slept with her boss and had no close friends to turn to for support? Had she seriously alienated herself because she'd been so engrossed with work?

No, she could admit the truth to herself. Commitment terrified her. Being dependent on someone, knowing they could leave at any moment and take her heart with them had her refusing to allow herself to open up to anyone. She didn't care if she was lonely. She'd rather be alone than broken.

Dropping her hands back into her lap, Zara lifted her gaze to Braden. He'd been so passionate earlier, so attentive to her needs sexually. But now he looked at her with care and compassion, and she truly had no idea what to think of him or even how to act. He could make her want things… things she'd never wanted before.

"This is all so strange to me," she admitted. "Before I started working for you, I'd heard rumors of how badass you were. Then I saw it firsthand when you threw Shane out of the party. Then you take in a kitten, snuggle with it, for crying out loud, and you look as if you want to hug me, and not for anything sexually related. I'm not sure which Braden I'll see from moment to moment."

His eyes hardened, his jaw clenched, but he didn't remove his hand. "The badass Braden trumps the nice one. I'm not a nice guy, Zara. I'm selfish, and I take what I want when I want it."

Shivers raced through her. He'd taken exactly what he'd wanted where she was concerned…not that she was complaining.

Zara covered his hand. "You're a nice guy when it counts. You'll never convince me otherwise."

He looked as if he wanted to say more, but he eased back and slid off the other side of the bed. She watched as he surveyed the boxes littering her bedroom.

"So you only have one more to go through," he stated as he headed for the largest box he'd brought up from the basement. She knew he was changing the subject, which had been her tactic all along. "It was heavy, so you may want to come over here to look through it, or I can pull out items and bring them to you."

Zara swung her legs off the bed and headed toward the box. "Let's see what this one has, and then we can discuss what I'll be selling."

Because the tender moment that had just happened couldn't happen again—clearly it had left them both shaken. She needed to keep her wits about her and remember that she was still his employee, she was still needing this reputable job to keep her business going in the right direction, and she needed to forget how this man made her body tingle in ways she never knew possible…and how he was acting as if he truly cared.

Twelve

They'd had a gourmet dinner of crackers, lunch meat, cheese and some fruit. Zara had grabbed a bottle of wine from the cellar, and now she sat on the chaise, legs stretched before her, her back against the side arm as she twirled the stem of her wineglass.

The poor kitten was going stir-crazy, so Zara had taken him for a walk through the house. Braden was already seeing their bond form, but he wasn't about to call her on it. She'd realize soon enough.

As the kitten pounced on her shoe, Zara watched him. "Should we give him a name or something?"

"Does this mean you're keeping him?"

Zara threw Braden a look. "I didn't say that. I just feel like he should be called something other than *Cat*."

Braden laughed. "Admit it, you like him."

"I'll call him Jack while he's here," she decided.

"Jack?"

Zara nodded. "Jack Frost."

Braden smiled at the perfect name. "Jack it is."

Zara didn't want to make commitments, didn't want to have to worry about anyone else but herself, and Braden understood her reasons. But at some point she'd have to put herself out there, even if it was with a cat. She was going to be one lonely person if she kept herself so distanced. He wouldn't know what he'd do without his family.

"So, what's it like having siblings?" she asked, staring into her glass…her fourth glass if he was counting correctly. "Being an only child sucked sometimes."

Braden shifted his back against the side of the bed, brought his knee up and reached out to pet Jack as he came over and slid against Zara's leg. Braden had stopped at three glasses of wine. He was a big guy, so he wasn't feeling anything, and one of them had to keep their wits about them. Apparently that responsibility fell to him.

"We had our moments," he admitted. "Laney is the baby, and she gets a bit angry when Mac and I look out for her. She's determined, stubborn, always putting others first, even at the sacrifice of her own happiness." He narrowed his gaze, which he knew she could see since they had lit candles and she was only a few feet away, staring right at him. "Sounds like someone else I know."

Zara took a sip of wine. "I prefer career driven."

Braden laughed as went on. "Mac and I tend to get along now, but when we were younger we pretty much caused havoc in the house. Mom passed when I was ten, Mac was seven and Laney was only four. That was about the time Ryker started coming around, too."

Propping her elbow on the arm of the chaise, Zara rested her head in her hand and settled the base of the wineglass in front of her, still holding on to the rim with those delicate fingers. "You speak of him quite a bit. You all are really close. I can hear the affection in your tone when you talk of your family."

When she discussed her parents, all that had laced her

tone was disdain. The only love he heard from her was when she told stories of her grandmother.

"We've always been a close family. My parents were adamant about that. We may fight, yell, even throw a few punches, but when it comes down to it, I know my family always has my back, and they know I always have theirs."

Zara smiled. "Unconditional love." She drained the rest of her glass, then sat it on the small accent table on the other side of the arm. "I bet when you all were younger you had snowball fights in weather like this."

Braden nodded, his hand stilled on the kitten's back as he replayed one particular day. "My brother, Mac, has a scar running through his brow as a souvenir from one of our snowball fights."

Zara's eyes widened. "He got cut from snow?"

"He got cut because our sister threw a snowball that had a rock in it. She's a lot stronger than she looks, but she had no idea about the rock. Trust me, she felt awful, and Mac played on her guilt for years."

She made a soft noise of acknowledgment, nearly a tender tone that had him almost hating how he was reliving these memories when she didn't have too many happy ones. But she wanted to hear them, and he actually enjoyed sharing stories of his family...so long as people didn't start butting into the family business and asking unnecessary questions.

"I bet you all had a big Christmas tree, family vacations, huge birthday parties."

"Yes to all of that," he confirmed. "The downfall of the siblings, when you're a kid, no matter what you got for a present, you had to share. I never liked that rule. When something belongs to me, it's mine for good."

Zara's lids lowered a touch, from the alcohol or from the double meaning she'd taken from his words. Had he subconsciously said that just for her benefit? Maybe, maybe not, but he wasn't sorry now that the words were out.

"This morning, when we…you know…"

"Had sex," he finished when she trailed off. He had no clue where she was going with this, but he knew exactly what topic she was dancing around when she couldn't even say the words.

"Yes. I didn't handle that very well." Her fingertip toyed with the binding running along the outer cushion; her eyes remained fixed on his, though, which only made her sexier, to realize that she wasn't afraid to face this head-on.

"I don't know," he amended. "I think you handled the sex perfectly."

A flirty smile spread across her lips. "I meant afterward. I'm not used to such a giving lover. I didn't know how to react, and with you being my boss, I thought it was easiest to just ignore everything and try to pretend we were on the same level playing field as before we stripped out of our clothes."

Braden didn't say a word. The wine was apparently making her more chatty than usual, and now that she was discussing the proverbial elephant in the room, he wanted to know what she had to say.

"I guess I should've said thank you," she added quickly. "Circumstances have us here together, and you could've been selfish, you could've totally ignored me after, but you didn't. You were…"

"If you say nice I'm going to be angry."

"Sweet."

Braden groaned. "I would've rather been nice."

He eyed her for another minute, more than aware of the crackling tension that had just been amped up in the past two minutes.

"I'm trying to thank you," she went on, talking louder to drown out his mumble. "It's refreshing to know there are guys like you out there."

Guys like him? He wanted to laugh, he wanted to confess just how ruthless he truly was and he wanted her to never look for a man like him in the future. Yes, he'd been caring in bed; yes, he'd rescued a cat. Those were qualities any man should possess. Braden didn't go above and beyond. For one thing, her pleasure brought him pleasure. Call it primal, territorial, whatever. When Zara had been turned on, that made him all chest-bumping, ego-inflated happy because he'd caused her arousal, her excitement.

"Does that mean you're looking for a guy who will treat you right, and you're done with the asshats you've been dating?" he asked.

"Maybe it means I want you to show me again how a woman should be treated."

Braden froze. The bold statement slammed into him. Nothing much could catch him off guard, but this woman kept him on his toes.

"Your wine is talking," he stated, attempting to blow it off, give her an out in case she hadn't meant to say that aloud.

"Maybe so," she admitted. "Or I'm just saying what I've been thinking all day. Every time I'd look at you or accidentally touch you, I'd think back to how amazing this morning was. Even though a relationship would be a huge mistake, I'm finding it rather difficult to stay over here while you're in my bed."

Had the heat cranked up more in here? Braden was sweating after that speech she just delivered.

Zara stretched out even more on the chaise and rolled on to her back, staring up at the ceiling as she continued to talk. "Wanting you isn't new, though. You know what you look like. I'm sure women throw themselves at you all the time. I don't want to be that typical, predictable woman."

"Baby, you're anything but typical and predictable."

Her soft laugh wrapped him in warmth. "I'll take that as a compliment and I like when you call me baby. But I meant that I wanted you when I first saw you, but this job had to take precedence and I refused to be so trite as to hit on my boss."

Oh, he would've loved had she come into his office that first day and had her way with him. Before his fantasy carried him away too much, Braden concentrated on her as she continued.

"Then I was mortified you had to see that whole incident with Shane, but when you and I were dancing, I wasn't thinking about Shane. I was thinking how great you smelled, powerful and manly."

Braden smiled into the dim light. She would be so embarrassed tomorrow when she woke and realized all she'd verbally spewed out tonight. But there was no way in hell he was stopping her.

"Now that you're stuck here, all I can think about is how amazing this morning was and how I'm going to lie here tonight and replay it in my mind."

Braden came to his knees and slowly closed the space between them. He laid a hand across her abdomen, startling her as she jerked to stare him in the eyes. Their faces were inches apart, so close he could ease forward just a touch and have that mouth beneath his in seconds. From this closer vantage point, he could see the slight flush in her cheeks from the wine, the moist lips where she'd licked them from being nervous, the pulse point at the base of her neck.

"Who said you had to lie here and replay it?" he asked, easing his hand beneath her shirt. His palm flattened out on her stomach, and the quivering beneath his touch only added to his desire for her. "Maybe that bed was lonely last night. Maybe I got sick of rolling over and inhaling your jasmine scent. Maybe I was awake all night wondering when you'd come to your senses and join me."

Zara lifted her arms, her hands resting on either side of her face. The innocent move, or maybe not-so-innocent, arched her back and pressed her breasts up.

"I couldn't join you, Braden. I don't have a good track

record with men, not that I'm looking for one right now, and I couldn't risk my job no matter how much I wanted you. Besides, I would've died had you rejected me."

That right there was the crux of her issue. Rejection. She'd been rejected by so many people. Well, maybe not so many in quantity, but definitely all of the important people, save for her grandmother. She feared rejection, and here he was using her. Taking advantage of a vulnerable woman was a straight ticket to hell.

"I wouldn't have rejected you," he murmured. "I was battling myself back at my party because I just wanted to drag you into a room, a closet, anywhere that we could be alone, and I could show you how much I wanted you."

He trailed his fingertips over her heated skin, earning him a swift intake of breath as her eyes drifted closed. "That wouldn't have looked very good for my reputation," she muttered. "I'm a professional and I can't afford for people to think I slept with you to get the job."

"Nobody will think that," he assured her. He'd make damn sure she had more jobs lined up than she could handle. He'd make sure she could choose the ones she wanted and didn't have to worry about taking them all.

"Keep touching me, Braden." Her voice, a throaty whisper, washed over him. "Your touch feels so good."

She was killing him. Those soft moans, her body all laid out on display. He'd told her he wasn't a nice guy and he was primed and ready to snap and take what she was blatantly offering. But he wouldn't want anyone else treating Zara disrespectfully. She deserved better than a man who couldn't control his hormones and took advantage of the fact she loved wine and couldn't hold it like the rest of his Irish family.

"Zara." He stilled his hand to get her attention, to let her know he couldn't take her to bed. But her soft snore greeted him. Braden sat back on his heels, kept his hand on her stomach and simply stared.

When was the last time she'd fully let go and relaxed? Did she trust anyone in her life on a personal level, or were all of her acquaintances the closest things she had to family and friends? Dating men who were users, jerks and not looking for commitment was a surefire way to keep yourself closed off from the world. Zara was excelling at being a loner. The irony wasn't lost on him that she planned parties and lavish bashes for people to mingle, socialize and enjoy the company of others, yet she refused to put herself in a position to enjoy anyone.

From the investigating he'd done before hiring her officially, he'd learned she'd had a small apartment in Boston, mostly kept to herself and rarely dated. She threw herself into her work, and it showed, but wasn't there more to life?

Braden snorted. Yeah, there was, and he was going to find it as soon as his family business was a bit more secure in a new territory.

As he watched her sleep, something shifted inside him. He didn't want that damn shift. He didn't want to care so much about Zara, about her loveless childhood and how it molded her into the fierce woman she was today.

All Braden wanted to do was wake her up, take her to bed and make love to her all night. Then he wanted to get home tomorrow and show Mac that tube so they could figure out how the hell to proceed from here.

Yet none of that was going to happen, so here he sat staring at the most complex, beautiful woman he'd ever known. Parts of her reminded Braden of his sister. He hadn't been feeding Zara a line of bull earlier when he'd said that, either. But Laney had something Zara didn't, and that was the strength and backing of a family.

It bothered him more than it should that Zara had nobody. He'd been fully aware of her living situation and family life before he'd hired her. He'd made a point to know exactly who Zara Perkins was so he could come at her the right way, the way that would ensure she trust him, work for him and allow him access into her home.

Granted, he hadn't planned on a snowstorm, but he wasn't looking a gift horse, or Mother Nature, in the mouth.

Braden sighed and raked a hand through his hair. He should rest, he should get back up and start searching. But he didn't want to do any of that. Not when Zara's body felt so warm beneath his palm, not when she was sleeping so peacefully and beautifully.

For once, he wasn't thinking work or how to get those coveted scrolls. No, for once Braden O'Shea was soaking in all of the goodness from another, hoping it would somehow rub off on him and make him not so much of a bastard. Because if Zara ever found out what he'd done, she'd hate him forever.

And that chilling thought scared the hell out of him.

Thirteen

Zara rolled over onto her side, coming to rest against a warm leg just as her arm crossed over a taut chest. She stilled, blinking into the darkness. No candles were burning, but the soft glow from the logs helped her get her bearings. She wasn't on the chaise where she'd been drinking her wine.

Wine. Zara froze. She'd gotten pretty chatty if she recalled correctly, but thankfully she was still dressed. So nothing had happened between Braden and her, but she was lying in bed beside him. Had he put her here?

Zara slowly started easing back to her side instead of crawling all over her temporary roommate.

"And here I thought you wanted to touch me."

Braden's thick tone filled the room.

"I didn't mean to… I had no idea we were…that you were…"

Lightning fast, Braden grabbed her arm and held her still. "Don't move. I put you here because I want you here."

Zara had to admit being in her own bed with her feather-down duvet was like heaven. Okay, fine, she loved being next to this man, knowing that he carried her and put her in bed, then climbed in beside her. What woman wouldn't get all giddy over that fact?

"Did I ask you to have sex with me again?" Mercy, the fact she had to even ask that question was even more embarrassing than the actual question.

"You implied you were willing."

Pathetic, party of one?

"Which just proves my theory that you're a nice guy."

In an instant, Braden had her on her back, her hands above her head, the entire length of his body on hers. "Do you feel light-headed at all? Headache? Dizziness?"

Breathless from their current state, Zara shook her head. "Why?"

"Because I'm about to strip you and take you up on that offer now. I want you to be fully aware of what I'm doing to you."

His lips captured hers before she could even comprehend what he was saying, but words were moot at this point. The fierce kiss, the tilt of his hips against hers and the way he gripped her wrists above her head were all very telling signs as to what he wanted. Added to that, her body had lit up from within, and she wanted everything he was willing to give her. She wasn't denying herself, not now, not with Braden.

He was right. She dated jerks. She did so to keep a distance and not form any relationship. So why shouldn't she sleep with a man who was considerate, obviously wanted her and wasn't asking for any type of commitment?

Oh, right. He was her boss. Well, at the moment, her boss was removing her pants and panties right along with them. Even as Zara's mind told her to put a stop to this, her body shifted so he could continue ridding her of the unwanted clothes.

She kicked the pants off her ankles and groaned when

Braden placed open-mouth kisses on her stomach. She threaded her hands through his hair. She'd already slept with him once; stopping now wouldn't change what had already happened. And Braden's promise of stripping her down was already proving to be amazing because he currently had his teeth on the hem of her shirt, sliding it up her torso.

When the material bunched at her breasts, she tried to pull her hands free to help.

"I've got this," he whispered. "Your only job is to relax and let me work."

Who was she to argue? He was her boss, after all.

He eased back enough to jerk the shirt over her head and toss it to the floor.

"If that cat pees on my—"

Braden's tongue trailed down her throat and into the valley of her breasts, cutting off any thought she'd had. Zara's back arched—she couldn't move much with his weight on her, but she wiggled beneath him enough to let him know he was absolutely driving her mad with this slow pace he'd set.

"Braden," she whispered. "Please."

"Anything."

He cupped one breast, stroking her skin with his thumb, his other hand trailing down her side and settling on her hip. His mouth, his hands—he seemed to be touching her all over at once. Zara's legs shifted anxiously, waiting for his next move. How could he be so thorough when she just wanted him to touch her where she ached the most?

Finally he slid his fingertips over her thighs, inching higher. Zara tilted her hips, near ready to beg him for more when he finally covered her with his hand. She eased her legs wider, giving him the access he needed.

While his fingers stroked her, he moved his other hand to lace their fingers together over her chest. His lips slid over her abdomen, and Zara thought she was going to shoot up off this bed if he didn't finish her soon.

"You're squirming," he murmured against her stomach. "You're going too slow."

His soft laughter filled the room. "I'm hanging on by a thread trying to give you pleasure, and you're complaining."

Zara pulled her hand from his and framed his face, forcing him to look up at her. "Put us both out of our misery. I want you. Now."

Braden crawled up her body, leaned over to the nightstand and pulled out a condom, quickly sheathing himself. When he rested his hands on either side of her head and hovered right above her, Zara's gaze locked on to his. Something flickered in his eyes, something she'd never seen from him before…or any other man for that matter. Before she could read too much into it, he plunged into her, making her cry out.

Gone was the slow, patient Braden. This Braden had snapped, was staking his claim and pulling her into his web of passion and desire.

His lips trailed over her shoulder, her neck, up her jawline as he continued to pump his hips. Zara could only grip his biceps and arch into him because he was in total control and doing everything absolutely perfectly.

Perfect. That was the one word that kept coming to mind every time she thought of Braden and how they were together.

When he kissed her, roughly, passionately, all thoughts evaporated. Her entire body heated, rising higher and higher as he increased the pace.

"Braden," she panted against his mouth. "Braden… I…"

He kissed his way to her ear and whispered, "Zara."

Her name softly on his lips when his body was so hard, so intensely moving against hers was enough to set her over the edge. She couldn't control the tremors racking her body; she couldn't control the way she screamed his name, clawed his shoulders.

Braden's entire body tensed as he arched back. Clenching his jaw, he stared down at her as he climaxed. The intensity of his stare stirred something so deep within her, so deep she was positive nobody had ever even uncovered that area before.

But Braden had. He'd uncovered so much about her, even more than she knew about herself.

When Braden eased on to his back, pulling her to sprawl on top of him, Zara could no longer deny the fact she was falling for her boss. And she could say that with certainty because he was the only man to ever care, to ever put her first, to ever pull feelings from her she hadn't even known she'd possessed.

The best part was that he did every bit of that without even trying. He just…was. He was everything she hadn't known she was looking for, and here he was, holding her so tightly after he'd made love to her in her own bed. His heart beat against her chest, and Zara had never been more aware of another the way she was with Braden.

The question now was what did she do about these feelings she never wanted? They were too strong to ignore, they were too scary to act on, but she'd never backed down from fear before.

Now she just had to figure out how to be strong, keep her business with the O'Sheas and keep Braden in her personal life for good.

Braden woke to a sleeping Zara on his chest, her hair spread all around him. Something had happened in the middle of the night…something that had nothing to do with the sex. There had been a new level introduced. How the hell had that happened? He'd seen something in Zara's eyes and he knew full well it was more than desire, more than lust.

But what scared him most was what she may have seen in his own eyes. He knew what he'd been feeling when they'd been together. Even if he was only admitting it to himself, he was feeling more for Zara than just physical attraction.

Raking a hand over his face, he reached to the bedside table for his phone and turned it on. The battery was starting to get low, but as soon as the phone powered on, his texts lit up. Apparently the road level was downgraded, and he could get out now. Did he tell Zara, or did he continue to stay here and search her house? He'd found the one tube that could be holding a scroll and he desperately wanted to get it into Mac's hands.

The electricity was still out, but maybe the electric company would be coming through soon, since there were no driving restrictions now.

His entire home had a backup generator. Possibilities swirled around in his mind. Zara nestled closer to his side, a soft sigh escaping her lips. When her warm breath fanned across his bare chest, he knew right then that he would be going home today…and she'd be coming with him.

That primal, territorial need he had for her had intensified. The ache to see her in his home, in his bed was nearly all-consuming.

Braden shot off a quick text to Mac that he would be home later with Zara and the container. Yes, it was presumptuous to assume she'd be coming with him, but he wouldn't take no for an answer. He saw exactly how much he affected her, he felt it, and after last night, she may wake up more confused than ever; but until Braden knew what the hell was going on between them, he wasn't about to leave her alone to start thinking of all the reasons they wouldn't work.

Not to mention he didn't want her out of his sight until he learned what was in this tube, because if it did indeed hold one of the scrolls, he would have to search this house again.

Braden set his phone back on the nightstand and turned toward Zara, wrapping both arms around her. As he pulled her body flush against his, he couldn't help but wonder how he'd gotten so far into her world. He'd started with wanting to gain enough trust to get into her home, and while she'd interested him from the start, he'd be lying if he said he hadn't wanted to sleep with her; but no way in hell had he planned on getting emotionally involved.

Damn it. This complicated things.

"I'm getting spoiled," she mumbled against his chest. "Waking to a warm, naked man who's holding me. Not being able to work, eating junk all the time."

Braden raked his hands up her back, loving the feel of all that smooth, silky skin beneath his palms. "Get dressed. The roads are better so we're heading to my house."

Zara jerked back. "Your house? Are you going to ask or just demand? I'm fine right here, you know."

"My house has a backup generator, so we'll have full amenities." He kissed her temple, hoping to soften her even more. "You're more than welcome to stay here, but why don't you come with me until your house is up and running?"

She tensed beneath him, and he wasn't about to give her the chance to back out. Softly he covered her lips with his. "I want you in my bed, Zara," he murmured against her. "I need you there."

Knowing he was fighting dirty, he allowed his fingertips to trail back down. Cupping her bottom, he pulled her against his hips. "But if you don't want to join me, just say so."

Zara groaned. "You're not playing fair."

"I'm not playing at all." He nipped at her lips. "I have some work to do, but I promise we'll pick up right here later."

Her brows drew in slightly. "I don't know, Braden."

"I do." He rested his forehead against hers, knowing she needed tenderness. "If we didn't work together in anyway, would you come to my house?"

She hesitated.

"I'm not asking for anything more," he added. "I'm just not ready to let you go."

"You make it impossible to say no."

Braden laughed, kissed her softly and tipped her face up. "That's my plan. Now let's get dressed and get out of here."

As he rolled over and came to sit on the edge of the bed, the cat darted out and rubbed against Braden's ankles. His sister would definitely take this little guy in if Zara didn't. That girl took in so many stray animals, she needed to live out in the country where she had land for such things. Having a home in the middle of Boston wasn't ideal for a make-shift animal shelter.

Braden rubbed the cat's back before coming to his feet. He'd pulled on his boxers and pants when he realized Zara was still in bed, the sheet pulled up beneath her arms, covering all the delicious spots.

"What's wrong?"

She toyed with the edge of the pillowcase. "What will your family say about me coming home with you? I mean, they know me as the events coordinator. Are they going to think I'm… I don't know."

He wanted to put her uncomfortable state to rest and move on. "Just say it. What are you afraid they're going to think?"

Her eyes met his. "That I'm using you for this position."

Guilt weighed heavy on him, but he brushed aside the unwanted emotion and crossed back to the bed, taking a seat on the edge and reaching out for her hand.

"First of all, you were hired long before we slept together. Second, it's nobody's business what we're doing. And lastly, they would never think that."

Zara's eyes searched him as if she were trying to tell if he was lying or hiding something. He couldn't very well tell her his family would never think she was using him because he'd been the one to use her in the first place. She could never know the real reason he'd hired her new company. No way in hell would he want her hurt in such a manner.

Because even if the scrolls were discovered in this house, Braden wasn't so sure he wanted to give up seeing Zara.

Suddenly the quest for his family's heirlooms and the need to be with this woman were totally separate issues, both important and both he refused to back down from.

Fourteen

Zara walked through the hallway of the O'Sheas' home. Unlike the other night when she was working and in the ballroom, now she was on the second floor, following Braden to her room…which she had no doubt would actually be his room.

In one hand he pulled her suitcase, in the other he held the kitten. Everything about this seemed a bit domestic, a bit too personal. Yes, sex was personal, too, but what they'd shared last night had gone so far beyond sex, but she had no clue about the territory she'd entered and she couldn't spend too much time thinking on it or she may run screaming.

And had Braden asked her to come to his home when he'd been dressed and not rubbing all over her body, she could've used some common sense and told him this wasn't the smartest of ideas. She was safe staying in her house with the gas heater. She'd eaten just fine, thanks to the stash of Pop-Tarts, and she'd been warm. What more did she need?

Zara adjusted her laptop bag on her shoulder. Braden

had stepped into the house and promptly handed the mystery tube to Mac. They'd exchanged a look, and Zara knew they'd just had some silent conversation that only worked when such a deep bond was formed. She had no idea what was so important about this find, but whatever it was, she trusted him to clue her in since the item was from her grandmother's house.

"You can work in here." Braden stepped aside, gesturing for her to enter the room first. "There's a desk in the corner by the double doors. I need to speak with Mac, and I could be a while."

He pulled her suitcase over to the closet and turned to face her. "Will you be all right?"

Zara glanced around the spacious bedroom. The king-size bed sat on a platform on the far wall. The dark, rich four posters were masculine, matching the deep blue bedding. Of course a man like Braden would have his bed be the dominant feature in his master suite. The sitting area with leather club chairs and a mahogany coffee table only added to the overall masculine theme of the room.

"This is your bedroom." She didn't ask as her eyes met his.

Still holding the kitten in one arm, he crossed to her. Each step he took seemed to be in tune with her heartbeat.

"I told you this is where I wanted you. Nobody will bother you in here. The staff knows to stay away from my quarters, and Mac keeps a guest room on the other side of the house. We have total privacy here."

Zara shivered at the veiled promise, but at the same time, the prospect of being totally alone with him, on his turf where she may be able to learn even more about him, held so much appeal.

"Go on," she told him with a smile. "I'll be fine. I actually have several things to work on, and now that I don't have to worry about my battery, I can focus for several hours. Do you need to leave the kitten with me?"

Braden shook his head. "Nah. He likes me. Not as much as he likes you, but I'll let him run around for a bit." Stopping at the doorway, Braden turned, offering her a lopsided grin. "I'll have dinner brought up later. I plan on spending the entire evening with you and no interruptions, so make sure you get that work done because you're mine."

That man did have a way with delivering promises. The impact he could make on her body without even touching her was astounding. But she couldn't stand in the doorway all day and daydream about how sexy and amazing Braden was.

For one thing, she wasn't moving in. She was here temporarily, and she needed to remember that. For another, she was behind on work. She had to get her spreadsheets updated for the upcoming events, Braden's included. In the next two months, she had seven events planned, some big, some small, but Zara prided herself on treating each event as if it was the only one she worked on. She wanted her clients to feel special, to feel as if she cared only for them and no one else.

Zara headed to the antique desk in the corner near the doors that led out on to a balcony. The thick snow blanketed the open space, but Zara's imagination worked just fine. What she wouldn't give to work on a terrace during the warmer months. How inspiring and refreshing to be outside on the days she worked from home.

Once she booted up her computer, she tried not to focus on the giant bed directly across from her line of sight. If she stared too long, she'd start fantasizing even more about what would take place there later, and since she already knew how talented the man was in bed, her fantasy just sprang into mind without her even trying.

Zara closed her eyes and sighed. She seriously had to get a grip on this situation and her feelings. Right now he was downstairs working with his brother, and Zara needed to remember she had a job to do, as well. The weekend was over. Even though the snow still covered a good portion of the area in Boston and the surrounding towns, Zara still had to think ahead. When these upcoming events rolled around, the snow would most likely be gone, and her clients were expecting a spectacular party.

Zara pulled up her schedule and made mental notes as well as jotting down some handwritten ones. She did nearly everything online, but still reverted back to pen and paper at times. She might do some things old-school, but that was okay. She attributed those skills to her grandmother.

And thinking of her grandmother brought her mind back around to Braden and what he'd found, if anything, inside that tube.

"Damn it." Braden slammed his fist on the desktop. "Where the hell did it disappear to?"

"You don't even know one of the scrolls is what was in here." Mac carefully put the cap back on. "There were no other tubes?"

Braden rested his palms on his desk and shook his head. "Nothing. There were still some boxes, though. Zara hadn't even unpacked her own things, yet. Between all of that and her grandmother's things, I could've spent days searching that house."

Standing on the other side of the desk, Mac laid the tube down and crossed his arms. "You were there for two days, and from what I can tell you managed one empty tube and sleeping with the woman you're using. You're in quite a mess, brother. We'll get the scrolls eventually, no need to seduce your way to them."

Fury bubbled within Braden. He leaned forward, holding Mac's gaze. "Don't be an ass. What Zara and I do is none of your concern, and I'm more than capable of searching. I know my position here."

Mac smiled, completely uncaring as to Braden's building anger. "Sounds like your lady's gotten to you. Why don't you just tell her what you want? At this point she trusts you. You guys played house for two days, you brought back a damn cat and now she's up in your room. If you tell her you need to search her house, I doubt she'd turn you away."

Braden pushed off the desk. He couldn't tell her. Not now. It was because she trusted him that he couldn't come clean with what he needed. Once she discovered he'd lied from the beginning and only initially hired her so he could get close, she'd start to question everything between them, and he couldn't have that.

"I'll find another way," Braden assured Mac. "When will Ryker be back?"

"He made it back to the States, but the airport is closed. He flew into Provincetown and rented a car. He should be here this afternoon."

Turning to face the floor-to-ceiling window facing the snow-covered property, Braden racked his brain on a solution. He'd been so damn sure there was a scroll inside that tube. He had to focus, keep his head on straight or he'd find himself in an even bigger mess. He was the O'Shea in charge now, and he needed to damn well act like it.

"Ryker needs to get into Zara's house while she's here," Mac stated simply.

"No." Braden shook his head, tossing his brother a glance over his shoulder. "I won't do that."

Damn it. What had happened to him? Three days ago Braden would've jumped at the chance to have Zara here preoccupied in his bed while Ryker went through her house. But now...well, now he couldn't go through with it.

"You're falling for her."

Braden jerked around. "I am not."

"I can't blame you," Mac went on as if Braden's denial meant nothing. "She's beautiful, sexy, a businesswoman. Clearly everything you'd ever want in a woman."

Yeah, she was. That was part of the problem, because he couldn't take things to the next level with her. For one thing, he'd only just gotten to know her, and when he said he wanted a wife and a family, he meant it. He didn't just want a woman to keep his bed warm. Braden wanted that bond his parents had. But the obvious reason Zara couldn't be that woman was because he'd lied to her from the get-go. Braden wanted a wife, a family, yes. But he wanted it to be the real deal, and there was no way he could start a relationship with someone he'd lied to, was continuing to lie to.

And how the hell had his mind gone into wife mode when he thought of Zara? That was ridiculous. She didn't do relationships, and he was using her. Definitely no happily-ever-after for them.

"Don't get carried away." Braden rounded the desk, pulling his phone from his pocket to check his messages. "Have you heard from Laney?"

"Yesterday I did. I guess Carter is staying with her during the storm."

Braden grunted as he scrolled through his email. "I need to take a shower and change from these clothes. Once Ryker gets here we all need to have a meeting."

Mac nodded. "And what about your houseguest?"

Braden gripped his phone and eyed his brother. "She's not your concern."

"You know she's going to find out what's going on. You've brought her here, she's going to hear talk or get suspicious as to why you want back in her house."

Gritting his teeth, Braden was well aware of all the concerns in having Zara here, but he wasn't ready to let her go.

"You let me worry about Zara," Braden warned. "Once Ryker gets here, we'll work on a plan. I'd be more comfortable if Laney was here, too, but she's stubborn."

"Carter wouldn't let her come."

Braden laughed. "The day that schmuck keeps my sister away from me is the day he disappears from her life for good."

Mac nodded in agreement. "I'll text her and tell her I'm

having Ryker pick her up on his way here. She needs to be in on this meeting anyway."

"Give me fifteen minutes. We'll just meet in here. I'll have the cook prepare a late lunch for us."

Braden headed toward the doorway, then stopped and glanced over his shoulder. "Don't argue if Laney acts like it's a problem to come. Ryker will take care of any issues. Just text him."

Mac laughed. "You know Laney and Ryker are like oil and water, right? Are you wanting a fight? It's best if I try to run interference before he gets there."

Braden shrugged. "I trust Ryker to take care of it, and Laney will know why we need her here. It's none of Carter's business, and I don't give a damn if Ryker offends him."

"Our little sister is going to arrive, and I'm pointing her in your direction when she unleashes her anger."

Braden thought of the woman currently upstairs in his bedroom. "I can handle an emotional woman." He hoped.

Fifteen

"I didn't need to be manhandled by the family bouncer."

Braden sat behind his father's old desk, now his, and looked across to his sister who refused to take a seat. With her arms folded, she shot death glares between Braden, Mac and Ryker. She may not be happy, but she was here.

"If you'd just said we needed to have a family meeting, I would've had Carter bring me," she continued, zeroing in on Braden. "I don't appreciate being told I was coming and my ride would be Ryker."

The man in question leaned against the wall by the door. His thick arms crossed, he'd yet to take his coat off, and he'd not said a word. Braden knew the man was processing everything, but he also didn't have a care in the world...least of all an angry Laney.

"Carter isn't invited to my house." Braden eased back in his chair and met his sister's fiery gaze. "I know you like him, but I don't, and you're well aware of my feelings on that matter. Ryker was coming in from the airport, and it was easier for him to get you. Now, are you going to have a seat or stand there and pout because you don't like your mode of transportation?"

Laney narrowed her eyes. "It's the lack of respect I'm pissed about."

"I respect you, Laney." He smiled when she finally took a seat next to Mac on the leather sofa. "If I didn't, you wouldn't have been called to this meeting."

Braden glanced up to Ryker. "Close that door."

Once the door was closed, Ryker moved on into the room, sinking into the oversize leather chair next to the sofa. Braden eased forward, resting his forearms on the desk.

"We'll discuss what happened with you in London later," Braden promised, nodding to Ryker. "First, we need to discuss the scrolls. I've spent the last two days in Zara Perkins's home, and so far all I've found is an empty tube that may or may not have held one or all of the scrolls. I'm sure they're stored separately, because together they could be ruined."

Laney shifted, leaning onto the arm of the sofa. "Did she know you were looking?"

"No. We were going through some of her grandmother's boxed-up things, and that's when I found this tube."

He pulled the container from below his desk and sat it up for them to see. "I was unable to get it open, but when I brought it back, Mac managed to get into it. There was a miniscule section that looked as if it had been broken before, so he pried that part open."

Ryker was first to reach for the tube. He examined it thoroughly before resting it on his leg. "Tell me where you looked in her house, and I'll start my search in other areas."

Because Ryker assumed he'd be the next plan of action. He never questioned his duties, his position. He'd been the muscles, the enforcer, the behind-the-scenes man for the O'Sheas for years. Braden knew Ryker felt an intense sense of loyalty because he'd been taken in when his home life was extremely lacking.

"I don't want you going in again," Braden countered, earning him raised brows from Ryker. "Zara trusts me, and I don't want you going into her house while she's here."

"You've got to be kidding me," Laney stated, eyes wide. "We need to find these and get them back where they belong. Either tell her what's going on or let Ryker look. And what the hell is she doing here?"

Braden ignored Mac's smirk. "She's staying here until her power comes back on, and that's all you need to know."

"So you're sleeping with her, and you've earned her trust, you say, yet you can't ask her to have a look around?"

That pretty much summed up his predicament, but he wasn't going to get into this with his baby sister. Whatever was going on with Zara was private.

Besides, the guilt that slid through him was getting quite uncomfortable. He was using Zara, no way to sugarcoat that. If any man treated Laney like this, Braden would destroy him.

"She doesn't have to know," Ryker chimed in. "I'm quick and thorough."

Mac eased forward to face Ryker. "Braden has suddenly developed a conscience where his woman is concerned."

Angry that his credibility was coming into question, Braden fired back at his younger brother. "Would you betray Jenna?"

Mac's eyes narrowed. "Jenna is my best friend, nothing more. I've known her for years. And, no, I'd never betray her for any reason."

"Then shut the hell up, and let me handle this."

Raking a hand over his face, Braden truly had no idea how to deal with the situation. "The scrolls may not even be in the house at this point. They could've been moved or accidentally tossed out. But, I have to believe had they been sold, we would've heard about it. Documents with Shakespeare's earliest works would've hit the media worldwide. Even if sold on the black market, we would've heard whispers. Our reach is far enough in the underground world."

"So how are you going to search the house?" Ryker asked.

"When I take Zara back home, I'm going to find a reason to stay." That wouldn't be too hard, considering their current state. "I'll search where I haven't. I won't leave anything untouched. I don't want to lie to her any more than necessary, so we're not breaking in."

"And what are you going to do if Zara finds out you've lied to her?" Mac asked.

"She won't find out," Braden assured him. She couldn't find out, because if she did, all this work would be for nothing. Not only would she permanently block him from searching, she'd never trust again. He'd made so much progress in only two days, he refused to believe anything bad would happen. And it was a risk he was willing to take to get all he wanted.

Zara had become too important too fast. He wasn't ready to sever their personal tie. Scrolls aside, he wanted her. And, if he told her even a portion of the truth, she was so distrusting that he wasn't sure she wouldn't cut him out of her life. She had every right.

"The cook has prepared a late lunch," Braden stated, coming to his feet. "I need to speak with Ryker privately."

Mac and Ryker stood, but Laney remained seated, stubborn as ever. "And when can I go home?" she asked.

"Whenever Ryker wants to take you."

Ryker glanced to Laney. "Might be a while. I still need to eat and crash. I had a bit of a run-in with the London police, and I'm jet-lagged."

"I'll call a cab," she said through gritted teeth.

"No, you won't," Ryker commanded.

Braden bit the inside of his cheek to keep from smiling. Mac turned his head to hide his smile, as well. Ryker could go without sleep for days. He was a force to be reckoned with, and if he wanted to do something, he'd do it. Apparently he didn't want Laney to leave yet, which was fine with Braden. The more she was away from Carter, the better.

Before Laney could protest, because she no doubt would, her cell rang. Pulling her phone from the pocket of her jeans, she glanced at the screen, then up to Braden. Without a word, she came to her feet and moved to the opposite side of the room where she answered with her back to them.

"You know he's calling to check up on her," Mac whispered.

Braden nodded in agreement. "I don't see what the hell she puts up with him for."

"She's defiant." Ryker's eyes remained on Laney. "She may see something in him, but she's staying with him out of spite because you two make a big deal about it."

Braden eased a hip on his desk and crossed his arms. "And you don't? I'm sure you didn't get out of her house without a verbal sparring match with Carter."

Ryker sneered. "I can handle that prick."

"I don't know when I'll be home." Laney's slightly raised voice carried across the room. "Of course I'm at my brother's house. Where else would I be?"

Braden's blood boiled, and a little of what Ryker said started to ring true. Maybe in Mac and Braden's attempt to protect her, they'd driven her deeper into the arms of a controlling asshole. Damn it. He needed to talk to her one-on-one.

Mac headed for the door. "I'm getting something to eat. I'll be around if you need me."

Braden pulled his gaze from his sister and stepped closer to Ryker. "Do I need to know anything about London?"

Ryker's dark eyes met his. "I handled it."

"With no trace back to us?"

Nodding, Ryker's jaw clenched. "I even managed to gain

the trust and cooperation of two of the boys in blue. Next time I go back, we'll have no worries."

Relief slid through Braden. He knew whatever Ryker had done, he'd done his job well. "And the item is secured?"

"It's in the Paris office, ready to go back to its rightful owner."

Braden slapped Ryker on the back. "Go eat. I'll clean things up with Laney and take her back home."

Ryker's brows lifted. "You're taking her back willingly?"

"She makes her own decisions. I'm just hoping she sees Carter for who he is before it's too late, because if he crosses the line more than he has, he'll have bigger problems on his hands than just checking up on her."

Ryker's thin lips pulled into an eerie grin. "I'll take her back after I eat. I'd like to have a talk with him."

Braden shook his head. "I'll take care of it. You go relax."

Ryker looked as if he wanted to argue, but finally he nodded. After throwing Laney one more glance, he left the room.

While waiting for her to finish her call, Braden put the tube in the lock cabinet by the door. He didn't want that container going anywhere for now.

Finally Laney turned, slid the phone in her pocket and started toward the door. Braden stepped in her path and hated that look of sadness that stared back at him. While he wanted to unleash his anger and tell her to drop that jerk, he knew she wouldn't listen to words.

In a move that surprised both of them, Braden glided his arms around her shoulders and pulled her against him. He kissed her on the head and whispered, "I'm sorry I was a jerk to you."

Laney squeezed him back, resting her head on his shoulder. "You're always a jerk, but you never apologize."

Laughing, Braden eased back and smoothed her dark hair away from her face. "I just want you happy and to be with someone who deserves you. I just don't like how Carter treats you."

"He treats me great when we're together," she said with a slight smile. "His ex cheated on him, and he's leery. I can't blame him after hearing the stories."

Braden would save his opinion on that topic. From the rumors he'd heard, it wasn't Carter's ex doing the cheating at all. But Braden still had a tail on Carter, so time would tell.

"You can stay and eat, or I'll take you home. Whatever you want."

Laney tipped her head and narrowed one eye at him. "Who are you and what have you done with my big brother?"

He shrugged. "I told you, I just want you happy."

Her features softened as she ran a finger between his brows. "Your worry lines aren't as prominent as they normally are. If I had to guess, I'd say Zara is to thank for the new Braden."

"Zara is…" Hell, he didn't even know what to say.

Laney patted his cheek. "It's okay. I can tell your feelings for her are strong, and I won't say a word. Just promise me you won't hurt her. I don't know her personally, but if you're having these emotions, then I'd say she is, too. Be careful where your hearts are concerned."

Braden swallowed and feared that when all was said and done, someone's heart would be hurt.

Ignoring that lump in his throat, he looped his arm through Laney's. "Why don't you stay and eat? Then I'll take you back."

Laney looked up at him with bright eyes. "I love you, Braden. Dad would be proud of you."

Another point that worried him. He hoped like hell he did the O'Shea name proud, because his father, grandfather and great-grandfather had done an impeccable job of building up a reputation. Some may be skeptical, but the name was respected and sometimes feared. No one messed with the O'Sheas. And once Braden guided the family into an even more reputable area, he could hold his head high, knowing he'd done the right thing.

Braden led Laney toward the kitchen. Once he got her back home, he could focus on Zara. Their time alone couldn't come soon enough.

Sixteen

Braden was surprised when he stepped into the master suite and Zara was nowhere in sight. A hint of her signature jasmine perfume lingered in the room.

He turned toward the attached bath and smiled. Looked as if she was a step ahead of him. He undressed as he moved toward the wide doorway. His shirt fell off his shoulders to the floor, he stepped out of his shoes, hopped out of his socks and shed his pants and boxers. By the time he stepped into the bathroom, he was more than ready to join Zara.

But he stopped as soon as his feet hit the tile. There in the sunken garden tub was Zara. She'd apparently packed bubbles because she was neck deep into them, her head tipped back, hair piled on her head and eyes closed. Was she sleeping? She wasn't moving.

Braden took a few moments to take in the sight of Zara relaxing in his tub. He'd never used it, never had a need. He grabbed a shower and that was it. This sunken bubble bath never looked so good.

Damp tendrils clung to the side of her neck, her pink lips parted on a soft sigh. Braden could barely restrain himself. He'd never wanted a woman with such a fierce ache before, and the knot in his gut told him this need wasn't only physical anymore. If everything between them were merely physical, Braden would've let Ryker go into her place and look around. But he couldn't do it.

Zara shifted, her eyes opened, instantly locking on him. A slow, seductive smile spread across her face.

"I meant to be done by the time you came up. But this is too relaxing." She lifted one bubble-covered arm, reaching out to him. "Join me?"

Braden wasn't about to turn down an invitation like that, even if he'd smell like flowers when he got out. Being with Zara, no matter the circumstances, was totally worth it.

Zara scooted forward, giving him room to step in behind her. When his legs stretched out on either side of her, Braden pulled her back against his chest. She rested her head on his shoulder and peered up at him.

"Did you get your meeting taken care of?"

He scooped up bubbles and swiped them over her bent knees. "I did and now I'm all yours. Did you manage to work?"

"I added another event," she stated, her voice lifting with excitement. "Parker Abrams was at your party the other night. His assistant sent me an email about working on his corporate event he hosts once a year for his employees. Apparently their last coordinator was caught making out with Parker's intoxicated son. Great news headline, bad for business. But how am I any different? I'm sleeping with my boss."

Braden smiled. "That's great news for you. I promise to keep our fling a secret."

Her lids closed, and Braden wanted to take back the words. This was starting to feel like more than a fling. He knew it, even if he didn't admit it out loud. There was something deeper than intimacy going on here. Short-term was the only way he'd worked before, but now…he didn't necessarily want to keep Zara a secret. She deserved more… they deserved more.

Zara rubbed her hand along the arm he had wrapped around her stomach. "I feel weird discussing business with you when we're naked. It's wrong…isn't it?"

Nothing about this moment was wrong. Nothing about having Zara smiling, happy and naked was wrong.

Braden nuzzled against her neck. "Then maybe we shouldn't talk."

Zara's slight groan had him reaching up to cup the side of her face, turning her so he could capture her lips. But the woman in his arms went a step further and turned until she faced him. Braden straightened his legs when she straddled his lap.

"I was lying here dreaming of you," she told him as she poised herself above him. "I have no idea how we got to this point, but I don't want to be anywhere else."

Encircling her waist with his hands, Braden stroked her damp skin with his thumbs. "I don't want anything between us, Zara."

"I've always used protection, and I'm on birth control." She tipped her hips, enough to nearly have his eyes roll back in his head. "What about you?"

"I'm clean and I've never been without a condom."

She quirked a brow in silent question. Braden eased up enough to claim her mouth at the same time he thrust into her. That instant friction, skin to skin, no barriers, was so new, so all-consuming, he wanted to take a moment and just…feel.

But Zara started moving, starting those pants as she tore her mouth away and gripped his shoulders. When she tipped her head back and bit her lip, Braden was absolutely mesmerized by the woman who'd managed to have complete and total control over him. So much so he was letting her into his private life, into his home. He'd never brought a woman into his bed.

Zara was different. He'd known it from the moment she'd stepped into his office. And now she was his. Would he ever let her go?

The thought of losing her chilled him, but he refused to think on that now.

Braden slid his hands up her soapy sides and cupped her breasts. Sliding his thumbs back and forth earned him another groan as she arched her back.

"Look at me," he demanded. He needed her to see him, to see them. Every primal part of him suddenly took over. "You're mine."

Those wide eyes locked on to his, and her mouth opened in a silent cry as he quickened the pace.

"Say it." Braden went back to gripping her waist, holding her still so he could gain back control. "Say you're mine, Zara."

"Yes," she cried. "Only yours."

When his hand dipped in the water and touched her intimately, she shattered all around him. Braden would never tire of seeing her come undone, of knowing he caused her pleasure. This was his, she was his. No other man would experience Zara so long as Braden was around, because he wasn't kidding and he hadn't been swept into the heat of the moment when he'd demanded she say she belonged to him.

Just as her trembling stopped, Braden squeezed her waist and let himself go. Zara leaned down, whispering something into his ear. He didn't grasp what she was saying; it didn't matter. This woman in his arms was all he needed for tonight, for tomorrow.

And now Braden was starting to wonder if she was the woman he needed forever. If she was, how the hell would he ever be able to build on anything when their initial meeting was all based on a lie? On him using her?

As Zara lay spent against him, Braden knew one thing

for certain. He either needed to let her go once he searched her home, or he needed to come clean with how they'd met in the first place.

Either way was a risk. Would she understand? Would she see that he'd had no choice in the matter, but once he'd gotten to know her all bets were off?

She had to understand, because Braden refused to lose her. Having her walk away wasn't an option.

Someone smacked her bare backside.

Zara jumped, twisting in the silky sheets and thick duvet. Sweeping the hair out of her eyes, she glared up to see Braden staring down at her, a wicked grin on his face and a twinkle in his eye.

But he was holding a cup of coffee. "That better be for me," she grumbled, reaching for the mug. Jack clawed at the side of the bed until Braden lifted him up.

"Of course. I also managed breakfast."

He reached to the nightstand and presented her with a plate. Zara eyed it before pulling the napkin from the top. A laugh escaped her.

"I know full well you do not stock s'mores Pop-Tarts in your house, considering you hadn't had them before I introduced you to them." She plucked one off the plate as she took a sip of the steaming hot coffee, black, just the way she liked it. "So how did you manage this?"

He cocked his head and raised his brows as if her question was absurd. Of course he had someone go out in this ridiculous weather just to get her a box of Pop-Tarts. The idea warmed her more than it should. It was a box of processed junk that cost a couple bucks, but he'd done so out of...what? Love? No, he didn't love her, but he obviously cared for her.

"Hurry up and eat," he told her. "I have another surprise for you."

With the Pop-Tart between her teeth, she narrowed her

eyes and bit off a hunk. Jack stretched out on Braden's pillow next to Zara. "What?"

He stepped back from the bed, and she took in the sight of him wearing—a ski suit?

"I hope you brought warm clothes. If not, I'll find something for you. Laney most likely has some clothes in her old room."

"Where are we going?" she asked, a bit nervous at how energetic he was this morning. Apparently the two times he'd woken her in the middle of the night hadn't worn him out.

"Just eat, put on warm clothes and I'll go see what else I can find." He leaned down, kissed her on the forehead and eased back just enough to look her in the eyes. "Trust me?"

Zara swallowed, nodded. "I wouldn't be here if I didn't."

Something flashed through his eyes, but just as quick as it appeared, the image was gone. Braden nodded down to her plate. "Eat up. You're going to need your energy."

"After last night, I'm exhausted."

His mouth quirked up in a grin. "Compliments will get you everything."

Zara rolled her eyes. "Easy there, tiger. Your ego is showing."

"My ego is never hidden," he countered as he walked to the door. "I'll have a heavier coat and thick gloves for you downstairs. Meet me by the front door in twenty minutes."

Zara gave him a mock salute, which earned her a chuckle as he walked out and closed the bedroom door behind him. She had no clue what he had planned, but obviously something outside. Was Braden an outdoorsy type? What did she truly know about the man she was falling for?

She broke off another piece of her pastry and smiled. She actually knew quite a bit. He was loyal and he was caring, though he'd never admit it. Family meant everything to him, and he wanted his own one day. He may have a reputation as a hard-ass, a man to be feared in the business world, but the Braden O'Shea she saw was loving.

Zara finished her breakfast and coffee, then set her dishes on the bedside table. She unplugged her phone from the charger and checked messages. Then she wished she hadn't. Three texts from Shane asking if she was all right. The first one was a simple question, the second was more demanding and the third was flat-out demanding. Arrogant jerk. Without replying, she laid her phone back down and started getting ready for…whatever it was she was doing this morning. She had emails to get to, but for now she wanted to be with Braden because he'd gone to the trouble of surprising her, and he seemed excited. Zara didn't know if she should be scared or worried.

The sooner she got dressed, the sooner she'd find out what Mr. O'Shea had planned.

Seventeen

"You're kidding."

Bundled up like an abominable snowman with layers upon mismatched layers, a bright yellow cap on her head and red snow boots, Zara stared at Braden as he knelt down in the knee-high snow and started forming a ball. The man may be a ruthless businessman, but this playful side was just as sexy and appealing.

"Do I look like I'm kidding?" he shot back over his shoulder. "We're building a snowman. Get down here and make balls."

Zara snorted. "You're going to freeze yours off," she muttered.

"Cute. Now help me."

Surveying the pristine blanket of snow, Zara squinted her eyes at the glare from the sun's reflection. She shoved her gloved hands into the pockets of Laney's old ski coat. Apparently she'd had some old things in her closet, and Braden claimed his sister wouldn't care.

Zara wasn't sure what had her more scared, the fact that she was getting in deeper with this family or that Braden was showing her his playful side.

It was the snowman. Something so simple, so traditional hit her right in the gut.

Braden glanced back over his shoulder, then pushed to his feet. "You're frowning."

"You probably did this all the time growing up," she stated, looking at the mound he'd started. "It's ridiculous how something like this freaks me out."

Braden stepped closer, peered down at her until she met his gaze. "You're supposed to be having fun. I want you to experience all the simple things, and I want to be the one to experience them with you. For now, we're starting with a snowman. Maybe later we can make snow cream or have hot chocolate with little marshmallows."

What did he mean he wanted to be the one to experience things with her? Was he thinking long-term? Was he saying he wanted something permanent?

"Where are we going with this?" she asked.

Braden braced his hands on her shoulders. "Wherever we want." He nipped at her lips. "But right now, we're making a snowman, and we're going to have fun. Then I'm going to kick your butt at a snowball fight."

Zara laughed. "You can try, but don't take inexperience for weakness."

"Is that a challenge?" he asked.

"Consider yourself warned." Zara took in a deep, cool breath and sighed. "Now, let's get to making some big balls."

Laughing, Braden smacked another cold kiss on her lips. Together they worked rolling one giant ball. Zara had no idea building a snowman was so much work. Despite the twenty degree temps, she was actually starting to work up a sweat. By the time they got the third ball rolled and on top of the middle one, Zara was nearly winded. Her muscles were hurting, and for mercy's sake she was clearly out of shape. Apparently eating junk and planning parties didn't help build up the endurance.

And here she thought her running regimen kept her endurance up. Apparently, she needed to change her workouts to walking in deep snow and using her core to keep her balanced.

"I'm going to need to soak in that tub again," she told him as they stood back to admire their work. "My muscles are crying."

The wicked grin he shot her sent shivers of arousal coursing through her. "I could be persuaded to give you a massage."

"During the bath?"

"I'd say we both deserve to soak our tired muscles."

Zara glanced back to the snowman. "This thing doesn't look finished. Should we have a carrot or something?"

Braden laughed. "I brought out a bag of various things. It's on the porch."

As he maneuvered through the snow to the porch, Zara got the most wonderful idea. Before he could turn back to see her, she quickly made two snowballs. Compact in each of her palms, she held them until just the right time.

The moment he turned around with the bag in his hand and stepped off the porch, Zara pelted him right in the face. She couldn't even fully enjoy his look of shock because she was doubled over with laughter and trying to gather more ammunition.

Before she could straighten, a wet, cold blob smacked her on the side of her head, barely missing her exposed cheek.

Zara tried to get to the snowman to use as a shield, but she ended up slipping in the snow and falling headfirst into the snowman, sending it toppling.

"No," she screamed as her body landed on the head.

Braden tackled her from behind. "That's what you get for fighting dirty."

He rolled her in the snow and pinned her down. She couldn't catch her breath for laughing. Braden straddled her as he trapped her hands beside her head.

"Still laughing?" he asked. "You may have got the jump on me, but who's in charge now?"

"It was worth it." Zara attempted to control herself, but his face was wet from the snowballs that had assaulted him. "I'm sorry I killed our snowman, though."

"You don't look sorry. You look smug."

"And you look cold," she countered. "I guess I kicked your butt at the snowball fight since you only got my hat."

Braden leaned down, his lips hovering just over hers. "You know what they say about paybacks," he muttered before he kissed her thoroughly, passionately…promisingly.

She hadn't even noticed he released her hands until icy cold snow was shoved into the top of her coat.

"Braden," she yelled as he jumped off her. "You put snow down my top."

She hopped up, dancing around, trying to get the blistering snow off her bare skin. "That's not playing fair."

"I gave you a warning about paybacks," he called as he scooped up another snowball.

Zara ducked as the ball flew over her head. "Oh, buddy. It's on."

Soaking in the garden tub had definitely done wonders for the sore muscles. Not to mention the fact Braden took full advantage of massaging every inch of Zara before he made love to her.

After their epic snowball fight, which they finally declared a tie, they came back in, and thanks to the chef, who was now going to get a raise, Braden and Zara had steaming cups of hot chocolate with marshmallows. Braden hadn't even had to request the treat.

Now they were spent in every way as they lounged beneath the covers in his massive bed.

"You're going to make it hard for me to go home," she muttered, snuggling deeper against his side. "Besides the hot sex, I've been undressed so much here, I may never want to wear pants again."

Braden's hand slid over her bare backside. He wasn't ready for her to leave. "Fine by me. Keeping you in my bed won't be a hardship."

Zara trailed her fingertips over his taut abdomen. "It's going to be a bit unprofessional of me to host parties while naked in your bed."

"You'll definitely be remembered."

These past few days had been more than he'd ever thought possible. Zara had embedded herself so deep into his life, he needed to come clean because he wanted to build something stronger, something permanent with her.

Once he explained why he'd needed to get into her house, she'd understand. They'd forged a bond so intimate and so fierce, he knew she would understand. Her grandmother had meant the world to her, so that family loyalty she would be able to relate to. Even though her parents hadn't been the most stellar of people in her life, Zara would see where he was coming from.

Then they could discuss the future. He just wished like hell his hand hadn't been forced, because he didn't want to tell her he'd lied to her. Right now she looked at him as if he were everything she'd been searching for but afraid to hope for. He didn't want to be the one to disappoint, to crush her and make her untrusting again.

"I need to tell you something." The words were out before he could fully gear himself up for this talk. "I'm not sure where to start."

Zara stilled against his side. Damn it, he hadn't meant to start out like this, instantly putting her on the defensive.

"You've asked before where this is going." Braden shifted to his side so he could face her. Lying in bed wasn't the ideal place to start this, but she was naked so she wouldn't run out angry. "I don't want you just in my bed, Zara. I want more."

Her eyes widened, either in panic or in shock he wasn't sure.

Reaching for her hand, he brought it to his chest and held her palm flat over his heart. "I know this has been fast, but the attraction was there the moment you came into my office. Seeing you at the party the other night only intensified things. But spending so much time with you over the past few days, I've realized that I care for you more than any woman I've had in my life other than my sister and my mother."

"Braden." Zara closed her eyes. "I want this, so much. But everything about long-term scares me. I mean, I can't even unpack all of my clothes at my new house. I want things, I want stability and a foundation. I've just never had that in my life, and… I'm scared."

Her words came out on a whisper, her breath tickling his bare chest, her declaration slicing him in two.

"I know you are, and that's why I want to be completely honest with you." Damn it, was that him trembling? "You're the woman I want in my life because you make me want to be honest, you make me want to be that guy you trust and think is such a good person."

Zara slid her hand from beneath his and eased back. "What do you mean be honest?"

"There's so much you need to know, and I have no idea where to start."

Braden sat up, rubbing his hands over his face. He was either the stupidest man alive or he was brilliant for coming clean like this and risking her trust. Surely once she learned the truth, the truth that came straight from him, she'd understand. Finding out any other way would make him look like a jerk, and understandably she'd be pissed. But by confessing his sins straight to her, Braden was confident she'd forgive him and they could move forward.

Could things be that easy?

Her hand rested on his shoulder blade. "Braden. You're scaring me."

Yeah, he was scaring himself, too. But this was worth it; *she* was worth it.

"My family has had some priceless heirlooms missing for decades." He opted to start all the way back at the beginning as opposed at the end when he'd started using her. "We had an ancestor who was an Irish monk during the sixteenth century."

"I have no idea how this affects us," she stated, coming to sit up beside him.

"Just listen."

Braden turned, facing her because he'd never backed down from what he wanted, and he was facing Zara head-on because he'd never wanted anything more.

"My ancestor transcribed nine of Shakespeare's works and they were written on scrolls. They were passed down from generation to generation, but during the Great Depression they were in a house that belonged to my family. They lost everything and were forced out before they could get the scrolls."

Braden searched her eyes as he grabbed her hand. "Those scrolls were left in the house, and we've been searching for them since."

"I still don't get any of this," she told him, shaking her head. "What do these scrolls have to do with us?"

"The house that belonged to my family until the Depression is yours, Zara."

"What?" she gasped. "Wait a minute, you think I have some documents that supposedly have works by Shakespeare hidden in my home?"

He watched as she processed all the words, then her shock morphed into hurt right before his eyes. Before she even spoke, his heart clenched in pain for her. He never knew he could physically hurt simply because someone he cared for was in pain.

"Did you search my house?" she asked, agony lacing her voice as she scooted back from him and clutched the sheet up around her neck as if she needed a shield of protection.

Braden swallowed the lie that could easily slip out. He wasn't that guy, not with her. Not anymore. "Yes."

Her lips clamped together as moisture gathered in her eyes. "And helping me go through my grandmother's things. That was another way for you to search?"

He nodded as lead settled in his gut.

"That was why you flipped out when you saw me holding that tube." Her eyes darted away as she spoke, as if she were playing the day back through her mind and realizing what he'd done. "You were in such a hurry to get back here, you wanted that opened so you could see inside it."

"There was nothing in it."

Tear-filled eyes swung back to him. "So now what? You need to do another search? Why didn't you just ask me in the beginning?"

Another gasp escaped her seconds before a tear slid down her cheek. She didn't bother to swipe it away, and that wet track mocked him. He'd done this to her. He'd hurt her, on purpose, but he'd had no other way initially. Not only that, he'd justified his actions.

"You hiring me wasn't because of my abilities at all," she whispered, scooting back. "You were using me from the start."

Before he could defend himself—and what could he say that wouldn't sound terrible—Zara sprang from the bed and started pulling clothes from her suitcase.

"I've been such a fool," she declared as she pulled on a pair of panties. "You've been playing me for months. I refused to believe the rumors about your business, about how ruthless and conniving the O'Sheas are. Now I know the truth. I won't let you use me again."

Eighteen

Zara's hands shook—from anger, from hurt, from the urgency to get the hell out of here. She couldn't get dressed quick enough.

"You're not leaving."

Zara yanked a sweatshirt over her head. "If I have to walk home, I'm not staying with you another second. I refuse to be with a liar and a manipulator, with a man who claims to care for me, yet you lie about everything."

Braden stood, grabbed a pair of boxer briefs and jerked them on before coming around the side of the bed. "There's so much about my business I can't share with you, Zara. We do what we have to do, and, yes, we use people, we've lied, we've cheated. But everything you and I have shared was genuine and real."

"Real?" she cried as she turned to him, her hands propped on her hips. "How can anything be real when the trust was clearly one-sided? Do you know how hard I fought what was happening between us? I kept telling myself that we couldn't get involved, that anything I felt for you was all superficial. Your power, your charm, everything about you drew me in, and then you went and showed me that sweet, caring side that had my guard coming down."

Zara refused to give into the sting of tears. She blinked them away before continuing, because if he wanted honesty, he was about to get it.

"I believed everything you said to me," she went on, her tone softening because the fight was going out of her. "I believed every touch, every promise. The fact that you sought me out to purposely use me cuts me like nobody else's actions or words ever has. How did you plan on getting into my house once you hired me? Seduction? You succeeded. I guess this storm really played well into your hands."

Another thought gripped her. "Shane warned me your family were liars and manipulators. I ignored him because I thought he was jealous. Looks like he might have had my best interest at heart after all."

"Zara."

He started to reach for her, but she stepped back, bumping into the small table her suitcase laid on. She skirted around it, never taking her eyes off him.

"Do you think I'm going to let you touch me? You did this. You destroyed something I was starting to hope for, something I'd already settled into. Damn it, Braden, I was falling for you, and you betrayed everything good that I had in my life. My self-confidence, my business, us."

She let out a lifeless laugh at his pained expression. "There never was an *us*, though. There was you sneaking behind my back, using me, and then there was me being naive and hopeful."

"Would you listen to me?"

Braden took a step forward and came within inches of her. Zara refused to back up, back down. She would put up a strong front before him if it killed her. She could collapse later in the privacy of her empty home.

"The deceit started when I hired you for who you were. I can't deny that. And, yes, I wanted to find a way into your house by gaining your trust. But the moment I got into your house, the second I touched you intimately, something changed for me. I still wanted to find what I came for, but I also wanted you and not just in bed. You did something to me, Zara. I can't let you go."

He seemed so heartfelt, so genuine, yet none of that mattered because it all came down to the fact he'd lied and betrayed her.

"You have no choice," she retorted, crossing her arms over her chest to keep more hurt from seeping into her heart. "You should've come clean before you took me to bed, because now all I think is you slept with me to gain my trust. You manipulated me, used my feelings."

Zara glanced around the room and let out a sigh. Ignoring Braden, she pushed past him to gather her things from the bathroom. Her eyes darted to the garden tub where memories had been made. Never again would she be a fool over a man. She should've listened to her heart in the first place.

Grabbing her lotion, toothbrush, bubble bath and razor, Zara came back out and dumped it all into her suitcase. She didn't care if anything leaked over her clothes; she had bigger issues at the moment.

With a swift jerk, she zipped up her luggage and turned back to Braden, who still hadn't moved. "I want someone to take me home. Not you."

The muscle in Braden's jaw ticked as he nodded. "Ryker is still here. I'll have him take you."

Zara extended the handle on her suitcase and started for the door. When Braden reached for it, she shot him a look. "Don't touch it. From here on out, I need nothing from you."

Before she could open the door, Braden slapped his hand on it, caging her between the wood and his hard body. "I'm letting you walk away because you need to think about this, about us. But I'm not giving up on you, Zara. You know in your heart everything between us was real. You felt it in my touch. That's something even I can't lie about."

Zara closed her eyes, wishing she could stop his words from penetrating so deeply into her heart. He'd already taken up too much space there. Surrounded by his heat, his masculine scent, Zara needed to get out of here where she could be alone and think without being influenced by this sexy man…a man she'd thought had a heart of gold. He only proved those men didn't exist.

"Let me go," she whispered. "I can't be here. I can't do this. Romance isn't real after all, is it?"

When his hand settled on her shoulder, she nearly lost it. Because no matter what he'd done to her, she couldn't just turn off her feelings.

"Don't shut me out," he whispered against her ear.

Steeling herself against his charms, his control over her, she shifted so his hand fell away. "You shut yourself out."

"Let me get dressed and I'll find Ryker for you."

Zara threw him a look over her shoulder. "I'll find him. I've already told you from here on out, you're not needed."

Pushing away, she opened the door and headed out into the hall. She'd never met this Ryker Braden had talked about, but surely she could find him and get the hell out of here.

She'd wait outside in the freezing cold if she had to. It couldn't be any colder than the bedroom they'd shared.

Awkward was such a mild word for this car ride back to her house. And because the roads were still covered, the trip took twice as long.

Zara didn't dare glance over to her driver. The man was built like a brick wall with coal-black hair and dark eyes. She could easily see why he was the O'Sheas' go-to guy. He had that menacing, brooding look down perfectly. Fitting for being the right-hand man for a lying, cheating family.

And the scar running along his neck? The man had barely

said a word to her other than "hi" and "the truck is over here," but he had badass written all over him.

"I've never pried into Braden's personal life."

Zara jerked in her seat at the deep tone and the fact he was actually going to bring up the proverbial elephant parked in the truck with them. "Then don't start now," she countered.

"I owe him," Ryker said simply before continuing. "He's never brought a woman back to the house, so whatever is going on between the two of you, it's serious. The O'Sheas are a private family. Other than the parties in the ballroom, no outsiders come into their home."

And that told her more than she needed to know. They were all hiding something.

Zara stared out the window. "You may owe him loyalty, but I owe him nothing. He's a liar."

Silence enveloped them once more. Zara folded her arms, pulling her coat tighter around her. She couldn't get warm, and it had nothing to do with winter hanging on for dear life.

"What did he tell you?" Ryker finally asked. The cautious way he phrased the question put Zara on alert.

She turned in her seat to face him, no longer caring how menacing this man was. "I assume you know full well why he wanted in my house, since you're like a brother to him."

Ryker's silence told her everything she needed to know. She refused to discuss this further with a stranger—not only a stranger, but one who was devoted to Braden.

As they neared her house, Zara's anger bubbled and intensified. Not only had Braden lied to her, he'd had a whole damn team of people in his corner. She hadn't thought of this sooner, but no doubt his brother and sister knew, too. She'd been made a fool by the entire family.

Ryker pulled on to her street, rounded the truck into her drive and put the vehicle in Park. Just as she reached for the handle, he spoke up once again.

"I offered to break into your house while you were staying with Braden." Ryker's dark eyes met hers, holding her in place. "He refused because he didn't want to betray you anymore."

A lump formed in her throat. "I'm glad he feels guilty."

"That wasn't just guilt. You know exactly what he feels for you."

Zara didn't want to think about what Braden's true feelings for her were because he had a warped way of showing them. Added to that, was she seriously sitting here having a heart-to-heart chat with a man who looked like an extra from a mafia movie?

Jerking on the handle, Zara stopped. She wanted to keep the upper hand, she wanted Braden to know she was in control of her life. What better way than to call him on his betrayal?

Zara glanced back to Ryker. The man's intense gaze still locked on her.

"Come on in," she invited. "You want to know if those coveted scrolls are here. I have no idea, but if they are, they're technically mine since I own the house. But you're more than welcome to come and look."

"And if I find them?"

Zara shrugged. "Then it sounds like Braden and I will have some business to discuss."

Ryker eyed her another minute, and she didn't know if she was more afraid if he came inside or if he didn't.

Nineteen

"The hell you say?"

There was no way Braden heard right.

"She invited me inside to look around," Ryker repeated.

Braden sank down into his leather office chair and processed Zara's shocking actions. Ryker remained standing on the other side of the desk, the man never ready to fully relax.

"I didn't go," Ryker added. "Whatever is going on between the two of you is something I want no part of, and it's so much more than the scrolls at this point."

Braden didn't want to be part of this mess, either, but unfortunately he'd brought it all on himself and he was screwed.

"I'll take care of this," Braden promised. "You have more work to do. We have a piece in Versailles that needs to be acquired before the May auction, too. I have the specs here."

Braden slid the folder across his desk. Without picking it up, Ryker flipped it open and started reading. Laney had done all the online investigating. She was a whiz at hacking without leaving even the slightest clue anyone had done so. She was invaluable to the family.

Braden knew Ryker would take things over from here, which was good because Braden had no energy to put into this project right now. His mind was on Zara and the fact she'd so easily invited Ryker into her home to search.

Was she playing a game? Mocking him? Was she seriously just going to let him search with no strings attached?

As much as Braden wanted to rush over and figure out what the hell she was thinking, he also wanted to give her space. He wouldn't give her too much, but he wanted her to miss him, to realize that they were good together and his actions had been justified in the beginning.

Ryker tapped the folder on the desk. "I'll take care of it. I'm heading to my apartment, if you need me for anything."

Braden nodded and waited until Ryker had stepped out before he braced his elbows on his desk and rested his head in his palms. What the hell was he going to do? He'd messed this up. In the beginning, had he known he would've fallen for her, he would've confessed what he wanted. But he'd never known any other way than to take what he wanted and not worry about feelings or personal issues cropping up.

Braden cursed himself as he slammed his fists on to the glossy desktop. Just as he pushed away, his cell vibrated. Glancing at the screen, Braden didn't recognize the number. He wasn't in the mood to chat, but he never knew when it was a business call. For the O'Sheas, business always carried on, no matter what was going on in their private lives.

Braden grabbed the phone and slid his fingertip across the screen. "Hello."

"What the hell did you do to Zara?"

Stunned by the rage-filled tone, it took Braden a minute to place the caller. "Why are you calling me, Shane?"

"I went by her house to check on her, and she'd been crying."

Braden wasn't stupid; he figured Zara had cried, but he

wanted to give her space. Still, the thought of her alone in that big house, crying with no one to hold her, comfort her, other than the cat, gutted him.

No one, but the prick Shane.

"How the hell do you know I did anything?" Braden asked.

"Because I know you, O'Shea. And now that she's done with you, I'm moving full-force into winning her back. Just thought you should know."

That arrogant, egotistical tone slammed into him.

"You went to her house?" Braden jerked to his feet. Gripping the phone, he started for the door. "Stay away from what's mine. You won't be warned again."

Braden disconnected the call and quickly shot off a text to Ryker. Yes, he was in the same house, but Braden wasn't wasting any time. He wanted Shane dealt with right now, and while Braden would love being the one to do so himself, Braden had someone else who needed his attention even more.

Zara tugged on the old bed until it was beneath the window. She'd worked up a sweat, but finally her bedroom was rearranged. She needed it to be different, because every time she'd walked in here, she'd seen Braden. He consumed her entire home, and Zara was trying like hell to rid the house of memories. Unfortunately, they were permanently embedded into her mind, her heart.

She'd only been home an hour when her electricity kicked back on. Making good use of the time, she washed her sheets and comforter. There was no way she would've been able to crawl into bed surrounded by Braden's masculine scent... and she was almost positive Jack had an accident.

She stared over at the chaise she'd pushed near the door. She truly had no idea where to put that now that she'd changed the bed.

Zara circled her room, stopping when her eyes zeroed in

on a sock, a piece of cardboard and a small towel where her bed used to be. That kitten had started a stash.

Just the thought of the kitten, of how Braden hadn't thought twice about rescuing it, had her eyes burning all over again. She'd experienced a wide variety of emotions in the past few hours. Anger, sorrow, fury and then emptiness.

All of that stemmed from Braden. She refused to even think of all the emotions she'd felt when Shane had stopped by. Unfortunately, he'd caught her during the sorrow stage.

Zara headed down to the first floor to check on the status of her sheets. They should be dry by now, and she needed to keep focused and stay busy. She didn't want to contemplate how bored she would be once she ran out of things to do. Even work wasn't appealing to her right now.

Just as she hit the bottom step, her doorbell rang. The last thing she wanted was a visitor, especially if Shane decided to come back. Now she'd hit her anger stage, and he'd be sorry if he decided he still couldn't take no for an answer.

The stained-glass sidelights provided no clue as to who her visitor was. Zara checked the peephole in the old door and gritted her teeth. She didn't want to get into this. She truly did not want to rehash all the good, bad and sexy with the man on the other side of the door.

But she knew Braden O'Shea well enough now to know he wasn't going away without a fight. Well, if he wanted a fight, she was ready to give him one.

Jerking the door open, Zara blocked the entrance and stared at her unwelcome guest.

"Ready to search the house?" she asked sweetly.

With his hands shoved in his black wool coat, collar up around his stubbled jawline, Braden still looked sexy. Why did he have to be so damn perfect to look at?

"I don't want to search your house," he told her, his jaw clenched. "I want to talk, and if you don't want me inside, I'm more than willing to stand on your porch. The choice is yours."

She gripped the edge of the door. "I could slam this door in your face and not give you a second thought."

"You could," he agreed. "But you're not a heartless woman, Zara. And no matter what you feel now, you also still have feelings for me. You're not the type of person who can just turn those off."

Hesitating, trying to figure out what to do, Zara gave in and pushed the door wider. Turning on her socked feet, she headed into the living room. The door closed behind her, but she kept her back to the doorway because right now she couldn't even face him. If he wanted to talk, he was more than welcome to do so, but Zara didn't know if she had the strength to face him head-on.

So much for that fight she'd geared up for. Just seeing him, hearing that sultry voice thrust her back into the sorrowful stage.

"Why are you here?" she asked, wrapping her arms around her waist. "Haven't we said enough?"

"Are you going to look at me?"

Swallowing, Zara shook her head. "No."

"Fair enough."

Braden's footsteps shuffled behind her, and she braced herself for his touch, but it never came. Still, the hairs on her neck stood on end. He was close, definitely within reaching distance, yet he didn't reach for her.

"There's nothing I can say to undo what I did."

Yeah, he was so close, she could feel the warmth of his breath when he spoke. He wasn't going to make this easy on her.

"When my father was in the hospital, the doctors weren't sure if he'd make it through the heart surgery. Dad knew, though. He knew the outcome. I could tell by the way he took my hand, asked me to find these scrolls no matter what."

Zara bit her lip to keep it from trembling. Braden's words, thick with emotion, were killing her. He did all of this for his family, the family he loved and a family that stood together through life's trials. Even though she didn't have this type of bond, she was starting to see just how important it was, and maybe Braden had been put in a rough place, torn between what he wanted and what he was bound to.

"I knew I was next in line to be in charge of everything, legal or otherwise." Braden laughed. "You're the only woman I've ever become this close to. That scares the hell out of me, Zara. My family is… We have secrets. To know you have that much power over me, to know that at any moment you could turn on me and ruin my family if you knew everything. I'm willing to risk it. That alone tells me how much I love you."

Zara whipped around, but Braden held a finger over her lips.

"I'm not done," he told her. "I saw how hard my dad searched for these scrolls. We believed they were still here, somewhere. We recovered an old trunk that had been here, but it proved to be a dead end a couple months ago. But when he died, I vowed to honor his wishes, to be head of the family and someone he'd be proud of. I made it my mission to find them, no matter the cost. And I knew I had to start with your home."

His hand slid from her lips, and she had to stop herself from licking where he'd touched. She was still reeling from his confession of love. Did he mean those words? Or was he just sorry he'd actually lost at something? The scrolls… and her.

"I knew a young woman lived here, and once I found out your profession, I knew it would be easy to meet you. Everything after that fell into place so fast…"

Braden shook his head, ran a hand over his face. The stubble on his cheeks rasped against his palm. He shut his eyes for the briefest of moments before opening them. Closing the miniscule gap between them, Braden placed his hands on her shoulders.

"If I'd know how fast, how hard I was going to fall for you, I would've done things differently. But the past is something even I'm not powerful enough to change. All I can do is promise you I won't lie to you again."

Zara wanted to be tough, to step away from his touch, but she couldn't bring herself to move.

"What makes you think I'll believe anything you're saying?" she asked, surprised her voice came out stronger than she actually felt. "Maybe you're just upset that you didn't find the scrolls. Maybe you still need me for this house, and you want my trust back for that reason alone."

"If I wanted this house searched tomorrow, it would be done without you knowing about it."

Zara knew he was telling the truth. And yet, he hadn't sent Ryker when she'd been at Braden's house. That had to count for something…didn't it?

"Right now, all I care about is you," he went on. "I've never begged for anything in my life. I've never had to. Damn it, Zara. I have no idea what to do to get you back. I'm in territory I've never been before."

His raw honesty paralleled her own. "You think this is familiar to me?" she cried. "I've never had a man tell me he loved me. I have no idea whether or not to believe you."

Those powerful hands slid up to frame her face. Braden tipped her face up. She had no choice but to look him straight in the eye.

"You want to believe me," he murmured. "You want to believe it because your feelings are so strong and you want to hold on to that happiness… A happiness only I can give you."

Zara reached up, gripped his wrists. She wanted to pull them away, but she found herself hanging on. "I want to be done with you, Braden. I want to be over you, but I can't just ignore what I feel. You hurt me so deep. I've never been cut that deep before. My parents, guys I've dated, I've always known where I stood with them. But with you, I thought I was in one place, but I wasn't even close."

Braden's thumbs stroked her skin, sending her nerves into high gear. Why did he have to come back? Why couldn't he have just let the break be clean?

"Never again," he promised. "You'll never wonder where you stand with me. You're it for me, Zara. I know you have a fear of commitment, I know where we stand right now is shaky, but I'm not giving up. I want you in my life permanently."

One second she was listening to him profess his love, his loyalty, the next she was leaning against him, kissing him. Her mouth moved over his, her hands still gripped his wrists, but she'd needed more contact, needed Braden.

When she eased back, she licked her lips and looked into his eyes. "I can't promise you anything. All I can promise is that we work together to see where this goes. You hurt me, Braden. That's not something I can forgive so easily."

He nodded, sliding his thumb across her bottom lip. "I can understand that, and it's more than I deserve. But I'm going to be patient where you're concerned. I don't want anyone else with me. I don't want to spend my life with another woman, so if we have to take this slow for you to see how serious I am, then so be it."

She hated to bring up the bone of contention between them, but she couldn't leave it hanging in the air.

"If you want to search this house, you can."

The muscle in Braden's jaw ticked, his lids lowered and he let out a sigh. "I'm not doing anything with this house or the scrolls until you and I are on solid ground."

Zara gasped. "You're serious," she whispered.

"I've never been more serious about anyone in my life." His lips slid over hers again for a brief second. "I meant what I said about loving you. I want to fulfill my father's wishes, but I will love you first and always."

Zara threw her arms around his neck, the thick coat getting in her way when she really wanted to feel him without barriers. "I hated you," she sobbed, hating how her emotions had betrayed her, and now she was an emotional wreck. "I moved my bedroom furniture around, I washed all the blankets and sheets trying to get you out of my room."

His soft chuckle vibrated against her. "You wasted a lot of time and energy, because I'm about to take you back upstairs and make love to you."

She eased back, swiped at her face and smiled. "Everything is still in the dryer."

In a swift, unexpected move, Braden scooped her up into his arms and headed for the steps. "If I recall, our first time wasn't in the bed anyway."

Zara toyed with the ends of his hair. She didn't care where he took her, she would go. They were starting fresh, and she knew in her heart this was meant to be. He was the man who would show her what love was, show her what loyalty and commitment were.

This was the man she'd spend the rest of her life with.

Epilogue

"Calm down, Laney. What happened?"

Zara sat up, pulling the old quilt around her as she listened to the urgency in Braden's tone as he talked to his sister on the cell. The kitten snuggled against her side.

"Don't go anywhere. I'm sending Ryker. He's closer than I am."

With a curse, he disconnected the call and punched in another number.

"Is she okay?" Zara asked.

"No."

Braden reached around, tucking her against his side as he held the cell to his ear. The fact he was still seeking her during a family crisis only added to the promise he'd made only hours ago to keep her first in his life.

"Ryker." Braden's bare torso tensed as he spoke. "Go to Laney's house. She needs you to help pack some things and get her back to my house safely. Carter cheated on her, and now he's trying to get her to open her door. I just hung up with her, and she's hysterical. You're closer than I am, which means you'll need to be nice. I'll be home shortly and meet you guys there."

Once he disconnected the call, he turned into her arms. "I'm sorry."

Zara smoothed her hand over his forehead, pushing away a strand of hair. "Don't be. The fact that you're helping your sister makes me love you more."

Braden froze. "You love me?"

"I fell in love when you brought the kitten inside," she confessed. "I didn't want to admit it then or when you told me. But I can't keep it inside. I know you had your reasons for lying. I don't like them, but I understand them. I know your family loyalty runs deep, and I know when you say you love someone, you mean it."

He rested his forehead against hers. "You have no idea how relieved I am to hear you say that. To know that you believe I love you, and it has nothing to do with my family's history, this house, or those scrolls."

"Is your sister okay? Maybe we should get some clothes on and head to your place."

Braden kissed her before easing up. "Would you want to pack some things and stay with me for a while?"

Zara stared up at him, marveling at the way that body always had her complete focus. "Define a while."

He shrugged. "We can start with one day and gradually ease you into forever."

Zara smiled, jumping to her feet. "Forever. That word always scared me before."

"And now?" he asked, wrapping his arms around her and pulling her flush with his body.

She smacked his lips with her own. "And now I want to hold on to it, I want to hold on to you. Forever."

* * * * *